P

MW01614537

"ONE SMALL STEP FOR NANS, ONE GIANT LEAP FOR NANKIND"

Stephen Haughan

To Ina

Enjoy x

PESHWARI NANS PART II
ONE GIANT LEAP FOR NANKIND

BY
STEPHEN HAUGHAN

PESHWARI NANS PART II

Against all odds, plucky pensioners Esther and Minnie achieved the seemingly unachievable in their classic Morris car. Journeying from their humble home in London England to the steamy heartlands of India, conquering not only their fears but rugged terrain, cultural differences and age-related stereotypes.

Through sheer grit, determination and a healthy supply of tea and biscuits, these endearing elderly sisters keep a heartfelt promise and in doing so win the hearts of millions the world over, dwarfing A-list celebrities and sending internet servers into meltdown.

The Peshwari Nans have been reborn, but the burning question on everybody's lips is, do they return home to their tiny East London tenement, their carpet slippers and cosy existence, or journey on throwing caution to the wind in defiance of age and of course the inevitable?

CHAPTER ONE.

Having left Raipur, Ravi, and the flamboyant festival of Holi behind them, Esther and Minnie, our intrepid octogenarian travellers in their classic 1960's Trafalgar blue Morris, positively relished the uncertainty of what lay ahead.

Jasvinder's dying wish had been fulfilled, albeit in a far more chaotic manner than the sisters had originally anticipated, but nevertheless the deed was done and the burden of responsibility had been lifted from their shoulders.

'Samosa, dear?' Minnie asked, offering a platter of provisions gifted to them by the good townsfolk of Raipur to her sister.

'Oh no I couldn't possibly, Minnie dear,' Esther said, puffing her cheeks and raising a hand. 'I had the bhajis, the biryani, the bhuna and more balti than I've eaten in a lifetime, not to mention the poppadums and pickles.'

'Likewise, Essy dear,' Minnie confessed whilst devouring a tasty triangular treat. 'But I'd hate to offend our generous hosts.' In the spirit of intercontinental harmony Minnie went on to consume a further four vegetable samosas, five onion bhajis, a whole naan bread and several fistfuls of Bombay mix, depositing an ample amount into her lap in doing so and leaving a solitary chickpea on the pewter platter. 'Mmmm, mm, mmm,' she mumbled licking her fingers and lips and passing the platter over her shoulder. 'Simply delicious, hands down the best bhajis bar none, and I've eaten a few in my time. Have I told you, dear, Cyril and I frequented the Bengal Palace every Thursday for their lunchtime buffet, well it was two for one for OAP's, you see.' Minnie referred yet again to her former lover,

'Yes, dear,' Esther said, rolling her eyes and slowing before a fork in the road. 'Sadly more often than I'd care to remember, now which way?' she asked, looking in either direction.

'Cyril always had the jalfrezi,' Minnie rambled. 'Heaven only knows why because it played him up something chronic the very next day.'

'Minnie, which way?' Esther again asked.

'Ghandi's revenge he called it,' Minnie said, unfazed. 'I'd have to put the lavatory paper in the refrigerator and a finger full of Sudocrem up his…'

'Minnie!' Esther barked, stopping her sister short, but it was too late, the grotesque image of Cyril bent forward gripping the hand basin with his corduroy trousers and Y front at his ankles, and her sister poised with a pot of cold cream at his rear, was now firmly lodged at the forefront of her mind. 'Which way?'

'Oh!' Minnie said, rising in her seat, 'I see.' Their onward journey had been thus far unplanned and night was fast descending.

'Left or right?' Esther added.

'Hmmmmm.' Minnie pondered for a moment. 'I haven't the foggiest, dear,' she eventually admitted.

The recently renovated road sign pointed to Nagpur to their left at ninety kilometres and Jabalpur to the right at one hundred and fifty. The sisters sat for a minute or two with Vivien's flickering headlights illuminating their options. 'Hmmmmm,' Esther also mumbled, 'Nagpur or Jabalpur, I know let's flip a coin!'

'We haven't any, dear,' Minnie confessed. 'I spent the last of our savings on these delightful souvenirs.' She reached down at her feet and produced a tacky plastic effigy of the Hindu god Ganesh with its distinctive elephant's head and a crudely carved Taj Mahal money box. 'I was assured by the stallholder that these are highly prized collectables,' she added, admiring her supposedly shrewd purchases. 'But I knew that already, I have a nose for antiquities, you see.'

'Oh yes, yes, I can see that,' Esther smirked. 'It's just a shame you haven't an eye for them.'

'What was that, dear?' Minnie asked, momentarily distracted by the exquisite detailing of the Taiwanese injection-moulded plastic figurine.

'Nothing, dear,' Esther said, tapping the wheel. 'So, which way?'

'I have it!' Minnie squealed, turning to snatch the chickpea from the discarded platter before switching it from her right to left hand several times in rapid succession. 'Father used to do this with a sixpence, do you remember?' she asked. 'If you guess correctly, Essy, we go left to Nagpur and vice versa.' Minnie held out her two clenched fists, one of which contained the pea.

'Ohhhh, I never was any good at this,' Esther moaned as with a shaky hand hovering over Minnie's, she tapped each hand in sequence whilst reciting a childhood rhyme. 'Eeny, meeny, miny, moe, catch, a, tiger, by, the, toe, if, he, hollers, let, him, go, eeny, meeny, miny, MO!' She jabbed at Minnie's left hand. 'It's that one, Mo!' she said excitedly.

'Correct!' Minnie chirped, revealing the chickpea before popping it into her mouth. 'Left it is, dear.'

'Right you are,' Esther smiled, selecting first gear and proceeding.

Soon the open countryside was cloaked in darkness without another solitary soul travelling the road to Nagpur. Vivien's lights picked out the potholes, stray dogs and scattered debris which Esther skirted with increasing anxiety. 'Damn you!' she cursed when yet another scrawny mongrel dashed across their path, its eyes wide and piercing as it turned and fled in the opposite direction.

Minnie reached and locked her door, clinging to her seat belt, silently praying Vivien's mechanics would not fail them in such an isolated and altogether eerie location. A half-moon put in an appearance sporadically through broken cloud illuminating the ripples on the adjacent paddies from stirring buffalo and rising catfish.

'What the?' Esther suddenly shrieked, slamming on the brakes, catching her sister off guard and sending her lurching forward into her safety belt.

'Dear God!' Minnie gasped clutching her hat. 'Essy dear, whatever's the matter?'

'T, t, t...' Esther stammered 'It's a t...'

'A what, dear?' Minnie asked, lifting the straw brim from her eyes and peering over Vivien's dashboard to see a huge adult male Bengal tiger stretched out in the road ahead, its head raised, looking in their direction.

'Heavens, Essy, it's a tiger!' Minnie shrieked, making a grab for her sister's arm 'Essy, Essy, it's a tiger!'

'I know, I know!' Esther snapped, frantically locking her own door.

'Turn around!' Minnie said, tugging her sister whilst the sprawling beast licked at its front legs and dragged itself up onto all fours, inquisitive at the dazzling intrusion, 'Turn around, Essy, quickly!'

'I can't!' Esther replied with very little room to manoeuvre. 'It's not safe!'

'Safe!' Minnie exclaimed. 'Essy, that, that thing is headed this way so I suggest you get us the hell out of here, and pronto, darling!'

'Yes, yes you're right,' Esther said, watching the striped predator saunter towards them, sniffing at the night air and picking up the scent of petroleum and the sisters' lily of the valley. Esther clumsily selected reverse gear, rattling the teeth in Vivien's gear box beneath them. The grinding startled the approaching animal which stopped in its tracks, flicking its snake-like tail from side to side apprehensively weighing up its quarry.

Esther reversed whilst turning the wheel and cursing the futility of her rear facing mirrors. 'Oh hell!' she cried, striking the grass verge with a jolt and grappling for first gear.

'Essy, Essy, Essyyyyyyy!' Minnie cried, observing the tiger's sudden aggressive approach with teeth bared.

'Yes, yes, alright, Minnie!' Esther said, panic-stricken and fumbling with the stick between them, but in an instant the Bengal tiger lunged, reared up and slammed its enormous front paws onto Vivien's bonnet.

'Oh no, no, no, no Essyyyyy!' Minnie screeched, clinging to her sister. 'Essy, pleaaaaase!'

Esther flung the stick into first and stamped on the accelerator, but almost immediately stalled the car, alarming the beast outside. 'No, no, no!' she herself cried, grappling with the keys and jangling the many charms which hung alongside them. With a deep bellowing roar the tiger recoiled and sprang on its hind legs into the air and up onto Vivien's bonnet, scrambling and scratching at the offside wing in doing so. 'ARRRRRRGH!' Esther and Minnie both screamed when confronted at close range, the weight of the animal rocking their aged car.

'Essy, do something!' Minnie begged, clinging to her sister.

Aghast, Esther released the wheel and cowered in her seat as the big cat's face loomed at the windscreen, its gaping mouth opening to lick at the glass revealing its menacing teeth, one of which had been broken recently during a fight with an equally aggressive wild boar, neither animal gaining the upper hand and retreating to lick their wounds.

Vivien's bonnet popped and buckled somewhat whilst the tiger pawed at her aluminium aerial, bending it this way and that, playfully at first before tearing it from its mount, when it sprung and whipped its face. With her sister mortified, Minnie took matters into her own hands, leaning to thump at Vivien's horn which obviously startled the tiger, sending it pouncing to the ground, snarling and hissing, tense and recoiling once again, but the beast did not retreat as its only meal in several days had been a lame egret found floundering at the paddy's edge and the occasional bullfrog which hardly served to sustain it.

The Bengal tiger had strayed from a protected reserve, one of several set up to monitor their dwindling numbers. Throughout previous decades these regal beasts have been hunted to near extinction fuelled by the illegal but highly lucrative trade in their body parts, and of course their magnificent skins. Farmers also shot and poisoned those that strayed too close, threatening their livestock and themselves for that matter, pitiless to the plight of their national animal having cultivated much of its ever shrinking natural habitat.

'Essy, start the damn car!' Minnie yelled, shaking her sister bodily. 'Hurry for heaven's sake!'

'Oh, oh yes!' Esther replied, reaching for the keys once again.

The tiger rounded Vivien and approached Minnie's door. 'Hurry, dear!' she again cried, cringing and inching closer to her sister as the animal reached and gripped Vivien's roof rack, standing some six and a half feet tall at Minnie's window and rocking the timber-framed car with ease and jostling the petrified pensioners inside.

Vivien's engine fired up and Esther again gripped the wheel and stabbed at the accelerator, spinning the rear wheels and sending a cloud of dirt and dust into the air, dislodging the tiger but propelling them only as far as a deep pothole where a front wheel sank to the axle, stopping the car violently once again. 'OH COME ON!' Esther cried angrily whilst her sister straightened her spectacles. Esther poured on the power, increasing the dust storm behind them. 'Damn, damn, damn!' she cursed, pounding the wheel and alternating forward and reverse in an attempt to dislodge them, but to no avail. Again the hungry tiger approached the passenger door clawing at the Trafalgar blue panelling.

'GO AWAY!' Minnie yelled, slapping at the window. 'GET AWAY WITH YOU!' Snarling, the beast pawed at the flimsy glass that separated them, tantalisingly close to the hearty meal inside.

'Come on, Vivien darling, please!' Esther begged, tearing the hat from her head and tossing it over her shoulder whilst wrenching at the gear stick.

With a powerful paw the big cat prised open the tiny triangular quarter light window beside Minnie and reached inside, extending its claws and lashing out. 'ARRRRRRGH, ESSYYYYYY!' she screamed, almost sharing her sister's seat at this point and thus hindering their escape attempt.

'Minnie, the stick, I can't….' Esther barked, grappling at Minnie's knees. 'Get out of the way, will you!'

The salivating tiger tore at Minnie's seat, thrusting the end of its nose inside also. 'Essy, helllp!' Minnie screeched with the flaying claws an inch or so from her shoulder.

'I CAN'T, I CAN'T!' Esther cried, rummaging amongst the hem of Minnie's skirt for the gear stick. 'Minnie, move, damn you!'

'Hell no!' Minnie replied, clinging ever tighter.

Rocking back and forth, Esther tried in vain to free them, grappling with the gear shift and her trembling sister; she then reached and wrenched open the glove compartment, rummaging blindly inside. 'Here!' she said, pulling out a ball of wool with a pair of eight-inch knitting needles wedged inside. 'Stick it, stick it, dear!' she yelled.

'Are you serious?' Minnie asked, flicking the tiger-torn foam from her lap and observing her shredded seat.

'Of course I am!' Esther insisted.

Minnie reluctantly tugged a needle from the wool, gripping it dagger-like in her shaking hand.

'Hurry, dear!' Esther urged, but even in this life or death situation Minnie struggled with her conscience. 'I can't, Essy!' she said, looking the ferocious tiger in the eye. A lesser individual would have instinctively plunged that needle deep into that glaring eye in a heartbeat and lose no sleep at having done so, but Minnie being Minnie this heinous solution to their dilemma proved wholeheartedly unacceptable.

'What are you waiting for?' Esther raged beside her. 'Just do it!'

'I'm sorry, Essy!' Minnie confessed, cowering from the beast. 'I just can't!'

The beast was hungry through no fault of its own and its kind had been persecuted enough. Esther, on the other hand, had a far more irrational approach, namely the desire to savour several more of their so-called twilight years with each of her extremities intact.

Tossing the needle down at her feet and leaning further away from the tiger's relentless thrashing, Minnie then reached behind amongst her numerous Raipur purchases.

'MINNIE!' Esther screeched in her ear. 'WE ARE GOING TO DIE, NOW TELL ME, WHICH PART OF THAT DO YOU FAIL TO UNDERSTAND?'

'Yes, yes, one moment, dear,' Minnie said, tossing cheap trinkets from her back. 'Ahhhh, here it is,' she said, producing a brown paper packet. 'I got this for Richard and his friends, I think it'll put a stop to his ridiculous shenanigans.'

Peshwari Nans Part II

Esther's grandson Richard had a penchant for pain, of the chili variety. He and his friends would ritually seek out the fiercest of sauces, powders and entire pods and record one another consuming them. This self-inflicted masochism was a rite of passage for any self-respecting thrill seeker, but Minnie was about to turn up the heat, taking the chili challenge to an all new volcanic level; she had sought the advice of a prominent chili farmer in town who agreed to concoct for her a blend of five of the hottest dried chilies known to man, the hottest of which being the infamous bhut jolokia, or ghost chili, originating from the Assam region of northern India. Resembling many of its fiery kind, the ghost chili pepper was literally in a league of its own because when its levels of the heat-provoking capsicum were measured using the Scoville scale it weighed in at a staggering one million units, five times hotter than the blistering habanero. Minnie broke the bag's wax seal and reached inside, scooping a quantity of the crimson powder into the palm of her hand.

'MINNIE!' Esther urged her frantically.

Minnie kicked out at the passenger door to startle the tiger momentarily. 'HEY!' she yelled, raising her hand to her mouth and blowing the red hot contents towards the animal's open mouth.

'What are you doing?' Esther asked, hoping for an altogether more brutal response.

'Just wait a second, dear,' Minnie assured her sister. Sure enough the tiger immediately ceased its savage onslaught, retracted its claws and snout and dropped from the car. Esther and Minnie leaned across tentatively to see the big cat shaking its head and drooling uncontrollable as the searing capsicum began to take effect; it clawed at the dirt road with streaming eyes. 'Sorryyyyyy,' Minnie called through the open window.

'Braaaavo,' Esther said with a hand on her sister's shoulder. 'Bravo.'

Before long the potent powder proved too much for the tiger to bear and it turned and sprinted for the rice paddy with its tail tucked firmly between its hind legs. Skidding at the water's edge, the stricken beast lapped and lapped greedily, but moments later the heat returned tenfold and, whimpering like a cat stuck up a tree, the tiger took off across the basmati plantation at breakneck speed, producing a series of ripples like a skimming stone before it disappeared from sight as did the moon.

'What was that?' Esther asked, licking the end of her finger and dabbing her sister's hand,

'NO, ESSY!' Minnie shrieked, but the bhut jolokia concoction had already made contact with her sister's tongue.

'OH GOOD HEAVEN'S!' Esther cried. 'OH, OH, OH, MINNIE!' She shook her head and opened her burning mouth. 'Dear Lord, help me, Minnie, help me, God damn it!'

Minnie found this mildly amusing as she wiped her hand clean on a shred of seat foam. 'I did try to warn you, dear,' she smirked.

'Yes, yes, never mind that!' Esther barked. 'Do something, will you, oooooooooh hurry, Minnie, hurryyyyyyyyy!' Tears ran down her reddened cheeks as she clawed at her protruding tongue.

'Alright, alright,' Minnie laughed, retrieving a pot of mint yoghurt from her supplies. 'Here, dear, take a sip of this,' she said.

Esther tore off the lid, threw back her head and proceeded to empty the cooling contents into her mouth.

'And in case you were wondering, dear,' Minnie informed her, 'It's soya.'

'I don't care what the hell it is!' Esther blurted, swilling the yoghurt over her burning tongue before draining the entire pot and fishing out the remains with her fingers. 'Ahhhhhhhhh,' she sighed as the heat marginally subsided. 'Minnie, dear,' she said, panting, 'I do believe that poor animal would've gotten off lightly if you'd have jabbed it in the eye with the knitting needle.'

Minnie wrapped the chili powder and placed it behind them, still very much amused at her sister's predicament, 'Shall we go, dear,' she said, settling in her shredded seat.

'Well yes, of course,' Esther replied, leaning from her window and sucking in the cool night air. 'If I can only get out of this blasted hole.'

'Oh yes, of course,' Minnie replied. 'Leave it to me, dear, I have a plan.' First making sure the tiger was long gone, Minnie opened her door and stepped outside to survey the depth of their problem. 'Oh yes,' she said confidently, 'I'll have us out of there in a jiffy, dear.' Tottering to the grass verge, Minnie grappled amongst the long grass plucking out several stones of varying sizes. 'I saw this in a movie once, dear!' she called over her shoulder whilst tossing the stones toward the hole.

'*Ice Cold in Alex*, I think it was, with John Mills, Sylvia Syms and Anthony Quayle, do you remember?' she asked, struggling with a particularly cumbersome rock. 'Mother had an enormous crush on our Mister Mills!'

'Yes, yes I do!' Esther called back. 'But I still have no idea what you are doing!'

'Never mind, dear!' Minnie said, tipping each stone into the hole. 'Just rock Vivien back and forth and leave the rest to me!'

Esther did as she was asked, alternating forward and reverse gears, and each time her sister dropped another rock into the pothole which duly disappeared beneath the spinning wheel until Vivien miraculously began to rise from the rut in the road. 'Don't stop, dear!' Minnie yelled at the wheel side. Soon the hole was full enough for one last stab at the accelerator in first gear and out Vivien popped. 'There!' Minnie shrieked, dropping back onto her bottom.

'Splendid, Minnie dear!' Esther said, stepping from Vivien to help her sister to her feet. 'You truly are a marvel at times, do you know that, darling?' she added with a hug.

'Oh it was nothing, dear,' Minnie replied, brushing the dirt from her skirt.

The moon again emerged and the sisters looked on in horror at the condition of their beloved Vivien; the Bengal tiger had inflicted deep gouges into the fragile bodywork and ash framing. 'Oh look at her, dear,' Esther told Minnie, who kept one eye on the rice paddy.

'Perhaps we should go now,' Minnie suggested.

'Oh yes, yes of course,' Esther agreed whilst hurriedly rounding the car to retake her seat.

Before climbing aboard Minnie opened the rear doors and retrieved a red and white spotted linen tablecloth and draped it over her tattered seat. 'Riiiight,' she said, buckling her belt. 'Ready, dear?'

Esther took a brief moment to gaze in wonderment at her plucky sister before leaning to plant a kiss on her wrinkled cheek and patting her knee. 'Bravo indeed,' she again said while releasing the handbrake.

During their onward journey the sisters quietly sat contemplating what could quite easily have been had the tiger gained access to Vivien, Esther also shuddering at the thought of a larger dose of Minnie's blazing bhut jolokia blend and sympathising somewhat with the Bengal beast.

'How about the Great Barrier Reef dear?' Minnie eventually asked out of the blue.

'What?' Esther asked, snapping out of her daze. 'What are you talking about, dear?'

'Our destination, dear,' Minnie reminded her. 'We have yet to decide.'

'Oh good heavens, you're right!' Esther replied, having been a tad preoccupied.

'We could snorkel, dear,' Minnie said excitedly. 'I've always wanted to snorkel, the closest I ever got was a rubber hose in a tin tub in front of the fire, do you remember, I managed to stay submerged for a full three and a half minutes until the Lifebuoy soap began to sting my eyes and you climbed in beside me and plugged the hose with your finger?'

'Ohhhhh yes,' Esther laughed, 'Yes, yes I do, you came up thrashing and splashing so hard you damn near put the fire out, anyway I was thinking more along the lines of the United States, dear, we could cruise Route 66, visit the Grand Canyon and maybe try our luck at Las Vegas, what do you say?'

'Hmmmmm,' Minnie pondered. 'How about Antarctica, we could fit Vivien with a set of skids and have a team of dogs pull us to the Pole.'

'Are you mad?' Esther asked, wide-eyed. 'We barely survived last winter with the pittance the government call the fuel allowance and you want us to go to Antarctica of all places; may I remind you, sister dear, that we are pensioners whose mortality rate is greatly increased when exposed to colder climates, therefore I really must insist we favour the tropics, somewhere kinder to our aging bones, like Egypt perhaps.'

'Oooooh yes!' Minnie squealed. 'Egypt, now you're talking, dear, the Nile, the pyramids and the souvenirs, ooh, Essy, think of the souvenirs.'

'Precisely,' Esther agreed. 'I hear you can purchase a replica sphinx that doubles as a door stop, a mummified money box and a King Tut teapot.'

'Really!' Minnie gasped, clasping her hands together and positively salivating at the prospect of perusing the gift shops and souks for worthless tat and trinkets to add to their cluttersome collection. 'Well, what are we waiting for then, Essy dear, Egypt it is.' The historical value of such a visit would of course play second fiddle to such a wanton spree.

'Hurry, dear!' Esther insisted. 'Consult the all-powerful Oz and plot a course immediately.'

'You mean Mister Google?' Minnie said, delving for their electronic device. 'Don't worry, dear,' she assured her sister. 'I'm all over it like a rash, or is it a dose of salts, I can never remember.'

'No, no, no, dear,' Esther informed her. 'That's a cure for diarrhoea, I'm sure of it.'

Minnie powered up the tablet and tapped at the screen, which lit up her face highlighting every crease and crow's foot. 'Oooh' she said, looking up to sniff at the gentle breeze creeping through the quarter light. 'Is that jasmine, dear?' she said as the heady scent of citrus blossom enveloped Esther also.

'No, no, no, dear,' Esther replied categorically. 'I have one or two scented candles infused with jasmine.'

'One or two!' Minnie smirked, having ridiculed her sister for years over her obsessive collection of candles and burners emitting every scent imaginable, and a few you could never, from cranberry and cider apple to Norwegian spruce.

Esther was drawn to them like the proverbial moth mesmerized by the dancing flame. 'I made quite an exciting discovery in Raipur,' she said, referring to her own recent purchases. 'A set of floating bath candles, saffron, paprika and garam masala scented and a dozen tandoori tea lights.'

'Oh the joy,' Minnie said sarcastically, having lost interest. 'Oooh here, dear,' she added, offering up the tablet. 'If we head to Mumbai we can take a freighter to Dubai and then overland through Saudi Arabia, across the Red sea and along the Nile to Cairo, simples.'

'Freighter?' Esther asked, straight-faced. 'On the ocean?'

19

'Yes, dear,' Minnie replied. 'Well, the Arabian sea to be more precise, followed by the Gulf of Oman and then the Persian Gulf.'

'A freighter?' Esther again asked with a sneer. 'I'm not so sure I like the sound of that, surely there has to be another way.'

'Well yes, yes there is,' Minnie admitted. 'But it'll add a further two and a half thousand miles to the journey.' Minnie's chosen route would eat up a colossal four thousand two hundred and seventy-one miles alone. 'No, no, dear,' she insisted. 'This makes perfect sense.'

'But, but, Minnie dear,' Esther pleaded.

'Oh come now, dear,' Minnie smiled. 'I'm not asking you to cross the Atlantic on a raffia raft, for Pete's sake, these mega ships are unsinkable, Essy.'

'One word, two syllables,' Esther said abruptly. 'Titanic.'

'Esther Reynolds!' Minnie snapped, slapping the tablet screen. 'Do you or do you not wish to go to Egypt, huh?'

'Well, well yes,' Esther admitted, craving the candles Cairo had to offer.

'And,' Minnie added, 'Do you wish to get there by the shortest bottom-numbing route possible?'

Esther shifted her aching bottom in her seat. 'Of course, dear,' she replied. 'I was merely concerned about the….'

'That settles it then,' Minnie intervened. 'We board the freighter at Mumbai, now what is that delightful aroma?' She wound down her window to catch a faceful just as Vivien's lights illuminated the first of Nagpur's many orange groves.

Known as the orange city because of the locally cultivated citrus produced in vast quantities and exported far and wide across the continent and beyond, Nagpur lay in the very heart of India with a population of around twenty-three million Hindus, Buddhists, Muslims, Sikhs and Christians, a melting pot of faiths as it were.

'Oranges, dear!' Minnie said, surprised somewhat. 'How extraordinary.'

'Yes, quite,' Esther agreed, finding the lush green orange groves a welcome change from the open windswept rice paddies, and she then let out a gaping yawn.

Minnie's eyes too grew heavy as she slumped against her door.

'Not long now, dear,' Esther assured her, passing a road sign. 'Another five kilometres and we'll find a room for the night.'

'Mmmm a roooom,' Minnie said dreamily.

It was close to midnight when the sisters entered the orange city, Esther fighting the effects of fatigue whilst Minnie slept open-mouthed beside her, her heavy rattled breathing grating on her sister enormously.

Nagpur is a thriving commercial hub of a city so therefore never sleeps, and the streets were marginally congested with taxi cabs, motorcycles and the high performance cars of the wealthy who gathered after dark to cruise and pitch for a place in the pecking order of Nagpur's business elite, many of them trading in the fruits and vegetables sold at the renowned Sitabuldi market, a commercial mecca for farmers and traders alike.

Stopping at a red signal, Esther drew alongside a gleaming canary yellow Ferrari with two male occupants, heads bobbing inside to their deafening stereo. 'Excuse me!' she called, winding down her window. 'Excuse me, could you point me in the direction of the nearest hotel?' but having raised her tone Esther was still no match for the pounding drum and bass beside her.

'I SAYYY!' she yelled, waving a hand. The passenger in designer shades tapped his friend's shoulder and gestured to Esther, and the two of them then pushed their glasses up onto their slick black hair and looked Vivien up and down before bursting into fits of laughter.

'I'm looking for a hotel!' Esther reiterated. The lights changed to green and the Ferrari driver immediately left Esther at a standstill with the merest tap at his accelerator. 'How rude!' Esther said, proceeding in a safe and altogether stately manner.

Several blocks into the city, Esther soon saw the familiar glowing sign up ahead of a popular hotel chain, but at the upper end of the market and one she'd never had the privilege nor the means to experience, but they were both exhausted and she did have an overdraft limit, seldom used but there for emergencies all the same. 'Minnie, Minnie, dear,' she said, nudging her sister. 'Minnie, wake up!'

'Mmmm, mmm,' Minnie moaned. 'Let me sleep, Cyril.'

'I'll give you Cyril!' Esther said, jabbing at her sister's arm. 'Minnie, wake up will you?'

Minnie roused and sat up bleary-eyed as Esther pulled up beneath the hotel's lavish entrance canopy, but was immediately ushered to a private but dimly lit car park to make way for an approaching Rolls Royce.

Esther clambered out and stood at Vivien's rear doors, expecting their bags to be collected, but the willing hotel staff busily attended to the millionaire Hindus that emerged from it, 'Helloooo!' she called but got no response.

'I'll get them, dear,' Minnie said, and keen to be beneath the sheets of a soft warm bed, she straightened her back, handed her sister the tablet and gathered up their luggage.

'Are you sure, dear?' Esther asked, locking Vivien behind them and again glancing at the many scratches on her beloved car. 'You poor dear,' she said.

'No really, I'm fine, Essy,' Minnie said with a bag in each hand.

'I was talking to Vivien,' Esther told her, leading the way to the foyer.

The sisters approached the hotel desk, both of them dead on their feet. 'Good evening, we'd like a room please,' Esther said, setting the tablet down 'Nothing too fancy, mind.'

'Fancy?' the night receptionist asked, straightening his tie.

'Yes you heard me,' Esther said, a little grouchy at this point. 'We're not made of money, you know, so just a simple twin will suffice.'

'I am sorry, madam,' the Bangladeshi receptionist said with a basic grasp of the English language. 'We have no simple room.' He scribbled a figure on a scrap of paper and slid it across to Esther. 'This is price of our most modest suite,' he informed her.

'How much?' Esther gasped, examining the slip. 'Are you quite sure this is your cheapest room?'

'Positive, madam,' the receptionist replied.

'Leave this to me, dear,' Minnie said, ushering Esther to one side and playing the fame game. 'Now look here, sonny,' she said, peering over her spectacles. You do know who we are, don't you?'

The receptionist looked the sisters up and down disapprovingly, 'I am sorry, madam,' he confessed. 'I do not.'

'The Nans,' Minnie said, hoping to jog his memory, 'The Peshwari Nans.'

'I am not knowing this name,' the receptionist again admitted before leaning to sweep the sisters aside as the millionaires approached and they conversed in his native tongue.

'Oh really!' Esther moaned.

'Can we afford it, dear?' Minnie asked, taking the slip from Esther's hand.

'Barely, dear,' her sister replied, looking about the foyer and catching sight of an ATM machine. 'I'll need to double check the account.' Retrieving her debit card from her purse, Esther approached the cashpoint and tapped in her PIN number and stood with Minnie at her side, 'What the?' she suddenly gasped when her balance was displayed; it seemed that Karl Bodine, the wealthy American gaming guru had been true to his word and transferred a large amount of money into her account, the first of many payments to be made after they were the unwitting catalyst that spawned his now billion-dollar entertainments empire. 'Minnie, look, it must be a mistake!'

'No, dear,' Minnie disagreed. 'It's that nice Mister Bodie, don't you remember?' Minnie craned her neck over her sister's shoulder. 'Does this mean we can afford an upgrade, dear?' she asked, eyeing the balance in excess of seventy thousand pounds.

'Undoubtedly, dear,' Esther smirked, retrieving her card and marching back to the desk. 'I sayyy!' she said, interrupting the conversation and addressing the distinguished guests. 'I say which room are you staying in?'

'I'm sorry?' one of the businessmen asked.

'Your room?' Esther again asked. 'Which is it, if I might ask?'

The gentleman's friend offered up their key fob. 'Room four eleven, the penthouse,' he said proudly.

'Ahhh thank you,' Esther said, turning to the receptionist. 'And my good man,' she said, clinging to her card. 'Tell me, is there a room four twelve by any chance?'

'Yes, yes of course,' the receptionist replied, again looking her over. 'We have three penthouse suites but…'

'Then we'll take it!' Esther said abruptly.

'But, madam,' the bemused receptionist smirked. 'Each suite is costing ninety six thousand rupees, per night, now if my calculation is correct that would convert to almost a thousand of your British pounds, I tell you what, madam, my cousin owns a humble bed and breakfast establishment just outside of town, I could telephone him for you if you wish.'

'I said,' Esther said, prodding at his desk, 'We'll take it!'

'Yes, yes we will,' Minnie echoed. 'Now if you're not to carry our bags I suggest you find somebody who will, and be quick about it, my sister and I have had a beastly night and we'd like to put our feet up if you don't mind.'

'Yes, room four twelve,' Esther said, sliding her card toward him. 'I think you'll find we have the wherewithal.'

The flustered receptionist and his wealthy male guests stood stunned when the payment transaction was authorised by Esther's bank.

'I'll trouble you for the key if you don't mind,' Esther said with a wry smile.

'Yes, yes of course, madam,' the grovelling receptionist said, fumbling for the fob and slapping a bell on his desk to summon his bellboy. 'Vivaan, Vivaan!' he yelled as the boy came scurrying down the stairs. 'Vivaan, take these bags and escort our most eminent guests to their suite, hurry, boy, hurry!'

The bellboy looked at both parties before making a grab for the businessmen's bags. 'Ahem!' Esther said, tapping his shoulder and dangling her fob under his nose. 'I believe we were here first.'

'Yes, Vivaan!' the receptionist barked, leaning to slap the boy about the ear. 'The ladies, see to the ladies, you fool!' He then bowed to the sisters. 'A thousand apologies,' he added. 'Please, enjoy your stay.'

'Thank you,' Minnie said, following her sister. 'Oh and errrr!' she called back. 'Have someone fetch up a pot of tea, will you please, preferably chamomile, there's a good man.'

'I will be seeing to it right away, madam,' the now subservient receptionist replied. 'Right way, no problem indeed.'

Escorted to their penthouse suite, Esther and Minnie by this time were in no mood to marvel at its elaborate detailing and priceless carved antiquities. The bellboy placed their bags beside the sumptuous seven-seater sofa and hovered at the door.

'I'm sorry, young man,' Esther informed him. 'I'm afraid we haven't a rupee between us.'

'No problem,' the bellboy smiled, reaching inside his gold-braided crimson tunic and producing a hand-held card reader. 'I accept Visa, Mastercard, Amex, Delta and travellers' cheques.'

'My, you are a resourceful chap, aren't you,' Esther smirked, handing over her card and entering her PIN once again. 'Minniiiie,' she then called after seeing the boy out. 'Minnie dear!' Her sister had hastily tracked down the bedroom leaving a trail of clothes in her wake and hopped between the sheets of her queen-sized bed. 'Oh there you are,' she added, having gathered Minnie's shoes, petticoat and skirt. 'I'll cancel the tea, shall I?' Minnie offered no reply. 'I said I'll cancel the tea, dear!' she said a little louder, but Minnie was sound asleep with the velveteen bedspread pulled up around her ears. 'Yes you do that, dear,' Esther said to herself whilst neatly folding her sister's clothes and returning to the lounge to telephone reception. 'It's Mrs Reynolds, dear, I'm afraid we won't be needing the tea after all,' she explained 'Could we possibly postpone till say nine-thirty in the morning?'

'But of course, madam,' the eager receptionist replied. 'I trust you are liking the suite?'

'I'm sorry, dear, what?' Esther asked, yawning once again.

'Your penthouse, madam,' the receptionist reiterated. 'Would it be meeting with your approval?'

'Oh,' Esther replied, giving the room a fleeting glance whilst loosening her blouse. 'Yes, yes it would be, thank you, now I'll bid you goodnight, sir.'

'Very good, madam,' the grinning receptionist replied, standing proudly at his desk. 'I trust you will be having dreams of sweetness,' he added before reaching to polish his brass name plate.

'You mean sweet dreams,' Esther said, kicking off her own shoes. 'Thank you, I shall, good night.' She replaced the telephone receiver, turned out the light and hobbled through to the bedroom massaging her aching behind in doing so.

Supercharged in the lap of luxury, the sisters rose around nine the following morning. 'I left the water in for you dear,' Minnie said, emerging from the bathroom wearing a cosy hotel housecoat.

'How thoughtful, thank you,' Esther said in passing.

At nine-thirty sharp the chamomile tea arrived. 'There you are, dear,' Esther said, joining her sister on the opulent glass-fronted balcony with the steaming pot. 'Oh, oh thank you, dear,' Minnie said, looking up from the tablet. 'Do you know, dear,' she added, having researched their current global position, 'That Nagpur is quite literally the geographical centre of India, isn't that remarkable?'

'No, no I didn't, dear,' Esther confessed refilling her own cup.

'And,' Minnie continued, 'There are no less than six national parks around Nagpur where tigers can be found.'

'Ohhh great,' Esther moaned. 'Well we won't be stopping any longer than necessary, dear, that's for sure.' The sisters stood in their housecoats looking out over the sprawling city and down at the teaming streets below. Moments later there was a knock at the door. 'I'll get it, dear,' Minnie said, preventing her sister from rising from her seat. 'Good morning, young man,' she said greeting the bellboy at the door. 'Would you like some tea?'

'Don't be daft, dear,' Esther said, having followed Minnie inside. 'Look at him, he's barely out of short trousers, what would he want with a herbal infusion? I'm sorry, dear, we haven't any fizzy pop,' she told the boy.

'Oooh, young man,' Minnie said, wagging a finger. 'You don't want to be drinking any of that rubbish, dear It'll rot those gorgeous pearly white teeth of yours.'

'Nonsense, dear,' Esther chuckled. 'My Jack had all his own teeth right up until the day he died and he drank oodles of cream soda and cherryade.'

'Oooh, cream soda,' Minnie said dreamily. 'I remember father would make the most amazing ice cream floats when we were children, with two whole scoops of Cornish vanilla.'

'Ohhh yes,' Esther recalled, leaving the bellboy bemused. 'But, dear,' she added. 'I think you'll have to go an awful long way to beat a knickerbocker glory.'

'From the Wimpy,' Minnie said, licking her lips. 'With a cherry on top!'

'Mmmmm,' Esther moaned. 'I remember it like it was yesterday, lashings of whipped cream and strawberry sauce.' She then turned to the perplexed bellboy. 'I'm sorry, why are you here?' she asked.

Minnie raised a finger before the boy could answer. 'I do believe Father had a banana long boat,' she said, reminiscing. The girls were treated fortnightly to their favourite desserts, the knickerbocker glory, a gargantuan glass of whipped cream, fresh fruit, jelly, strawberry sauce, chocolate sprinkles, a wafer and that all-important glazed cherry for good measure. They would sit bobbing with anticipation in the window seat of their local Wimpy fast food restaurant while their tasty treats were prepared, then race one another to the bottom of their glasses until they were positively queasy and full to the brim.

'Yes, why are you here?' Minnie too asked, breaking from her daydream.

'I, I cannot remember,' the boy replied, his head spinning with their tales of dreamy desserts. 'Oh, oh yes!' he then said, slapping his own forehead. 'I almost forgot, I'm afraid I have some terrible news for you both.'

'Terrible news,' Minnie said with a hand to her mouth. 'Oh dear, Essy, he has terrible news.'

'Oh good heavens,' Esther too gasped. 'Whatever's happened, what is it?'

'Well,' the boy continued, hesitant to break the news. 'I arrived for work this morning on my bicycle and I could not help but notice your rather odd mode of transport outside.'

'Vivien,' Esther enlightened him. 'Yes what about her, oh and she's not odd, dear boy, she's unique, rather like my sister.'

'Why thank you, dear,' Minnie smiled rubbing her sister's back.

'Yes, yes, your Vivien,' the boy added. 'I'm afraid I have to inform you she has been the victim of a terrible injustice, I have never seen the likes of this in Nagpur, never, your Vivien has been set upon by vandals.'

'Vandals!' Esther cried, clutching her chest. 'Oh good Lord no!'

Minnie scurried to the balcony and peered over the ledge while her sister was helped down onto the sofa. 'Not my Vivien,' Esther gasped, suffering from a shortness of breath. 'Not my darling Vivien.'

'It's alright, dear!' Minnie called from the balcony. 'She's just as we left her!'

'Oh thank heavens,' Esther sighed reclining.

'But, Missy,' Vivaan said, joining Minnie outside. 'Look, look at your Vivien, she has been the victim of a most barbaric assault, if you wish I will telephone our chief of police immediately.'

'No, no, dear that won't be necessary,' Minnie said remaining surprisingly calm. 'It wasn't vandals, my love, it was a tiger.'

'A tiger!' Vivaan shrieked, looking down around the hotel grounds with the colour draining from his face. 'A tiger, here in Nagpur!'

'No, no, no,' Minnie chuckled. 'We encountered the blighter some twenty or so kilometres outside town.'

'And you are unharmed?' Vivaan asked, looking Minnie up and down.

'Not a scratch, dear,' Minnie replied, returning to her sister. 'I tell you it'll take a lot more than an oversized pussycat to get the better of us, eh dear?'

'Well,' Esther replied unconvinced. 'If it wasn't for you, dear, and your blazing hot chili powder I very much doubt we'd be here to tell the tale.'

'Chili powder?' Vivaan asked, bemused.

'Yes, that's right,' Minnie said, reaching for her bag. 'Perhaps you'd like to try a pinch?'

'NO!' Esther snapped before Vivaan could reply. 'Believe me, young man,' she told him, 'If you value your life, and your internal organs for that matter you would be well advised to avoid it like the plague.'

As he looked the sisters up and down once again the penny soon dropped with the young bellboy as he clasped his hand to his head and dashed back to the balcony. 'Holy Hindus!' he cried, firstly looking down at Vivien and then back in at the sisters. 'It's you, the naan breads, I, I mean the Peshwari Nans!' he shrieked, rejoining the sisters. 'It is, is it not?'

'Yes, dear, in the flesh,' Esther replied, reaching for his hand having been partially swallowed by the marshmallow-like sofa. 'Now help me out of this thing, will you.'

'Yes, yes of course, Missy!' the boy said, eagerly hoisting Esther free, bowing repeatedly to the pair of them. 'A thousand apologies for my foolish intrusion,' he added. 'Please forgive me.'

Minnie took hold of the lad to curtail his enthusiasm. 'That's quite enough of that, young man,' she said, patting his back. 'Now would you be a dear and fetch us some more tea?'

'Yes, yes, yes, yes of course,' Vivaan rapidly replied. 'I will bring for you the finest tea in all of India, you will see!'

'As long as it's herbal, dear,' Esther told him. 'And if at all possible,' she added, gesturing to the cheap hotel crockery, 'In a china cup, it makes a world of difference, you see.'

Vivaan plucked a cup from their tray, 'I do not believe it!' he said angrily. 'I will speak to the manager immediately on your behalf and insist the kitchen staff are thrown out on the street for such an insult, you have my word.'

'Oh that won't be necessary,' Minnie intervened. 'I'm sure they meant well; by the way do you think you could rustle us up a slice or two of toast and marmalade, I'm positively famished and my sister and I make a point of never leaving the house without breakfast, isn't that right, Essy, dear?'

'Oh no, never,' Esther agreed. 'You're quite right, dear.'

'Toast, yes, yes, of course,' Vivaan chirped. 'We have white bread, brown or our very own chapatti.'

'Oh I don't mind, dear,' Esther smirked. 'Just as long as it isn't a tiger loaf.'

'Ohh very good, dear,' Minnie laughed, cottoning on instantly. 'Oh and crumpets,' she told Vivaan. 'Now I know it's a tall order but if you do happen to have any we'd be eternally grateful.'

'Crum-pets,' the lad pondered. 'Crumpet, I'm sorry, what is this crumpet?'

'You don't know?' Esther asked wide-eyed. 'Oh my dear boy, you have led a sheltered life, haven't you, a toasted crumpet is sheer bliss on a plate, it's a hot buttered slice of heaven itself and the greatest start to any day you could ever wish for.'

'Hear, hear,' Minnie said, applauding her sister's gushing compliments.

'Crumpets,' the boy echoed. 'I will find them for you,' he said, dashing to the door. 'I will find these holiest of holy crumpets even if I have to search the whole of Nagpur, you have my word as bellboy of this fine hotel!' With this he left and sprinted to the elevator to move heaven and earth if he had to, to please their honourable guests.

The sisters freshened up and dressed before Vivaan returned some thirty minutes later pushing a hotel trolley. 'Madams,' he said when Minnie opened the door. 'Breakfast is served.' Removing his hat, he stood rigidly beside the silver domed salvers. 'Your toast and marmalade,' he gestured, removing the first lid. 'And,' he added, proudly lifting the second, 'Your beloved crumpets.'

Sure enough, what lay beneath appeared in every sense of the word to be a heap of six or seven steaming crumpets.

'Oh how wonderful!' Minnie said, clasping her hands together at her chest. 'Well done, well done indeed.'

'Mmmmm,' Esther mumbled, taking a bite with a dash of marmalade, 'Wonderful indeed, how on earth did you come by them?'

'Well you see,' Vivaan explained, 'We were not having your crumpets here in Nagpur so I telephoned my cousin in New Delhi who has an uncle in Bangladesh who in turn has a brother in your very own Bradford city, do you know it, Missy?'

'Oh yes,' Esther replied. 'I believe it in the north of England, somewhere between Leeds and Huddersfield if my memory serves me right.'

''Well my cousin's uncle's brother,' Vivaan explained further, 'He located the recipe for your crumpets and relayed it back to me and I was giving it to the kitchen staff to prepare for you.'

'Remarkable,' Minnie said, plucking a crumpet for herself. 'Oh and I see you found some china too, you are a clever boy.'

'Yes, yes the finest china for you,' Vivaan said proudly. 'Our esteemed Prime Minister Narendra Modi himself drank from these very cups during his recent visit to Nagpur.'

'Well thank you, dearie,' Esther said with a smile and a mouthful of crumpet. 'You must let us give you something for your troubles.'

In an instant Vivaan whipped out his card reader and rattled off his usual patter for paying guests, 'That is most kind, I accept Visa, Mastercard, Amex, Delta and…'

'Yes, yes, dear,' Esther said, interrupting his flow and inserting her card. 'You know,' she added, 'If you're not running your own chain of hotels one day, young man, I'll be more than surprised.'

'Thank you, madam,' Vivaan said politely. 'I was uneducated as a child but now I study each and every night until the early light, you are right I will, I will have my own hotel, you'll see.'

'Well, you reap what you sow,' Esther smiled, entering her PIN and gifting the boy more rupees than he could possibly earn in an entire year. 'And that, young man, is for the crumpets,' she informed him.

'Holy Hindus, Missy,' the lad again gasped, eyeing the astonishing amount. 'A thousand blessings upon you both, no, no, ten thousand blessings!' He immediately hugged the two sisters before remembering his place. 'Oh, I am sorry, so sorry,' he said bowing again and backing toward the door. 'Please, enjoy your breakfast and thank you, thank you once again.' With a flash of his tunic he turned and skipped out the door holding the card reader aloft in celebration. 'VIVAAN MUKHERGEE!' he yelled his name out loud 'HOTEL MANAGER!'

The sisters later left the hotel to discover that Vivaan had washed and scrubbed Vivien from top to bottom with a bucket and sponge, leaving her marginally closer to her former glory and had also placed a large quantity of crumpets wrapped in white linen on her bonnet. 'Ahhhh,' Esther said, reading the note attached aloud. 'Once again I thank you for your gift and for gracing our hotel with your most illustrious presence.'

'Ahhh, how thoughtful,' Minnie said, cradling the much coveted crumpets.

Setting off once again, Esther and Minnie picked their way through the hustle and bustle of mid-morning traffic in downtown Nagpur, en route passing the renowned zero mile stone marking the exact geographical centre of the Indian continent. The monument consisted of four raging horses and a pinpointing pillar exquisitely carved in local sandstone.

After an hour or so of fraught manoeuvring and much horn blowing, Nagpur was finally behind them and they were able to breathe the clean country air once again, although the sun was rising in the hazy cloudless sky and temperatures were beginning to soar.

'Water, dear?' Minnie asked, handing her sister the flask she had astutely filled that very morning.

'Thank you, dear,' Esther said whilst steering around an ox-drawn cart and a group of barefooted children soaked to the skin having repeatedly leapt into an adjacent drainage ditch to cool themselves.

'Shall we, dear?' Minnie asked, suggesting the sisters stop and join the jubilant juveniles.

'Heavens, no!' Esther replied resolutely, driving on by and turning up Vivien's crotchety fan to its highest level, which barely ruffled her silver hair. 'That looks like a hot bed of typhoid, tuberculosis and diphtheria if you ask me,' she added, ever the cautionary sister.

'Ahh yes,' Minnie reluctantly agreed. 'You're probably right, dear.' She glanced over her shoulder in passing at the raven-haired youths who were clearly having the time of their lives, evoking echoes of her own childhood, when jumping into muddy puddles and collecting slugs and snails was the norm, something alien to later generations whose paranoid parents imprison their children behind double locked doors, showering them with expensive electronics to stimulate their captive minds, when all they really need is a pair of Wellington boots, a stick and a vivid imagination.

The distance between Nagpur and Mumbai was a back-breaking eight hundred and fifty kilometres and one that couldn't possibly be completed in a single day in a

Morris Traveller at forty miles per hour; therefore an additional overnight stop would be required. After careful consultation with Mister Google and his marvellous mountain of maps, Minnie suggested the midway city of Aurangabad in the Maharashtra region, a little known destination but nevertheless containing not one but two UNESCO world heritage sites, the awe-inspiring Ajanta and Ellora caves. These monumental rock dwellings built by Hindus and Buddhists as far back as the second century are said to contain the finest examples of primitive paintings and carvings ever discovered to date.

'Right you are, dear,' Esther agreed, leaning from her window to catch what little breeze there was.

'Here, dear,' Minnie said, offering the flask once again. 'I'm afraid that's all there is.'

'You have it, dear,' Esther insisted, putting her younger sibling first. 'I'll be fine, honestly.'

Minnie tipped what little water remained onto a face cloth and reached to dab her sister's reddened face before removing her hat to fan her.

'Thank you,' Esther sighed, relieved momentarily.

Minnie ran the towel around her own neck before any traces of moisture rapidly evaporated.

The welcome sight of a tiny village greeted the over the brow of the next hill and more importantly a dripping standpipe at the side of the road. 'Thank heavens,' Esther said, licking her parched lips. Stopping, the sisters gathered whatever containers they possessed and hastily filled them to the brim, then took it in turn to pump water over the other sister's grateful head. 'My God, that feels glorious,' Esther remarked, sweeping her sodden hair from her eyes and wiping the excess water from her face.

'I'll second that, dear,' Minnie agreed, filling her straw hat and dumping it onto her head.

The sisters then took a moment to reflect on their recent irrational decision to continue their travels rather than return home to their former humdrum existence, 'No regrets dear?' Esther asked.

'None whatsoever,' Minnie replied, taking in the evocative sights and sounds of the mystical Indian mid-west. 'How about you, dear?' she too asked. 'You have Elizabeth and young Richard back home after all.'

'Yes you're right, I do,' Esther said, picturing her loved ones. 'But I've been there for them, Minnie dear, their entire lives, I've been a shoulder to cry on when Elizabeth and Richard's father sadly separated, and a financial lifeline when my grandson, God bless him, spent every penny of his student loan in the first three weeks of term, so no, Minnie dearest, I have no regrets at all.'

'Splendid!' Minnie said, lifting the water containers into Vivien's open rear doors.

Quenched and ever determined, the sisters took to the road once again, and in high spirits Minnie soon broke into song. 'Paaack up ya troubles in yer old kit bag and smile, smile, smiiile!' a firm favourite of their father's.

Esther looked across and did just that, beaming from ear to ear and recalling him warbling the wartime ditty as he returned home from the Red Lion public house late on a Friday night, and she then joined her sister's rousing rendition. 'While you've a Lucifer to light your faaag, smile, boys that's the styyyyle!' She reached across and squeezed Minnie's hand fondly. 'Whaaaaat's the use of worryiiiing!' they both sang, swaying from side to side. 'It never was worth whiiiile, so pack up ya troubles in yer old kit bag and smile, smile, smiiiiiiiile!'

'Ha, ha, that brings back memories, dear,' Esther said jovially.

'Doesn't it just,' Minnie agreed. 'Do you know I can still hear Mother scolding him from the street door; will you be quiet you'll wake the girls!'

'Ahh, little did she know eh,' Esther reminisced. 'We never slept until Father was home, oh how we laughed and laughed as Mother hoisted him in from the doorstep with a wagging finger and an attempted straight face.'

'I do miss those days,' Minnie said, dropping her head and toying with a loose button on her cardigan.

'Me too,' Esther said with the slightest of lumps in her throat. 'We had nothing, dear, but I believe we were truly happy, in fact I cannot for the life of me remember a day without laughter in our house, what with Father being such an incorrigible practical joker.'

'Oh good heavens yes,' Minnie said with her smile immediately returning. 'Do you remember he put that huge plastic spider in the bottom of Mother's porridge bowl and swore us to secrecy, we sat and watched almost bursting as she ate her breakfast, and then roared with laughter when she scooped the horrid thing into her mouth.'

'Yes that's right,' Esther laughed 'She chased Father around the parlour with a rolled up copy of the *Radio Times*.'

'Crikey yes,' Minnie chuckled. 'And the time he told us there was buried treasure in the back garden, then sat and watched as we dug up his potatoes.'

'Yes I remember that,' Esther said scowling. 'He sat with a bottle of stout and his feet up while we dug over the entire vegetable patch, at the time, I tell you, I was not amused.'

'Me neither,' Minnie echoed. 'Oooh those blisters, mind you, dear, I'd give anything to do it all over again just to see that look on his face when we dug up the very last King Edward, he laughed so hard his deckchair collapsed and he dumped his stout into his lap.' The sisters' reminiscences served to pass the time of day and soon they were entering Aurangabad.

Parking in the centre of town, Esther and Minnie decided to stretch their legs and take in the sights before seeking out temporary lodgings. 'Here, dear,' Esther said, handing her sister a number of rupees, 'I took the liberty of obtaining some cash from our hotel in Nagpur, well, a girl needs some pennies in her purse after all, now shall we shop?'

'Oooh yes, let's,' Minnie said, eagerly pocketing her spends. Hand in hand they strolled along the thriving high street. 'Excuse me, sir,' Minnie said, stopping a road sweeper in the midst of his duties. 'I wonder, could you tell us if Aurangabad has a branch of the Heart Foundation by any chance?'

The sweeper, who spoke no English, whatsoever looked at the sisters as though they were visitors from Mars. 'Or possibly the RSPCA?' Minnie added 'You know, second-hand, thrift or tat whatever you prefer to call it?' Again the road sweeper looked on blankly.

'Oh never mind,' Minnie said, having very little patience for the man. She then attracted the attention of a fresh fruit peddler. 'I sayyyy!' she called. 'Are there any jumble sales of possibly church bazaars in town today that you know of, or maybe a car boot perhaps?'

'Jumble?' the greengrocer asked. 'What is jumble, madam?'

'What is jumble!' Minnie exclaimed. 'What is jumble!'

'My good man,' Esther intervened. 'A jumble sale is a veritable voyage of discovery, a chance to delve into the realms of the unknown as it were, it's, it's like searching for the lost city of Atlantis, Eldorado or King Solomon's mines!'

'Hear, hear!' Minnie agreed.

The sisters' life-long love of second-hand goods piled high and sold for a pittance stemmed from their grandmother Enid, who was indeed a grandmaster, or mistress for that matter, in the art of the rummage as she called it. Enid scoured the local rags for news of upcoming jumbles, fetes and bazaars and endeavoured to be first in line when the doors opened. Once inside the church or schoolhouse she would methodically but speedily sift through the garments, glassware, silverware, crockery and porcelain with military precision. Enid's elbows were legendary in the business of bargain hunting, fending off any would-be rival scavenger with a rib-crunching jab. Amongst her most illustrious finds were a pair of pearl earrings worn by Queen Victoria, a chamber pot once filled to the brim by Charles Dickens, Christopher Columbus's croquet mallet and a stuffed and mounted stoat rumoured to have bitten the Bard himself, Will Shakespeare. Enid had a nose like no other, a sixth sense as it were; if the needle in the proverbial haystack were remotely valuable or held some divine provenance she would find it.

Minnie tugged at her sister's arm. 'Look, dear!' she said, taut with excitement. 'Look!'

A Pakistani pensioner hobbled in their direction carrying a tattered standard lamp under one arm and a crudely painted replica portrait of Mother Theresa under the other. 'I'll bet you a pound to a penny, dear,' Minnie added, still tugging at her sister's sleeve, 'She's one of us.' By one of them she meant a member of the ancient order of collectors, united in a common goal and passionately devoted to the rummage.

'I do believe you're right, dear,' Esther said stopping in her tracks. The two of them stood shoulder to shoulder preventing the pensioner from passing with her wares, unless of course she divulged the source of such rich pickings. 'Ahh, good afternoon,' Esther said with a smile whilst eyeing her purchases, 'My sister and I are, ahem, fellow thrifters, if you get my drift.'

'Sorry?' the woman replied, clinging tightly to her tat.

'Now, now,' Minnie added, standing firm. 'It's alright, my dear, we were just wondering where it was you purchased such fine items?'

The Pakistani gripped her finds with whitened knuckles, reluctant to reveal the source. 'No understand, no understand,' she said furtively.

'Oh come now, my dear,' Esther said, attempting to befriend their fellow rummager, 'We're new in town and want to know where the action is, if you get my drift, it's OK, we'll keep this just between the three of us.' She turned to her sister. 'Minnie dear, show the good lady our credentials,' she said nodding.

Minnie looked around before rolling up her sleeve to reveal not one but six charity rubber wristbands in a variety of colours purchased at the counters of their regular haunts for a pound each, haunts such as Oxfam, Age UK and their firm favourite The Salvation Army.

'Ahhhh yes,' the woman gasped, setting down her portrait and reaching to stroke the coveted bands. 'My apology, my apology,' she said with a courteous bow, and she then looked over her shoulder before pulling the sisters close and lowering her voice. 'One hundred yard, take a left,' she whispered as though giving up the whereabouts of an ancient pharaoh's tomb. 'Two hundred yard, take a right, twenty-five paces, take another right, six paces, take a left.'

'Are you getting this, dear?' Esther asked her sister.

'Yes, dear,' Minnie replied. 'Every word of it.'

'Look for the green door,' the woman added, scooping up her tacky painting. 'Knock three times and ask for Mohammed,' she informed them, glancing over the other shoulder, 'You tell him Indira sent you.'

'Indira,' Esther replied. 'Right you are, my dear, thank you, oh and have no fear, your secret is safe with us.'

In exchange for such pearls of wisdom Minnie slipped the Cat Protection League's band from her arm and handed it to their ally, whose eyes lit up as though receiving a precious accolade. 'Wait, wait!' she said, rolling the sleeve of her sari to her upper arm to reveal an equally impressive collection of charity bands. 'For you,' she said, tugging a black and yellow striped wristy belonging to Aurangabad's very own Tiger Trust.

'Oh I couldn't possibly, dear,' Minnie said, moved by the reciprocal gesture.

'Please, please,' Indira insisted. 'For you.'

'Well, oh alright,' Minnie smiled, stretching the band over her fingers. 'Look, dear,' she told her sister. 'It's for the tigers, isn't it marvellous?'

'Hmmmm,' Esther said, unnerved at the mention of the T word. 'Yes, quite.'

'You like?' Indira asked, offering her arm for Esther and displaying some two dozen bands stretching from her wrist to her elbow in a rainbow of dazzling colour.

'My, that's a magnificent haul you have there, my dear,' Esther remarked, eyeing the indented inscriptions from some of India's most noteworthy charities.

Minnie bowed to Indira's superior bandsmanship, affording her the respect she so rightly deserved.

'I must go,' Indira said, eager to be on her way for fear of prying eyes. 'Tell no one,' she said in parting, and in an instant she disappeared into a narrow passageway and was gone.

'Excellent!' Esther said rubbing her hands together. 'Right, Minnie, lead on.'

'Me?' Minnie exclaimed.

'Yes, you!' Esther replied sharply. 'You do remember the way, don't you?'

'The way?' Minnie asked. 'Ohhhh, the wayyyy, well.'

'What do you mean, well?' her sister snapped. 'Now think, Minnie, this is important.'

'Yes I'm trying, dear,' Minnie moaned, her memory blurred by Indira's rubber revelation. 'I know we have to take a left, dear,' she eventually said. 'Yes, yes it's definitely a left.'

'And?' Esther asked expectantly.

'Ahh,' Minnie said, her mind a complete blank. 'Now if I were to hazard a guess, dear, I'd say it was a right, no, no wait I could be wrong.'

'Ohhh great,' Esther groaned. 'Minnie!' she then barked. 'Do you or do you not know the way, yes or no?'

'Errrrr, no,' Minnie confessed.

'NO!' Esther yelled. 'What do you mean no, Minnie, how could you be so stupid, this is tat we're talking about, now think, cast your mind back, was it a left next, or a right?'

Minnie thought long and hard. 'I have it, dear!' she suddenly shrieked. 'Yes, yes I remember now, follow me,' and she marched off confidently with Esther scurrying behind her. 'One hundred yard,' Minnie mouthed. 'Take a left.' Minnie followed Indira's instructions into the Aurangabad backstreets. 'Now was it six paces left or six paces right?' she said, stopping at an intersection.

'Miniiiiie!' Esther moaned. 'I thought you said you had it?'

'Well I did, dear,' Minnie said, looking left then right whilst toying with her tiger band. 'But, but…'

'But you've forgotten, haven't you?' her sister snapped. 'Oh that's juuust great.'

'No, no, give me a moment, dear,' Minnie said in her defence. 'You know I have a nose for these things.'

'No, actually I don't,' Esther remarked, the pair of them completely and utterly lost at this point.

'There, dear!' Minnie suddenly chirped, catching sight of a green door some sixty or seventy yards away. 'I told you, dear,' she added, striding forth again. 'Follow me!' Esther rolled her eyes and trudged after her sister.

'Knock three times,' Minnie said to herself at the door, and she did just that with Esther at her side. 'Mohammed?' she asked when a middle-aged gent answered. 'Indira sent us.' She took hold of her sister's hand and marched inside, leaving the owner speechless at the door. 'Where is it then?' Minnie asked, looking around the sparsely furnished room. 'Where's the tat?'

'Tat?' the gentleman replied, still stood at his door 'Tat?' 'Yes, yes the goods,' Minnie added picking his tin plate from the side table. 'This is hardly worth rolling up our sleeves for.'

'Minnie?' Esther said, realising their faux pas.

Leave this to me, dear,' Minnie said, silencing her sister with a raised hand. 'He's obviously hiding something, where is it?' she asked again, raising her voice. 'I realise we're from out of town but we've just as much right to browse as the rest of them.'

'Minnie!' Esther again said, taking hold of her sister's arm. 'We should go.'

'Go!' Minnie exclaimed. 'Not until he's shown us the goods, dear, I didn't come all this way to leave empty-handed, now, my good man, I suggest you spill the beans, where's the pottery, the paintings and the second-hand clothes, come on, out with it.' She looked behind then at a curtain strung across a doorway. 'Are they out back?' she asked. 'Yes, yes they are, aren't they.' She broke away from her sister and wrenched aside the curtain dividing the back room from the lounge, only to see the gentleman's wife and three children sitting at the dinner table eating a meagre meal of boiled rice and chapattis. 'Oh,' she said, struck dumb for a moment.

'Oh indeed!' Esther said, looking for herself. 'I'm ever so sorry,' she explained to the shell-shocked family. 'There seems to have been a grave misunderstanding on my sister's behalf, please forgive the intrusion.' She tugged her sister from the curtain in order to beat a hasty retreat when something caught her eye. 'Just a minute, Minnie,' she said, pausing to admire a solitary salt shaker on the rickety kitchen table. 'Excuse me, madam?' she said with a glint in her eye. 'I couldn't help but admire your charming salt pot, could you tell me, is it a Davenport by any chance?' The mother shrugged her shoulders, unfamiliar with the English manufacturer of fine chinaware. 'The salt, dear,' Esther reiterated. 'You see I believe I have the matching pepper pot.' She then took the liberty of plucking said pot from the table and examining it closely. 'It is, it is!' she said, wide-eyed with her heart now racing. 'Oh my God, what a find, what a find!'

'What is it, dear?' Minnie asked, peering over Esther's shoulder.

'Look, dear!' Esther gushed. 'It's the matching Davenport we've been looking for.'

'I don't believe it!' Minnie remarked. 'Here, of all places, Essy, it's a miracle, that's what it is, Oh good heavens, dear, my heart's pounding.'

'Mine too,' Esther replied, caressing the tiny salt shaker. 'My good man,' she said, addressing the father. 'Please, I beg of you, would you allow me to purchase this phenomenal piece of china from you?'

'This?' the man said, unaware of its sentimental significance.

'Yes,' Esther said, fending Minnie off as she tried to take it from her. 'I'm willing to pay whatever it is you want, go ahead, sir, name your price.' Her solitary pepper pot had played on her mind for several years but try as they might the sisters had failed to find its partner so to speak.

'Take it, take it!' the Indian gent said, eager to be rid of the intrusive sisters. 'Please,' he added, gesturing to the open door.

'Don't be ridiculous,' Esther smirked. 'I couldn't possibly expect you to give such a prize piece away, after all it's a Davenport for Pete's sake, no, no, you must let me pay you.'

The gentleman's wife had gotten the gist of the conversation and leapt from her seat. 'One thousand rupees!' she said, keen to provide for their children, the family left penniless after a recent illness.

'No, no, no, Sanita!' her husband said, shaking his head and ushering the sisters toward the door 'Please, take it' he said once again.

'Wait!' Esther said, breaking away. 'One thousand you say?' One thousand Indian rupees equated to just over ten English pounds but was still enough to feed the family for a fortnight or possibly a month at a push. 'Here,' Esther said, peeling several notes from her purse. 'Shall we sayyyy, fifty thousand?' and she thrust the money into Sanita's hand before the mother knew what was happening.

'No, no, please,' Sanita said on closer inspection.

Esther had paid a staggering five hundred pounds for the Davenport shaker 'Ah, ah, not another word,' she insisted.

'But, Miss,' the husband objected at his wife's side. 'We cannot accept this.'

'You can and you will,' Esther said resolutely. 'Believe me, I am more than satisfied with the transaction,' she added.

Minnie tugged at her sister's sleeve. 'You see, dear,' she said, looking extremely pleased with herself, 'I told you I had a nose for these things, didn't I.'

'Shut up, Minnie,' Esther said, still a tad miffed at her sister. 'And get out.' She pocketed the precious salt shaker and backed out the door. 'Thank you so much,' she told the flabbergasted couple. 'And once again my sincere apologies for the intrusion.'

Sanita and her husband stood spellbound for a moment or two after Esther closed the door and then jumped for joy; they now had enough money to feed and clothe their children for the foreseeable future, and all because of a simple salt shaker they had purchased for a couple of rupees from the very shop the sisters so eagerly sought, though quite how the Davenport piece migrated there will forever be a mystery.

Minnie crossed the street towards another green door. 'What about this one, dear?' she asked her sister, her hand hovering over the knocker.

'No, wait!' Esther barked, looking around at several other doors of a similar colour. 'Oh good grief this really is intolerable,' she groaned, but then towards the end of a fruitless search Esther glimpsed a battered brass fire bucket hanging from a hook outside one residence in a side street, with of course another green door. 'Could it be?' she said, leaving Minnie standing at the roadside.

'Wait for me, dear!' Minnie cried, feeling altogether uneasy in the strange town and hurrying behind.

Taking a deep breath, Esther raised her fist and rapped three times on the peeling premises' door. A jangling of keys could then be heard inside and the sliding of four heavy iron bolts. 'Mohammed?' Esther asked when a shadowy figure peered around the door. The occupier, an elderly bearded Indian nodded. 'Oh thank goodness,' Esther said with a hand to her chest. 'It's lovely to meet you, Mister Mohammed,' Esther added. 'A mutual friend of ours sent us, Indira?'

'Ahhhh yes,' the man said, smiling and opening the door just enough for the sisters to slip through. 'Quickly, come inside,' he told them, ushering them in before checking the street in either direction and hastily closing the door.

'Oh my word!' Esther gasped on first inspection of the brimming store. The dusty dank room was full to capacity with everything Esther and Minnie's hearts could have desired, clothes piled high to the ceiling and jigsaws galore, so much in fact that all but a narrow hazardous passageway remained amongst the clutter.

Minnie ran her hand over the box of a two-thousand-piece puzzle of the Taj Mahal. 'I think I've died and gone to heaven, dear,' she told her equally awestruck sister.

'That makes two of us,' Esther agreed, toying with a set of cork coasters, each of them depicting a playful kitten on the topside.

'Take your time,' Mohammed said, leaving the sisters and disappearing out back to tend to his supper.

'Oh we will!' Minnie called after him whilst rolling up her sleeves in readiness. 'I've waited for an opportunity like this my entire life,' she confessed.

The sisters found it near impossible to contain their excitement; they had found their Shangri-La, their Nirvana, their promised land and they were going to rummage until their crooked arthritic fingers bled if it meant leaving no stone unturned. 'Shall we, dear?' Esther said as though at a starting gate.

Minnie had no time to reply as she dived straight in, immersing herself in a pile of romantic novels, the scent of the aged paper and the occasional erotic text titillating her to the point of ecstasy. 'Look, dear, look!' she said, holding aloft a set of dominos dating back to the Second World War with a dent in the tin lid marking the impact of a stray enemy bullet.

'Put them aside, dear,' Esther told her, having started a pile of prospective purchases of her own, a sturdy pair of winter boots, two silk neck scarves and a wicker lampshade.

The sisters worked the enormous heap of tat from either side, each of them unable to see the other, just the clanging and thumping of disturbed paraphernalia and their frequent squeals and shrieks giving away their approximate location.

'Good grief!' Esther gasped, tugging a storm lantern from beneath a pile of crocheted cushions. 'I remember Grandfather visiting the outhouse in the middle of the night with one of these, that and a risqué magazine stuffed down his trousers.'

'What was that dear?' Minnie asked appearing with an armful of CDs, cassettes and vinyl 78's,

'Grandfather,' Esther said again. 'In the loo with his mucky magazines.'

'Oh heavens yes,' Minnie smiled. 'Look, dear,' she added, displaying her discoveries. 'Matt Munroe, Gilbert and Sullivan, Louis Armstrong and a favourite of ours, Danny O'Donnell, it's a double album but disc one is missing.'

'Danny O'Donnell!' Esther said dreamily. 'Oh, Minnie he has the voice of an angel, doesn't he, and such a charming young man.' The Irish crooner and now household name could literally charm the nylons off the ladies' legs with hits such as *Tipperary Girl, Light a Candle, The Way Dreams Are* and of course, *Morning Has Broken.*

'It's only five rupees, dear,' Minnie said eagerly.

'Oh my, that's an absolute steal,' Esther said, flushed with enthusiasm. 'Put them by, dear, put them by,' she said, and then something familiar over her sister's shoulder caught her eye. 'Minnie,' she said with her heart rate rising to critical levels. 'Minnie, I daren't look, dear, could you tell me, is that or is that not a Paul O'Grady mug behind you?'

'Where?' Minnie said, spinning one hundred and eighty degrees on the spot. 'Where, Essy, where?'

'Over there amongst the bric-a-brac,' Esther informed her 'Is it, Minnie darling, is it?'

Minnie approached the cluttered shelf with trepidation. The handle of a coffee mug could be seen alongside a Capodimonte and assorted cruet sets with a partial image barely visible.

'Can you reach it, dear?' Esther asked, close behind her sister.

Minnie's hand trembled as she reached out, and for brief moment the earth seemed to slow on its axis.

'Careful, careful, dear!' Esther warned when her sister dislodged a ceramic gravy boat.

With her heart in her mouth Minnie gripped the handle and teased the mug from between the crystal and chinaware.

'My God!' Esther said, grabbing her sister's chiffon blouse. 'Minnie, look, it is, it's him, Minnie, it's our beloved!'

Sure enough when exposed, the mug featured a photograph of a smiling Paul O'Grady, the nation's favourite presenter and former drag queen with one of his many rescue dogs clasped lovingly to his chest.

'How on earth?' Minnie said, taking a step back and stumbling on a stack of women's magazines.

'CAREFUL!' Esther shrieked, making a grab for the mug with no concern for her sister's safety. 'Oh thank heavens,' she added, snatching it from Minnie's clumsy hands and wiping the dust from the cherished image. 'I daren't put it down,' she told Minnie who regained her footing and straightened her spectacles. The thought of another customer stealing it from under their nose was a notion too dire to even contemplate.

'No, dear, you're right,' Minnie agreed, continuing her search.

Any self-respecting pensioner would have given their false teeth to be in Esther and Minnie's position that fateful day, Mohammed's emporium was an Aladdin's cave to any would-be collector of clutter, knick-knacks and complete and utter tat.

Before long the sisters had amassed a mountain of second-hand items. 'Oh dear,' Esther said, surveying the hefty haul which they would undoubtedly have trouble cramming into a minivan let alone Vivien. 'We'll have to whittle it down, dear,' she begrudgingly told her sister.

'Whittle it down!' Minnie said defensively. 'But, but how, dear?'

The pair set about the painful task of deciding an object's right to a place in their hearts and their Morris based on three things; its size, its beauty and its emotional value. 'Now, dear,' Esther said, sifting through their pickings. 'The framed print, yes or no?'

'Oh yes, Essy!' Minnie said, clutching the cheap reproduction. 'It's the Sydney Opera House, Cyril promised he'd take me there, well, before we separated that is.'

'Esther set down the cranberry glass bowl she was cradling. 'Yes, tell me again, Minnie dearest?' she asked. 'Why was it you and Cyril went your separate ways?'

Minnie cleared her throat. 'Well it was a number of reasons actually,' she said, finding it a strain to relive. 'One of them being the fact that he'd been carrying on behind my back with Daphne from the library, the slut, she promised to waive his fines if he took her out to dinner, and Cyril never returned his novels on time.'

'Really!' Esther exclaimed. 'Daphne with the blue rinse and the cheap perfume?'

'Yes, that Daphne,' Minnie said, grimacing. 'The thought of her stamping his library card makes my blood boil, it does, Essy.'

'OK,' Essy agreed, 'We'll keep the Sydney Opera House, now what about the wind chime, I don't know about you but I rather like it, I thought I could hang it outside the kitchen window to keep the pigeons from you-know-whatting over my geraniums, I won a silver ribbon for my window box last year from the local horticultural society, of course Marjorie won gold for her polyanthus, the bitch, I swear she bought those from Waitrose the day before judging was due to commence, but I'll get my hands on that trophy you'll see, if those blasted pigeons would just defecate elsewhere.'

'You're right, dear,' Minnie said, sympathising with her sister and her bitter neighbourly feud. 'We simply must keep the wind chime, after all it's a matter of principle.'

A full fifteen minutes later the sisters had begun to make a little headway, just a little, mind. 'It's no use, dear,' Esther said, eyeing the yes and no piles. 'We must be more mercenary, for Vivien's sake.'

'Yes, dear, I know,' Minnie agreed, clinging tightly to her romantic Mills and Boon novels. 'I thought I'd read all of these but clearly I was mistaken.'

'I'm sorry, dear,' Esther said, prising them from her sister's vice-like grasp. 'But we simply haven't the room, not if you insist on keeping the fireguard and the clothes horse.'

'I do indeed,' Minnie replied, stroking the collapsible wooden frame. 'I'll be able to dry all my passion-killers in front of the fire at once.' Minnie had previously strung one or two pairs of her huge reinforced undergarments above the gas hob to dry which grated on her sister no end.

'OK, the clothes horse is a definite yes,' Esther confirmed. 'But the Mills and Boons I'm afraid will have to stay, I'm sorry, Minnie, but we have to draw the line somewhere.'

With a heavy heart and the odd muffled objection, Minnie replaced the paperbacks.

Eventually after much deliberation and one or two heartfelt decisions Esther and Minnie had reduced their purchases to a more manageable level. 'I sayyyyy!' Esther called toward the rear of the premises. 'We're ready to settle up now!'

Mohammed appeared, mopping curry sauce from his beard. 'Very good, very good!' he said with a glint in his eye. 'Now let me be seeing.' He totted up the 'yes' pile in his head. 'I can do for two thousand rupee if you please,' he finally said with his hands clasped. 'And if you are wanting carrier bag I'm afraid I am having to charge an extra five rupee, government legislation you see.'

'Oh God, not here too,' Esther groaned, having begrudgingly purchased carriers back home. 'Oh very well,' she agreed. 'We'll take half a dozen to begin with.'

Minnie began to pack their assorted wares. 'Two thousand rupees for all this, dear,' she said with a grin. 'I just can't believe it.' A little over twenty pounds had netted them a handsome load.

'Well thank you, Mohammed,' Esther said with two bags in each hand. 'If my sister and I are ever again in this neck of the woods you can rest assured we'll be paying you another visit.'

'Undoubtedly,' Minnie agreed, weighted down herself. 'So if you could please put the paperbacks aside I'd be eternally grateful.'

Mohammed opened the door and again checked the street outside before allowing the sisters to leave. 'Good day to you,' he said, slamming the door shut behind them and shoving across the heavy bolts.

'Peculiar fellow,' Esther remarked retracing their steps along the street.

'I say, Essy, would you like me to lead the way?' her sister asked, attempting to keep up.

'No I would not!' Esther said sternly. 'You have an appalling sense of direction at the best of times, Minnie, oh and before you say you have a nose for it, believe me you do not.'

'Oh,' Minnie sulked while pausing to set her heavy bags down. 'I see.'

'No you don't!' Esther barked, looking back. 'That's just it, you never ever see!'

With reddened hands and aching limbs the sisters eventually arrived back to where they'd left Vivien and loaded their booty into the back.

'Now, lodgings?' Esther said, looking around with a host of hotels to choose from.

'There dear,' Minnie piped up. 'That looks adorable, can we stay there, pleaaaaaase?'

'The Moon and Seven Heavens?' Esther said, looking across the street at the smaller of a group of boarding houses. 'Are you sure, dear?'

'Oh yes, quite sure, dear,' Minnie said, tugging her overnight bag from the back of the car. 'I read about it on the travel advisor thingy, apparently a Mr and Mrs Forsythe from Tewskesbury gave it a five-star rating from cleanliness and old world charm.'

'Five stars you say?' Esther pondered. 'Well I'll take your word for it, Minnie.' She also eyed the palatial Aurangabad Hilton on the next block but decided to give her sister the benefit of the doubt, after all, Mister Google and the tablet had stood them in good stead thus far. 'I suppose if it's good enough for our fellow Brits,' she agreed, retrieving her own bag and locking Vivien.

CHAPTER TWO.

The following morning raised voices could be heard by those on the street outside the Moon and Seven Heavens hotel as Esther and Minnie emerged. 'Five stars!' Esther barked, enraged at her sister's poor choice of accommodation. 'That's the last time I listen to you, I swear, Minnie, the last time, I didn't sleep a wink, a blasted wink!'

'Oh come now, dear,' Minnie said, trailing behind. 'Don't you think you're being a tad melodramatic?'

'Melodramatic!' Esther growled on the hotel steps. 'Melodramatic, this place needs a demolition order, that's what it needs, my back is in pieces after spending the night on that mortician's slab they call a bed, and room service, ha, don't get me started on room service, a filthy paper cup of dishwater passed off as Darjeeling and a naan bread as hard as a flipping discus!'

'But, Essy,' Minnie said, amid her sister's ranting. 'The Forsythes said...'

'The Forsythes!' Esther snarled with visible bags under her eyes. 'I tell you, Minnie, if I ever have the misfortune to meet the Forsythes I'll give them a piece of my mind, five stars indeed, ha!'

In her haste Minnie had read the only online five-star review for the Moon and Seven Heavens; the remaining three hundred and forty visitors rated it with only one star with comments such as 'Utterly disgusted!' and 'Unfit for human habitation!' and a whole host of other disparaging remarks. Mister and Mrs Forsythe, however, found the hotel a step up from their squalid, rodent-infested caravan and thus rated it favourably whilst touring the sub-continent.

'A wrecking ball!' Esther said looking back. 'That's what it needs, a blasted wrecking ball, Seven Heavens my backside!'

Minnie scratched at her neck, having been feasted upon by a thousand bed mites. 'Well at least the view was pleasant from our balcony, dear,' she said attempting to soften the blow.

'Balcony!' Esther scoffed. 'I wouldn't set foot outside that room for all the tea in China, not if I valued my life anyway.' The wooden makeshift balcony had indeed seen better days, dry rot and decay had rendered it treacherous and unable to withstand the weight of a small child. 'And what view exactly?' Esther asked, spinning in the middle of the road to confront her sister.

'The petting zoo,' Minnie replied. 'Did you not see it, dear, they had cows, chickens, pigs, sheep and goats, I thought we could pay them a visit before we left town, what do you think?'

'Minnie!' Esther gasped in disbelief 'That was no petting zoo, that was an abattoir, you fool, they were there to have their throats cut.'

'What!' Minnie said, shell-shocked. 'No, Essy, surely not!

'Errrrr, yes,' Esther said, enlightening her hapless sister. 'How many petting zoos do you know with a one hundred percent mortality rate, eh?'

'An abattoir?' Minnie said, struggling to come to terms with the glaring facts.

'Yes, Minnie, an abattoir,' Esther insisted, hurling her bag into Vivien. 'The fellow covered in blood hadn't just cut himself shaving for Pete's sake, now get in will you, and give me that blasted tablet, I'll write a review alright, the Moon and Seven Hells more like!'

Minnie loaded her bag and slipped in sheepishly beside her sister, who prodded at the tablet screen venomously. Minnie then raised a finger. 'I thought we could give them two stars dear,' she suggested. 'After all Mister Muktar did carry our bags up five flights of stairs and supply us with those rather charming candles, which I feel gave the place a certain ambiance, don't you, dear?'

'Mister Muktar carried our bags, Minnie!' Esther reminded her sister, 'Because the elevator had been condemned as had the electrics, hence the candles.'

'Oh,' Minnie said, lowering her hand, 'I see.'

'Minnie, if you say that once more!' Esther raged. 'I swear I'll…'

'Alright, alright!' Minnie said, interrupting. 'You're right, dear, I never see, do I?'

The sisters left Aurangabad with mixed feelings, elated at having made several meteoric finds at Mohammed's and aggrieved at having spent the night at the ill-fated Moon and Seven Heavens hotel, although the word hotel should be used loosely in connection with the run down, ramshackle residence.

'Ooh look, dear!' Minnie said, once out of town. 'A pair of swans, how lovely.'

Esther merely glared across at her sister with contempt, feeling altogether irritable having tossed and turned the entire night whilst her sister slept beside her like a baby, occasionally robbing her of the only suspiciously stained sheet in the room. 'You know they mate for life, dear don't you,' Minnie added referring to the swans. 'Can you imagine spending you entire life with the same person?'

Esther again glared at her sister. 'Yes, Minnie,' she said, stiff lipped. 'Yes I can,' but her flippant remark sailed way over her sister's head.

Minnie settled in her seat, contented after a restful night. 'Ahhhhh,' she sighed with a wistful smile. 'Next stop Mumbai, dear, I'm so excited, I've heard so much about the place, apparently.' she added, retrieving the tablet and tapping at the screen.

'Oh God,' Esther groaned whilst suffering terribly from sleep deprivation.

'Mumbai,' Minnie said, clearing her throat, 'Has the highest population of any Indian city, around twenty million, dear.'

'Marvellous,' Esther said expressionless.

'Also,' Minnie continued unabated, 'There are more billionaires currently residing in Mumbai than anywhere else in the entire country, and, dear, I don't know about you but I was not aware that Mumbai and Bombay are one in the same, Bombay is Mumbai and vice versa, amazing, simply amazing.'

'Riveting, dear,' Esther said, yawning.

'It says here, dear,' Minnie added, reading Mumbai's Wikipedia entry, 'Mumbai lies on the west coast of India and has a deep natural harbour making it a major sea port in the Arabian sea, the Arabian sea, dear, our gateway to Dubai.'

'Please, don't remind me,' Esther moaned, dreading the thought of boarding a freighter.

'Now I've made all the arrangements,' Minnie informed her sister. 'We board the Northern Star in three days, apparently we are to report to a Captain Kofti at ten a.m. sharp or she sails without us.'

'And wouldn't that be a crying shame,' Esther replied, tongue in cheek.

'Now, now, dear,' Minnie said, raising a finger. 'I'm sure once you find your sea legs you'll embrace it with zest and vigour.'

'The only thing I'll be embracing, dear,' Esther said, vehemently opposed to any nautical excursions, 'Is a bucket, now are you quite sure there is no reasonable alternative?'

'Positive, dear,' Minnie said, reading on. 'Mumbai, the city of dreams,' she said enthusiastically. 'The gateway to India!'

'Minnie!' Esther said, squeezing Vivien's wheel tightly. 'Please!'

'Oh right you are, dear,' Minnie agreed, giving her sister a little breathing space, but moments later offering one or two more pearls of wisdom. 'According to the interweb, dear, we have a further three hundred and twenty kilometres to go before we reach Mumbai, oh and apparently the Taj Mahal Palace hotel comes highly recommended, it's been given five stars on the travel advisor thingy.'

'Not by the blasted Forsythes, I hope!' Esther snapped, irritable still.

'No, dear,' Minnie smirked. 'The Taj Mahal has in excess of a thousand five-star reviews, shall I make a reservation?'

'I'm warning you, Minnie!' Esther said, pointing a finger in her sister's direction. 'If this is another of your foolhardy discoveries I'll, I'll…'

'Oooh look, dear!' Minnie quickly intervened. 'An elephant.' Sure enough, a bull elephant wallowed in an adjacent river, partially submerged and blowing gallons of water onto its broad back through its trunk. Minnie hastily took a photograph and then another of her sister's scowling face.

'Stop it!' Esther barked. 'What are you doing?'

'Updating our social media whatsits,' Minnie informed her. 'I've been inundated with tweets, emails and PMs.'

'PMs?' Esther asked. 'What the devil?'

'Private messages, dear,' Minnie enlightened her sister. 'It's quite the done thing nowadays, anyway we have a responsibility to our followers and I for one might add take that very seriously indeed.'

'Well that's your department,' Esther scoffed, 'I am purely logistics.'

'Yes I know that, dear,' Minnie said, snapping a group of workers harvesting wheat and maize nearby. 'We each have a role to play,' she added.

'Hmmmm,' Esther muttered, avoiding further potholes in the poorly maintained mid-west roads.

For once Minnie had chosen wisely with the Taj Mahal Palace hotel and with a hundred or so kilometres to go she could rest easy, safe in the knowledge that Esther would have no cause for complaint whatsoever; she might even thank her younger sister, now that surely would be a red-letter day.

Minnie continued to delight their legions of followers over the course of the following three or four hours as the sisters passed unhindered through Shrirampur, Sangamner, Purushwadi, Shendi and Murbad. Each of these steamy townships and villages offering a unique insight into the lesser publicised but culturally rich heartlands. Shrirampur, for instance, formed around the once thriving sugar cane industry, and Purushwadi, a thousand meters above sea level and home to the little known but simply breath-taking firefly sanctuary, a phenomenon to rival the famed Northern Lights themselves.

Approaching Mumbai, Esther and Minnie began to attract the odd wave from fans who immediately recognised Vivien as she approached with her distinctive throaty exhaust and shrill horn, which was put to good use as the roads were simply teaming with pedestrians, hand carts, livestock and market traders galore. 'Essy, isn't it wonderful,' Minnie remarked as they entered the densely populated city.

'I don't know about that, dear,' Esther replied with her stress levels peaking.

All around mutterings of 'Peshwari Nans' could be heard, and yet again several flower garlands were strung across Vivien's roof rack and hung from her pitted chrome wing mirrors. Hoteliers and restaurateurs, learning of the sisters' arrival, dashed out into the streets to vie for their business, as a favourable review from the Peshwari Nans could undoubtedly turn a mediocre business into a major player overnight. In the hands of the sisters the pen was indeed mightier than the sword, and as the Moon and Seven Heavens had learned, it could quite easily have the opposite effect.

Esther's scathing condemnation of their previous accommodation in Aurangabad with its broken elevator and tepid brown bath water had forced its closure until major refurbishment works were carried out, and the owners had heeded Esther's advice and brought in the wrecking ball to reduce the ramshackle residence to rubble.

The frantic Mumbai business owners jostled one another, yelling enticements at the sisters above their neighbours. 'I GIVE YOU GOOD PRICE, GOOD PRICE!' and 'TWO FOR ONE ON CHAMOMILE TEA!' another promised. 'PLEASE I HAVE AIR CONDITION AND JIGSAW IN EVERY ROOM!'

'Did you hear that, dear?' Minnie asked, tugging at her sister's arm. 'A jigsaw in every room, I wonder if there's one with a piece missing.' She took out her lucky charm, a jigsaw segment featuring a human foot found in a puzzle purchased in Prague during their previous escapades; she kissed the piece and tucked it back into her pocket, convinced of its talisman-like qualities.

Toward the seafront and the port of Mumbai the bedlam intensified, as thousands upon thousands of Indians, Pakistanis and Bangladeshis filled the streets paying no heed to the honking mid-afternoon traffic and all hopes of a highway code had been dashed days before reaching this sprawling metropolis.

Everybody without exception seemed to speak at double the decibels of anything the sisters had every encountered, so much so it unnerved the elderly

Londoners. 'Take a left, dear, take a left!' Minnie said, guiding her sister toward their destination. 'Go around him, dear!' she gesticulated. 'What are you waiting for?'

'I can't, for heaven's sake!' Esther said, grimacing. 'There's a blasted cow in the road!'

The heat was unbearable and the noise skull splitting; a fellow motorist began yelling obscenities in Bengali when Esther- failed to give way. 'TO THE RIGHT, YOU FOOL!' she yelled back out the window, quoting her own highway code, 'TO THE RIGHT!'

Wailing bhangra music provided the soundtrack to the madness that is Mumbai, blasted from taxi cabs and cheap Taiwanese transistor radios alike. 'Why does it have to be so loud?' Esther asked, wincing. 'I'm sure I'm getting one of my heads, Minnie.'

'Oh I think it's rather catchy, dear,' Minnie replied, bobbing in her seat and eyeing the traditional dress of the locals. 'I rather fancy I might purchase a sari, dear' she said, checking the myriad of clothing retailers. 'What do you think?'

'Whatever,' Esther said, whilst dismissing a chapatti peddler at her window. 'No thank you!' she told the young Indian boy, who was quickly joined by up to a dozen of his countrymen offering everything from sandals to samosas through the open window. 'No, no!' Esther said, over and over. 'No thank you, I said!'

Minnie reached across with twenty rupees in her hand. 'I'll take two samosas, a rubber cobra and a solar fan please,' she told the gathering.

'Minnie!' Esther said through gritted teeth. 'Please don't encourage them'

'Oh, Essy,' Minnie smiled. 'The poor things are only trying to make a living, I really do feel for them.' Minnie waved the rubber snake under her sister's nose in passing. 'Sssssssssss!' she chuckled

'Get that away from me, you fool,' Esther said, swatting the life-like cobra.

Minnie tucked into her samosas whilst waving the snake around the car.

'Will you put that down!' Esther raged. 'Sometimes, Minnie, I swear I'd like to….'

'I got this for you,' Minnie said, interrupting once again and licking the sucker on the back of the solar fan; she then promptly stuck it to Vivien's windscreen, and almost immediately the tiny propeller began to whir blowing cooling air into Esther's reddened face.

'Oh,' Esther remarked, going off the boil. 'Errrrrr, thank you, thank you, Minnie, that's awfully kind of you.' Only Minnie could go from zero to hero in a heartbeat.

Approaching the vast seven-storey Taj Mahal Palace, the sisters couldn't help but marvel at its architectural stature. 'It's, it's like Windsor Castle, dear,' Minnie gasped, leaning from her window.

'Don't be daft, it's nothing like Windsor Castle,' Esther replied defensively. 'But it is rather impressive, I'll grant you that.' Kings, queens, popes and presidents had graced its stately suites.

Esther parked Vivien between two gleaming Bentleys and swung her aching legs one at a time out the door, while Minnie gathered her purse and the tablet. 'Oh wow!' she said, looking across the harbour at the heart-stopping gateway bridge. 'Isn't that something, dear?'

'Yes, yes,' Esther said, red-faced once again at the back doors wrestling with Minnie's collapsible clothes horse. 'Help me with the bags, will you,' she asked, but Minnie had wandered to the water's edge, snapping several of the super yachts moored alongside. 'Minnie!' Esther called, tossing her fireguard aside to retrieve their luggage.

Minnie sidled back, toying with the pearls around her neck. 'I've just seen Richard Branson, dear,' she told her sister. 'He sends his love.'

'Yes, yes, never mind that,' Esther said, having worked up a sweat. 'Here.' She thrust Minnie's bag to her chest. 'Now don't wander off,' she warned her. 'And try not to antagonise the locals.'

'Antagonise, dear?' Minnie asked, clattering the wing mirror of a Lamborghini in passing, the driver of which glared at her. 'Afternoon!' she said with a regal wave. 'Lovely day!'

A hotel footman approached the couple in the car park. 'Excuse me, excuse me, Miss!' he called on seeing Vivien's tarnished condition and assuming the sisters were penniless tourists. 'You cannot be parking there, this is the Taj Mahal Palace.'

'Yes, yes, we know,' Esther informed him. 'We have a reservation.'

'You do?' the footman said, raising his eyebrows. 'Really?'

'Yes, in the name of Reynolds,' Esther added. 'Now be a dear and take our baggage would you, can't you see we're senior citizens?'

'Yes, yes, of course,' the footman said, hastily relieving the sisters of their luggage. 'Please accept my humble apologies, I saw your vehicle and thought…'

'Oh, Vivien,' Esther said, looking back at her cherished car. 'Yes, I see what you mean, the old girl has been through the wringer of late.'

The footman then called to one of the hotel's many chauffeurs. 'This is Lari,' he told Esther. 'He number one mechanic in all of Mumbai.'

'Lari?' Esther replied. 'Like the lamb?' Lari looked on blankly. 'Never mind,' Esther added, 'Thank you, dear, but I believe it's a panel beater we need.'

'I can fix,' Lari said eagerly. 'And I can paint for you.'

'Oh I doubt that very much,' Esther scoffed, whilst Minnie tweaked her hat using a Porsche window as a mirror. 'She's a 1965 Morris, dear, they don't make them anymore, my love.'

'Trafalgar blue,' Lari said proudly. 'British Leyland colour BU37, I can mix for you.'

'Oh,' Esther said, gobsmacked. 'How on earth?'

'I told you, Miss,' the footman intervened. 'Lari number one in Mumbai.'

'Can you really fix my Vivien?' Esther asked, clutching her chest. 'Can you?'

'Absolutely, madam,' Lari said, grinning. 'Tell me how long you stay?'

'Three days,' Minnie piped up. 'We sail for Dubai in three days.'

'I fix in two days,' Lari said confidently, 'As good as new, you see, madam.'

'Oh that would be wonderful,' Esther said, feeling an emotional surge. 'Now I assure you money is no object young man,' she told him with a hand on his shoulder. 'And I know it's a tall order so just do your best with her, do you hear?'

'No problem, no problem,' Lari said as Esther handed over the keys and glanced over her shoulder at Vivien once more. 'I will do for you number one job,' he told her. 'Number one job indeed.'

'Thank you, Lari,' Esther said. 'And thank you too,' she told the attentive footman. 'Now lead on, my good man.' She turned to her sister who was still preening herself in the parked Porsche's window. 'Minnie, come away!' she insisted, tugging her sister and snatching a car aerial from her hand.

'What?' Minnie asked. 'It just came off, dear.'

Esther quickly discarded the broken antenna and dragged her sister toward the foyer. 'What did I say, what did I say?' she said, scolding her sister all the way to the front desk. 'Oh hello,' she then said in a lighter tone. 'I believe we have a reservation, under the name of Reynolds, this is my sister, Minnie, for all she's worth.'

'Pardon, dear?' Minnie asked, having been distracted by the sheer scale of the hotel lobby itself,

'Ahhh yes, madam, I have you here,' the hotel manager said. 'And may I say on behalf of the Taj Mahal Palace what an honour it is to have you both here.' He leaned a little closer. 'I personally am a huge fan of yours, a huge fan indeed.'

'Oh er, thank you,' Esther replied, handing over her card.

'And you, madam,' the manager said, offering Minnie his hand. 'You must be Minnie, may I say you are every bit as beautiful as I'd imagined, every bit, madam.'

'Really?' Minnie said, flicking her hair from her eyes. 'Well thank you, thanks awfully, but I must give full credit to the Avon lady, she calls twice a week with her cosmetics and they are a life saver, I tell you, I'd wrinkle like a rhino without them, dear.'

The manager bent and kissed the back of Minnie's hand.

'Oooh errr,' Esther said, a tad jealous. 'Perhaps you two would like a room of your own.'

A commotion could then be heard behind them and the sisters turned to see one of India's most famous sons descending the hotel stairs, flanked by his vast entourage and of course the ever present paparazzi. Internationally acclaimed Bollywood movie director Raj Govinda literally commanded the sort of attention heads of state could only dream of. Mumbai was the home of Bollywood, which in box office sales alone dwarfed its American cousin, and Raj Govinda, born the son of a peasant farmer, ruled the roost with net personal earning running into the billions.

The eager paps poked microphones in his direction. 'Mister Govinda, Mister Govinda!' they yelled whilst battling with his burly bodyguards. Raj's movies had scooped every major award and accolade the Bollywood industry had to offer and made megastars of their leading actors. The two movies that he will undoubtedly best be remembered for and which are now iconic in their own right are, '*Two Pints of Cobra and a Mutton Curry* and '*Bang, Bang, Bangalore'* both of them grossing twice the amount of such big hitters as *ET, Titanic* and *Avatar*.

'Who's that, dear?' Minnie asked at her sister's side.

'I haven't the foggiest,' Esther replied, eyeing the pot-bellied balding director in his lurid yellow open neck shirt with one of India's top supermodels on his right arm.

'He looks like Uncle Ted,' Minnie remarked. Esther and Minnie's Uncle Ted, now deceased, was an equally chubby chap who worked the Whitechapel market in the late 1960's cutting keys and sharpening knives on his pedal-powered grindstone, his own portly podge acquired through years at the bar of the Blind Beggar where he routinely down a dozen pints of stout and consume copious packets of scampi fries.

Raj mopped his brow with his silk scarf and eyed the ample breasts of his latest conquest, the gold chains around his neck clamped between his treble chins. He suddenly threw up his arms and halted the procession when spotting Esther and Minnie at the front desk. 'STOOOOOP!' he yelled, silencing everyone in the immediate vicinity. 'That's it, that's it!' he said, hitting himself about the head. 'Thank you, Lord, thank you, thank you,' he added, looking to the heavens before pushing his way through the crowd. 'Out of my way!' he yelled. 'Out of my way!' Sweating profusely and followed by the mob, Raj waddled to the desk. 'Excuse me,' he said, decidedly out of breath. 'Do forgive the intrusion but, but are you not Esther and Mimmie, the Peshwari Nans?'

'Minnie, dear,' Minnie said, correcting him. 'And yes, yes we are.'

'Ohhhhhh!' Raj cried, thanking the gods once again. 'I knew it, I knew it! It is a sign, I tell you, a sign, Esther and Mimmie have come to Mumbai!'

'Errr, that's Minnie,' Minnie again informed him.

Raj's astute business mind kicked into gear immediately. 'I have it, I tell you,' he said, tugging his assistant to his side and dismissing his hot young girlfriend. 'I have the one, I have the one!'

'The one, sir!' his assistant too gasped. 'Really?'

By 'the one' Raj meant the Bollywood blockbuster to beat all others, the movie he'd dreamt of making his entire life. 'Ladies, ladies,' he said excitedly. 'I am sorry once again for the intrusion but I have a proposition I wish to put to you.'

'I'm sorry too, dear,' Minnie said dismissively. 'But I'm not on the market.'

'No, no, no!' Raj laughed. 'I am not wanting a wife. I am wanting a leading lady, two leading ladies in fact.'

'Leading ladies?' Esther asked. 'I'm sorry but I don't follow you, who are you anyway?'

Raj's entire entourage gasped at Esther's naivety, but Raj found it refreshingly hilarious. 'My apologies,' he said, wiping his sweat-drenched neck.

'Please, allow me to introduce myself, Raj Govinda, I er, I suppose you could say I am in the movie business.' This amused his followers greatly. 'Bollywood movies to be precise,' he added.

'Bollywood?' Minnie asked.

'Yes, Mimmie, Bollywood movies,' Raj replied proudly.

'Errrr,' Minnie said, raising a finger. 'Actually it's Minnie.'

'Yes of course,' Raj replied, his head now spinning with prospective plots. 'I have a script,' he informed the bewildered sisters. 'But until now I have found nobody worthy to play my heroines.'

'Us?' Esther asked with a smile. 'You cannot be serious.'

'Madam,' Raj said, straight-faced. 'I have never before been so serious, not in my whole life, never, please tell me you will consider my proposal, please.'

'Yes we'll do it,' Minnie blurted without hesitation.

'WHAT?' Esther barked, spinning to confront her sister. 'We will do nothing of the sort.'

'Oh but, Essy, the movies,' Minnie pleaded.

'No!' Esther replied unflinching. 'Minnie dear, I can't believe you are even contemplating such a ridiculous notion, I'm sorry, Mister, what did you say your name was?' she asked the director.

'Govinda, Raj Govinda,' Raj said, clicking his fingers and snatching his cheque book from his assistant. 'Please you can name your price,' he told the sisters. 'Any price, you must do it, you must, we will make cinematic history together, Mimmie, talk to your sister, tell her.'

'The name's Minnie,' Minnie insisted once again.

'Yes, yes, my apologies, Mimmie,' Raj said, beside himself with excitement at this point.

Esther stood firm. 'No, no, I'm sorry, Mister Govinda, it's quite out of the question, besides we have no acting experience whatsoever.'

'You speak for yourself,' Minnie piped up. 'I once played a star in the school Nativity.'

'Yes that's right,' Esther scoffed. 'You had to stand there dressed from head to toe in tin foil without a single line, my God, Minnie, that hardly makes you Scarlet O'Hara now does it.'

'Please,' Raj begged with his hands clasped and his dream movie within his grasp, an epic so incredible that his name would live on for eons to come.

'Also, Minnie,' Esther added in her defence, 'As you quite rightly pointed out, we sail in three days, albeit against my better judgement.'

'No problem, madam,' Raj smiled. 'I will be needing you for just one and one half days, that is all, please won't you reconsider?'

'Pleaaaaase, Essy,' Minnie grovelled. 'It'll be fun, won't it, Mister Govinda?'

'It will indeed, Mimmie,' Raj remarked with his heart pounding in his bloated chest.

The surrounding paparazzi jostled for position with cameras flashing, this was truly a momentous meeting, Raj Govinda and the Peshwari Nans in talks, opportunities that fantastic were only ever witnessed once in a news hound's lifetime.

'Please, Essy, can we, can we?' Minnie continued, tugging at her sister's sleeve 'You're right, I didn't have a speaking part in the Nativity but you've got to admit I had stage presence.'

'Oh you had presence alright,' Esther scoffed. 'Right up to the point when you fell off your cardboard cloud and crushed the blasted manger, the donkey bolted dragging the three wise men with it and the Virgin Mary went home in tears.'

'Ohhh,' Raj said, addressing Minnie, 'You have some experience then?'

'Oh yes,' Minnie said confidently. 'Yes, it's in the blood you see, our great-grandfather had a Punch and Judy stand at Frinton-on-Sea.'

'Punch and Judy?' Raj asked. 'What is Punch and Judy?'

'What is Punch and Judy!' Minnie said aghast. 'Mister Govinda, my dear, you have not lived, sir, you have not lived.'

Mister Govinda turned to his assistant, demanding they research the British seaside puppetry tradition. 'So you will do it, yes?' he then asked the sisters.

Minnie looked at her sister the same way she did when they were children and she'd eaten all her sweets before her big sister.

'Ohhh alright,' Esther said as she invariably did back then, sharing her packet. 'Anything for a quiet life, I suppose.'

'Yes!' Raj shrieked. 'I will send a car for you in the morning, say around nine?'

'Yes, nine is fine, thank you,' Minnie said enthusiastically. 'Errrr, one more thing,' she added, 'What's the movie about, are we to star opposite a dashing young leading man, and maybe become embroiled in a sensuous love triangle fighting for his affections?'

'Errr, not exactly,' Raj replied, eyeing the eavesdropping media. 'I am sorry, I cannot say too much at this time, but all will be revealed tomorrow, you will see, I promise you it will be the most momentous movie Bollywood has ever seen, now get some rest tonight, ladies, filming can be a little arduous at first.'

'Right you are, dearie,' Minnie said shielding her eyes from the flashing cameras. 'Right you are.'

Raj Govinda was swept away by his people with the majority of the Indian media at his heels, but one or two remained with the sisters for the lowdown on their recent travels and their eventual destination. 'Well, I won't say where we're headed,' Esther told them. 'My sister and I would like some privacy you know, but I will tell you where we've been.' She began divulging the details of the previous few days. 'And then we came across a tiger!' she said pausing for breath.

'Oh yes!' Minnie intervened. 'It had great big snarling teeth, we were frightened to death, weren't we, dear?'

'Yes, yes, I was coming to that,' Esther said, offended at Minnie's interjection. 'Now where was I?'

'Tell them about the chili powder, dear!' Minnie blurted at her side.

'Yes, yes, dear!' Esther snapped. 'I was about to if you give me a moment.' She took another deep breath. 'As I was saying,' she proceeded once again, 'We came across a tiger.'

'Chili powder, you say?' a reporter asked Minnie.

'Yes that's right,' Minnie replied, cutting her sister off yet again. 'My sister Essy wanted me to stick the beast with a knitting needle but I didn't have the heart so I simply blew a handful of hot chili powder into its nose and sent the blighter packing as it were.'

Esther glared at her sister as the reporters gathered around Minnie for further details, leaving her alone at the desk.

'Your key, madam,' the hotel manager said, tapping Esther's shoulder. 'I hope you do not mind,' he added,

'But I took the liberty of seating you at my table for dinner this evening, I am entertaining one or two of India's leading lights and I thought you might find the company scintillating.'

'Oh how kind,' Esther said, removing her hat and shaking her silver locks.

'Say, seven-thirty?' the manager asked, summoning his bellboy who whisked the sisters' baggage away.

'And then,' Minnie added, with the reporters eating out of her hand, 'I bought a rubber snake!' She whipped out the quivering cobra and waved it in the air, startling the gathering at first. 'Marvellous, isn't it?' she chuckled. 'I bought it for the little lad next door, you see he had a pet slow worm but his mother sucked it up with the Henry hoover, the dear boy was devastated.'

'Minnie!' Esther said, tapping the key on the desk impatiently. 'Are we done here?'

'Oh!' Minnie said, pocketing her souvenir snake. 'But, Essy, I'd forgotten to tell them about the crumpets, dear.'

'Don't bother,' Esther said, taking her sister's arm and leading her away. 'Good day to you,' she told the scribbling reporters.

Taking the elevator to the sixth floor, the sisters tracked down their room, tipped the waiting bellboy handsomely and gasped at their magnificent surroundings. The Taj Mahal Palace surpassed all expectations and then some, putting their previous opulent accommodation in the shade. The balcony terrace offered breath-taking views of the Mumbai harbour and the Arabian sea beyond. 'Essy, look!' Minnie said, exploring. 'Look at the size of this thing,' she pointed out the enormous four-poster bed almost eight feet wide. 'I could roll over three times and still not bother you in the night, dear.'

'There is a God after all,' Esther muttered under her breath.

'What was that, dear?' Minnie asked, flopping back on the bed spread-eagled.

'I said I must give Richard a call!' Esther said, thinking fast. 'And see how that daughter of mine is doing, mind you I daren't mention the tiger incident, the poor dear will hit the roof.' Esther was right to be conservative with the truth, her daughter Elizabeth had recently been readmitted to the secure facility which had previously released her on probation. She had taken the news of her mother's onward travels extremely badly, having assumed she'd return home from Raipur, so badly in fact that it took five hospital porters and two police officers to remove her from her ransacked two-bed semi having sedated her three times. 'Now how does this contraption work?' she said toying with the tablet.

'Here, dear,' Minnie intervened, having become quite the aficionado. 'Right, Essy dear,' she said powering up the device. 'Would you like to text, whatsapp, snapchat, private message, tweet, email or skype?'

'What?' Esther asked, her head spinning 'I just want to talk to the dear boy, that's all.'

'Right you are, dear,' Minnie replied, tapping away until Richard finally appeared on the screen.

'Ahhh there you are, my darling,' Esther said, taking the tablet from her sister. 'Can you hear me, I said can you hear me, Richard!'

'Yes, Gran,' Richard replied, turning down the volume at his end. 'How are you, hi, Minnie!'

'Afternoon, Richard dear!' Minnie called whilst unpacking her knitwear. 'Your grandmother and I are in Mumbai!'

'I know,' Richard replied. 'I saw your photos.'

'How's your mother?' Esther asked. 'Has she simmered down since we last spoke?'

'Errrrr, not entirely, Gran,' Richard said, looking about the place at his botched repairs. 'When you said you weren't coming home just yet she had what you might call an episode.' Elizabeth's episode had lasted all of four hours with a tense stand-off at one point when she'd clambered out of the bathroom window, scaled the drainpipe and climbed onto the roof; she was eventually talked down by a trained negotiator after she'd hurled several slates down at the curious neighbours.

'An episode you say?' Esther asked 'Well is she alright, can I speak to her?'

'She's er, she's just having a lie down at the moment, Gran,' Richard said, lying through his teeth of course. 'Don't worry, I'll tell her you called.' Elizabeth was lying down alright, strapped to a hospital bed in a locked and padded room thrashing in her restraints and screaming abuse at her captors.

'Well, OK,' Esther said, blowing Richard a kiss. 'I just wanted to touch base with you, give your mother my love and take care, darling.'

'Will do, Gran,' Richard replied, plucking a piece of broken china from between the sofa cushions. 'You take care too, yeah, love you loads, byyye!' Signing off,

Esther tracked down her sister to their rooms very own cocktail bar. 'There you are,' she said, clambering onto a stool while Minnie tinkered behind.

'Look, dear,' Minnie said, brandishing a recipe booklet for such alcoholic classics as the Harvey Wallbanger and the Singapore Sling. 'I thought I might try my hand at a Long Island Iced Tea.'

'Oooh, iced tea,' Esther said enthusiastically. 'That sounds heavenly right now.'

'Right let me see,' Minnie said, squinting at the instructions and removing one or two bottles while her sister spun on the revolving stool wistfully.

'Shall I put the kettle on dear?' Esther asked,

'No, no, dear that won't be necessary,' Minnie informed her while pouring a healthy measure of white rum into two tall glasses and reaching for the vodka. 'There you go, dear,' she said moments later after crudely concocting the cocktail.

'Is it herbal, dear?' Esther asked, sniffing at her glass.

'I don't know Essy,' Minnie replied, taking a mouthful. 'But it tastes jolly good.'

Esther tentatively tasted hers. 'Mmmmm, oh that's simply divine!' she said licking her lips. 'Iced tea, you say?'

'That's what it says,' Minnie said, having polished off half of her drink already. 'Would you like another, dear?' Minnie asked, refilling the shaker.

'Ohh yes please,' Esther replied, making short work of her cocktail. 'What tea did you say it was, dear?' she then asked, handing Minnie her glass and eagerly awaiting another.

'Long Island, dear,' Minnie said, rattling the shaker like a pro and charging both glasses to the brim.

The sisters downed a further three cocktails each and sat reminiscing about the relatives they had loved and lost. 'Here's to Aunt Maud!' Esther said, clinking her sister's glass. 'The finest concert pianist to ever grace the Albert Hall in my opinion.'

'Hear, hear!' Minnie agreed. 'And Uncle Stan!' she too cheered. 'The best bin man Bromley by Bow has ever seen, and a true gentleman to boot; would you like another, dear,' she then asked.

'Ohh, why not,' Esther replied, throwing caution to the wind. 'After all it's only iced tea.'

Minnie mixed another batch with increasing levels of alcohol and the pair proceeded to toast everybody from Buddy Holly to Oliver Cromwell.

'Oh good heavens!' Esther suddenly said, checking her wristwatch. 'Look at the time, dear, we're to be at dinner in half an hour!'

'Crickey, you're right!' Minnie agreed, draining her glass and helping her sister down from her stool, the pair of them a tad woozy.

The sisters tottered about their spacious apartment in their undergarments having hurriedly showered. 'Where are my pearls, dear?' Esther asked stumbling over the pouffe.

'I don't know, dear, Minnie replied 'Have you seen my dentures by any chance?'

'They're where you left them!' Esther reminded her sister whilst hunting for her pearls, an identical set to her sister's and a treasured parting gift from their mother. 'In the jewellery box!'

'Right you are, dear,' Minnie said, bumping into the door frame en route to the bedroom. 'Found them!' she called back to Esther, who held one of two dresses in front of her. 'Oh and I found your pearls too!' Minnie added, wrestling with the two tangled sets around her neck.

'Ready, dear?' Esther eventually asked around five and twenty past the hour.

'Born ready, Essy dear,' Minnie replied, pinning an emerald brooch to her chest 'Born ready.'

Clinging to one another for stability, Esther and Minnie took the elevator to the ground floor and followed their noses to the hotel restaurant, a place where fine dining and exquisite ambiance went harmoniously hand in hand. 'Ahhhh, ladies,' the hotel manager, said rising from his seat. 'Please, please come sit.' He dragged two chairs from beneath the circular table occupied by six members of India's elite; two actors, a bhangra starlet, the port of Mumbai's harbour master and his wife and the front runner in the Indian prime ministerial elections.

'Hellooooo,' Minnie chirped, clattering one or two diners' chairs as she made her way to the table.

Each of the seated guests rose to greet the sisters, offering their hands and bowing as though in the presence of royalty.

'Hellooooo, hellooooo,' Esther too said in turn.

'Esther and Minnie!' the manager proudly announced his guests of honour. 'The Peshwari Nans.' All heads in the restaurant turned to face them and the name reverberated around the cavernous room from table to table. 'Peshwari Nans, it's the Peshwari Nans,' they whispered. Many looked on, envious at the manager's remaining guests at being seated with such celebrities.

Minnie flopped down onto her chair, upsetting an empty wine glass in front of her. 'Ooops,' she chuckled, grappling to right the crystal goblet.

'Impeccable timing!' the manager said, retaking his seat. 'I was about to order drinks, what would you ladies like, anything just name it.'

'Oh well,' Esther said, rubbing her hands together. 'I know I speak for my sister when I say we'll have a couple of your finest iced teas if you please.'

'Iced tea?' the manager asked. 'No champagne?'

'Oh no, no, no, dear,' Esther said, shaking her head. 'The bubbles are likely to give me a bilious attack, the iced teas will do nicely, thank you.'

'As you wish,' the manager said, clicking his fingers to summon the waiter.

Minnie eyed the harbour master's naval regalia beside her. 'I had a man friend who was a pilot,' she said, mistaking the emblems for those of an aerial nature. 'He flew Hurricanes and Spitfires during the war, what do you fly?'

'I'm sorry?' the harbour master replied, baffled entirely. 'I do not fly.'

'You don't!' Minnie exclaimed. 'I see, air traffic control then is it, make a note of that dear,' she told her sister beside her. 'The wing commander here has no head for heights.'

'What, no!' the harbour master in an attempt to explain.

'That's quite alright, dear,' Minnie smirked. 'There is absolutely no shame in it, no shame whatsoever.'

'Although,' Esther said, leaning across her sister, 'If you haven't the stomach for aviation, dear, maybe you should have considered a career at sea, just a suggestion, that's all.'

'No, wait, you do not understand!' the harbour master floundered.

'It's alright, dear,' Minnie said patting his hand. 'My sister and I won't think any less of you.'

The flummoxed harbour official was about to retaliate further when his wife got a grip of him. 'Do not be making a scene, my dear,' she told him, looking around at the prying eyes.

The drinks then arrived and the sisters were handed their iced teas. 'What in earth?' Esther remarked, taking a sip. 'Minnie dearest, I hate to admit it but this isn't a patch on yours, my love, not a patch at all.'

'Oh no you're right, my dear,' Minnie agreed, sampling the non-alcoholic beverage. 'Excuse me!' she called to the departing waiter 'I say, young man, this is iced tea, is it not?'

'Indeed, madam,' the waiter replied humbly.

'Long Island iced tea,' Minnie added. 'My sister and I are no fools I'll have you know.'

'Oh no, no, madam,' the waiter said in a bid to explain. 'This is…'

'Pathetic, that's what it is,' Esther told him in no uncertain terms. 'I say, my dear' she said, addressing the would-be prime minister. 'Have the blighters watered down your whisky too?'

'Please, madam,' the waiter squirmed, removing hurriedly removing their iced teas. 'I will bring your cocktails immediately.'

Minnie wagged a finger, 'See to it you do, young man,' she said over her spectacles.

The hotel manager glared at his waiter as though the mistake was his own. 'Hurry, hurry!' he snapped.

'I do hate to make a scene,' Esther confessed. 'But if you don't stand up for what's right you may as well turn belly up and let them walk all over you, am I right, Minnie dearest?'

'Quite right, dear,' Minnie agreed.

Their cocktails duly arrived much to the sisters' approval. 'Thaaat's better,' Esther smiled, patting the waiter. 'It's not your fault, dear,' she told him. 'I'd imagine it's hotel policy.'

The red-faced manager hastily changed the subject. 'Ladies, ladies please allow me to introduce Sanita Sharma, our number one best-selling bhangra artist.' Sanita reached out a slender hand.

'Pleased to meet you, dearie,' Esther said offering hers.

'Oooh,' Minnie said, eyeing her jewellery. 'What a charming necklace, dear, if you don't mind me saying you look like the Queen of Sheba, doesn't she, dear.'

'The Queen of Sheba,' Esther echoed. 'My sentiment entirely.'

The blushing bhangra star clasped her hands together and bowed to the sisters. 'Thank you, thank you kindly,' she said, revealing several glitzy bangles on her wrist.

'Oh and I just love you bracelets, dear,' Minnie gushed 'Beautiful, absolutely beautiful.'

'Yes, beautiful,' Esther again echoed after downing yet another Long Island iced tea. 'Two more, please!' she called, attracting the waiter's attention. 'Keep them coming, young man!'

Peshwari Nans Part II

Sanita leaned to examine Minnie's charity bands. 'I am liking your bangles too,' she said in return.

'Really!' Minnie gasped, slipping a crimson band from her wrist. 'Here, dear,' she said, offering it across the table. 'Red Nose Day 2012, my sister and I baked cookies and raised four pounds fifty for Comic Relief.'

'Oh thank you so much,' Sanita said, caressing the band and slipping it over her hand. 'Red Nose Day?' she then asked.

'Yes, dear,' Esther replied. 'We could have raised a whole lot more but my sister here fell asleep in front of the television and burnt the second batch.'

'Oh come now, dear,' Minnie said defensively. 'I'd challenge anyone to stay awake after three helpings of sherry trifle and half an hour in front of the electric fire.'

The party dined extravagantly with Minnie spoilt for choice when it came to meat- and dairy-free alternatives. 'Oh this is delicious.' she said. nibbling warm French bread and a delightful butternut pate. 'My compliments to the chef.'

After dinner it was time for yet another cocktail. 'Cooeeeee!' Minnie called, slurring ever so slightly and waving her glass above her head while the remainder of the table sipped coffee.

Esther looked about the place and the sombre couple seated at the adjacent table. 'Has somebody died?' she asked. 'Crikey, Minnie, it's like a blooming morgue, dear.'

Minnie tapped her sister's shoulder and pointed out a grand piano in the corner of the room. 'Do you think you can still tinkle the ivories, dear?' she asked.

Peshwari Nans Part II

'Ooh, I could give it a go, dear,' Esther said, brimming with Dutch courage.

'Shall we, dear?' Minnie asked rising from her seat.

'Why not?' Esther replied, dragging herself to her feet.

'Do excuse us for a moment,' Minnie told the hotel manager. 'My sister and I have a few old time music hall memories we'd like to share with you.'

Slightly inebriated, the sisters lurched between the tables, again nudging one or two guests in the process. 'I sayyyyy!' Minnie said at the microphone stand while her sister slid along the piano bench and raised the lid. 'Nothing lifts the spirits more than a good old-fashioned sing-along so pay attention and join in once you've gotten the gist, OK?' She whispered a possible opening number into her sister's ear. 'Take it away, Essy!' she said, bracing herself.

Esther hadn't played piano for many years and clattered several wrong keys in proceeding. 'Sorryyyyy!' she said, pausing to compose herself.

'That's quite alright, dear,' Minnie said sympathetically. 'Take your time.'

Again all heads in the Taj Mahal restaurant turned their way as Esther began to play. 'Ahem!' Minnie said, bursting into an old time classic. '*Roll out the barrel, we'll have a barrel of fun, Roll out the barrel, we've got the blues on the ruuun!*'

The seated guests, the majority of them Indian nationals, looked at one another astounded by the sisters' bravado, but they were the Peshwari Nans and had carte blanche as far as the awestruck manager was concerned. He too began to mouth the words, '*Roll out the barrel*' then those around him began to steadily follow suit, not wanting to offend their honoured guests.

Minnie then treated the company to a verse or two of *Mother Kelly's Doorstep, Underneath the Arches* and of course *Run Rabbit Run*. All chairs were turned to face the performing sisters and hands clapped along in time. 'I sayyyyy!' Minnie called again to the attentive waiter. 'Two more of those delicious teas of yours, please, oh and while you're at it get our friends a drink too!'

'Everybody?' the waiter asked, looking around the restaurant.

'Yes, everybody!' she replied. 'OK, folks, shall we try that once more from the top?' she asked. All the ensemble nodded, having listened intently to Minnie's rousing rendition of *Maybe it's Because I'm a Londoner*. 'Ready, dear?' she asked her sister.

'As I'll ever be, dear,' Esther replied, cracking her knuckles and striking up the opening notes.

Minnie and as many as eighty guests and staff members broke into song. '*Maybe it's because I'm a Londoner, that I love London towwwn, I get a funny feeling inside of me, just walking up and down, maybe it's because I'm a Londoner, that I love London towwwwwwwwwn!*' Everybody leapt to their feet applauding feverishly as Minnie helped her sozzled sister to her feet and the pair took a shaky bow.

'BRAVO, BRAVO!' the hotel manager cried, clapping the loudest.

With privacy being a rare privilege in today's world the entire proceedings were once again recorded on a plethora of hand-held devices and launched onto the World Wide Web, immediately causing a surge of national pride back home.

Peshwari Nans Part II

Esther and Minnie staggered back to the manager's table to a hero's welcome 'Wonderful, wonderful!' said the harbour master's wife, still clapping. 'You are so right, my dears, there is nothing quite like a cockeny knees up.'

'You mean cockney, dearie,' Esther said correcting her.

The manager helped the sisters into their seats. 'The Taj Mahal has witnessed something truly amazing here tonight,' he said, wiping a tear from his eye. 'The likes of which I am doubting we will ever be seeing again.'

'Oh I don't know about that, my lovely,' Minnie said, draining her drink 'There's always tomorrow night.'

Esther and Minnie amused their hosts for a further hour and a half with personal anecdotes, some a little too personal for comfort. 'So I said to Cyril' Minnie said, surrounded by raised eyebrows. 'I'll do anything for love, my dear, but I won't do that.'

The harbour master's wife gasped, took hold of her husband's hand and dragged him from the table. 'Cheerio!' Esther said, waving them goodbye.

Soon the restaurant was all but empty and only the sisters and the manager remained, now seated at the bar. 'Ladies, may I say,' he said, popping the cork on a rather expensive prosecco, 'In all my years as hotel manager of the Taj Mahal I have never had a night as wonderful as this, and I have entertained some of the world's biggest names, the biggest I say, but you have enchanted me beyond my wildest dreams, my wildest dreams!'

'Oh you're too kind,' Esther slurred, offering her glass.

'I just wish you could have met our mother and father,' Minnie told him 'Saturday nights around Mother's battered upright piano were sheer bliss, singing until the early hours, you see my sister and I have no need of wealth and fame, we're far too old for all that nonsense, it's family that matters the most and binds us together, it's always been about family, without it we have nothing.'

'Hear, hear!' Esther said raising her glass.

'I agree,' the manager said, toasting his own aged parents. 'I am fortunate,' he told them. 'My mother and father are still alive in Jodhpur, I know I should visit more but the hotel….'

'Now then!' Esther said, raising a hand. 'Let me stop you right there and offer you a piece of advice; this hotel is made of bricks and mortar, is it not?' The manager agreed. 'So,' Esther continued, 'It'll be here long after you and I are dead and buried, but your family, your family, that's flesh and blood, do you hear me, nothing, nothing is more important than that.'

'Nothing,' Minnie reiterated. 'You know, dearie, you only miss what you had when it's gone, visit them before they are gone too, please.'

The sisters' drunken words of wisdom resonated with the hotel manager, who had forgone family commitments to further his career, an oh so familiar story repeated the world over. Parents and elderly relatives sat watching and waiting from a million windows for a familiar face to tread the garden path and knock at the door they once left, and sadly many of them passed away alone at the expense of a child's promotion or absent-minded complacence.

'Family!' Esther said, clinking her sister's glass.

'Family, dear,' Minnie replied, leaning to kiss her sister's cheek. 'I love you, darling,' she added softly.

'Ditto,' Esther smiled, returning the kiss.

'You are right!' the manager said, offering his own glass with a lump in his throat. 'I will go, I will go to Jodhpur right away, my father he loves our games of chess on the veranda, I can remember as a small boy he would sit and patiently explain to me the significance of strategy and cunning in the game, and my mother, oh my mother she makes for me the most wonderful Chana masala every time I come home to stay, I swear if she could she would still tie my shoes.'

'That's love, dear,' Esther told him. 'Plain and simple.'

The sisters were eventually escorted back to their room by the thankful manager, during which the three of them raised the elevator roof with a spine tingling rendition of *Land of Hope and Glory*.

CHAPTER THREE.

The sisters were woken the following morning by the sound of rapping knuckles on the door. 'Madams, madams!' the bellboy called. 'Your chauffeur is here!'

'What, what?' Esther groaned, opening an eye. 'Oh,' she then said, looking down to see that she was still fully clothed and sprawled on top of the bedspread. 'Minnie!' she said, seeing her sister's side of the bed empty and unruffled. 'Minnie, where are you, oooh my head.' Stretching and wincing, she rolled from the bed, clutching her temple in standing. 'Dear Lord,' she moaned, checking her dishevelled reflection in the full-length mirror. 'Minniiie!'

'Madams!' the bellboy again called knocking a little louder.

'Yes, yes, yes, I'm coming!' Esther said, trudging to the lounge where she discovered her sister draped at one end of the sofa sound asleep, open-mouthed with the remote control in her hand and the television still playing re-runs of popular Indian soap operas. 'Minnie, what are you doing?' she asked, hurrying as best she could to the door. 'Yes what is it?' she asked the boy 'What do you want at this ungodly hour?'

'Your chauffeur, madam,' the lad replied. 'He is waiting for you, and so is Mister Govinda.'

'Mister Govinda?' Esther asked, the events of the previous evening a blur.

'Yes, yes, Mister Govinda!' the bellboy replied fidgeting, having been strict instructions to fetch the sisters. 'I must tell you he is not a man to be kept waiting.'

'Mister Govinda, Mister Govinda?' Esther pondered. 'Ohhhhhh that Mister Govinda, yes, yes, I remember now, that foolish sister of mine has gotten us roped into a movie of his, I believe.'

'You must hurry!' the boy said in an attempt to coax Esther out the door.

'Hurry?' Esther smirked. 'My dear boy, I'll do nothing of the sort, I have to bathe, change my clothes, fix my head and put on a new face before I'd even contemplate leaving the hotel, no, no, you'll have to tell them to wait.' With this she closed the door in the anguished boy's face. 'Minnie, get up!' she then said, snatching the remote from her sister's limp hand and switching off the television. 'Minniiiiiie, this was your blasted idea so get up right this minute, do you hear me?'

Minnie fluttered her eyes and wiped the dribble from the corner of her mouth. 'Mmmmm morning, dear,' she mumbled.

'Don't you 'morning dear' me!' Esther growled. 'I'll give you iced teas, my damned head is pounding.'

'Really, dear?' Minnie said, sitting upright and stretching out her arms. 'Funny, because I feel fine.' Minnie was of course lying but thought it best under the circumstances. 'Perhaps it was something you've eaten.'

'Oh dear God!' Esther then gasped as the mist rose in her mind, revealing in graphic detail their alcohol-fuelled riotous restaurant revelry. 'Minnie, I played piano!'

'Yes, dear, you did,' Minnie said, raising a smile. 'And rather well too, I thought.'

'Good heavens, we'll be a laughing stock,' Esther said with a hand to her mouth. 'Minnie, however will we face them?'

Minnie dragged herself from the sofa and made her way to the bathroom with her sister in tow. 'That's the last time, Minnie, I swear it' Esther moaned. 'The last time I ever listen to you, I know I've said it before but I mean it this time, Minnie, Minnie!'

'Where are you going, Essy? Minnie said, stopping her sister at the bathroom door. 'I need to take a shower.'

'So do I,' Esther informed her. 'We have no time therefore we'll have to share.'

'Very well, dear,' Minnie agreed.

Although their hotel room was huge the shower was surprisingly small in comparison as the pair soon discovered. 'Minnie will you kindly remove your knee from my buttocks!' Esther said whilst pressed against the glass screen.

'I'm trying to, dear,' Minnie replied with a head full of lather; the sisters shuffled in circles as though their feet were manacled together standing in turn beneath the spraying spout, their wrinkled bodies forced against the cold marble walls.

'Oh my eyes, my eyes!' Minnie cried, thrashing momentarily as the foam ran down her face.

'Get off me, you fool!' Esther yelled, fending off her sister's flailing elbows.

Hungover and dehydrated, the sisters drained a dozen miniature bottles of tonic water from the mini bar, dragged on dresses and pulled their straw hats down over their hastily brushed hair.

'Will you do my lippy, dear?' Minnie asked, offering Esther her cosmetics. 'My hands are shaking something awful.'

'Ohh, give it here,' Esther sighed, having crudely applied her own lipstick and enough foundation to render over the finer cracks. 'Will you keep still!' she said, straying from her sister's lip line on more than one occasion. 'Ohh, that'll have to do,' she added impatiently. 'Come now, your Mister Govinda is waiting apparently.'

'Oooh yes,' Minnie said, perking up ever so slightly. 'I'd almost forgotten, we're going to be in the movies.'

'I'd rather be in bed,' Esther again groaned, bracing herself before opening the door.

The bellboy, who had waited tapping his toes in the corridor, suddenly scurried toward the elevator. 'Come, come!' he said, stabbing at the buttons.

'Yes alright,' Esther replied, slipping on a pair of dark glasses in a futile attempt to conceal her identity. 'Minnie, I cannot believe you got me tiddly,' she said, scolding her sister whilst pulling her hat further down. 'With a little luck they'll have forgotten all about it.'

Descending to the hotel lobby, they emerged to find the place abuzz with staff and guests galore heading hurriedly in all directions. 'Oh blast,' Esther cursed, dropping her head while her sister sauntered behind her.

'Morning!' Minnie called to a few familiar faces, attracting exactly the sort of attention her sister was so desperate to avoid.

'What are you doing?' Esther barked, but it was too late, they were soon spotted by a pair of Bengali newlyweds who stopped in the middle of the lobby, having dined alongside the sisters the night before. In high spirits the happy couple both began to sing at the tops of their voices, having memorised the lilting lyrics to one of Minnie's childhood favourites, a song first written in 1892 by Harry Darce, telling the tale of a courting couple and their bicycle made for two. '*DAISY, DAISY GIVE ME YOUR ANSWER DOOOOOO, I'M HALF CRAZY ALL FOR THE LOVE OF YOUUUUU!*' Suddenly all around also stopped and dozens of smiling faces turned the sisters' way.

'Oh please God, no,' Esther cringed as they joined in the belting chorus. '*IT WON'T BE A STYLISH MARRIAGE, I CAN'T AFFORD A CARRIAGE, BUT YOU'LL LOOK SWEET UPON THE SEAT OF A BICYCLE MADE FOR TWOOOOOOOOOOOOO!*'

'Oh how charming, dear,' Minnie squealed, clapping her hands. 'Don't you think?'

Esther shamefully hurried to the door as rapturous applause echoed throughout the lobby whilst her sister paused to soak up the adulation. 'Minnie!' she snapped, beckoning. 'Come away, will you!'

'Goodbyyyyyye!' Minnie said, waving. 'Bye, bye!'

Raj Govinda's chauffer stood waiting beside a sleek black limousine as the sisters left the hotel. 'Morning!' Minnie called, lowering each foot in turn down the hotel steps. 'Lovely day!'

'Get in, will you!' Esther said, prodding her sister's backside as she bent at the limousine door.

'Oooh, dear, look,' Minnie said, dropping onto the broad bench seat and discovering the rose glass cocktail cabinet beside her.

'Don't you dare,' Esther warned her. 'I mean it, Minnie, don't you even think about it, I've already got a bass drum banging in my head, the last thing I need right now is the rest of the blasted orchestra.'

'Right you are, dear,' Minnie said, reclining somewhat.

The chauffeur closed the door behind them and hopped in the front. 'Good morning to you,' he said cheerfully. 'I must say I am feeling truly blessed for driving you this fine morning.'

'Really?' Esther said nonchalantly. 'You don't want to know how I'm feeling right now.'

'Please,' the driver said, looking in the rear view mirror. 'Help yourself to refreshments.'

Esther opened the tiny fridge in front of her. 'Oh marvellous,' she sighed, removing a carton of freshly squeezed orange juice and plucking two champagne flutes from an adjacent rack. 'Here,' she said, topping up her sister's glass and flopping back into her seat. 'Thaaat's better' she added once hydrated but still shaking nevertheless.

Making their way out of Mumbai, the limousine navigated the bustling streets with relative ease, many of the other road users simply moving aside when seeing Raj's private plate GOV 1 approaching, such was the respect he commanded amongst his people. Raj Govinda's iconic movies and television shows were watched by millions and repeated nightly and the man himself was considered second only to the great Mahatma Gandhi. Having purchased the sole rights to the nation's cricket coverage, Govinda TV towered a mile above its closest rivals; in short you either watched his channel or you didn't watch television at all.

'I sayyyy, where are we going?' Minnie asked, looking up ahead.

'Baramati, Miss,' the chauffeur replied. 'Mister Govinda owns a thousand acres of arable land where the set for this movie was built some nine and a half years ago, it has been in limbo as we say, until now that is, he has assembled the finest cast of actors in all of India to star alongside you, the very finest I tell you.'

'Oh,' Esther said, feeling a tad intimidated. 'He has, has he?'

They drove for a further two hours into the countryside and eventually reached the region of Baramati where Raj had ring-fenced his sprawling lot. Security guards patrolled the rustic entrance gates, waving the limousine through as they approached; a further five minutes went by without seeing a soul until they came up on Raj's encampment, a gathering of gargantuan trailers each housing an A-list Bollywood star. 'Ahhhh welcome, welcome!' Raj said, rising from his director's chair with open arms, surrounded by cameramen and sound engineers having thrashed out the details of the day's filming. 'Esther, Mimmie!' he called as the chauffer opened the rear door and helped the sisters alight.

'Errr, that's Minnie, I'll have you know,' Minnie said, clinging to her sister for support.

'Yes, yes, of course,' Raj said with a broad smile etched on his face. 'Come, come sit with me.' He ushered the sisters beneath a white linen gazebo and offered tea.

'Oooh, yes please,' Minnie said, wasting no time. 'Look, dear, it's Darjeeling!' she told her sister, who surveyed the mountain of movie-making equipment being routinely unpacked by an army of technicians.

'Yes, yes thank you, dear,' Esther said, taking a cup but very much in awe of her surroundings.

'You like?' Raj asked, joining her. 'Welcome to the movie business.'

'I've never seen anything quite like it,' Esther confessed, almost missing her mouth whilst raising her cup. Mile after mile after mile of audio and visual cabling was unloaded from five heavy trucks, as were munitions, heavy artillery and upwards of a thousand antiquated rifles. 'Errrrr,' Esther said, raising a finger. 'What are those for?'

'The movie,' Raj said proudly, 'It will be an epic, Miss Esther,' he went on to explain. 'Never before has the uprising been shot in such graphic detail, never.'

'Uprising?' Esther asked whilst Minnie tucked into the lavish buffet laid out before them. No expense had been spared for Bollywood's elite, the finest cuisine had been flown in from across the continent. 'What uprising?'

'What uprising!' Raj said with raised eyebrows. 'The Great Uprising, Miss Esther,' Raj explained, horrified at her apparent ignorance of the most poignant and also turbulent period in Indian history. '1857,' Raj continued 'During the time of the British Raj, is it not ringing a bell in your head, Miss Esther?'

'Listen, dearie,' Esther replied. 'The only thing ringing in my head right now are those blasted iced teas.' She glared at her sister.

'What was that, dear?' Minnie asked, licking the hummus from her lips.

'Iced teas!' Esther snarled.

'Oooh, yes please,' Minnie said, scooping a chapatti full into her mouth. 'I'm all in favour of a hair of the dog, dear.'

'You see,' Esther told Raj. 'The woman's a bumbling fool.'

The theme of Raj's Bollywood blockbuster was far from an original concept having been screened and serialised on numerous occasions, but Raj's adaptation was to take the bloody blight in India's history books and show it in a way that obliterated the boundaries of acceptability, laying bare the true horrors of the conflict as though tearing down the walls of a slaughterhouse revealing the stench and gore within.

The rebellion, also known as India's First War of Independence, began with a small band of mutinous Sepoys (Indian army recruits) who were dissatisfied with their lives under the rule of the then British East India company. The rebellion began in the town of Meerut but soon spread further afield and their rampaging ranks swelled. These bloodthirsty mutineers began the systematic slaughter of British men women and children and all who stood with them. The woeful war crimes eventually filtered back to Great Britain and horrified a nation, who demanded swift and merciless retribution. Thousands of British soldiers were shipped overseas to quell the rampaging rebellion by whatever means necessary, but some officers took this caveat to the extreme, hanging deserters by the dozen and even strapping them to the business end of a loaded cannon and blasting their body parts to the four winds as a warning to others.

'So errrrrr,' Esther pondered. 'Where exactly do my sister and I fit into this period drama of yours?'

'You, my dears,' Raj smiled. 'Are the catalyst that brought the avenging British troops to our shores in great numbers, great numbers indeed to put an end to the great uprising, and end it they did.'

Shortly after, the British East India Company was dissolved and replaced with the British Raj, a new restructured army offering equality to all and not just the senior ranks. Queen Victoria was eventually named as Empress of India in 1876 and presided over the country until she died on January 22nd 1901.

'The catalyst, you say,' Esther said, watching the weaponry being carried over the brow of a nearby hill. 'Riiiiight.'

'Essy, dear,' Minnie mumbled with a mouthful of vegetable vindaloo. 'You really should try the buffet.'

'Minnie, they have guns,' Esther told her gorging sister, curious as to the nature of their impending roles. 'Guns, Minnie dear.'

'Yes, yes, dear,' Minnie said, oblivious. 'But they also have pakoras too, and a rather refreshing Mango Lassi, you really ought to try it.'

'What?' Esther said, breaking her concentration. 'Minnie, what are you doing, come away will you, you'll give yourself indigestion.'

'Oh, yes, yes of course,' Minnie finally agreed whilst reaching for the bhajis. 'Did you say guns, dear?' she asked, joining her sister.

'Yes dear, guns,' Esther said, scowling. 'What on earth have you gotten us into, that's what I'd like to know.'

Raj ushered the sisters to an adjacent trailer. 'This is for you,' he told them. 'I trust you will find it to your liking, costume and make-up will be along shortly,' and with this he was off, clipboard in hand, barking at set designers and special effects personnel alike.

The sisters' trailer, although resembling a large caravan, was a million miles from the battered tin can they regularly holidayed in at Canvey Island as children. The six-berth luxury home from home oozed glamour and opulence with its floor laid in shimmering cobalt blue quartz tiling with specks of flaked gold suspended in the highly polished glaze; deep velour cushions smothered the curvaceous cream corner couch and petite crystal chandeliers hung from the rhinestone-encrusted roof. 'Ohhhh, Essy,' Minnie gasped. 'A girl could get used to this, don't you think?'

'Well,' Esther said, coming round to the idea. 'I see what you mean, dear, yes.'

A short while later as the sisters reclined having kicked off their shoes, there was a knock at the door and the wardrobe assistants entered carrying the sisters' heavy cotton costumes; ankle-length evening dresses several layers thick complete with figure-snatching corsets and bloomers. 'Oh how heavenly,' Minnie said, fingering the pleats. Two make-up artists then arrived along with a wig fitter, and each set about transforming the eighty-somethings into Victorian ladies. 'Look, dear,' Minnie said, shaking the auburn curls that hung around her ears, 'I feel like Greta Garbo.'

'Greta Garbage more like,' Esther smirked, frustrating the make-up girl. 'Sorry, dear,' she said, turning back and puckering her lips.

Raj reappeared carrying with him two scripts for the sisters to peruse. 'OK,' he said, sitting beside them as the finishing touches were applied to their attire. 'You, Essy, are to play Lady Belinda Bagshot, the dowager Duchess of Derbyshire, living here having sold the family estate belonging to your late husband, and you, Mimmie…'

'Minnie,' Minnie said, plucking Belgian chocolates from a tray beside her.

'Yes of course,' Raj continued. 'You are to play Tilly, the chambermaid.'

'Chambermaid!' Minnie exclaimed.

'Yes!' Esther laughed, clenching a triumphant fist.

'But, but Mister Govinda,' Minnie beseeched the director. 'Why am I to be the chambermaid when I have a wealth of previous experience?'

'You were a tin foil star,' Esther said, mocking her sister's first year Nativity debut. 'Get over it.'

'Yes, but,' Minnie moaned. 'A chambermaid.'

'Yes, a chambermaid,' Raj reiterated. 'But you have a pivotal role, my dear, quite pivotal indeed.'

'Pivotal role, my foot!' Minnie again moaned. 'She gets to play a dowager Duchess and I'm her skivvy, the story of my blooming life that is.'

Esther couldn't help but see the funny side. 'Oh come now, dear,' she smirked, 'I promise I'll go easy on you.'

'Essy!' Minnie remarked. 'That's rich coming from you, well answer me this, Esther Reynolds, who is it that draws the short straw every time and has to plunge the bunged up lavatory U-bend, me that's who, me, Essy, every damned time, and while we're on the subject...'

Raj could only spectate as Minnie spewed her pent-up grievances. 'I'm sure that's a double-headed sixpence you keep tossing because for the last five times in a blasted row I've had to degrease the oven racking and clean behind the refrigerator, do you know I now have enough fluff to stuff a double duvet.'

'Ladies, ladies,' Raj implored them. 'Can we please focus?'

'Yes, dear,' Esther told her sister, tongue-in-cheek. 'Can you please focus, oh and that reminds me, the kitchen sink is backing up again and the kettle needs descaling, I'll toss you for it when we get back home.'

'Ohhhhh no, no, no, no,' Minnie said, shaking her curls. 'If you think I'm falling for that old chestnut you are very much mistaken, very much indeed.'

'Best of three?' Esther asked her naive sister.

'Oh alright,' Minnie foolishly agreed. 'At least I'll have a fighting chance.'

Of course Minnie hadn't a hope in hell of defeating her sister, whose sixpenny piece did in fact feature the head of King George V on both sides, and traditionally she always called first.

'Ladies, please,' Raj begged, brandishing the scripts. 'Your motivation!'

'Oh sorry, dear,' Esther said, checking her regal reflection while her sister looked altogether dowdy beside her.

'OK,' Raj said once again. 'We have erected a house on the other side of the hill, your house is, Esther, or should I say Lady Belinda where you reside with Tilly,

your butler and nine other menial staff members, the
year of course is 1857 and news of the uprising has
spread to this region, the staff have begun boarding up
the windows and doors when word of the advancing
rebels arrives, soon the mutineers have laid siege to the
house baying for your blood.'

'Oh dear,' Esther said, clutching her chest. 'Our blood,
you say?'

'Yes and they mean to have it,' Raj said, hoping to instil
a sense of character into the sisters. 'These mutineers
will stop at nothing, nothing, I tell you,' he continued.
'Your staff return fire with what little munitions you
possess but the butler and the gardener are both fatally
wounded in the exchange leaving just the women of the
household, your cooks, the cleaner and of course Tilly.'

'My chamber maid,' Esther reminded her sister, whilst
flashing her dazzling costume jewellery.

'Yes, yes, yes, alright!' Minnie snapped. 'But I tell you,
I'm not happy about this, Mister Govinda, not one
iota.'

'Please, Mimmie,' Raj said, his frustration increasing.

'It's Minnie!' Minnie said, aggrieved at his constant
mispronunciation, 'Not Mimmie, or Milly for that
matter, Minnie.'

'Yes, yes, yes,' Raj replied. 'If we could please move on.'

'Carry on, dear,' Esther said sympathetically. 'So the
men are dead, are they, leaving us women holed up in a
house surrounded by cutthroats, am I right?'

'Exactly,' Raj smiled, elated that the plot was finally
sinking in.

'Chocolate, dear?' Minnie said, offering her sister the
now sparse tray.

'Pay attention, Minnie,' Esther said, pushing the tray aside. 'You don't want to fluff any of your lines, now do you.'

'Are you forgetting, dear?' Minnie said puffing her chest somewhat. 'I have a near photographic memory, do you know, Mister Govinda,' she added detracting from the subject once again, 'Essy sends me to the supermarket for groceries without a list and I return triumphant every time, don't I, dear?' Her sister was busily scrutinising her script, 'I said don't I, dear,' Minnie reiterated, 'I never forget a thing, do I?'

'What's there to forget?' Esther scoffed. 'The nice young man in the van delivers our essentials, you, my dear, are only entrusted with fetching the occasional packet of biscuits, possibly a loo roll and my Sudoku magazines, and by the way I'd hardly call purchasing two copies of *Men and Muscle* magazine a triumph, would you, what on earth were you thinking?'

'I'm sorry, dear, I was distracted,' Minnie said in her defence after inadvertently choosing the bodybuilding bi-weekly over her sister's regular cryptic classic. 'You see I won two pounds on a scratch card and it went completely to my head.'

Raj, the wardrobe assistant, the make-up artist and the wig fitter sat spellbound by the sisters' nonsensical exchange.

'What do you mean, it went to your head?' Esther asked her sister. 'And will you put those chocolates down, you'll give yourself indigestion.'

'Well, dear,' Minnie replied setting down the tray, 'I must have been distracted when I telephoned the lottery people to confirm my scoop, I spoke to a charming young lady, Sharon I think her name was, from Newcastle Under Lyme apparently, anyway I explained that I'd just purchased my ticket along with the Garibaldi biscuits, Sharon said she prefers a fig roll but I said oh no, dear, it's a Garibaldi or nothing as far as I'm concerned, oh and she has a Yorkshire terrier named Spike which I thought was adorable.'

'Minnie!' Esther said in a bid to silence her sister and sensing Raj's frustration.

'Anyway,' Minnie said, oblivious. 'Sharon kindly explained that I could cash in my chips as it were right there at the counter, well as you can well imagine I was over the moon, dear, with my winnings I bought a packet of extra strong mints, a quarter of lemon drops and a tin of mushy peas, they do say it goes to your head, doesn't it.'

'Mushy peas?' Raj asked, having been drawn into to the rambling tale.

'Of course, dear,' Minnie said abruptly. 'You can't have chips without mushy peas, it simply isn't done.'

Raj threw his hands in the air. 'Ladies, please, the movie!' he said before dismissing his assistants.

'It's alright, dear,' Esther assured him whilst glaring at her sister, 'I'll beat it into her if I have to.'

Raj explained the sisters' cameo role in the movie, a catalyst indeed because after the incident at the Duchess's house the British arrived in force to smite the rebellion and change the course of Indian history forever.

Although short-lived, the Peshwari Nans' pivotal parts were truly the icing on the cake for the sixty-five-year-old director who planned to retire on an all-time high when the movie premiered.

A further two hours were needed to drum the scripts into the novice sisters with Minnie's attention meandering at times. 'Do excuse me while I use the facilities,' she said at one point, hoisting herself from the sofa and heading for the lavatory, and then returning a short while later to explain in great detail the inner workings of the self-sanitising trailer toilet with its awe-inspiring soft close lid.

'Dual flush you say?' Esther remarked 'Whatever next?'

'Yes, dear,' Minnie said, brimming with enthusiasm for the Winnebago's WC. 'And heated too, oh Essy, it was heavenly.'

Esther switched places with her sister. 'I hope you don't mind,' she told Raj, heading for the lavatory to see for herself,

'No, no, no, not at all,' Raj said, lying through his teeth of course. 'That's quite alright.'

Filming eventually got underway on the set, opening with Esther, or Lady Belinda Bagshot as it were, barking orders at Tilly to fetch more coal for the fire and run her mistress a hot bath.

'Yes, m'lady, yes, m'lady,' were the majority of Minnie's opening lines.

'Oh and bring me some cheese will you, Tilly,' the Duchess said whilst reclining in her wingback chair and loving every minute of it.

'Oh really, Essy!' Minnie growled, slipping out of character.

'CUUUT!' Raj screamed, having warned her several time previously. 'Mimmie dear, please remember it's m'lady you are addressing.'

'Yes, dear,' Minnie replied, flustered and red-faced. 'And will you please remember it's Minnie for Pete's sake!'

Running behind schedule after several more of Minnie's mishaps, the day's filming ended with news arriving of the recent uprising and the possibility of mutineers heading their way. 'Tilly dear, would you help Jackson board the windows,' Lady Bagshot said whilst taking tea.

'Yes m'lady' Minnie replied through gritted teeth.

'Oh and fetch me my slippers, will you,' her mistress added over her horn-rimmed glasses 'There's a good girl, oh and do keep an eye on the fire too.'

'ESSY!' Minnie stormed 'If you wish I could stick a broom up my backside and sweep the blasted floor!'

'CUUUUUUUT!' Raj said before calling time on the day's proceedings. 'Miss Mimmie, please you must adhere to the script,' he told her, a little exasperated to say the least.

'Yes, yes, I know!' Minnie said angrily. 'But why on earth does Lady blasted Bagshot have to gloat the way she does?'

'Minnie dear,' her sister said, placing an arm around Minnie's shoulder. 'I'm merely adding emphasis to the character, that's all.'

Minnie shrugged off her sister's affections. 'And relishing every minute of it no doubt,' she sulked.

The sisters were driven back to the Taj Mahal where Esther flatly refused to dine in the restaurant that evening for fear of re-enacting the raucous events of their previous visit. Instead she opted for a light supper in their room and an early night with one or two magazines she'd picked up in the foyer.

Minnie, on the other hand, attempted to amuse herself with a cup of cocoa and a pack of playing cards, but after two hands of Patience hers soon ran out. 'Oh blast,' she said, discarding the hand and pacing the room. 'Essy dear!' she called. 'I thought I might stretch my legs, dear, would you care to join me?' but peering into the bedroom she saw her elder sister fast asleep with the glossy magazines open on the bed. 'Oh right you are, dear,' Minnie said, quietly closing the door. Slipping quietly from the room after relieving the refrigerator of a bar of chocolate, Minnie swung her handbag over her shoulder and took the elevator back down to the lobby. 'Good evening,' she said to a passing porter whilst looking around for the hotel manager.

'He has gone, Missy' the porter informed her whilst burdened with baggage.

'To Jodhpur.'

'To his parents?' Minnie asked.

'Yes, Missy,' the porter replied, hurrying on his way.

'Oh how lovely,' Minnie remarked, and she wandered around the foyer aimlessly before venturing outside to take in the night air.

'Taxi, Missy?' a cab driver called having just dropped a fare.

'Oh, oh no thank you, dear,' Minnie replied with a wave. 'I'm merely stretching my legs.'

'I give you good price!' the driver insisted, holding open the rear door. 'Take you nice place!'

'I said no thank you,' Minnie reiterated. 'I'm quite alright, young man.' She then thought for a moment. 'Nice place you say?' she asked, looking up toward their apartment window.

'Yes, Missy, nice place good price,' the driver said, flashing a smile. 'Nice place, restaurant, night club, casino…'

'Oooh a casino!' Minnie said with a twinkle in her eye. 'Would they by any chance have a blackjack table?'

'But of course, Missy,' the eager taxi driver said, beckoning. 'Come, come I take you, good price.'

'Well lead on, my good man,' Minnie said, wasting no time and climbing in the back of his yellow New York style taxi cab.

'Don't worry, Missy,' the driver said, hopping in the front. 'I give you good price, very good price.'

Minnie rolled her eyes, 'I'll be the judge of that, young man,' she informed him, clinging tightly to her handbag.

Minnie was driven all of two hundred yards to the harbour where a huge super-yacht was berthed. 'Casino, Missy,' the driver said, opening the rear door.

'What, already?' Minnie gasped, with the Taj Mahal still very much in plain sight.

'Yes, yes, best casino in all of Mumbai,' the driver said, gesturing to the hulking vessel towering above them and just a stone's throw from her hotel.

'Well, well, how much is the fare?' Minnie asked.

'One thousand rupees please,' her driver told her, holding out his hand.

'One thousand!' Minnie exclaimed. 'One thousand, but that's over ten pounds and you've barely driven a quarter mile, that's preposterous.'

'This is good price, Missy,' the driver informed her yet again. 'One thousand please.'

'No, no, no,' Minnie said, taking out her purse. 'I'll give you a hundred and not a penny more, I do believe that's fair.'

'Ohhhhh please, Missy, the price is very good, twenty thousand rupees for a quality ride in my premium taxi cab.'

'Good price my foot!' Minnie said, getting a tad riled. 'You, sir, are nothing but a charlatan and I'll be blowed if I'll give you a penny more than a hundred, so take it or leave it.'

The taxi driver regularly fleeced the guests of the Taj Mahal, many of them millionaires and paying his vastly exaggerated prices without batting an eyelid, but Minnie was no pushover, she'd haggled with the best hawkers Whitechapel market had to offer, and like her sister emerged victorious every time.

'Oh OK!' the driver relented. 'Eight hundred rupees and you are taking the food from my belly so you are.'

'I'm afraid you'll have to do better than that,' Minnie scoffed, standing her ground. 'My sister and I have been known to walk a mile and a half to save the bus fare and haggle till we were blue in the face over the price of a packet of tea, so what's it to be?'

'Five hundred rupees,' the driver replied, mopping his perspiring brow and smudging his bindi spot in the process, 'OK, OK, three hundred and fifty rupees, please.'

Minnie waved a quantity of rupees under his nose. 'I'll give you one hundred and fifty for your damned cheek,' she said abruptly. 'I suggest you take it before my generosity wanes.' There then followed a brief but tense stand-off with eyes locked and lips pursed.

'OK, OK!' the beleaguered driver conceded. 'One hundred and fifty rupees!' He snatched the money and leapt back into his cab cursing in Bengali under his breath.

'Thank youuuu!' Minnie called after him as he left in a hurry. 'Do enjoy the remainder of your evening, won't you!' She turned and strolled triumphantly toward the yacht with its carpeted gangway and burly suited doormen. 'Excuse me,' she said with the guards looming over her, 'I'm here for the casino.'

The two Indian ex-Olympic weightlifters sneered at the frail unassuming woman beneath them and resumed their conversation. 'I sayyyyy!' Minnie said, raising her voice, 'I have money you know.'

'Your money no good,' one of the men told her, under strict instruction to turn away anyone who didn't fit the casino's strict entry requirements, glamour and sophistication being two of them.

'Oh,' Minnie said, dejected somewhat. 'I'm a guest at the Taj Mahal, I'll have you know,' she added, hoping to sway them. 'And a close personal friend of Mister Govinda, perhaps you've heard of him.'

'Govinda!' both men said in unison whilst stiffening their stance. 'Raj Govinda?' one added.

'Precisely,' Minnie chirped. 'That's the fellow, he and I are collaborating on movie at the moment, but never mind, I can see you are men of principle and I admire you for that, I'll bid you good night.'

'No, no wait!' both men cried, stopping Minnie in her tracks. 'Please,' the larger of the two added, 'I think there has been a mistake, Missy, a grave mistake on our behalf, a thousand pardons to you, come, please.'

'Really, oh you're too kind,' Minnie said, taking them both by the arm as they led her up the sloping gangway. 'Thank you, my dears,' she said on deck. 'I'll see to it Mister Govinda hears of your chivalry.'

'Thank you kindly, madam,' they both replied, knowing full well how generously the director tipped on his regular visits to the floating casino. 'Thank you kindly indeed.'

Minnie made her way below decks, plucking a glass of bubbly from a waiter's tray in passing. 'Hellooooo, helloooo' she called to many of India's super rich seated at the roulette, blackjack and poker tables.

'Madam,' the floor manager said politely, approaching her. 'Perhaps you would like to purchase some chips?'

'Oh no, dear,' Minnie replied, clutching her stomach. 'After what I've eaten today I'll go bang, my dearie.'

'Excuse me?' the manager asked, mystified. 'Ohhhh very good, madam, very good,' he then chuckled. 'No, no I am meaning the gambling chips, for the tables you see.'

'Ohhhh I seeeee,' Minnie smirked. 'Do excuse me, won't you.'

'That's quite alright, madam,' the manager said courteously; he then leaned and looked a little closer. 'Please forgive me, madam, but are you not one half of the Nans, the Peshwari Nans?'

Peshwari Nans Part II

'Yes, love,' Minnie said, sipping her champagne. 'Oh good God that's as dull as dish water!' she exclaimed, screwing up her face and thrusting the glass into a passing waiter's hand. 'If that's anything to go by it's a good job I gave the chips a wide berth.'

'Madam, we have no chips' the manager first told her before grabbing at the waiter's arm. 'Bring our guest the Bollinger,' he barked. 'Hurry, man, hurry!'

Minnie wandered between the tables having purchased a stack of chips of the plastic variety, popping one or two down on the roulette table and watching the tiny bouncing ball come to rest in the red segment. 'Fiddlesticks!' she cursed before placing the opposite bet and losing once again. 'Ahhhh blackjack,' she then said with a broad smile, wrenching herself up onto a stool between two leggy Indian glamour models. 'Good evening, good evening,' she said but receiving only a nod in reply from the pair who regularly appeared on the cover of India's best-selling fashion magazines advertising Gucci, Dolce and Gabbana, and Yves Saint Laurent to name but a few. 'Riiiight,' Minnie said, cracking her knuckles and playing it safe at first, betting only a few rupees at a time while those seated around the table with her, the high rollers as it were, parted with thousands without batting an eyelid. Suddenly a loud and obnoxious Japanese customer called out from behind 'HEYYYYYY, HEYYYYYY, I KNOW YOU!' he cried, spilling his complimentary champagne, in which he'd overindulged. 'I KNOW YOUUUU!'

'Yes dear I'm sure you do,' Minnie said as he approached. 'What are you doing?' she then asked as he threw his arms around her neck and pressed his cheek against hers, reeking of alcohol and expensive cigars.

'You that Nan right?' he slurred, rocking Minnie from side to side.

'Yes, dear,' Minnie said, attempting to shrug off his pestering hands.

'HEY, EVERYBODY!' he then yelled, turning dozens of heads. 'LOOK, LOOK, IT'S THE NAN!'

'Please I'd rather not draw attention if you don't mind,' Minnie told him as he manhandled her and reached for his phone.

'Take a selfie, take a selfie!' he insisted, stretching his arm out in front of them and planting a slobbering kiss on her cheek whilst capturing the moment, but as he posed for another with Minnie grappling beneath him a firm hand then grasped the collar of his jacket and hoisted him from the table.

'Didn't you hear the lady,' the intervening man told the drunkard, whose father had business interests with the yacht's owners.

'GET YOUR HANDS OFF ME!' he cried, writhing in his white tuxedo with his tie askew and the neck of his shirt open. 'DO YOU NOT KNOW WHO I AM?' Then spinning to confront his assailant the gambler immediately froze open-mouthed. 'Wait!' he gasped 'You Mister Bond, Mister Jame Bond!' Sure enough Minnie's saviour was the suave British actor who'd played the inimitable 007 in four consecutive movies before passing the baton.

Holidaying in Mumbai with his family, the Brit had left his hotel for the same reasons Minnie had. 'You want your selfie, here!' he grimaced, snatching the gambler's phone, pulling him close to his chest and snapping the pair of them before thrusting it back into his hand and shoving him toward the door. 'Now I suggest you leave before I do something you'll live to regret.'

'Yes, yes, I leaving!' the staggering pest said, having watched the actor systematically destroy an entire army of bad guys on the big screen. He stumbled on the stairs as he left, looking lovingly at his recent snap. 'Jame Bond!' he said in awe. 'JAME BOND!'

'Thank you, my dear,' Minnie said, offering her hand.

'Think nothing of it,' her fellow countryman said, taking out his own phone having recognised Minnie's familiar frame. 'May I?' he asked, reaching for a photograph of the two of them.

'Yes, yes, of course,' Minnie said snuggling in close to the dashing gent and posing cheek to cheek.

'My wife,' the actor said, pocketing his phone. 'She's a huge fan of yours, and your sister of course, is she not with you?'

'No she's soaking her teeth, dear,' Minnie said, giving him a little more information than he required. 'Oh and by the way' she added 'She's a huge fan of yours too, my sweet, she'll be positively green with envy when I tell her.' After a moment or two of small talk the former Bond left the casino leaving Minnie bursting at the seams to break the news to her sister of their meeting, a spot of karma she thought after the days fetching and carrying for the Dowager Duchess.

Minnie's fortunes at the blackjack table swung back and forth from rags to riches and vice versa. Soon she was down to her last two thousand rupees, around twenty pounds, but she ignored the calls from her fellow gamblers for her to quit and put it all on one last-ditch hand. Minnie was immediately dealt an ace and a king and scooped the handsome pot in front of her, 'Oooooh, lucky me,' she squealed as to her complete surprise a priest sat down beside her with a fistful of the lowest denomination of chips. 'Evening, Father,' Minnie said, looking him up and down whilst he wagered a few rupees without uttering a word and winning twice his original stake almost immediately.

'Well done,' Minnie said, tossing in her losing hand beside him. 'I'm sorry, I hope you don't mind me saying,' she added after some deliberation 'But isn't this sort of thing frowned upon by the big man upstairs?'

'Big man?' the priest asked, sliding a larger amount to the centre of the table.

'Yes, you know,' Minnie replied gesturing above their heads. 'The head honcho, A number one, top of the heap as Sinatra once said.'

'Ohhhhh,' the priest said, cottoning on. 'You mean…'

'Yes of course,' Minnie added. 'Aren't you afraid you'll be struck by a thunderbolt or plagued by leaches or whatnot?'

'No, no, no, I am here doing his bidding,' the priest chuckled, winning the next hand and drawing the pot toward him.

'His bidding?' Minnie exclaimed. 'I'd hardly call this a vocation, and no doubt you are gambling with the coffers from the collection plate, dear God, you ought to be ashamed of yourself.'

'Please allow me to explain,' the priest replied, nodding to the dealer for another hand.

'I wish you would,' Minnie said, horrified at his apparent misuse of church funds.

'Before I become priest,' he explained whilst sneaking a look at his cards, 'I was big, big gambler, very big, but I lost my beloved wife to malaria and as you can imagine I was devastated beyond consolation.'

'Oh I am sorry to hear that, dear,' Minnie said, changing her tone immediately. 'Yes I rather think you would be.'

'I tried to take my own life on several occasions just to be with her,' the priest confessed. 'But the Almighty, he came to me in a blinding vision, ohhh, Missy, it was so beautiful, it was then that I realised I must use my gift at the gambling tables to do good things, for the poor and the homeless of Mumbai, so here I am, I run a humble mission for the orphans and street children of which there are many.'

In fact the figures for Mumbai's forgotten children, many of them sleeping in the open streets at the mercy of the elements and perhaps worse, ran into the tens of thousands.

'Oh how lovely,' Minnie said, patting his hand. 'That's extremely commendable and I'm sorry I misjudged you, I'm sure your dear wife would be immensely proud of you, good for you sir, good for you.'

Minnie went on to increase her own pot after three consecutive wins, with the priest's fortunes beside her wavering. 'All of it, my dear,' Minnie told the dealer, pushing her entire stack of chips to the centre of the table.

'Are you sure, madam?' the courteous dealer asked.

'In for a penny, in for a pound,' was Minnie's reply, with the priest having to bet only a few rupees during his rare run of bad luck Examining her hand, Minnie's heart fluttered as she rose from the stool and stepped down. 'There, dear,' she said, sliding the cards face down toward the priest. 'I'm going to turn in for the night, perhaps you might like to play my hand.'

'Sorry?' the priest asked, bemused. 'But, but if you win?' Minnie tucked her handbag under her arm and made for the door. 'Give it to the children!' she called back with a wry smile before disappearing out of sight.

The priest took a peep at Minnie's cards and almost fell from his stool; of course the hand was unbeatable and almost one hundred thousand rupees was soon pushed his way. 'Congratulations, Father,' the dealer said, knowing only too well how many hot meals the princely pot could provide, herself hailing from those very same streets. Looking around at the closing door, the priest was convinced that he'd just been in the presence of an angel, a further reaffirming sign from his Lord and Master. The vulnerable orphans would indeed eat well and receive vital health care, warm clothes and shoes for their calloused feet.

Minnie descended the gangway. 'Madam,' one of the doormen said, greeting her on the quayside and taking her arm. 'Please, allow me to escort you to your hotel.'

'Oh, are you sure, dear?' Minnie asked. 'I'd hate to trouble you.'

'No trouble at all, I assure you,' the burly bouncer replied, leaving his post. 'I would consider it a great pleasure.'

'Well thank you,' Minnie told her escort. 'That's awfully kind of you, sorry I didn't catch your name?'

'Tariq,' the doorman replied. 'My name is Tariq, and I have a question I would like to put to you if I may.'

'Yes, yes of course,' Minnie agreed. 'Ask away!'

'My mother,' Tariq explained. 'She is having a birthday very soon, she will be seventy-two years of age and I am wondering what a woman of that age would really want on that most special of days?'

'Oh how sweet of you, dear,' Minnie said, whilst gripping his muscular arm. 'May I ask do you have children?'

'Yes, two young boys,' Tariq informed her. 'Full of mischief, the both of them.'

'Well if it were me,' Minnie said, offering her words of wisdom. 'Nothing would make me happier than a visit from my son and his two little tearaways, with perhaps a bunch of fresh chrysanthemums and a tin of assorted biscuits, oh and a jigsaw, yes definitely a jigsaw, I can highly recommend the Mona Lisa, with twenty thousand pieces she'll still be doing the damn thing when she's seventy-five.'

'Your hotel, madam,' Tariq said as Minnie reeled off her own personal wish list.

'Crystalized ginger!' Minnie added excitedly. 'Believe me, Tariq my love, she would simply die for a box of crystalized ginger, and potpourri, dear, you really must give her potpourri.'

'OK, OK,' Tariq said, his head now spinning. 'So if I am not mistaken, you are recommending to me the potpourri, the ginger that is crystalized, the Mona Lisa jigsaw, the biscuits that are assorted in their tin, flowers and a visit from her grandchildren?'

'Yes, dear,' Minnie replied. 'Oh and slippers, my darling, you can't go wrong with slippers.'

'Slippers,' Tariq said, adding them to his mental list. 'You have been most informative, Missy,' he added, bending to kiss her hand. 'I will bid you goodnight and the sweetest of dreams.'

'And you, dear,' Minnie said, entering the hotel. 'Night, night!'

Creeping back into their room, Minnie undressed in the dark. 'Damn, damn, damn and blast!' she cursed, stubbing her big toe on the bed leg; she then slipped into bed without waking her sister and lay with her hand over her mouth with her toe throbbing something terrible. Eventually the pain subsided and Minnie pulled up the duvet under her chin and lay staring out the window at the starlit sky until her eyes grew heavy.

Esther woke her sister the following morning after several failed attempts, unaware of her nocturnal ventures. 'Will you please get up!' she said as Minnie rolled to the opposite side of their bed, pretending not to have heard. 'Tilly!' she then barked, inadvertently slipping into character. 'Do as you're told!'

'It's Minnie!' Minnie said, flinging the sheets aside angrily. 'Your sister, remember?'

'Yes, yes, whatever,' Esther said, tossing her sister fresh underwear. 'Now go freshen up, the car will be here for us in an hour.'

'It's not fair!' Minnie moaned, harping on about their given roles. 'I don't see why I have to be the chambermaid, Tilly fetch this, Tilly fetch that!'

'Oh do be quiet,' Esther smirked, relishing the day's filming and her position as the Dowager Duchess.

'Oh!' Minnie said, popping her head out from the bathroom. 'You'll never guess who I bumped into last night, dear.'

'Last night?' Esther asked, puzzled. 'What do you mean last night, you were hear with me, weren't you?'

'Initially, dear, yes,' Minnie informed her. 'But then I popped out to the casino across the street.'

'The casino!' Esther cried, dashing from the bedroom. 'You mean you were out on your own, without me?'

'Yes of course,' Minnie smiled. 'You know I'm partial to a hand or two of blackjack, and after all I was bored and not at all sleepy.'

'Yes but, Minnie!' Esther said, horrified at her sister's flagrant irresponsibility. 'On your own, for heaven's sake'

'My dear, I was fiiiine,' Minnie laughed. 'Besides I met a heartthrob of yours while I was out, Mister Brosnan, AKA 007.'

'You did not!' Esther gasped. 'You didn't, my Piercey, my Piercey Brosnan?'

'In the flesh,' Minnie said proudly. 'And very dashing he was too.'

'You're lying!' Esther stormed, having had a foolish crush on the Irish-born actor ever since he first played the British secret service agent in 1995 in the movie *Goldeneye.*

'Check the tablet, dear, if you don't believe me,' Minnie said, tapping the door frame nonchalantly. En route to the bathroom Minnie had accessed the former Bond's social media page and come across the photograph he had proudly posted of the two of them.

'It's a lie, I tell you,' Esther growled, snatching the tablet from the sofa. 'Youuuuu bitch!' she then cursed on seeing the two of them in such close proximity. 'How could you?'

'He really is quite a charmer, isn't he, dear,' Minnie said, gloating and loving every second of it. 'And far more handsome in the flesh.'

'You cow! Esther said, tossing the tablet down. 'You knew I was sweet on him so you threw yourself at him like a, like a cheap hussy!'

'Actually,' Minnie informed her sister, 'He came to my rescue, you see there was this rather intoxicated Oriental gentleman making a complete ass of himself so Pierce gallantly stepped in to defend my honour, I must say I felt like a Bond girl for a moment there.'

'Rescue!' Esther snapped. 'Minnie, what on earth were you doing?'

Minnie proceeded to inform her jealous sister of the night's events. 'Well,' she began, taking a deep breath. 'I took a taxi across the street, and of course I haggled over the price, as you do, then after my close and altogether memorable encounter with Mister Bond I met a rather remarkable priest.'

'In the casino?' Esther remarked whilst hunting for her shoes.

'Yes, dear!' Minnie called running a hot bath. 'Remarkable, quite remarkable, oh and then Tariq brought me home and we discussed potpourri!'

'Potpourri?' Esther said as her sister closed the door. 'What the devil?'

Raj's chauffeur arrived promptly at nine to find the sisters ready and waiting in the hotel foyer. 'Morning, dear!' Esther called as he opened the rear door once again. 'Lovely day!'

'Good morning to you,' the driver replied, tipping his cap. 'I trust you are well this fine and pleasant morning.'

'Maaaaaarvelous,' Minnie said, lifting the hem of her flowing skirt to climb aboard.

Arriving on location Esther and Minnie once again spent an hour and a half in their trailer with Raj's team, transforming them into the pompous Lady Bagshot and the dainty but downtrodden chambermaid Tilly.

'Fetch my pearls, will you, Tilly!' Esther asked, slipping prematurely into character. 'Hurry, girl!'

Minnie glared at her elder sister. 'I'll do nothing of the sort, you cheeky mare,' she said angrily. 'May I remind you, Essy that until Mister Govinda calls action I am still your sister, and not your skivvy.'

'Yes, yes, of course you are,' 'Esther agreed. 'Now about those pearls?'

'Ohhhh damn you,' Minnie said, reaching for her sister's accessories.

With the house now surrounded by an army of deserting Sepoy renegades, Esther and Minnie took up their positions as Lady Belinda and Tilly in the drawing room which had been locked from the inside with the front entrance doors heavily bolted. They were told that the remaining members of staff, each of them Indian, had fled hoping to be spared by their fellow countrymen, but instead they were bludgeoned to death with a dozen rifle butts for serving their British masters. 'Tilly, come away from the window!' the Duchess called, cowering in the corner of the room.

'But, Madam,' Tilly replied, wrenching the rifle from the lifeless butler's hand. 'We've gotta do something, I heard cook talking and apparently these bugger's ain't taking no prisoners.'

'Aren't, Tilly!' the Duchess said from afar. 'The correct pronunciation is aren't, how many more times do I have to tell you.'

Tilly was born in South London, the illegitimate daughter of a prostitute, and the Duchess had taken pity on her when her horse and carriage had bowled her over in the street giving her a lifelong lilting limp. 'Madam, this ain't no time to talk proper!' Tilly replied, examining the weapon having never before held a gun let alone fired one. 'Flippin 'eck!' she cursed, attempting to cock the antiquated weapon.

'Tilly, what are you doing?' her mistress called. 'Come away at once, will you, hurry, we must hide, it's our only chance!'

''Ide!' Tilly yelled. 'Madam, there ain't no use in 'idin, soon them bleeders are gonna bash the soddin' door in!'

'Tilly!' the Duchess snapped. 'I'll trouble you to keep a civil tongue!'

Tilly took aim through the narrow slit in the hastily erected boarding, closed her eyes and fired. 'OH BLIMEY!' she cursed when the weapon violently recoiled, bruising her shoulder immediately, but loading again nevertheless and firing indiscriminately at the hordes outside. 'GOTCHA!' she then cried, punching the air. 'Madam, ar got wunna them buggers!'

'Did you?' the Duchess asked, peering around the sofa. 'I say, well done, Tilly, well done indeed.'

The countless mutineers gathered on the front lawn meant that even if Tilly were blindfolded with one arm tied behind her back it would have been virtually impossible not to have struck at least one of them. 'Ar got anuvva one, madam!' she cried excitedly, having mastered the loading process, but their supply of munitions was dwindling fast.

The Duchess bravely ventured out from her bolthole to see for herself. 'So you did, Tilly, so you did!' she shrieked, stooping to peep through a cracked board and charged with a glimmer of hope. 'Oh but, Tilly, there are hundreds of them, what are we to do, what are we to do, Tilly?'

Tilly gripped the rifle with whitened knuckles and gritted teeth. 'We're gonna give 'em what for, madam,' she growled, firing and felling another Sepoy. 'That's what we're gonna do, give the buggers what for!'

During those fraught moments the Duchess looked upon her chambermaid in a whole new light; the woman whom she'd ill-treated to a degree for several years was now courageously defending her against insurmountable odds, and although wincing and petrified Lady Belinda stood beside Tilly as a hail of returning fire splintered the birch boarding of her beloved house.

Raj Govinda and his team watched from the wings as the two untrained novices pulled off the performance of a lifetime with all but a few misplaced lines. As far as Minnie was concerned she was defending her sister and needed no additional motivation.

'GET DAAN, MADAM, GET DAAN!' Tilly screeched, pushing her mistress to the floor before fatally wounding another rebel. 'TAKE THAT, YA BUGGER!' she yelled through the boarded window.

The Duchess looked up in awe of her hired help who was all but a few years younger than herself. 'Thank you, Tilly dear,' she said, patting Tilly's thigh tenderly. 'And please, please forgive the way I've behaved towards you, I've been positively beastly at times, I know I have.'

'Oh it don't matter, madam,' Tilly replied, counting the last of their ammunition and pocketing two shells in her pinnie. 'Nuffing don't matter no more.' She then dropped to one knee beside her mistress. 'Listen, madam,' she said, looking the Duchess in the eye. 'Don't you be frettin' about me coz ar know what you done for me when I ad nuffing, you took me in and give me a roof over me 'ead so ar should be fankin you.'

'Oh, Tilly,' the Duchess said, caressing her maid's cheek. 'What would I have done without you?'

There were echoes of the sisters' day-to-day relationship in that tender moment. 'I, I want you to do something for me, Tilly,' the Duchess asked as the riot outside grew louder.

'Course, madam, anyfing' Tilly replied sitting beside her. 'Anyfing, you know that.'

'I want you to do it,' the Duchess said, gesturing to the rifle. 'Not those out there.'

Tilly retrieved the shells from her pinnie pocket. 'What do you fink ar was savin these for, madam,' she confessed with a lump in her throat. 'But to be 'onest ar don't fink ar can do it.'

The Sepoy raiders began beating on the entrance door in greater numbers. 'You have to, Tilly, please,' the Duchess begged. 'Please, do this one last thing for me, please, Tilly.' She gripped the rifle barrel. 'You have to, Tilly,' she reiterated. 'You have to do it now!'

Tilly clambered to her feet with her knees trembling as Raj held his breath; this was it, the moment he had dreamt of. 'Ar can't, madam!' Tilly said with the tears beginning to flow.

'Do it Tilly, please I beg of you!' the Duchess said gripping Tilly's skirt as the hordes broke through the entrance doors, flooded into the entrance hall yelling and screaming and made for the drawing room, pounding the panelling with fists and rifles. 'TILLYYY!' Lady Belinda yelled. 'PLEAAAAASE!'

Minnie's tears at this point were wholly genuine as she shakily raised the prop rifle to her sister's head. 'Oh God, oh God!' she sobbed. 'Ar'm sorry, ar'm sorry, ar'm sorry, forgive me, madam, please forgive me!'

The door was then splintered from its hinges as Minnie closed her eyes once again and pulled the trigger with her heart literally breaking in her chest. The Duchess slumped to the side, slid down the wall and lay motionless as Tilly, now panic-stricken and in floods of tears, attempted to reload, but trembling uncontrollably as she was she fumbled and dropped the remaining shell. 'Bugger!' she cursed, looking up in time to see the whites of the rebels' eyes before as many as twenty of them took aim and gunned her down on the spot. Staggering and vomiting theatrical blood, Minnie fell beside Esther, managing with the life rapidly draining from her to rest her bloodied head on her sister's chest.

'AAAAAAAAND CUT!' Raj yelled leaping from his director's chair and rushing to the sisters. 'YOU DID IT, YOU DID IT!' he shrieked, throwing his hands in the air. 'By golly you did it, and it was magnificent I tell you, truly magnificent!'

'Oh thank you,' Esther said, hoisting herself up onto her bottom.

'Was it really?' Minnie asked. 'Really magnificent?'

'My dear Mimmie, my apologies, Minnie,' Raj said, elated beyond words. 'You have made me the happiest man alive I am telling you, my dream, my dream has been fulfilled!'

'Did you hear that, dear?' Minnie said helping her sister to her feet. 'We were magnificent!'

'No, dear,' Esther said proudly. 'You were magnificent, and I'm sorry I ever doubted your ability and also for mocking your Nativity, you really do have it in your blood, my dear, there is no doubt about it, none whatsoever.'

'Do you mean that, dear?' asked Minnie with the broadest smile etched on her face.

'Truly?'

'Yes truly,' Esther said as the extras filed from the room toward the set canteen. 'Are we done, dear?' Esther asked Raj back at their trailer. 'Only I'd like to get out of this blasted corset, the damn thing's cutting me in two.'

'Yes, yes, my dear,' Raj said, positively bobbing with excitement, and he then left them to change back into their everyday clothes.

Before doing so Esther and Minnie looked one another up and down. 'Tilly,' Esther said with a smile.

'M'lady,' Minnie replied; the pair then burst into fits of laughter, never in their wildest dream could they have foreseen the events of that day. Hugging passionately the sisters savoured every last moment as movie stars, possibly adding their names to the list of such iconic screen sirens as Elizabeth Taylor, Lauren Bacall, Bette Davis and Audrey Hepburn.

That evening at Raj Govinda's request Esther and Minnie were invited to Mumbai's most lavish of restaurants, the three time Michelin star awarded Bollywood Balti and incidentally owned by the director himself.

'Hellooooo, hellooooo!' they both said arriving and mingling amongst cinematic royalty as it were.

'Hiiiiii,' a familiar face said from the crowd, it was the young Asian heartthrob who had starred alongside them as Lady Belinda's head gardener. 'May I just say,' he added, turning side on to squeeze between his fellow actors, 'What an absolute pleasure it was working with you ladies, personally I thought your performances were breathtaking, simply breathtaking.'

'Ohhhh how nice of you to say,' Esther replied. 'Myself I thought we were mediocre at best.'

'Ohhh no, no, no,' the handsome young man said categorically. 'When Mister Govinda said you were amateurs you could have knocked me down with a feather, a feather I tell you.'

'Amateurs,' Minnie protested. 'Let me tell you my dear, without the North Star the Nativity is nothing, nothing I tell you.'

Of course the youth knew nothing of Minnie's childhood acting debut 'Nativity?' he asked, bemused.

'It's a long story, dear,' Esther said, waving across the room to Raj. 'I'd hate to bore you with it, do excuse me will you,' she told the popular pin-up as the crowd graciously parted for her.

Minnie on the other hand stayed a while to explain to the young A-lister the complexities of wrapping oneself in tin foil and perching motionless on a cardboard box. 'And I suppose I've been a star ever since,' she bragged, patting the lad's hand and heading to join her sister, leaving him lost for words. 'Thank you, thank you,' she told the onlookers who bombarded her with favourable comments. 'Oh really you're too kind.'

Raj ushered the sisters to his table. 'Come, come sit!' he called. 'I owe you so much, so, so much, I tell you I have been walking on air since this afternoon, walking on air I say!'

'Well,' Esther said, sitting beside him. 'I'm just glad we were able to help, that's all.'

'Yes, yes it was so exciting,' Minnie squealed. 'And the toilet facilities in our trailer were mind-boggling I tell you, weren't they, dear?'

'Oh yes, mind-boggling,' her sister agreed.

Minnie reference to the trailer's state of the art WC had the guests seated around them in hysterics. 'A soft close seat,' she raved. 'Who'd have imagined?'

'Minnie, my darling,' Raj said, with his arms outstretched, 'I will buy for you a thousand of these lavatory seats if you so wish.'

'Ooooh,' Minnie said, clasping her hands together. 'You, Mister Govinda, are too kind, sir, too kind by half.'

A steady flow of celebrities approached the sisters requesting they sign their starched white napkins.

'Ladies, ladies,' Raj said, distracting them from their admirers, 'I have a proposition I wish to put to you.'

'Oh really,' Esther replied, handing back a monogrammed napkin. 'A proposition, you say, how intriguing, Minnie dear, he has a proposition.'

'What's that, dear?' Minnie asked, cupping her ear.

'He has a proposition, dear!' Esther said a little louder.

'Don't you think it's a little too soon, dear,' Minnie replied with her sister's best interests at heart. 'I mean with Jack barely cold in the ground and all.'

'You're right,' her sister said adamantly, 'I'm sorry, Mister Govinda,' she told the director. 'I'm extremely flattered but…'

'No, no, no!' Raj laughed. 'I assure you it is not that sort of proposition, I would like you both to stay here in Mumbai.'

'Stay?' Esther asked, giving Raj her fullest attention. 'What do you mean, stay?'

'Stay,' Raj reiterated. 'I was to retire after this picture but you two have awoken a hunger in me, a hunger to make more, together we could take the world by storm, by storm I tell you.'

Minnie leaned a little closer. 'What did he say, dear?' she asked.

'He wants us to stay, dear,' Esther informed her.

'Stay!' Minnie gasped. 'Here, in Mumbai!'

'Yes,' Esther replied. 'In Mumbai.'

'Oh,' Minnie said, stunned somewhat. 'But, but what about Cairo, dear, we have plans.'

'Minnie dearest,' her sister said, gripping her hand, 'I thought you would relish the idea of a career on the silver screen, treading the red carpet in your finest twin set and pearls.'

'My darling sister,' Minnie smiled. 'Had you asked me that forty years ago I'd have bitten Mister Govinda's hand off but I'm far too long in the tooth for all that nonsense now, don't get me wrong, sir,' she told the director, 'I've enjoyed the experience immensely, but I think I speak for the both of us when I say the lure of the open road far outweighs the smell of the grease paint as they say.'

'Please,' Raj said, clasping his hands in prayer. 'I beg of you, reconsider, Bollywood has been waiting for such a breath of fresh air as yourselves for a very long time, believe me.'

'That's awfully kind of you to say, Mister Govinda but,' Esther said with a hand on her heart, 'My sister's right, we are far too long in the tooth to be embarking on a new career, we consider ourselves free spirits now and believe me we're having the time of our lives, what little there is remaining, so I am afraid we will graciously decline your kind offer, but I assure you we are both extremely flattered.'

'Extremely flattered,' Minnie echoed as yet another napkin was dangled before her.

The star-studded even went swimmingly with Esther and Minnie enthralling the guests with tales of a bygone era. 'By the time I received the hand-me-downs,' Minnie said with a crowd gathered around them, 'The shoes had been repaired a dozen times and the knickers had sagged beyond all recognition, do you remember, dear?' she asked her sister.

'Yes of course,' Esther chuckled. 'Well they had had three previous owners in our family alone and were second-hand at the point of purchase.'

'Amazing, amazing!' Raj said, taking notes beside them. 'And you say your grandfather was killed by a doodlebug during the war?'

'Yes that's right, God rest his soul,' Esther replied. 'The Golden Fleece in Mortimer Street took a direct hit during the blackout, he and a lady friend of his had been canoodling in the snug at the time, of course Grandmother had no idea he was playing away so to speak, she thought he was playing bar billiards with the chaps from the station, he was a police officer you see and quite a celebrity by all accounts, you see it was his dogged determination that led to the eventual arrest of Doctor Christie, the infamous serial killer or the Rillington Place strangler as he was dubbed.'

'Oh yes,' Raj said, nodding repeatedly. 'I have heard of this man. Number ten, was it not?'

'That's right, dear, Ten Rillington Place,' Esther told him. 'The blighter murdered his wife along with as many as seven other women, a nasty piece of work by all accounts, and as for my grandfather, well after appearing in every Fleet Street rag the ladies positively threw themselves at him.'

'And who could blame them,' Minnie intervened. 'He was a very handsome young man, rather like an early Richard Burton I always thought.'

The conversation went on late into the night with the anecdotes flowing freely as did the wine. 'So, you are leaving tomorrow,' Raj eventually said with a heavy heart. 'And you say there is nothing I can do to change your mind?'

'Sorry, dear,' Esther told him. 'We were promised our car would be restored and returned in the morning before we set sail for Dubai.'

'Your car?' Raj said as several guests began to leave. 'My dears, I will buy you a dozen automobiles, what would you like, Mercedes, Aston Martin perhaps, Porsche?'

'No, no, dear,' Esther refused. 'There is only one car for me, my Vivien, my marvellous Morris. She may not be fast and she may not be state of the art but she's got class and real panache.'

'She's a motoring icon, isn't she, dear,' Minnie added.

'That she is, dear,' Esther agreed. 'That she is.'

Raj took out his cheque book. 'Well I will see to it that you are rewarded handsomely for your services,' he told the sisters. 'Please, name your price.'

'Oh there really is no need, dear,' Esther said, raising a hand. 'You see we already have more than we need.' She referred to Karl Bodine's regular payments. 'And we thoroughly enjoyed the experience, after all.'

'Yes but..' Raj said, stunned at her honesty. 'You must accept payment, it is only right you see.'

'I tell you what, my lovely,' Minnie piped up. 'Do you know the mission on Kashmiri Street?'

'Yes, yes, I do,' Raj replied. 'You see I own this place and I insist the kitchen delivers all our waste food to the priest who looks after the children, a noble man, a very noble man indeed.'

'Yes, I met him recently,' Minnie confessed. 'Do you think you could make a donation on our behalf, whatever you see fit?'

'If that is what you wish, dear Minnie,' Raj replied. 'I will see to it personally that the mission receive a very generous donation, you will see, very generous indeed.'

Esther once again looked upon her sister with awe and admiration. 'You really do have a heart of pure gold, do you know that, sister dear,' she said, patting the back of Minnie's hand. 'Pure gold.'

'Oh don't be silly,' Minnie said, shrugging off the praise. 'It's just like you said, dear, we can't spend what we have already so what's the point of adding to the pot, surely that's just greed, isn't it, dear?'

Whilst millionaires and billionaires the world over stockpiled their wealth in heavily fortified vaults constantly striving to increase their dragon's hoard and sleeping with one eye open for fear of losing a single penny, Esther and Minnie ascended to the moral high ground, taking only what they needed to live out their days in relative comfort and nothing more.

Raj hugged the sisters outside his restaurant and held open the limousine door. 'Farewell, my friends,' he told them with a parting kiss. 'And thank you from the bottom of my heart once again for the picture of my dreams, please take the utmost care of yourselves and come back any time you wish, I will be waiting.'

'Thank you, Mister Govinda,' Esther said, returning the kiss to his cheek.

'Please,' Raj replied bowing graciously. 'My friends call me Raj, and you are now two of my closest friends.'

'Goodbye, Raj my sweet,' Minnie said, climbing into the limousine. 'And thank you, for making me feel like a star, I mean.'

'Oh but you are a star,' Raj said, closing the door behind them. 'Remember your Nativity.' He then bent to offer a personal message. 'Some would describe you ladies as rough diamonds,' he said, looking them in the eye. 'Me, I say you are polished jewels, both of you.'

'Ahhhh, you take care of yourself, my love,' Esther said, tugging her seat belt over her shoulder. 'And please don't retire, my dear, if you truly love what you do, do it until your very last breath.'

'Goodbye!' Raj said, waving as the sisters were driven away with their words of wisdom still ringing in his ears.

It was late by the time the sisters turned in for the night, a little after 1 a.m. to be exact. 'I've set the alarm, dear,' Esther said, winding up her clunky enamelled bedside clock. 'If we are to be on that blasted boat of yours before ten a.m. we will have to rise at eight o'clock sharp, do you hear?' She set the clock down and rolled over to find her sister already sound asleep, and with the rigours of the day steadily taking their toll it was only moments before she too drifted off.

Esther's clanging alarm rang for a full minute and a half the following morning before she reached out a fumbling hand and knocked it onto the floor where it continued to ring. 'Blast!' she sleepily cursed, rolling onto her side and grappling beside the bed amongst her carpet slippers.

'Switch it off, dear!' Minnie moaned, prodding her sister's back with a bony finger. 'Switch it off, will you!'

'Yes I'm trying to!' Esther barked in reply whilst knocking the timepiece out of reach. 'Oh hell!' she growled when forced to clamber from the bed and drop slowly onto all fours to hunt bleary-eyed for the offending clock.

'Thank heavens,' Minnie said when it was eventually silenced. 'Now if you'll just give me five more minutes, dear.'

Esther peered over the mattress at her dozing sister. 'I will not!' she said, hauling herself to her feet having gotten out of bed a little quicker than she would have liked and paid the agonising price for doing so. 'Get up, Minnie,' she told her sister. 'We haven't time for your shenanigans this morning.'

Cocking a deaf ear once again Minnie slithered deeper beneath the sheets.

'Ohhh no you don't,' Esther warned her, tugging at the duvet. 'You get out of that bed right now or it'll be the cold flannel for you, young lady.'

'God!' Minnie exclaimed, peering from her nest. 'You sound just like Mother.'

'No, dear,' Esther said, pushing her feet inside her slippers. 'If I was your mother I'd have put you up for adoption long before now, now get up for Pete's sake!'

'Oh, Essy!' Minnie said, sitting up sharply to confront her sister. 'You don't mean that, you take that back right this minute!'

'Shan't,' Esther said, leaving the bedroom with her nose in the air.

'How rude,' Minnie groaned, swinging her legs over the side of the bed and feeling for her own slippers.

Esther had showered, dressed and begun to pack long before her sister had fully woken. 'Minnie!' she said, bearing down on her case to fasten the clasp, 'Will you hurry.'

'Yes, yes,' Minnie replied wistfully whilst gazing from the window out over the rail side streets of Mumbai, where thousands upon thousands of Indian refugees lived beneath canvas sheeting and rusting corrugated iron. As many as half of the teaming metropolis of the former Bombay lived in abject poverty, eking out a bleak existence begging and hawking cheap trinkets aboard the heavily crowded commuter trains while their children danced and sang to entertain the travellers for a rupee or two per day. She thought of her chance encounter with the benevolent priest and the mountainous task he faced day in day out with an ever increasing flock arriving at his door in desperation. 'Yes, yes, I'm coming, dear,' she said, shuffling to the bathroom.

A short while later the Taj Mahal bellboy carried their luggage to reception leaving the sisters to enjoy a light breakfast in the hotel restaurant. 'More tea dear?' Minnie asked, offering the pot.

'Oh yes, please,' Esther replied, but was immediately startled, dropping her cup when the bellboy raced to their table.

'Missy, Missy, come quick!' he cried, clinging to his hat. 'Come quickly, come see come see!'

'What the?' Esther shrieked as her sister poured tea onto the tablecloth. 'What, what's wrong, boy?'

'Missy, come see!' the lad again cried, wide-eyed.

'Oh dear, whatever's happened?' Minnie asked, setting down the china pot. 'Essy, what's happened, dear?' Fearing a disaster the sisters rose from the table.

'Come, come!' the bellboy urged.

'Dear Lord, what is it, young man?' Esther asked, leaving her breakfast of toast and beans while her sister reached back and snatched a slice from her plate and nibbled from one corner whilst trailing her sister.

'Come see, Missy!' the buoyant boy said, positively skipping across the foyer.

A crowd had gathered outside as though surrounding an accident victim. 'Oh good heavens!' Esther said with a hand to her mouth. 'What is it?'

The crowd parted on their approach, stopping the sisters dead in their tracks. 'Oh my word!' Esther squealed.

'Ohhhh, Essy,' Minnie said equally astonished. There before them, sitting purring in the road was Vivien, looking absolutely resplendent in the early morning sun. All traces of the Bengal tiger's ferocious attack had been beaten from her bodywork and the minutest of blemishes carefully filled, sanded and prepared for a complete respray in British Leyland colour BU37, Trafalgar blue.

'Ohhhh, Vivien darling,' Esther gushed with her hands clasped to her cheeks, 'Just look at you.'

Lari stood proudly at her side, smiling and polishing her Morris emblem.

'Essy, look,' Minnie said, peering in through the open passenger window at her reupholstered seat.

'But, but how?' Esther asked, running a hand across her car's curvaceous wing.

144

'I told you, Missy,' the doorman said. 'Lari best mechanic in all of Mumbai.'

'Yes, yes I know you did but…' Esther said in awe. 'Are you quite sure she is my Vivien?' Opening the driver's door, Esther pulled down the sun visor to reveal a faded black and white photograph of her wedding day, with Jack wearing a suit he'd borrowed from an undertaker friend. 'It is!' she said, looking around the gleaming interior. 'It is my Vivien, it's, it's a miracle, Minnie, that's what it is.'

'A miracle indeed dear,' her sister agreed. 'A miracle and a marvel.'

Esther approached the grinning chauffeur. 'Ohhhh, Lari,' she said with open arms. 'How ever did you manage it, dear, and so quickly too?'

'Your Vivien was like the piece of cake,' Lari replied, bowing. 'And a pleasure to fix for you.'

'Did you hear that, Minnie dear?' Esther said, looking over her car again. 'He said it was a piece of cake, can you believe that?'

'The man's a genius,' Minnie remarked. 'An absolute genius.'

Vivien literally sparkled from top to bottom the same way she did way back in 1965 when she rolled off the production line eight thousand miles away in Great Britain.

Esther again flung her arms around Lari, overcome with emotion and gratitude. 'Thank you,' she said with a tear in her eye. 'Thank you, you remarkable young man, my Vivien looks, she looks…' Esther was momentarily stuck for words.

'Beautiful, dear,' Minnie piped up. 'She looks beautiful.'

'Yes, beautiful,' Esther had to agree. 'Absolutely beautiful.'

Lari had worked through the night in his wooden outhouse lit only by a flickering flame, using a handful of rusting second-hand tools and a spray kit once used to paint Mumbai's bustling locomotives.

'Remarkable,' Esther went on to say, stunned to the very core. 'Quite remarkable.'

The bellboy arrived with their luggage and promptly packed it in the rear and stood hovering with his ever ready card reader. 'I'll get this, dear,' Minnie told her overwhelmed sister, reaching for her purse and again tipping the lad generously.

'Thank you kindly, Missy,' the lad said before rushing to greet a party of Pakistani parliamentary candidates. 'Please allow me,' he said, pocketing his reader and snatching the bags of whom he perceived may be the most handsome tipper.

'Now,' Esther said, producing her own tartan purse. 'You must tell me how much I owe you for your troubles, go ahead, as I said you can name your price and I'll happily pay it.'

'Well,' Lari said, almost too embarrassed to say. 'There was some additional costs to the repair. The paint and the materials,' he added.

'That' quite alright, dear,' Esther agreed. 'Just let me know the total and I'll settle up with you right now.'

Lari's brother beside him urged him in their native tongue to fleece the foreigners but the humble chauffeur was having none of it. 'No, no, no,' he said, shaking his head and pushing his sibling aside. 'Missy, shall we say twenty thousand rupees?'

'For the paint?' Esther asked.

'No, no, Missy, for the entire job,' Lari said swiftly. 'Twenty thousand is my price.'

'Don't be ridiculous!' Esther laughed. 'Twenty thousand rupees is a pittance.'

'Yes, a pittance,' Minnie echoed, still admiring his handiwork.

'Oh no, no, that won't do at all,' Esther objected. 'I'll give you sixty thousand rupees for your labour and another twenty-five thousand for those incidentals, does that sound fair to you?'

Lari stood totting up the amounts in his head and then gasped. 'Eighty-five thousand rupees, Missy!'

'Oh I'm sorry, is that too little?' Esther asked. 'Shall we make it a round hundred?'

'What?' Lari said with a hand to his forehead. 'No, no, no, no, no, no, Missy, please I cannot accept this!' His brother jabbed at his ribs to silence his apparent lunacy.

'You can and you will,' Esther insisted. 'And I'll hear no more about it.'

Lari surely was a wasted talent as a Taj Mahal chauffeur, not only had he restored Vivien's appearance aesthetically but the uber-talented part time mechanic had also give her a thorough service, ensuring her roadworthiness and reliability for many miles to come.

Taking a lasting look at the grandiose Taj Mahal Palace hotel, the sisters thanked those gathered to see them off and for a most memorable visit to Mumbai. 'Goodbye and thank you so, so, much again,' Esther told, Lari leaning from her driver's seat.

'We best hurry, dear,' Minnie reminded her sister whilst checking her wristwatch. 'We only have thirty minutes before the freighter leaves.'

'Right you are, dear,' Esther replied, slipping Vivien's polished stick into first gear and raising the clutch as the crowd parted before them.

'Byyyyye, goodbyyyye!' Minnie called from her window with a regal wave.

Leaving the hotel complex, the sisters were immediately halted when faced with Mumbai's morning rush and although the harbour entrance where the Northern Star was moored was a mere quarter mile from the Taj Mahal and clearly visible, the gridlock that ensnared them gave the sisters cause for great concern. 'Oh, Essy,' Minnie said repeatedly checking her wrist. 'Twenty minutes, dear, we only have twenty minutes and the travel agent was most insistent we arrived with plenty of time to spare.'

'Yes, yes, Minnie,' her sister snapped, 'I'm well aware of that.' She leaned on Vivien's horn. 'Get out of the way, you fools!' she yelled as several pedestrians meandered between the standing vehicles hawking newspapers and cigarettes to the frustrated drivers who faced this morning mayhem on a daily basis.

'No, thank you,' Minnie said politely when a carton of cigarettes was thrust through her window and the trader rattled off his marketing spiel. 'I said no thank you,' she insisted, raising a hand as his patter became uncomfortably aggressive. 'My sister and I do not smoke so would you kindly peddle your poison elsewhere, no, I said no!'

A ship's booming horn then sounded as the Saudi-owned freighter made preparations to set sail. 'We have eight minutes, dear, eight minutes,' Minnie said, keeping her anxious sister regularly updated.

'Minnie!' Esther blurted, tapping Vivien's dashboard clock angrily. 'May I remind you that Vivien has kept excellent time throughout all the years that I've had her, which is more than I can say for that tacky timepiece of yours.'

'Tacky timepiece!' Minnie exclaimed, breathing onto the glass bezel. 'But, Essy, this is a Tiffany, and a present from Cyril.'

'Tiffany!' Esther scoffed. 'My dear, if that thing's a Tiffany I'll eat this hat of mine right now.'

'It is, it is, I tell you,' Minnie protested whilst winding her replica wristwatch. 'Cyril had asked me to spend the weekend at his caravan you see, well how could I refuse when he'd gone to such lengths to woo me.'

'Lengths!' Esther again laughed. 'Minnie, it's a cheap market knock-off, my dear, look at it for Pete's sake, the brass strap has turned your wrist green and the second hand is turning in the opposite direction, oh and in case you've ever wondered, dear, Tiffany is spelt with two f's.'

'Are you sure, dear?' Minnie asked, examining her gift more closely. 'But, but Cyril said it was a token of his undying love, oh dear God!' she then gasped recoiling when recalling their wet and windy weekend at Clacton-on-Sea where the only entertainment to be had was Cyril's battered board games and a frolic between the sheets. 'I daren't tell you what I had to give him in return,' she confessed.

'No, don't,' Esther said abruptly. 'Please don't, I've not long eaten, remember.'

Cyril had indeed duped Minnie into engaging in their first romantic interlude together at the leaking monstrosity he lovingly referred to as his state of the art home from home; this of course would be true if your home was a shanty town shack in tornado alley. The site where Cyril's listing love nest was situated had a ten degree gradient which meant that any fruit rolled regularly from the Formica table, but an astute move on his part nevertheless as Minnie would naturally gravitate to his side of the cramped cabin bed.

Cyril had saved coupons from the weekly *Radio Times* magazine and sent an additional thirty-five pence to cover postage and packing and later received the crude Korean copy of the Tiffany timepiece once worn by the late Queen Mother, a copy flawed in so many ways that even the most naïve would question its validity, but Minnie being Minnie was blown away and blinded by his apparent generosity and suspected nothing untoward, in fact she obliged him the entire stormy weekend to show her gratitude.

With mere moments to spare the sisters turned off the bustling street. 'WAIT, WAIT!' Minnie yelled from her window whilst the ship's mooring tethers were being withdrawn. Esther leaned on Vivien's horn once again, attracting the attention of the harbour master who was there to oversee the vessel's departure. 'COOOOEEEEEE!' Minnie called, waving a handkerchief. 'STOP THE BOAT, STOP THE BOAT, WILL YOU, DEAR!'

The harbour master immediately radioed the ship's captain who powered down the bow thrusters which were gradually pushing the vessel from her berth. 'You are just in the nick of time, madams,' the harbour master told the sisters. 'Hurry, please, leave your vehicle here and I will see it is lifted aboard, quickly, quickly, now!'

'Oh thank you, dear' Esther replied, stepping from Vivien and retrieving her bags. 'You will be careful with her, won't you,' she added, patting her polished bonnet.

'Of course, of course,' the harbour master said, signalling to the quayside crane driver.

The one hundred and twenty thousand ton Northern Star sat low in the water, having been loaded with some three hundred containers, but with her shipping line falling on hard times the Saudis had been forced to consider the option of carrying paying passengers too, providing sleeping and dining facilities albeit modest.

A contingent of the Indian army stood on deck looking out across their homeland packed in preparation for training manoeuvres in the deserts surrounding Dubai, and two chivalrous recruits raced down the gangway to assist the elderly ladies. 'Please allow me, madam,' one of them said, relieving Esther of her luggage whilst his friend took Minnie's arm.

'Oh how kind,' Esther said, gripping the rope rail.

'Thank you, young man,' Minnie smiled. 'I must say I do love a man in uniform, don't you, Essy, I said I love a man in uniform, dear!'

'You'd love a man in just about anything,' her sister said over her shoulder.

'What was that, dear?' Minnie asked with a shortness of breath and pausing on the steep gangway.

'Oh come now, dear,' Esther said, stopping halfway herself. 'You can't possibly deny, Minnie, that you have a promiscuous streak about you.'

'My dear, what are you insinuating?' Minnie asked angrily. 'That I'm some cheap floozy willing to drop my linen for every Tom Dick and Harry, is that what you're saying, is it?'

The two recruits stood bewildered as the two sisters got into a heated exchange, delaying the ship's departure further. 'OK, how many?' Esther asked abruptly.

'How many what?' Minnie replied, standing her ground.

'Men, of course,' Esther remarked. 'How many men have you had relations with, five, ten, fifty perhaps?'

'Oh I don't know!' Minnie said, thinking back.

'There you have it,' Esther said with a smug smile. 'You don't know, I rest my case.'

Minnie genuinely couldn't recall the number of lovers she'd entertained throughout her long life, 'It's nowhere near fifty, that's for sure,' she said in her defence, 'Now let me see, there was Cyril of course, then there was Albert from the gas light and coke company, he'd always stop for a cup of tea and a Chelsea bun after he'd read the meter.'

'I bet that's not all he stopped for,' Esther said, tongue-in-cheek.

'Yes well, alright,' Minnie confessed. 'I'll admit we were close, but in return he did turn a blind eye to all the penny washers I'd been filling the meter with.'

The harbour master waved frantically from the quay. 'Ladies, ladies!' he called. 'Hurry, she is waiting to depart!'

'What about Geoffrey?' Esther asked her sister.

'Oh yes,' Minnie confessed, 'I'd forgotten all about Geoffrey, from the undertakers, we met when we buried Aunt Maud, charming man, always had that aroma of embalming fluid about him though, but he comforted me in my hour of need, and in more ways than one,' she added as a mischievous smile crept across her face. 'Do you know we once did it across the front seat of his hearse, I wouldn't have minded but there was a cold corpse in a coffin in the back at the time, Miss Ripley it was, my old form tutor, I never did care much for the woman.' Minnie began to ramble aimlessly. 'Do you know she once gave me the slipper for flashing my stocking tops in return for chocolate and chewing gum.'

The boisterous boys on board called to their colleagues and heckled from above. 'Please, we should go,' one of them told Esther, continuing with her bags.

'Well I think you got off lightly, you mucky minx,' Esther said, leaning into her stride. 'I'd have caned you and kept you behind in detention with a thousand lines.'

'My darling,' Minnie said, hoisting herself on deck. 'I was merely using my God given gift for the greater good.'

'Gift!' Esther remarked, pausing again. 'What gift?'

'As an entrepreneur, dear,' Minnie chirped. 'I was providing a service in a niche market, it's a simple case of supply and demand.'

'Poppycock!' Esther sneered.

'It's not, dear,' Minnie said, defending her risqué actions. 'It's just how Ritchie Branson started out.'

'What, by flashing his underpants?' Esther scoffed, looking around the vast expanse of solid steel deck. 'Oh good Lord!' she then remarked as Vivien was craned aboard into the cargo hold. 'Do be careful, please!' she told the crew members charged with lashing the vehicle securely into place.

Minnie retrieved her bags from the serviceman and slipped three rupees into his hand. 'Thank you kindly, sonny,' she said, leaving him examining the pittance.

The ship's huge rectangular containers loomed above them stacked like Lego blocks and filled with export goods of all description, silks, spices and sporting goods produced in the sweatshops of India for a fraction of their eventual retail price. Global brands worn and sponsored by sporting superstars were complacent in the exploitation of the poorly paid minors but chose to turn a blind eye to the horrific and altogether life-threatening conditions within the country's textile industry. But perhaps blame should also be apportioned to the consumer whose greed and vanity fuelled these Dickensian and archaic workhouses.

'This way, ladies,' the sisters were told by a newly appointed member of the cabin crew who led them inside and below deck.

'Oh,' Esther said, expecting a more grandiose interior like those of the oceangoing cruise liners that ferried hordes of retirees around the Caribbean and Norwegian Fjords. Instead the Northern Star's adaptations to accommodate passengers were limited to say the least, she was first and foremost a working commercial freighter with a huge steel battleship grey superstructure, without a shred of carpeting, just cold hard checker-plating beneath the sisters' feet. 'Minnie!' Esther said. 'What on earth is this?'

'Cheap, dear,' Minnie replied, in awe of her surroundings. 'You know how I love a bargain.'

'Dear God, woman!' her sister raged. 'I've seen more creature comforts in a garden shed.'

'Oh come now, dear,' Minnie chirped, ever the optimist. 'I'm sure the cabins have been furnished to the highest specifications, after all the travel company did promise an unforgettable nautical experience aboard the pride of the Saudi fleet, oddly enough though, dear there were no customer reviews.' The reason for this omission was simple, Minnie's foolhardy booking had been the very first received by the shipping line after initial safety concerns and reported health and safety violations, leading at one point to the vessel's operating licence being revoked and only reinstated when the Saudi owners paid an undisclosed sum to corrupt maritime officials. 'I'll bet a penny to a pound too, dear,' Minnie added, 'They have a soft close lavatory seat.'

'Hmmmm,' Esther remarked, unconvinced at her sister's chosen mode of transport, but with Vivien now tethered below there was no turning back.

'Your cabin, Madams,' the sisters were told and their bags deposited at yet another steel door.

'I sayyyy,' Esther called to the departing seaman. 'Could you be a dear and ask the captain to proceed at a leisurely pace, I'm a little unsteady on my feet at the best of times, you understand.'

'Madam,' the sailor replied, returning. 'We are expected in Dubai in three days and we are already behind schedule so I am afraid the pace will be far from leisurely, I assure you of that.'

'Oh hell,' Esther cursed, turning to glare at her sister who quickly ducked inside the cabin.

'Miniiiie,' Esther called after her, snatching her back and starting after her, but then almost slamming head long into her back as Minnie stood aghast in the doorway. 'What is it?' Esther asked, unable to see. 'Minnie, out of the way, will you!'

Hesitant at first, Minnie eventually stepped to the side, wincing as she waited for her sister's reaction. 'What the?' Esther gasped, letting her luggage slip from her fingers. 'Minnie!'

Minnie desperately scoured the stark steel room for a single positive. 'Oooh look, dear, we have a window!' she said, hurrying out of reach to peer from their one and only tiny porthole offering very little in the way of natural light.

'I'll give you window!' Esther barked 'Minnie, please tell me there has been a misunderstanding and you haven't booked this floating tin can as our passage to Dubai?'

'Well,' Minnie said, equally stunned but doing her damndest not to show it. 'Oooh look, bunk beds, dear, how charming.' Again she aimed to convince her cynical sister of the cabin's less obvious qualities. 'Go on, you choose,' she said, allowing her sister first dibs.

'Choose what?' Esther asked, unimpressed.

'Top or bottom,' Minnie said enthusiastically.

'Neither!' Esther sneered. 'Minnie, if you think I'm spending a single night in this, this mausoleum then you, my dear, are very much mistaken, very much indeed.'

Minnie prodded at the unforgiving mattress while her sister ventured into the en suite. 'Oh and as for the lavatory seat!' Esther called back, 'There isn't one!'

'I beg your pardon, dear,' Minnie replied. 'No soft close lavatory seat?'

'No lavatory seat whatsoever!' Esther said, appalled at the cold stainless steel fixture and fittings akin to those in a maximum security prison.

'Oh!' Minnie said, peering inside.

'Oh indeed!' Esther raged. 'Minnie, where are the creature comforts you promised, the complimentary chocolates, the ambient lighting and the fine floral furnishings, where, Minnie, where?'

Minnie had indeed previously oversold the freighter to her sister with tales of traditional teak panelling, polished nautical brassware and panoramic views from their stateroom, as she so eloquently described it.

'Stateroom!' Esther laughed, whilst thumbing the near transparent toilet tissue. 'Stateroom, ha!' she stormed from the en suite as Minnie had also elaborated.

To say Minnie had been a tad economical with the truth would be a gross understatement indeed. 'I'll take the top then, dear,' she told her sister, tossing her hat onto the upper bunk. 'I'm fully aware you need to pee several times during the night so best you stay within reach.'

'Minnie, read my lips!' Esther said adamantly. 'We are not staying here!'

'Oh, right,' Minnie replied, having begun to unpack. 'Well, Essy, I suppose we could request an upgrade.'

'Request!' Esther again snarled. 'We'll insist on it, my dear, we'll address our grievances to the captain himself, come dear.' She took hold of her sister's hand and led her briskly from the cabin. 'OK, where do we find the blighter?' she added, looking each way along the ship's corridor. 'COOEEEEE!' she then called to a passing engineer. 'I sayyyy, could you tell me where we might find the captain?'

The Indian national spoke no English and merely returned a blank expression.

'The captain?' Esther again asked. 'El capitan!'

'Ohhhh capitan!' the man said, rubbing his hands on an oily rag and gesturing to their right. 'Capitan, capitan!' he said before hurrying on his way.

'Riiiight,' Esther said bracing herself for a confrontation, 'This way, Minnie my dear,' she said, grimacing. 'I'll have us that stateroom if it's the last thing I do you'll see, I'll not be hoodwinked, not by anybody.'

'Oh please don't make a scene dear' Minnie said, trailing behind and wringing her hands. 'I'm sure once we've unpacked our knick-knacks our cabin would feel more like home, it just needs a woman's touch, Essy, that's all, I have a yard or two of velour I could stich us a scatter cushion or two, and possibly matching pillow cases, what do you think, Essy, Essy dear, I said what do you think?'

Esther was having none of it, as striding now she made her way to the upper deck with the wheelhouse in sight.

'Wait, Essy!' Minnie moaned, stepping gingerly over the reels of steel cable.

'I sayyyyyy!' Esther called, ascending the iron stairs toward the ship's bridge. 'I sayyyyyy, I'd like a word if I may!'

'Essyyyyy,' Minnie whined, her heels clattering on the heavy checker-plating. 'Let's go back.'

'Right!' Esther said, bursting into the wheelhouse with her sleeves already rolled to her elbows. 'Who's in charge here?'

'Madam, Madam,' Captain Kofti said, approaching. 'You cannot be here, it is strictly forbidden.'

'Morning!' Minnie chirped, arriving moments later. 'Lovely day!'

'Oh shut up, Minnie,' Esther barked, standing her ground. 'Are you the captain?' she asked aggressively. 'El capitano?'

'Yes, yes I am captain,' the Jordanian naval officer replied, raising his hands. 'Please, please you must return to your cabin at once.'

'That's just it'! Esther stormed. 'My sister informed me she specifically requested a stateroom, so if you would kindly make the necessary arrangements for our upgrade then you'll hear no more about it.'

'Stateroom?' the captain said with a smile emerging. 'We have no stateroom, Madam, you have the finest quarters the Northern Star has to offer, larger than my own in fact,'

'No stateroom!' Esther said, riveted to the spot as her sister wilted behind her. 'But, but my sister booked, didn't you, Minnie?'

'Oh yes,' Minnie piped up, recalling nothing of the booking arrangements. 'I specifically booked a stateroom.'

'There, you see,' Esther confirmed. 'We booked a stateroom, now if you're telling me that this ship or boat or whatever it is has no such accommodation then my sister and I will disembark this instant and demand a full refund forthwith.'

'Disembark?' the captain said, looking over her shoulder at the shrinking port of Mumbai. 'I am afraid this is impossible, Madam,'

Esther turned to see the mighty freighter churning the water in its wake with a prolonged blast of its horn. 'What, wait!' she cried. 'You have to go back!'

'Out of the question,' Captain Kofti replied, signalling to his first mate to increase thrust.

'Stop, I say!' Esther said, prodding his shoulder. 'Stop, we want to get off!'

'You will get off, Madam,' the captain informed her, 'As soon as we reach Dubai, exactly three days from now, now if you would kindly return to your, stateroom,' he said with a wry smile, 'Your meals will be served in the galley.' He added, 'Please feel free to stretch your legs on deck but steer clear of the containers, this also is a restricted area, for your own safety you understand.'

'Yes but…' Esther said as they bid the Mumbai mainland a fond farewell, 'But, but.' She then spun to confront her sister but Minnie had already exited the wheelhouse and was hot-footing it down the iron stairs, having fully anticipated her sister's wrath. 'Miniiiiie!' Esther growled. 'Minnie, you did it again, didn't you!' She shuffled down the stairs after her sheepish sister.

'Minnie, just you wait, just you bloomin' well wait, my girl!'

'Essy, it's not my fault!' Minnie called back, pausing at the bottom to catch her breath.

'No!' Esther said, seething. 'It never is, is it, why on earth did I ever listen to you, answer me that?'

'Oh we've had worse, dear,' Minnie said, attempting to make light of their predicament.

'Yes you're right!' Esther yelled, gripping the rail. 'And you, Minnie, have personally arranged every one of them, haven't you!'

Minnie scurried across the deck with her sister in hot pursuit.

'Three days!' Esther cried, throwing her hands in the air. 'Three days aboard this blasted thing!'

Minnie pause to catch her breath. 'Alright, alright, dear,' she said, wheezing and clutching her chest. 'I'm sorry, it's all my fault as usual, there, I said it, now will you please calm down, dear, before one of us has a perishing heart attack.'

'I will not calm down, Minnie, not in the slightest,' her sister raged and began a lengthy tirade of abuse toward her sister, avoiding the more serious of profanities of course; neither sister would ever dream of unleashing the F-word no matter how perturbed.

Esther's wild gesticulating with flaying arms was of great amusement to those above them in the wheelhouse. 'The English!' Captain Kofti laughed. 'They are crazy, yes.'

Esther cornered her cowering sister. 'And where are the loungers?' she asked 'Where, Minnie, and where is the pool, you promised me a pool, and come to think of it where are the other passengers?' There wasn't another solitary soul on the Northern Star's deck, just a flock of defecating seagulls.

Reviews of the Mumbai to Dubai freighter crossing had been harsh to say the least with one disgruntled couple describing it as '*hell on high water*' and another venting their anger by penning a poisonous letter to the travel agent threatening legal action if a full refund was not forthcoming; all in all word had gotten around and the shipping lines paying passenger venture was all but dead in the water, so to speak.

'I'm not entirely sure, dear,' Minnie confessed. 'But look on the bright side, Essy, that's what I always say.'

'Bright side!' Esther scoffed. 'What bright side?'

'Well, dear,' Minnie explained. 'We won't have any trouble getting a lifeboat if the ship is….' She hesitated.

'Sinking!' Esther blurted. 'You were going to say sinking, weren't you, oh that's just great, that is!' Esther stormed to the side of the ship and looked down at the turbulent swell tossed up by the bow thrusters as the Northern Star manoeuvred steadily out of Mumbai harbour towards the open Arabian sea.

'Let's have some tea, dear,' Minnie suggested at her sister's side, 'You know thing always seem that little bit rosier after a nice cup of tea, oh and I have a packet of pink wafer biscuits we could share too, what do you say, dear?'

'Did you say pink wafers?' Esther asked, distracted from their seemingly dire situation.

'Yes, dear,' Minnie chirped. 'But do remember the two second rule, won't you.'

'How could I forget,' Esther replied whilst clinging tightly to her hat.

The two second rule referred to the length of time a pink wafer biscuit could be safely suspended in steaming hot tea before the unthinkable occurred, the dreaded snap off and the majority of the tasty treat tragically sinking to the bottom of the cup only to be hastily spooned out as unrecognisable mush. 'OK,' Esther agreed. 'But don't you dare think that lets you off the hook, young lady, not by a long chalk,' but Minnie knew better, a cup of cinnamon and rose-hip tea and a pink wafer or two and her sister would literally be eating out of her hand. 'And yes,' she continued, 'I will have the bottom bunk, but for my vertigo as well as my frequent lavatorial visits.'

'Thaaaat's the spirit, dear,' Minnie said, stepping over the steel door threshold and descending below deck. 'Beside, Essy,' she said over her shoulder, 'I hear the Arabian sea is as calm as a millpond this time of year so that makes for plain sailing and a pleasant voyage as far as I'm concerned.'

'Oh really?' Esther remarked. 'And who, may I ask, told you so?'

'Oh I had a reading dear,' Minnie confessed. 'From a renowned Swarmi in Mumbai, at least I think he was a Swarmi, anyway I paid him a large sum of money and got some very favourable answers in return, firstly he told me I'd meet a tall dark stranger.'

'Minnie!' Esther interrupted. 'Hadn't you noticed, Mumbai is full of tall dark strangers, you fool, I could have told you that myself and saved you the expense.'

'Yes, dear, but he assured me he was a mystic.'

'Mystic my foot,' Esther scoffed. 'He played you for the fool that you are, dear, and you believed him no doubt, hook line and sinker.'

'No, no, wait!' Minnie called after her sister who shuffled off along the barren corridor. 'He told me someday I'd receive a very important letter, well you know what that is, don't you?'

'Not another reminder from the council, I hope,' Esther said without turning, 'Always griping about the rent arrears, haven't they got anything better to do than harass us law-abiding senior citizens?'

'No, dear, from Her Majesty,' Minnie called after her. 'I'll hazard a guess that the fellow was hinting that I was going to live to be a hundred and receive my telegram from the Queen, I'd say that's a thousand rupees well spent, wouldn't you?'

'My dear Minnie,' Esther said, stopping at their cabin door. 'If you paid me a thousand rupees I'd tell you that you were going to live another fifty years, inherit a small fortune and marry the Michael Bublé fellow you're so sweet on,' and with this Esther disappeared inside leaving her sister to mull over those possibilities.

'Oooh, Michael Bublé,' she said dreamily. 'Yes, yes I can see him now in a skimpy loincloth peeling my Victoria plums and rubbing deep heat into my sciatica, I tell you, Essy I'd never let him leave the house.' She trailed in after her sister. 'Anyway, dear, the Swarmi said,' she added, 'With the monsoon winds not expected for another three months there would barely be a ripple on the surface the sea throughout our entire journey, and he was right, look, dear.' Minnie peered out the narrow porthole across the motionless

Arabian sea, mirror-like reflecting the wispy white clouds above them.

'Well I suppose so,' Esther said, pressing her face to her sister's.

'It'll be fiiiine, dear,' Minnie smiled. 'Now about that tea.' Minnie rummaged in the overhead locker. 'Bingo!' she cried, retrieving a battered electric kettle with its cord having been repaired several times with sticky tape. 'Shall I be mother?' she asked, having boiled and filled two chipped enamel mugs. 'I must say, dear, this is the life, isn't it' she added, stirring noisily while Esther wrenched the wafers open. The two of them sat swinging their legs on the bottom bunk, sniffing at the steam rising from their mugs and dunking dangerously close to the fabled two second mark.

'Well it comes close, dear,' Esther replied, still unsure of their surroundings, 'But I must say I'd have preferred something a little grander and more accommodating to senior citizens.'

'But, Essy dear,' Minnie said, plucking another wafer from the packet. 'I don't see myself as a senior citizen, more a teenager with seventy years of experience, I mean I still get a huge kick out of jumping in puddles and riding the roundabout, do you know?' she then said, leaning a little closer. 'I once knocked on Marjorie's door and attempted to duck out of sight before she opened it.' Marjorie was a neighbour and bitter rival when it came to one-upmanship, baking bigger and better cakes than the sisters to impress their peers at the Women's Institute and the bridge club.

'Oh how marvellous,' Esther squealed, instantly seeing the funny side of her sister's childish prank. 'But wait,' she added curiously. 'What do you mean, attempted?'

'Oh blast!' Minnie suddenly cursed when the wafer she was holding reached terminal tea capacity as it's known in dunking circles and snapped clean in two, the lower half descending rapidly to the murky depths of her tin mug. 'Well,' she said whilst fishing with a spoon. 'During my getaway the wheel sheared off my shopping trolley and I was left red-faced and stranded outside and came face to face with our adversary, well I had no choice, I had to pop inside and endure half an hour of her bombastic boasting while she explained in excruciating detail the advantages of having a five-tier walnut whatnot, I think young Richard would describe my actions as an epic fail.' Marjorie's recently purchase of a five-tier stand of bric-a-brac shelves had Minnie green with envy and wishing she'd never attempted the mischievous stunt.

'Epic fail?' Esther asked.

'Oh it's cyber-speak dear,' Minnie informed her far from tech savvy sister 'I wouldn't expect you to understand.'

'Oh but I'd like to, dear,' Esther confessed. 'I've noticed how effortlessly you now navigate you way around that tablet thingy and I was thinking it's about time I got on board, so to speak.'

Minnie puffed out her chest at her sister's compliment. 'Oh I'd be only too happy to show you the ropes, dear,' she said retrieving the device.

Throughout their lengthy lives Esther had always been the more talented of the two, the piano lessons for instance, she would quite happily sit and play Mozart's 5th symphony in C minor whilst Minnie hammered at the keys venting her frustrations at botching the mere basics, and their riding lessons at the city farm where Esther would take a muscular thoroughbred around a series of demanding obstacles whilst Minnie yelled and waved her arms in the air in an attempt to get her chubby pit pony to put one hoof in front of the other. But now the tables were finally turned, Minnie had the upper hand and her sister was the novice. 'OK,' Minnie said, shuffling her bottom to get comfortable on the firm mattress. 'Now let's begin with the basics, shall we.' Minnie went on to demonstrate the limitless possibilities this window to the world had to offer. 'So now you have email,' she eventually told her sister before embarking on a tentative voyage of the World Wide Web.

'Email?' Esther mused. 'I'm sorry, what's email again?'

'Look at it this way, Essy,' Minnie explained yet again. 'It's like sending a letter with a supersonic stamp attached, it literally arrives in the blink of an eye.'

'So er, would that be first or second class?' Esther asked, struggling to comprehend the sheer speed at which correspondence could be exchanged online. And if Esther was blown away by the paperless postal service she was about to be completely flabbergasted when her sister opened Pandora's box and led her into a wonderland more fantastical than that of Alice and the Mad Hatter himself.

'Go on,' Minnie said, coaxing her big sister, 'Ask it anything you like.'

'Anything?' Esther replied, her mind a complete blank at this point.

'Yes, dear, anything,' Minnie said proudly. 'Go on, it won't bite.'

Esther sat with her finger poised over the pad pondering life's complexities, scientific equations, the origin of man. 'What to ask, what to ask,' she muttered, spoilt for choice. 'Oh I know!' she chirped, tapping at the titanic search engine.

'What, dear, what?' Minnie asked, curious as to her sister's request in an almost endless ocean of information.

'Well,' Esther said, tapping with her tongue poking from her mouth and her face illuminated by the screen. 'I've been wanting a recipe for blueberry muffins.'

'Blueberry muffins!' Minnie smirked, 'My dear, you literally have a seat at the table with the all-powerful Oz and you ask about blueberry muffins.' Her reference to Dorothy's experience with the infamous wizard in the 1939 American musical fantasy drama went clean over her sister's head, Esther had tapped into culinary gold as far as she was concerned.

'There, you see, dear,' Esther said, delighted with her discovery. 'That's what I've been trying to tell you all these years but you just wouldn't listen, well it's there in black and white, you're supposed to let the mix rest fully before filling the muffin cases.'

'Good grief,' Minnie said, leaving her sister on the bunk barely scratching the surface of the tablet's encyclopaedic resources. 'I'm going to stretch my legs, dear' she told Esther, who sat wide-eyed. 'Are you coming, Essy?'

'Oh no, no, you go, dear,' her sister replied whilst fetching a pencil and paper from her handbag. 'I've stumbled across Jamie's jam roly-poly, apparently it's a firm favourite of the Prince of Wales.'

'Right you are, dear,' Minnie said, raising her eyebrows and leaving her sister perusing the web page of the popular celebrity chef. 'I shan't be long.'

'Take your time, dear,' Esther said without averting her eyes from the font of all foodie knowledge.

Minnie closed the steel door behind her with a clang and ventured left along the narrow corridor lit with low wattage fluorescent tubes, several of which flickered giving her shadow an almost animated appearance.

The port of Mumbai was now a nautical mile or two behind them as the Northern Star increased power to the main engines throwing up a trailing foaming swell behind them. 'Ahhh, Captain Kofti,' Minnie said, venturing on deck and greeting the officer. 'I wonder, could you please point me in the direction of the restaurant, I take it we are all inclusive?'

'Inclusive?' Captain Kofti replied with a ruffled brow.

'Yes,' Minnie said, feeling the hunger pangs returning even though she'd snatched a fistful of croissants before leaving the Taj Mahal that morning. 'And I take it it's a running buffet,' she assumed. 'My sister and I are rather partial to finger food, I'll have you know, oh and by the way we haven't been issued our wristbands yet, I'm sure it's just an oversight.'

'Wristbands?' the captain again asked.

'For the buffet, dear,' Minnie exclaimed. 'Now if you'll kindly direct me I'll pop along and load a paper plate or two, I do hope you have those delicious vegetable spring rolls with hoisin sauce, oh good heavens they are to die for.'

Captain Kofti looked down upon Minnie, bewildered beyond belief. 'Madam,' he said lost for words momentarily. 'You eat with the crew aboard my ship.'

'With the crew?' Minnie asked, finding the notion a tad odd. 'Well I must say that's extremely admirable of you, captain, allowing your staff to dine in first class with the passengers, extremely admirable indeed, now would the restaurant be to the port or the starboard side?' she asked in an attempt to impress the captain with her limited nautical knowledge.

'You mean the galley,' the captain informed her. 'It is down below, two levels to the right.'

'Yes, yes that's it, the galley,' Minnie said, peering back inside. 'Now about those wristbands?' She turned to find the captain had made the sharpest of exits to distance himself from this crazy old woman.

'Right you are, two levels down,' Minnie said to herself, clambering back inside with the bit firmly between her teeth so to speak. Descending whilst clutching the rail hand over fist, Minnie was spurred on by the thought of huge platters of elaborately carved fruit, melons modelled to resemble exotic birds of paradise surrounding a towering ice sculpture, such was her imagination. Quickening her step anticipation Minnie side-stepped a crew member in the corridor carrying a tray back to his quarters. 'Hellooooo,' she said politely. 'Lovely day!'

The seaman said nothing, inching past in the narrow confines.

Minnie glanced down at his upturned plate in passing concealing his supper. 'Ooooh what's the special, dear?' she asked with her stomach now rumbling 'The special, dear?' she asked again, tapping his plate.

'Soup,' the seaman said, expressionless.

'No, not the starter, dear, the special?' Minnie insisted. 'The main course?'

'Soup,' was his only reply as he hurried on his way.

'The man's a fool,' Minnie muttered, following her nose. 'Ahhhh,' she soon said with a smile, entering the ship's galley where the Indian army recruits sat amongst the Northern Star crew members. 'Hellooooo!' she chirped, picking her way gingerly between the bare board tables and receiving the oddest of looks. 'Lovely day!'

The recruits jostled one another playfully as they so often did whilst swilling mugs of hot overly sweet tea.

Joining the queue Minnie could hardly see the selection on offer. 'I sayyyy!' she said, tapping the shoulder of the Indian officer in front of her. 'Going anywhere nice?' she asked, making small talk whilst shuffling forward inch by inch.

'Excuse me?' the officer, replied turning.

'For your holiday?' Minnie added. 'Are you going anywhere nice, my sister and I are headed to Cairo, weeeell you have to see the pyramids before you die, don't you, dear.' Minnie's pleasantries did little to dent the officer's steely composure.

'Holiday?' he merely said, having been a lifelong devotee to the Indian army, seldom allowing himself a break from his official duties.

'Yeees,' Minnie added cheerfully. 'I suspect you and your lot are off on some thrill-seeking adrenalin fest, am I right?'

'Madam,' the officer said, tight–lipped. 'We do not have holiday.'

'No holiday!' Minnie exclaimed, aghast at the revelation. 'What do you mean you don't have holiday, that's preposterous, I mean everybody needs a holiday at some time or other, to recharge ones batteries and so forth, now if I were you,' she told the puzzled officer, 'I'd have a sharp word with your superiors and tell them that it is wholly unacceptable, stand up for yourself and issue your demands, man,' she told him in no uncertain terms.

'And when they give in,' she continued, 'Which I assure you they will, I can highly recommend a chalet bungalow break in Bognor Regis, my sister and I holidayed there in the 1970's and had an absolute whale of a time.'

'Bognor Regis?' the officer said, having completely lost his previous train of thought.

'Yes, dear,' Minnie replied enthusiastically. 'I tell you they have scones and potted preserves to make your mouth water.'

A gap in the queue ahead of the spellbound officer had formed 'NEEEEEXT!' the ship's cook called, clanging her ladle down on the stainless steel surface.

'Oh do hurry, dear,' Minnie told the Indian officer, nudging his forearm. 'Before all the canapés are taken.' Shuffling forward, Minnie craned her neck to peruse the galley's afternoon selection. 'Oh,' she then said, confronted with nothing but a large iron cauldron perched on a gas burner. 'I sayyyy!' she called from behind the officer. 'Are we too late, my dear?'

'Late,' the cook said, dragging the back of her hand across her dripping brow, 'What you mean, late?'

'For the starters, dearie,' Minnie replied. 'The appetizers, where are the appetizers?'

'We have not this appetizer,' the Egyptian cook informed her, lifting the lid from the solitary steaming pot. 'We have only soup.'

'Oh, I see,' Minnie said, despondent to say the least. 'And er, may I ask, what exactly is the soup de jour?'

'I am sorry?' the cook said, puzzled by Minnie's Frenchism.

'The soup of the day, dear?' 'Minnie explained. 'What is it?'

'Chicken,' the cook replied, plunging the ladle deep into the broth and scooping out a portion of breast meat and something that closely resembled the rear end. 'You see,' she told Minnie proudly, 'Is chicken.'

'Oh no, no, no,' Minnie sneered, screwing up her face. 'I'm afraid I couldn't possibly, I don't eat meat you see, do you have tomato and basil by any chance, or perhaps leak and potato?'

'I have potato,' the cook said, ducking beneath her counter.

'Oh great,' Minnie said with a smile of relief. 'In that case I'll take two, please.'

The Northern Star's cook reappeared brandishing two large raw baking potatoes. 'Potato,' she said, slamming them down in front of Minnie.

'Ahhh,' Minnie remarked, raising a finger. 'No, I meant as a soup, my dear, as a soup.'

The cook lifted the cauldron lid once again. 'You want soup?' she asked, straight-faced.

'No, no, of course not!' Minnie snapped, growing increasingly frustrated at the oceanic language barrier between them. 'I mean yes, but not chicken, potato!'

Growing tired of Minnie's apparent indecisiveness, the cook thrust both potatoes into her hands and turned to the next in line. 'NEEEEEXT!' she yelled, readying her ladle.

'No, no, wait!' Minnie pleaded but was immediately bundled along by the hungry crew members behind her. 'Oh blast!' she cursed, looking down at the meagre offerings in her hands and around the sparse ship's galley, a far cry from the bountiful banquet hall she'd envisaged; where were the exotic but edible table decorations, the solid silver napkin rings and the all-important ice sculpture, where indeed was the ice sculpture?' Disgruntled and famished even more so, Minnie trudged from the galley and back toward their cabin where she found her sister still deeply engrossed on her bunk.

'Minnie, this is remarkable!' Esther gushed. 'I've just traced our family tree all the way back to Guy Fawkes, it seems, dear, that we are related to the blighter!' Esther hadn't taken her eyes or fingers for that matter off the tablet screen all the while her sister had been gone, exploring the wonders of the universe with NASA and the fauna and flora of the Amazonian rain forest to name but a few of the exhaustive web pages. 'Oh and er?' she asked Minnie, 'What's with the potatoes, dear?'

'Oh,' Minnie said, her mind racing with her sister's shocking family revelation. 'Did you say Guy Fawkes, Essy, dear?' she then asked.

'Yes, dear,' Esther replied. 'Gunpowder, treason and plot, that Guy Fawkes.' The genealogical link with the infamous Mister Fawkes whose plot to blow up Parliament in 1605 stunned Minnie to the core. 'Well I'll be blowed, if you pardon the pun,' she said.

'Isn't that remarkable,' Esther added. 'Now what are you doing with those potatoes?'

'Oh these,' Minnie said, snapping out of her historical daydream. 'It's a long story, to be honest with you, but basically this is lunch.'

'But, but they're raw, dear,' Esther exclaimed, stating the obvious. 'Minnie!' she then snapped, 'Please don't tell me that as well as being housed in a tiny steel box closely resembling a death row prison cell, there are no restaurant facilities either, you assured me we were all inclusive and would be spoilt for choice aboard this vessel, and while we are on the subject where are our wristbands?'

'I'm afraid there aren't any, dear,' Minnie confessed. .No wristbands, no melon balls, no napkin rings and no ice sculptures.'

'No ice sculptures!' Esther raged, even more horrified then her sister. 'Minnie, you promised me a luxury liner with all the mod cons, instead you press-ganged me aboard a blasted tin tub with all the culinary class of a cockroach-infested cafeteria, how could you?'

'Oh but, dear,' Minnie said, pleading her case. 'Weren't we brought up to make the most of what we had, if we can survive rationing, Essy, I'm sure we can get through this, make do and mend and all that.' Minnie's wartime rallying cry fell on deaf ears.

'Make do!' Esther sneered at the raw root vegetables. 'Minnie, we have two raw potatoes, for Pete's sake!'

'Not for long, dear,' Minnie said, filling the kettle once again and cramming the two veggies inside. 'Necessity, dear,' she told her sister, 'Is the mother of invention.'

'Oh,' Esther said, stunned at her sister's ingenuity. 'I see, boiled potatoes it is then.'

'A firm favourite of ours,' Minnie replied, forcing on the lid. 'Am I right?'

'A firm favourite, dear,' her sister agreed, wriggling with anticipation.

Minnie's game-changing flash of inspiration lifted Esther's spirits momentarily, even more so when her sister produced two miniature bottles of dry gin from her suitcase and a slim-line tonic. 'Tipple, dear?' she asked, cracking the lids and filling their two mugs.

'Whyyyy not,' Esther agreed, toasting her sister's good health courtesy of the Taj Mahal's mini bar.

With their cabin filling with steam Minnie prodded and poked the potatoes occasionally with a knitting needle. 'Ahhh here we are,' she eventually said, scooping them onto two plates. 'Dinner is served,' she said proudly.

Esther rummaged for her newly acquired Davenport salt shaker and two plastic forks. The sisters sat side by side savouring their simple but satisfying meal. 'Do you remember, dear?' Minnie said whilst fanning her burning mouth, 'When Mother fed the four of us for a fortnight on a sack of King Edwards and a jar of mustard pickle?'

Peshwari Nans Part II

'Yes, yes I do, dear,' Esther replied, recalling with great fondness the day-to-day struggles faced during wartime Britain when necessity literally was the mother of invention. The humble potato, grown in coal sacks, dustbins, backyards and allotments bolstered an entire nation through their darkest hours; baked, mashed, chipped, fried or boiled the versatile vegetable was as much a saviour as the Spitfires of the Battle of Britain themselves.

'Mmmm, did you know, dear,' Esther said clearing her plate, 'That the potato was first farmed in Peru around 8000 BC.' Her recent internet induction had indeed opened her eyes to a limitless font of knowledge.

'No, no I didn't, dear,' Minnie marvelled.

'And that the Arabian sea on which we are currently sailing,' Esther added keen to share her recent finds, 'Has a maximum depth well in excess of fifteen hundred feet.'

'Remarkable, dear,' Minnie replied, sipping her G and T.

Both sisters had now joined the ranks of the tech savvy senior citizens, emerging from the dark ages into a light and futuristic world. These silver surfers, as they have become known, fearlessly embraced a brave new world, several of them becoming overnight web sensations uploading viral videos of themselves engaging in extreme activities such as cliff diving, wing walking and free climbing. A new breed of thrill seeker had emerged; with age on their side and death imminently looming they had absolutely nothing to lose, taking jaw dropping leaps of faith that many of their younger counterparts deemed suicidal and steered well clear of.

With the gin consumed and several rounds of virtual backgammon behind them, the sisters eventually tired and prepared for bed. 'Help me up, will you, dear,' Minnie said, lifting a leg and gripping her mattress.

'Oh really, Minnie!' Esther said, having already climbed beneath her own sheets. A disgruntled Esther rolled from her bunk, clasped both hands together forming a stirrup and bent to grip her sister's foot.

'Push, dear, push!' Minnie cried, clawing at her sheets. 'Esther, push, will you!'

'I am, you fool!' Esther shrieked with her sister's ample bottom thrust in her face. 'For heaven's sake!' she grunted. 'Get up, will you!'

Minnie huffed and puffed, wheezed and groaned her way up onto the top bunk, inflicting bodily harm onto her sister with her flailing feet in the process. 'Ahhhh,' she said, rolling onto her back and breathing a sigh of relief; she then glanced over at her red-faced sister who stood seething with her silver hair now a tangled mess. 'Be a dear, Essy, and turn out the light,' she merely said, oblivious before rolling to face the wall.

Esther counted slowly to ten in her head to reduce the level of anxiety and prevent herself from throttling her sister with her bare clenched hands.

Having spent the first night in rigid bunks aboard the Northern Star, the sisters woke to a rolling swell. 'Good heavens,' Esther said, disorientated and almost dislodged from her bed.

'Morning, dear!' Minnie called down, finding the experience exhilarating and peering through the porthole. 'Lovely day by all accounts.'

'Lovely day?' Esther remarked, clinging to her horse hair mattress. 'I'll give you lovely day, Minnie, I've hardly slept a bloomin' wink all night on this tombstone they call a bed, and the sheets, Minnie, they've irritated my psoriasis something terrible.'

'Oh, Essy,' Minnie said, leaning over the edge of her bunk with a smile, 'You know that's always been your trouble, you've always been a glass half empty kind of girl, haven't you, myself I prefer to view the world through rose-tinted spectacles, embracing the experiencing and...'

'Minnie!' Esther barked from her bunk below. 'Shut, up.'

'Right you are, dear,' Minnie agreed, clambering down to fill the electric kettle once more.

Esther hobbled around their cabin stretching and straightening her aching back, whilst Minnie whistled a merry tune and ran a duster over their metallic surroundings. 'What on earth are you doing?' Esther asked, finding her flitting insufferable.

'I'm sprucing up the place, my dear,' Minnie replied, breathing onto the porthole glass and rubbing it vigorously. 'Just because we are away from home dear doesn't mean we have to lower our standards, now does it, after all, cleanliness is next to godliness, isn't that what they say?'

'Cleanliness?' Esther sneered. 'You're a fine one to talk about cleanliness, how many times have I asked you to tidy your side of the bedroom, how many, Minnie, you have a mountain of magazines, hat boxes, tangled wool and toffee wrappers, it's like living in a blasted landfill sometimes, I swear, it's a wonder we aren't overrun with rodents.'

'Oh, Essy, I couldn't possibly part with the magazines,' Minnie said, pleading her case. 'The *National Geographic*s were a gift from Cyril, he had a monthly subscription you see, he said it was for the images of geological interest but I knew it was for the bare-breasted Polynesian beauties that often tickled his fancy, the hat boxes are where I keep my treasured photographs, buttons, bows, bits and bobs.'

'And that unsightly bird's nest of knitting wool?' Esther asked, having cursed her sister each time she'd attempted to hoover their bedroom.

'Well,' Minnie said, turning to confront her sister. 'That unsightly bird's nest of knitting wool as you so call it,' she said defensively, 'Will one day be a warm winter shawl, and a gift for you, my dear.'

'Oh,' Esther said, shocked and embarrassed at the same time. 'I see, well er, thank you, dear, that's extremely thoughtful of you.' She thought it best to let slide her sister's collection of golden toffee wrappers that had constantly frustrated her.

'Oh and as for the wrappers, dear,' Minnie added, 'I'm saving them for little Tommy next door, he's making a papier maché head of Tutankhamen for a school project you see, and I suggested them as imitation gold leaf.'

Again Esther was struck dumb by her sister's apparent generosity. 'Tommy, you say?' she asked, red-faced.

'Yes, dear,' Minnie chirped. 'He really is the most resourceful little chap, do you know for his chemistry assignment Tommy isolated the hydrogen molecule in his mother's kitchen with the aid of a microwave, a George Formby grill and a turkey baster, of course he won first prize and a trip to Switzerland to meet a former Nobel Prize winner to exchange complex equations, and all at the age of nine.'

Attempting to wash a short while later, both sisters cursed the steadily dripping hot tap in stark contrast with the jet of freezing water gushing from the cold. 'Damn it!' Esther cried, attempting to pluck a curling air from her chin and nipping her skin in doing so, 'I wish they'd keep this blasted ship still just for one moment.'

'We are at sea, dear,' Minnie said, stating the obvious and steadying herself whist dressing. 'Breakfast, dear?' she then asked, opening the cabin door.

'Of course, dear,' Esther replied, scurrying behind. 'I could eat a horse right this minute, figuratively speaking of course,' she added after receiving a disapproving glare from her sister.

Turning the corridor corner the sisters were immediately stopped in their tracks open-mouthed. 'Good, heavens,' Esther gasped, craning her neck to see beyond her grinning sister. Ahead of them several members of the Indian military were zig-zagging from room to room wearing nothing but their underpants, and with an average age of twenty-two they each cut a fine figure having been drilled vigorously on the parade ground for quite some time, six packs, biceps and pectorals were in abundance as were their firm gluteus maximus like pit bull puppies in the rear of their skin tight briefs.

'Good heavens indeed,' Minnie replied, feasting her eyes. 'Morning!' she called, fussing her hair. 'Lovely day!'

The shameless lads turned to reveal their more prominent muscles, forcing Esther to cover her sister's eyes. 'Do you mind!' she told them sternly.

'No, not at all,' Minnie replied, wriggling free and gawping wide eyed.

The recruits disappeared and the shell-shocked sisters tottered on their way. 'Well I never' Esther said grimacing while Minnie's mind wandered to a hedonistic place where those young recruits frolicked naked with her in a cool Caribbean lagoon. 'Minnie, Minnie!' Esther said, prodding her sister who had paused momentarily.

'Oh, oh sorry, dear,' Minnie said, coming to. 'I was miles away.'

Reaching the ship's galley Esther recoiled at its less than luxurious appearance. 'Minnie, please tell me this isn't the restaurant,' she said, dragging a finger across a dust-covered table.

'No, no, dear,' Minnie replied. 'Actually it's the galley.' Approaching, Minnie perused the empty steel shelves once again. 'Do you have any toast, my dear?' she asked the cook who stood stirring the self-same pot from the previous night. 'And maybe a pot of thick cut marmalade?'

'No,' the cook replied categorically. 'We have soup.'

'No, dear,' Minnie said, looking across the counter at the sparse provisions. 'We are wanting a spot of breakfast, my sister and I.'

'Soup,' the cook again informed Minnie, 'You want soup?'

'No, for heaven's sake,' Esther intervened. 'We would like some breakfast if that isn't too much to ask.' Her hunger pangs made her increasingly irate. 'You know, croissants, crumpets, that sort of thing.'

'Crumpets?' the cook asked, bemused.

'Yes, yes, do you have them?' Minnie asked expectantly.

'No, only soup,' the cook replied with her deadpan expression.

'Riiiiight,' Esther sighed, the gravity of their situation slowly sinking in. 'So er, what exactly is the soup of the day then, my dear?'

'Is chicken,' the cook said, beating he ladle on the side of the pot to dislodge the stale and congealed lumps.

'But, but,' Minnie stammered, 'It was chicken yesterday, was it not?'

'Is chicken every day,' the Yemeni cook informed her. 'You want?' In fact the same bilious broth had stood simmering in that cauldron for almost a week and a half with the cook, who had no formal culinary qualifications, occasionally adding another scrawny carcass, a stock cube or two and a handful of wilting vegetables that the ship's rats had previously dined on.

'Oooh look, dear!' Minnie said, leading her sister toward a vending machine before she exploded at the counter.

'Minnie!' Esther snapped. 'May I remind you I am a grown woman, I need more sustenance than a choccy bar and a packet of peanuts, for Pete's sake'

'They have Oreos,' Minnie said, pointing out a firm favourite of theirs. 'And party rings, dear.'

'Well why didn't you say so, dear,' Esther said, pushing her sister aside and emptying the loose change from her purse and then watching as packet after packet fell into the hopper bellow.

Laden with snacks, Esther and Minnie left the dingy galley and ventured up on deck where they were greeted by a cool north easterly breeze. There they stood gorging themselves at the rail looking out across the Arabian sea at the coast of Pakistan in the distance and its fine capital, the city of Karachi, a thriving hub to match Mumbai for population, wealth and commerce.

Minnie tossed several morsels into the air to be caught by swooping and screeching gulls.

'Don't encourage them, dear,' Esther said, ducking from the overly aggressive sea birds. 'I still haven't gotten over our trip to Broadstairs, you know.' During a day trip to the Kent coast the sisters feasted on ice cream from the world-famous Morelli's gelato parlour, peppermint rock from the numerous novelty vendors and sat overlooking the picturesque Joss Bay eating a steaming bag of golden chips with the smell of malt vinegar filling the air, and also attracting the attention of Kent's own flock of bullish birds who dived in formation, harassing the petrified pensioners before they fled discarding their traditional seaside fare, a tactic the gulls had perfected to great effect.

Captain Kofti approached the sisters with a smile. 'Ladies, ladies,' he said with open arms. 'I trust you are enjoying your trip with us.'

'Enjoying!' Esther immediately stormed, flinching from another flapping bird. 'My dear Mister Kofti,' she said, examining his identification embroidered to his breast pocket. 'To use the word enjoy would indeed be a gross overstatement, I am currently compiling a lengthy list of grievances that will be duly be sent to your superiors when we eventually reach dry land.'

Minnie appeared altogether more content, happily feeding a gannet that stood on the rail beside her. 'Who's a pretty boy then?' she said, sharing a party ring. 'Look, dear!' she told her sister. 'Isn't he gorgeous?' Minnie reached to pet the wild bird and received a nasty nip for her trouble. 'OUCH, YOU LITTLE BUGGER!' she cursed, snatching her hand away.

'Serves you right,' Esther sneered, inching away from the fearless feathered fiend.

'Grievances?' Captain Kofti asked. 'Why would you good ladies have grievances, the Northern Star is the flagship of our line, it is, how you say, the cat's tail.'

'The cat's whiskers,' Esther corrected the captain. 'The expression, Captain Kofti, is cat's whiskers and I am afraid I am going to have to wholeheartedly disagree.'

'What is wrong?' the captain asked, puzzled at the possibility.

'Wrong!' Esther remarked. 'Are you out of your mind, everything, everything is wrong, our bunks are hard, the waters cold, the lavatory seat is non-existent, you couldn't swing a church mouse let alone a cat in the shower, the dining facilities are deplorable and I swear I saw a rat in the corridor as big as a Yorkshire blasted Terrier!'

'Anything else?' the captain asked, finding her complaints trivial to say the least.

'Isn't that enough?' Esther asked, venturing to the stern toward the stacked containers.

Captain Kofti dismissed Esther momentarily. 'Please, that is a restricted area!' he called to Minnie. 'For your own safety you understand!'

'Oh, right you are, dear,' Minnie replied, peering over the side down at the emerald sea.

Esther tapped the captain's shoulder, keen for a satisfactory resolution to her dispute. 'Now, about my grievances,' she said, seeking some recompense perhaps.

The captain stood with his hands on his hips pondering the predicament. 'I tell you what I do,' he told her. 'Why don't you and your charming sister join me for dinner tonight?'

'Really?' Esther said, raising her pencilled on eyebrows. 'Dinner, at your table?'

'Of course,' the captain said, resting both hands on Esther's shoulders. 'You will be my guests.'

'Oh wow,' Esther gushed with an instant change of heart. 'Perhaps I may have been a little hasty, Captain Kofti, Minnie and I would be delighted to join you, thank you.'

'Excellent!' the captain smiled. 'I will send for you at precisely six o'clock, now if you will excuse me.'

'Yes, yes of course,' Esther said, brimming with excitement as the captain left. 'Did you hear that, Minnie dear?' she asked, approaching her sister. 'We are to dine at the captain's table.'

'The captain's table!' Minnie exclaimed, spinning from the rail. 'Really, oh Essy, however did you manage that?'

'A little leverage goes a long way, my dear,' Esther said proudly. 'With the evidence I had stacked against him I simply left him no choice.'

'Well done, you,' Minnie said, hugging her sister tightly, equally as thrilled.

An invitation to the captain's table on any oceangoing liner was a huge privilege and one usually denied to so many. 'Whatever shall I wear?' Minnie mused as the two of them sat on a coil of winch wire discussing dress codes and nautical etiquette. 'I just can't believe it,' she added on occasion. 'The captain's table.'

The Northern Star cruised several miles off the coast of Pakistan toward the gulf of Oman, where the shipping lanes became increasingly congested with tankers carrying billions of gallons of crude oil to their port and starboard.

'Coooeeeee!' Minnie called, waving her spotted handkerchief to another freighter passing in the opposite direction, as the predominantly Pakistani crew smiled and waved in reply.

Soon a chill wind blew in from the west, whipping up the sea around the colossal ninety-thousand-ton Northern Star. 'Come, dear,' Esther said, clinging to her hat and leading her sister inside.

'Oh but, Essy,' Minnie said, finding the whole experience exhilarating.

'Minnie dearest,' Esther warned her sister. 'You are unsteady on your feet at the best of times, I'm not having you taking a tumble and putting that hip of yours out again.'

'Oh, Essy, I'm fiiiine, look,' Minnie replied, doing a quick two-step, but staggering and gripping the steel rail when a rogue wave slammed into the freighter's hull.

'Get in here, you foolish woman,' Esther urged, dragging her sister bodily inside and reaching for the door.

Later that afternoon the sisters showered hastily in the near sub-zero water dripping pitifully from the rusting shower head. 'Minnie!' Esther said, rummaging through her make-up bag. 'Have you been at my foundation again?'

'No, dear,' Minnie replied, emerging from the bathroom positively caked in the stuff, 'oh well maybe just a little.'

'A little!' Esther snapped, snatching the empty tin from her sister's hand. 'It's a subtle cosmetic application, not a damned mud mask.'

'What do you think, dear?' Minnie asked, with her eyebrow pencil poised at her cheek. 'One beauty spot or two?'

'What?' Esther replied, still miffed at Minnie's constant plundering of her dwindling cosmetics supply.

'One spot or two?' Minnie reiterated.

'Oh,' Esther scraping the remains of her foundation, 'Definitely one, you don't want to oversell yourself, now do you, and, Minnie, what's with the cleavage, if you don't mind me saying you look as though you're touting for business.'

'How dare you!' Minnie said, horrified at her sister's disparaging remark whilst checking her reflection and tweaking the plunging neckline of her satin baby blue evening dress. 'My Cyril always said if you've got it flaunt it.'

'Yes, dear,' Esther reluctantly agreed. 'But that was way back when your whatsits resembled a pair of firm baked buns, now they're more like a couple of sagging baps.'

Esther's remark went way over Minnie's head as she grappled with the restraints of her stiffly laced corset. 'God, I can't breathe in this thing,' she cursed, red-faced.

'Me neither, dear,' Esther agreed, prodding and poking at her own midriff. 'Well you know what they say don't you, dear,' she added. 'Vanity comes at a price.'

Minnie stood struggling with the tiny clasp of a beautifully enamelled brooch 'Help me will you, dear,' she said, having pricked her finger several times.

'Give it here,' Esther said, taking charge and pinning the fake ruby-encrusted Indian elephant to her sister's gown. 'Oh, Minnie, that is beautiful,' she said, admiring the tacky market stall replica.

'Do you really like it, dear?' Minnie asked, caressing the costume jewellery. 'The nice young chap on the stall told me it was it's a lucky talisman blessed by the Maharaja himself.'

'Did he now?' Esther smirked, having heard her fair share of traders' exaggerated spiel. 'And tell me, how much did you pay for such an exquisite piece, two rupees, three perhaps?'

'No, dear,' Minnie confessed. 'It was an absolute steel at a thousand rupees, he wanted double that but I was having none of it.'

'A thousand!' Esther gasped. 'A thousand, Minnie, and you say it's personally blessed by the Maharaja himself?'

'Yes, dear,' Minnie said proudly. 'Those were his exact words.'

'Dear God,' Esther sighed. 'And they say there is one born every minute.'

A little before six there was a knock at the sisters' cabin door. 'Helloooo,' Esther said, greeting the first mate. 'Hurry, Minnie dearest,' she called over her shoulder whilst tucking her clutch bag under her arm.

Minnie grappled on all fours attempting to retrieve a shoe from beneath the bottom bunk. 'Yes, yes, dear, I'm coming,' she grunted.

'Minnie, quickly!' Esther urged, not wanting to keep their host and any other influential guests waiting.

'That's not it!' Minnie cursed, retrieving a Wellington boot discarded by the previous occupants.

The first mate peered inside to see Minnie's bottom in the air. 'I have it, I have it!' Minnie squealed, holding the shoe aloft and clambering puffing up the bed post.

'Well put the damn thing on and be quick about it,' her sister snapped, checking her own reflection one last time. 'Right,' she then said to the captain's assistant with her sister at her side. 'How do we look?' The pair had polished, preened and pampered themselves to perfection for their prestigious date.

The first mate looked on, bemused, and offered a polite reply. 'Very nice, very nice, madams.'

'Why thank you kindly' Minnie replied, the two of them having pulled out all the stops so to speak and overdosed completely with their favoured Lily of the Valley scent, draping themselves in pearls and wearing matching crimson feather fascinators in their hair.

'Right then,' Esther said, puffing her chest and lifting the hem of her dress from the floor. 'Lead on, my good man.'

Following the first mate, Esther and Minnie looked radiant whilst beaming with expectation as after their culinary calamity of the previous evening they were eager to dine in style. 'The captain's quarters,' the first mate informed the ladies, knocking on a similar steel door to their own.

'Come!' Captain Kofti called from within.

On opening the door the sisters literally could have been bowled over with a feather. 'Oh,' Esther and Minnie said in tandem.

The captain's cabin where their meal was due to take place was half the size of their own, cramped and cluttered with maps, charts and nautical paraphernalia and reeking of cheap Cuban cigars. 'Ahhhh come, come in!' the captain said, rising from his desk to greet them. 'Look at you, look at you,' he said, eyeing them up and down with a broad smile. 'You look like the queens of England.'

'Queen, dear,' Esther said, stepping inside and kicking a rum bottle aside. 'There is only one queen, I'll have you know.'

'Yes and that's me,' Minnie said, barging past her sister and fussing with her hair.

'Oh don't be ridiculous,' Esther sneered, gesturing to that plunging neckline. 'Her Majesty wouldn't be seen dead in that gown.'

'Oh really?' Minnie replied, folding her arms across her chest defiantly. 'Well take another look in the mirror, sweetheart, you look like the sugar plum fairy on Prozac.'

'How dare you!' Esther raged, having gone to great lengths to considerably enhance her appearance. 'Well you, my dear,' she said, retaliating while the captain and the first mate looked on speechless. 'You look like something the cat dragged in and spat out.'

'Ooooh, you bitch!' Minnie growled, clenching a fist, the two of them getting into a heated spat within the cramped confines of Captain Kofti's cabin. 'Well you look like Cinderella's ugly sisters all rolled into one!' Minnie laughed.

'Youuuuu cow!' Esther cried, prodding her sister.

'You look like Coco the bloomin' clown in that ridiculous make-up, may I remind you that you are eighty-four, not eight and a half.'

Minnie had indeed over-applied the layers of foundation, blusher and rouge just as a young child would when let loose in her mother's cosmetics drawer.

'You take that back, Esther Reynolds!' Minnie cursed, lunging at her sister.

'Ladies, ladies please!' Captain Kofti said, stepping between them. 'Please let us not fight!'

'She started it!' Minnie yelled over his shoulder whilst pointing a rigid finger at her sister's face.

'I did not, she did!' Esther replied childishly.

'Please, please!' Captain Kofti urged, with the sisters grappling to get at one another. 'Please let us just enjoy the evening, are you not hungry?'

Esther paused momentarily. 'Well, well yes,' she said, simmering somewhat, 'Actually we're famished'

'It's the brooch, isn't it?' Minnie said, still glaring at her sister. 'You're jealous of the brooch, aren't you.'

'Don't be ridiculous!' Esther scoffed. 'Me, jealous, of that piece of tat.'

'It's not a piece of tat!' 'Minnie replied defensively whilst straightening the elephant. 'It's a lucky talisman, and you're just miffed I found it first.'

Esther raised a smile. 'Well if that, that thing's a lucky talisman I'll eat my hat, and your hat too for that matter.'

Captain Kofti tried his level best to calm the warring sisters. 'Please, sit,' he begged. The captain's table as it were that the sisters had gotten so excited about earlier was nothing more than a knotty pine picnic table with a bench seat attached either side pushed up against the ship's steel hull.

'What, here?' Esther asked, having assumed they would be led to an elaborate dining hall perhaps.

'Yes, of course,' the captain replied, offering a seat. 'You are my guests, after all, chef will serve dinner in one moment.'

'It's not chicken soup by any chance, is it?' Minnie asked. 'Because if it is you know what you can do with it, young man.'

'Ahh,' the captain said, having pre-ordered from the standard Northern Star's limited menu. 'Please bear with me just one moment,' he added, making for the door. 'I will personally see to a suitable alternative.' With this Captain Kofti scurried from his cabin to interrupt the ship's cook, whom he met in the corridor. 'No soup tonight, my dear,' he told her, raising a hand.

'No soup?' the chef said, aghast. 'But, captain sir, you always have the soup.' 'Yes, yes but not tonight,' the captain replied, eager to appease his guests. 'Tell me, what else do we have?'

'Nothing, sir,' the chef simply said whilst clinging to a tray containing three steaming bowls of her now legendary signature dish.

'Nothing!' the captain remarked with a hand to his forehead. 'Are you quite sure?'

The disgruntled chef nodded with a grunt and turned back for the galley.

Meanwhile Minnie and Esther sat beside one another in the captain's quarters, neither uttering a word and deliberately avoiding eye contact with one another.

'Ladiiies!' the captain said smiling on his return, his arms laden with snacks from the ship's vending machine. 'It appears the chef has been taken sick and cannot cook for us this evening.'

'Huh!' Minnie mumbled. 'I dare say she had the chicken soup, serves her right if you ask me.'

'But,' the captain said, emptying his wares onto the table. 'As you can see we are always prepared for emergencies aboard the Northern Star.'

'Biscuits?' Esther said, unimpressed to say the least. 'So this is dinner, is it, and this I take it is the captain's table.'

'Yes, yes of course,' Captain Kofti said, sitting opposite the sisters and seeing absolutely no problem with the pathetic offerings.

'Oooh!' Minnie chirped, plucking the Oreos from the pile. 'It's not all bad, you know'

'Yes but…' Esther moaned, finding fault wherever she looked.

'Oh do be quiet, dear,' Minnie snapped, tossing her sister the Jammy Dodgers. 'As Mother always said, life is what you make of it, am I right?'

No matter how miffed Esther may have been, her mother's words rang true in her ears. 'Well, well I suppose so,' she conceded, tearing open the packet.

'Excellent, excellent!' the captain said, choosing a chocolate bar for himself. 'Now, tell me all about yourselves,' he asked. 'I am intrigued as to why you are undertaking this journey.'

'My God, where to begin,' Minnie replied, looking to her sister for inspiration.

'Ooooh,' Esther said, wriggling in her seat, 'Brace yourself, Captain Kofti,' she told him. 'What we are about to divulge will seem more like the fictional works of a deranged novelist,' a statement closer to the truth than either of the sisters could have imagined. 'It all began,' she said, shuffling closer to her sister, 'With our beautiful friend and neighbour Jasvinder.'

Captain's Kofti's eyes grew wider and wider as their tale unfolded in elaborate detail. 'You were at Auschwitz?' he marvelled.

'Yes, yes,' Esther swiftly replied. 'My Jack was there too, you see, during the liberation.'

'And you, Minnie,' the captain probed. 'You really dived from the high board?'

'But of course,' Minnie said, puffing her chest. 'It was a matter of national pride after all.' She referred to the barracking she'd received from a group of rowdy and obnoxious German swimmers in a Belgian communal pool.

'Wait, wait!' the captain said, halting Minnie and not wanting to miss a single detail. 'We must drink to your achievements.'

'Drink!' Minnie said, discarding her half eaten biscuit. 'Well maybe just a nip, dear.'

Esther tugged at her sister's arm. 'Do you think that's wise, dear?' she asked level-headedly.

'My dearest Essy,' Minnie said, pushing the remaining treats aside. 'It would be rude, would it not, to refuse the captain's hospitality, especially as he's gone to so much trouble.'

'Trouble?' Esther asked, looking around his unkempt cabin.

The captain reached into his desk drawer and produced a bottle of Lambs Navy Rum three quarters full and three heavy crystal glasses, heavy enough in fact to remain upright in the most buoyant of swells. 'Now,' he said, pouring them each a generous measure. 'Tell me more of your troubles with the Russian President.'

While the sisters enlightened the Northern Star's captain as to their Russian exploits with the Premiere they had inadvertently enraged, they hardly flinched when sipping the potent spirit.

'You say he shot at you?' the captain asked, rocking back in his seat.

'Oh yes,' Minnie replied. 'Several times in fact, but I do believe the blighter got his comeuppance.' She referred of course to the President's colossal misfortune when the military jeep he was pursuing the sisters in veered off the road and was unceremoniously dumped nose first into boggy marshland, with the world's media close at hand to capture the moment in glorious high definition.

Soon Minnie was sliding her glass across the table toward the captain, followed closely by her sister.

'Anyway that's enough about us,' she said, cupping her refilled glass. 'Tell us of your life at sea, it must be awfully exciting.'

'Yes, do tell,' Esther added. 'Is it as swashbuckling as they say?'

'Oh no, no, no,' Captain Kofti laughed. 'But I will admit it does have its moments, for example, during our last trip to Mumbai we lost all power to the main engines and began to drift dangerously close to the rocks off the coast of Karachi.'

'Really!' Esther gasped, clutching her pearls. 'What on earth happened?'

'Yes, captain, what happened?' Minnie also asked.

The captain poured a little more rum. 'We were forced to lower the anchor,' he told them, 'having averted a major maritime incident. With only moments to spare, I might add.'

Esther began to doubt the vessel's seaworthiness. 'So errrrr, these engines of yours,' she asked. 'I trust they have been thoroughly overhauled by a competent engineer?'

'Of course, my dear,' the captain replied confidently. 'We have the finest ship's engineer anywhere on the high seas, and may I say she makes a mighty fine chicken soup too.'

'You mean?' Esther said, putting two and two together and deducing that the ship's chef responsible for the hideous broth also doubled as the grease monkey. 'Oh good heavens!' she remarked. 'Surely there's a hygiene issue at stake here, captain.'

'Nonsense,' their host laughed, lighting a Cuban cigar much to the sisters' annoyance, 'I myself have had this soup for the past five years and look at me, I am as strong as an ox.' He unbuttoned his shirt halfway down to slap his manly chest.

'Yes, yes, very good thank you,' Esther said, unconvinced and fanning his smoke from her face. 'Do you mind?' she sneered.

'Oh I am sorry, where are my manners,' the captain said, offering the hand-crafted box across the table. 'Would you care for a cigar?'

'Good God no,' Esther said resolutely, horrified at the mere suggestion.

'May I have a tote?' Minnie asked.

'Minnie!' her sister snapped, aghast. 'You'll do nothing of the sort.'

'Oh but, Essy,' Minnie moaned. 'I've always been curious as to their appeal.'

'I strictly forbid it,' Esther said abruptly. 'And if Mother were here she'd be mortified, positively mortified, sometimes, young lady, I don't know what possesses you, I really don't.'

'Well, Mother isn't here,' Minnie said defiantly. 'And at eighty-four I'm hardly a young lady, in fact I'm old enough to do exactly as I please.'

'And old enough to know better,' Esther reminded Minnie robustly.

But standing her ground for once Minnie reached for the box and plucked out a plump cigar.

'Minniiiie!' Esther growled. 'Don't you dare.'

Snatching the captain's lighter from the table, Minnie pursed her lips in an exaggerated fashion, being a complete novice and flicking her thumb several times before igniting the tip. 'Ooooh,' she said without inhaling a thing. 'Not bad, not bad at all.'

'Really?' Esther asked. 'Are you sure?' Seeing that her sister had not violently convulsed, Esther's curiosity was aroused. 'No, ill effects, no nausea?'

'None whatsoever, dear,' Minnie replied, removing the cigar from her mouth and blowing absolutely nothing into the air. 'I don't see what all the fuss is about,' she added, flicking the glowing ash like a pro.

'Oh,' Esther said, having been led to believe that this odious cancer stick was the work of the devil himself. 'Hmmm, may I?' she then asked.

'Yes of course, dear,' her sister said, handing over the smouldering cigar.

Esther first looked her sister over once again, checking for signs of an adverse reaction, but of course there were none, in fact Minnie had more exhaled than inhaled in her naivety.

'Right, here goes,' Esther said, bracing herself and curling her cragged lips around the Cuban smoke and drawing in a lengthy lungful; what was to follow was as obvious as night following day and the ebb and flow of the tide. Esther's stomach immediately and her aged lungs contorted to near collapse, coughing, spluttering and wheezing. Esther's eyes filled to overflowing as she rocked back and forth in her seat, unable to catch her breath momentarily.

'Essy, Essy are you alright?' Minnie foolishly asked. 'Essy, Essy dear!'

'Of course I'm not alright, you fool!' Esther gargled. 'Dear Lord, get this blasted thing away from me!'

Snatching her glass of rum, Esther downed a double shot in a single gulp to douse the fire within.

'I don't see what your problem is,' Minnie said, blowing into the end of the cigar once again and attempting a smokeless ring.

'Ohhh no!' Esther growled, snatching the cigar and stubbing it out vigorously into the captain's ash tray then pouring herself another drink to take the ghastly taste away. 'If you don't mind?' she added, glaring at the captain until he too extinguished his cigar prematurely.

Several shots of the highly potent spirit later, the sisters began to experience that warm fuzzy feeling and a loosening of their inhibitions. 'So, tell me, captain,' a curious Esther asked. 'Do you have a girl in every port?'

'Or a whore in every harbour?' Minnie piped up, eager for the captain to spill the beans and brazen under the effects of the Navy rum.

'Well,' Captain Kofti replied, positively brimming with testosterone. 'Let me just say, if I were to name them all we would be here until sunrise,' he boasted. The captain had indeed bedded a bevvy of beauties during his nautical navigations. 'But one or two have a special place in my heart,' he added, slapping his chest firmly once again. 'There is Senora from Sardinia, she has eyes as blue as the deepest ocean and the breasts like the ripest cantaloupes.'

'Breasts like antelopes?' Minnie slurred, failing to see the connection.

'The melons, the melons,' Captain Kofti explained, cupping his hands to his chest. 'And Betina from Bahrain,' he said wistfully. 'Ohhhh, my Betina.' He went on to describe another of his land-based lovers in much more detail than Esther would have wished.

'Yes, yes alright, that's quite enough of that!' Esther said, growing ever hotter under the collar whilst her sister listened intently.

'Oh my Cyril did that,' Minnie chirped enthusiastically, referring to a sensual seaweed rub. 'With a little olive oil and balsamic vinegar.'

'Dear God!' Esther remarked. 'Were you making love, Minnie darling, or a blasted salad dressing, on second thoughts I don't think I wish to know.'

'Well, dear,' Minnie replied, informing her sister anyway. 'It began in the kitchen with the tossing of a few leafy greens, then Cyril wanted to introduce a little rocket of his own, and before we knew it we were going at it hammer and…'

'Please, Minnie!' her sister insisted. 'For the love of God spare me the details.'

'By the time we'd finished,' Minnie continued unabated, 'The lettuce had wilted and so had his rocket.'

Captain Kofti fell about laughing whilst Esther folded her arms across her chest and glared disapprovingly at her jovial sister. 'Some things, Minnie,' she reminded her, 'Are best kept to oneself.'

'Oh come now, dear,' Minnie chuckled. 'It's no worse than those weekly magazines of yours, and don't you tell me you buy them for the word search thingy neither, they are nothing but smut from cover to cover.'

Esther's regular indulgence of up to half a dozen so-called women's magazines had raised her blood pressure on more than one occasion with tales of forbidden love, hedonistic holiday romances and sinful seductions on the streets of suburbia. Such publications were never short of immoral material, offering upwards of two hundred pounds for each article published and therefore crammed with cringe-worthy carnal confessions, hardly works of literary genius but fuelling the desires of their loyal readership all the same.

'I, I buy them for the gardening tips, if you must know,' Esther said, quick to jump to her defence and excuse her voyeuristic obsession.

'But, Essy,' Minnie said in reply. 'We have no garden, dear, we have an aspidistra, three spider plants and a mother-in-law's tongue in the bathroom that require very little in the way of maintenance, so how many tips can one require?'

The sisters' houseplants had been in the family for many years and had remained relatively unchanged, maybe daring to flower once a decade but for the majority of their lives they sat inanimate in porcelain art pots on the window sill beside the liquid lavender soap and the discount denture grip.

Esther again glared at Minnie. 'Are you forgetting my seasonal window box?' she blurted. 'Our view of the estate from the kitchen simply wouldn't be the same without my green-fingered display.'

'View from the kitchen?' Minnie said, pouring another rum whilst the Northern Star steamed headlong into a raging storm. 'My dear,' she added, sipping her overfilled glass, 'Three winter pansies and a Tit box hardly make you Capability Brown, now do they.' Minnie's reference to the 18th century landscape designer responsible for creating many of the breathtaking parks and gardens of England, Blenheim

Palace, Warwick Castle and Harewood House to name but a few, only served to enrage her sister further.

'You're just jealous, Minnie, and you know it,' Esther said, grabbing at her glass as the ship listed to the left.

'Jealous!' Minnie scoffed, bracing herself too. 'Me?'

Captain Kofti sat back rolling his cigar between finger and thumb as the two sisters squabbled over the terracotta trough that graced their kitchen window sill. 'Yes, you!' Esther said, pointing a bony finger. 'Ever since I banned you from my box.' Esther had given in one time to her sister's constant bleating and allowed her to choose the theme for the summer of 2005. But instead of selecting from the vast array of complimentary flora the local garden centre had to offer, Minnie opted for a hideous and crudely painted garden gnome, three plastic windmills and a meerkat solar light, which if exhibited at the prestigious Chelsea Flower Show would have seen her forcibly ejected from the century-old event.

The Northern Star began to rise and fall with greater intensity but the sisters, brimming with Navy rum, hardly batted an eye. Suddenly Captain Kofti broke into song, as puffing his chest he belted out an ancient sea shanty telling the impassioned tale of a young deckhand sailing the seven seas in search of love, a rousing yarn which rang from the rigging of the tall ships of old.

Esther and Minnie ceased their petty feuding and listened intently, welling up at the climax when the deckhand's vessel ran aground in heavy weather and he was rescued by a Polynesian princess, the two soon becoming star-crossed lovers. 'Braavo, Braavo!' Minnie squealed, clapping theatrically at the captain's crescendo.

'Very good, sir!' Esther agreed before whispering a suggestion into her sister's ear.

'Oooh yes dear, let's,' Minnie agreed enthusiastically. The two of them raised their glasses and rocked from side to side with the rhythm of the rising swell outside and their high pitched rendition of Rod Stewart's iconic hit, *Sailing*.

> *'I am saaailing, I am saaaaaling'*

they began, albeit less melodically than the original,

> *'Hoooome again,*
> *crooos the seaaaaa,*
> *I am saaaling,*
> *stooormy waaters*
> *to be neaaar youuuuu,*
> *to be freeeeeeeee'*

Captain Kofti sat up spellbound at this ditty, unbeknown to him, with a surge of nautical emotion.

> *'Can you heaaaaaar me'*

the sisters continued,

> *'Can you heaaaaaaar me*
> *through the daaark niiiight*
> *faaaar awaaaay'*

Towards the end, the now swaying captain mouthed the words along with his warbling guests;

Peshwari Nans Part II

'We are saaaaaling
we are saaaaaaailing
hoooome agaaaaain
cross the seaaaaaaa,
We are saaaaaailing'
stoooormy waaaters
to be neaaaar youuuuu
to be freeeeeeeeeeeeeee!'

Captain Kofti raised his own glass and his voice too,

'TO BE NEAAAAAAR YOUUUUUUU
TO BE FREEEEEEEEEEEEE!'

'Excellent, excellent!' the captain gushed, clapping loudly. 'This is good, very good!'
'Isn't it just,' Minnie squealed. The ladies were indeed sailing stormy waters as the force eight gales gusting outside rapidly increased in velocity, toying with the gargantuan vessel as though it were a toy boat in a tub.
'Ooooerrr,' Esther exclaimed, gripping her sister's arm to prevent herself from spilling from the table. 'I believe I've had rather too much to drink, Minnie dearest.'
'Just one last tot, Essy darling,' Minnie insisted, thrusting her sister's glass into her hand. 'Here's to you, Captain Kofti!' she said, toasting their host and stubbing out her cigar. 'And the Northern whatsit and all who sail in her!' Minnie and her sister were now comfortably numb and oblivious to the raging typhoon

205

that was rapidly building on the other side of the steel hull.

'Yes thank you, Kofti captain,' Esther slurred, having mellowed dramatically. 'I never thought I'd hear myself say this but that rum of yours was quite simply divine, simply divine, sir, you must allow us to repay the favour, my sister Minnie and I have a bottle or two of homemade vodka back at our cabin, do feel free to pop along whenever you're not boating or whatever it is you do.'

En route from London to Raipur, the sisters had made the acquaintance of Monique and her elderly and somewhat randy father Ludvik at their guest house in Poland. Monique produced the elicit liquor in the basement of the family chateau and gifted the sisters several bottles on leaving. 'Yes do,' Minnie agreed. 'Come round any old time.'

'I say, dear,' Esther chuckled with a hiccup. 'Isn't that a cue for a song?'

'Do you know, dear,' Minnie replied, swaying a little more, 'I do believe it is,' and the two of them then treated the bewildered captain to a traditional catchy cockney anthem, predominantly performed whilst under the influence of alcohol.

'Come round any old time and make yourself at home'

The sisters linked arms to steady one another.

Put your feet on the mantel shelf
open the cupboard and HELP yourself,
iiiiiiii don't care if your friends have left you all alone

Peshwari Nans Part II

Captain Kofti snatched the rum bottle as it slid toward the edge of the table. 'To you!' he said, swigging from the neck and feeling very little effect unlike his elderly guests.

Esther rose from the table, helping Minnie to her feet. 'Crikey!' she said, staggering across the ship's sloping floor with her sister in tow.

Minnie began kicking her feet out as best she could. 'I feel like a Tiller girl, dear!' she shrieked, mimicking the leggy female dance troupe famous for their high-kicking routines during the 1890s.

Arm in arm, the sozzled sisters left the captain's cabin and made their way haphazardly back towards their own, ricocheting from either corridor wall in the process. *'Come round any old time!'* they sang at the tops of their croaky voices. *'And make yourself at home, rich or poor, knock at the door.'* At this point Minnie pounded on three of the adjacent cabin doors, rousing the slumbering Indian recruits inside who soon peered out bleary-eyed clinging to their door posts as the storm ensued. 'Helloooooo!' Minnie called back with a wave, 'lovely day!'

After trying several wrong doors the giggling sisters burst into their own cabin and were immediately bundled onto Esther's bottom bunk when the Northern Star listed violently to one side. 'Weeeeeeeee!' Minnie cried, finding the whole experience exhilarating as did her sister, who under normal circumstances would have undoubtedly donned her inflatable vest and scurried for the life rafts long before then, had she not succumbed to the captain's Caribbean tipple, that is.

The pair snuggled close together, each raising a clenched fist and belting out a lingering chorus of Rod's rousing anthem once again.

'WE ARE SAIIIIILIIIING, WE ARE SAIIIIILIIIING
HOME AGAIIIIN, ACROSS THE SEAAAAAAA,
WE ARE SAIIIIILIIIING, STORMY
WAAATERRRRS
TO BE NEAAAAAR YOUUUUU
TO BE FREEEEEE'

Esther kissed her sister's cheek and held her tightly in her arms.

'TO BE NEAAAAAAAR YOUUUUUUU
TO BE FREEEEEEEEE!'

Jubilant and unnerved by the near hurricane force winds battering the Northern Star, Esther and Minnie were literally rocked to sleep as she rose some seventy feet from towering peak to plummeting trough.

The following morning Esther woke to a pounding head, which incidentally was pressed against the cabin wall with her sister having taken up the lion's share of her narrow bunk. 'Minnie,' she mumbled, having difficulty operating her mouth, 'Minnie, will you please move!'

'Mmmmm,' Minnie moaned, wriggling closer still.

Esther reached behind and attempted to prise her sister from her but Minnie's entire body weight made this impossible, that combined with Esther's complete lack of energy following their late overindulgent night. 'Miniiiie,' she groaned. 'Get off!'

'I'm trying to, Essy dear,' Minnie replied, unable to roll away. It soon dawned on the pair that the bunk on which they lay and the entire ship for that matter was listing at a precarious and apparently permanent angle.

Minnie reached behind her and clawed at the mattress, hauling herself clear of her cramped sister. 'Ooooer!' she cried, stepping gingerly from the bunk onto the sloping floor. 'Essy dear, something is seriously awry.'

'Yes, my head,' Esther moaned, clutching her throbbing temples.

Minnie gripped the bunk posts and grappled her way into the bathroom where she stood clinging to the steel basin examining the hideous coating on her tongue.

The storm had long since abated and the heavy thunder and rain clouds blown eastwards leaving a white post-traumatic sky in its wake. Captain Kofti and his fellow officers gathered anxiously in the wheelhouse frantically discussing the apparent perilous predicament.

During the savage storm, affectionately known as Hurricane Irene which began a thousand nautical miles away, the Saudi freighter was relentlessly pummelled for a full four hours, and eventually one of the sturdy steel fasteners securing the cargo containers fatigued and failed, putting increased pressure on the ninety-nine remaining; one by one thirty more sheered and broke free allowing a layer of some thirty or so corrugated shipping containers to topple overboard, splashing down into the raging slate grey sea where they were instantly swept bobbing and scattered to the four ferocious winds.

Those containers that hadn't broken completely free now hung in the balance from the vessel's port side, their combined weight of well in excess of a hundred tonnes pulling the ship off kilter where she remained stricken, but with increased pressure now placed on the remainder of the securing shackles the situation was truly dire to say the least.

'Minnie, what's happening?' Esther called, sitting with her head in her hands on the edge of their sloping bunk.

'I haven't the foggiest, dear,' Minnie replied, filling the basin until the water trickled from one side. 'Perhaps we're cornering, dear, I'm sure the ship will right itself in due course.'

Esther shuffled alongside her sister, the pair disorientated by their angular surroundings. 'Dear Lord,' she groaned, checking her reflection. 'Never again, Minnie, I swear it, never ever again.'

The situation on deck suddenly took a severe turn for the worse when a dozen more shackles broke loose, shifting the balance of the Northern Star's remaining colossal load. 'Essyyyyyyy!' Minnie cried, clinging to her sister for stability and sliding to the adjacent wall. 'What's happening?'

'Well, according to you,' Esther said, wrenching her arm free, 'We are cornering, but somehow, Minnie, I have my doubts.'

The two of them scrambled hand over fist back to their bunks. 'Look, Essy!' Minnie said at the porthole, watching a blue shipping container gliding by, its shipment of textiles bound for the markets of Dubai.

'Good heavens!' Esther gasped, pressing her nose to the glass at Minnie's side. 'Minnie, get dressed,' she added. 'Get dressed at once!'

'What is it, Essy?' Minnie asked, remaining at the window. 'Are we, are we sinking?'

'Do as I say!' her elder sister barked. 'And no, we are not sinking, but as a precaution I think we ought to make our way to the upper decks, closer to the lifeboats so to speak.'

'Lifeboats!' Minnie squealed. 'So we are sinking, Essy, Essy, what are we to do, Essy, Essy?'

'Minnie, for Pete's sake!' Esther barked, shaking Minnie to her senses. 'Will you please stop that infernal whining and just do as I say, get dressed and gather your things, now Minnie, NOW!'

Making a split-second executive decision, Captain Kofti sent out a distress signal, fearing the worst.

'Sir, sir!' a young engineer then said on bursting into the wheelhouse.

'Sir, we have to cut them free, sir!' He gestured to the thirty or more containers hanging over the side of the ship straining the shackles of the remaining layer. 'Sir, it's our only hope, sir!'

'How, boy, how?' the captain asked at the radio.

'With the gas, sir,' the confident teen replied. 'I can cut them, sir, let me try, please, sir.'

'Out of the question,' Captain Kofti said, assessing the severity of the situation once again. 'It is too dangerous, boy, return to your station at once.'

'But, sir!' the boy pleaded. 'I can do this, sir, I know I can, just get me up there with the gas, please, sir, we do not have much time.'

The captain looked long and hard out of the wheelhouse window at his listing vessel, wrestling with his conscience. The lad was young, younger than his own son in fact and the newest member of the Northern Star's crew.

'Sir, I can do this,' the trainee engineer pleaded, wanting desperately to prove his worth and gain respect from his peers in an increasingly demanding industry.

'I cannot ask you to do this,' the captain said, watching yet another container break free and the horizon tilt a further two degrees. A reply to his SOS then came through, informing them that the closest rescue vessel was at least two hours away from their present position. 'Hurry, please hurry!' he yelled into the receiver before slamming it down and looking the boy up and down. 'You really think you can do this?' he asked with his options dwindling fast.

'Yes, sir,' the trainee replied, rubbing the palms of his hands on his grease-covered overalls. 'I believe it is possible, sir, if the crew can lift me and the gas bottles onto the containers, I know I can cut them free and right the ship.' The boy's brilliant theory was correct but foolhardy nevertheless.

'I just don't know,' the captain said, clinging to his wheel. 'It is very dangerous, boy, you do understand, don't you?'

'Yes, sir, I know,' the teen said, oozing confidence. 'But please allow me to try.' The young Turk, born in the capital Ankara, had always dreamt of working at sea and studied religiously to make it a reality, agreeing to work his first passage for free to earn his place amongst the crew.

'OK,' the captain reluctantly agreed whilst his more experienced mechanics worked tirelessly below to stem the ingress of sea water into the engine room. 'But be very careful, boy,' he added, looking the boy in the eye.

'I will, sir,' the boy replied, rushing from the wheelhouse, bounding down the staircase three treads at a time.

Esther and Minnie by now had made their way on deck, having slid the length of the corridor wall and hauled their suitcases hand over fist up the sloping stairs. 'Christ, Essy!' Minnie gasped as the enormity of the situation became glaringly apparent. 'Look!' Chains and shackles groaned and creaked under the colossal strain with the ship's centre of gravity steadily shifting.

Captain Kofti radioed the ship's crane driver to return to his post at once and lower the hoist to collect the boy and the oxyacetylene bottles used in the cutting of heavy steel. Then, catching sight of the emerging sisters, he quickly descended the stairs to confront them. 'You should remain below!' he called out to them in no uncertain terms. 'It is not safe here!'

'Poppycock!' Esther barked in reply. 'My dear captain,' she added on approach, 'It is obvious the ship is in dire straits so my sister and I are going to remain within spitting distance of the lifeboats, do I make myself perfectly clear?'

'Madam!' the captain replied, raising an authoritative finger. 'As captain of this ship I am ordering you to return to your cabin immediately.'

'Ordering me?' Esther growled.

Minnie tugged at her sister's sleeve. 'Errrm, what's he doing?' she asked, watching the young Turk being craned from the deck.

Captain Kofti watched too with his heart in his mouth. 'This is why it is dangerous,' he informed the sisters. 'The loose containers must be cut free in order to save the ship.'

'But, but he's just a boy,' Minnie remarked.

'Indeed, madam,' the captain agreed. 'A very brave boy, now would you please return to…'

'We're staying!' Esther said adamantly. 'Like it or not.'

'Very well,' the captain said under mounting pressure. 'But please remain here, and put on your life vests at once.' He snatched two yellow life preservers from an adjacent locker and thrust them into the sisters' hands. 'I must go,' he told them. 'Please, stay here,' he warned them before rushing back to the wheelhouse.

Touching down on top of a stack of precarious containers, the courageous lad dragged the ship's cumbersome cutting equipment clear of the hoist.

'Dear Lord,' Esther said whilst donning her latex vest. 'The boy's mad, quite mad.'

Esther and Minnie watched in awe, as did the captain and his crew, as the boy known only to them as Kadir manhandled the heavy bottles across three sloping containers, gritting his teeth and sliding several feet in doing so. 'Christ, I can't watch, Minnie dear,' Esther said, turning away momentarily, but then out of motherly concern she turned back, gripping her sister's coat sleeve.

'Careful, careful!' Minnie called when Kadir stumbled and the cutting equipment slipped from his hand and rolled toward the edge. Quick as a flash the athletic boy leapt full stretch to grasp the rubber hoses and haul them back some twenty feet, with the veins standing from his young arms and the whites of his eyes prominent.

'Good boy,' the captain said with his face pressed to the window. 'Good boy.'

Kadir eventually reached the buckling steel shackles, wedged the bottle between two containers and pulled on a pair of welding goggles, waving first to his captain before igniting the torch, sending a yellowish blue flame roaring from the nozzle. The boy set to work burning through the two-inch thick twisted steel, sending a shower of glowing molten sparks tumbling down the containers and into the sea below. Suddenly the first shackle broke free and Kadir rocked back as five hulking containers slid free and tumbled overboard, scraping and grinding those beneath them.

'That's it, Kadir, that's it, boy,' the captain said, clenching a fist.

Minnie stood transfixed at Kadir's selfless act of heroism. 'I've never seen anything quite like it,' she confessed. 'Look, Essy!' she gasped, watching a further three containers splash down and submerge before bobbing to the surface.

Tirelessly Kadir worked, sweating profusely to free another twenty-five shipping containers,

'Look, sir, look!' the first mate exclaimed, watching the Northern Star right herself by a few precious degrees. 'The boy is blessed, sir, he is blessed, I tell you.'

'Blessed indeed!' the captain replied jubilantly.

Smiling and waving once again Kadir approached a string of forty containers, wrenching the gas bottles behind him, his white cotton shirt heavily stained.

'Look, Essy, look!' Minnie squealed, feeling the vessel levelling beneath her feet. 'I do believe the boy has done it.'

'Marvellous,' Esther replied with an overwhelming sense of pride for the young Turk. 'Absolutely marvellous.'

Again Kadir cut the shackles in a hail of pyrotechnic sparks, some of which scorched his brave arms, causing him to flinch but continue with gritted teeth. The line of containers in varying colours lurched and groaned under increasing pressure as just two shackles remained. 'Yes, boy, yes,' the captain mouthed at the window whilst Esther clung to her trembling sister.

But suddenly, without warning the final shackle sheared to the deafening sound of scraping metal on metal and the entire row of containers with a combined weight of some seventy tons lurched free. 'Yes!' Kadir said, wrenching his goggles from his face and turning to face his captain to seek his praise. The rapid shift of momentum though dislodged the gas bottles and they too slid free; unbeknown to Kadir the red and blue hoses had become entwined around his right foot and he was dramatically torn from his seated position,

'NO, NO!' the captain cried, watching the boy grappling panic-stricken, unable to cling to the corrugated steel.

'Essy, Essy oh God!' Minnie screeched, burying her face in her sister's chest. 'Please God no!'

Weighing in excess of one hundred and fifty pounds, the oxyacetylene bottles pulled the wiry boy toward the edge while he wrestled to free himself from the tubular snare. Captain Kofti could not avert his eyes during the boy's horrendous death throes as it were. 'KADIIIIIR!' he himself screamed, rushing outside. But it was too late, the clanging bottles tumbled over the side and plummeted seaward with Kadir thrashing his arms wildly in tow, eventually piercing the water like twin torpedoes and dragging the gargling boy beneath the surface.

Esther covered her mouth. 'Oh no, no, no, no, no!' she screamed, pushing her sister aside and rushing to the rail in time to see the remaining containers topple overboard one by one to seal Kadir's fate.

'KADIIIIR!' Captain Kofti yelled, rapidly descending the stairs. 'KADIIIIIIR!'

Minnie stood rocking with her arms wrapped around her waist, 'Oh, captain, the boy, the dear, dear boy,' she sobbed.

As if in slow motion the creaking Northern Star rolled back to her former upright position and the piercing alarm that had been sounding the entire time ceased. The captain joined Esther, eagerly looking for signs of his young engineer as several crew members hastily lowered a lifeboat. 'CAN YOU SEE HIM?' he yelled over the side. 'CAN YOU SEE KADIR?'

The shaking heads from within the lifeboat told a chilling tale, the boy was gone, tugged to a watery grave at the bottom of the Arabian sea, the Northern Star had been saved but at a hefty price.

Esther and Minnie now wept in one another's arms with the distraught captain at their side, unable to fathom the sense of loss and longing. Kadir's infectious enthusiasm and exuberance during the previous weeks at sea had not gone unnoticed, becoming the topic of conversation around the galley tables and in the wheelhouse on many occasions. The boy's welding goggles and oily rags that were forever tucked into his back pocket were all that were plucked from surrounding sea during the frantic search.

'It's my fault, it's my fault,' the captain said with his head in his hands. 'What have I done?'

Esther gently rubbed the captain's back, mopping her eyes with her handkerchief. 'The dear boy gave his life to save us,' she told him. 'I doubt there is a greater sacrifice.'

'Kadir is dead because of me,' the captain replied, inconsolable in his grief. 'I will never forgive myself, never.'

Suddenly a cry rang out. 'CAPTAIN, CAPTAIN LOOK!' Spinning, the captain and the sisters dashed to the rail and peered over the side to see the ship's first mate waving from the lifeboat and gesturing to a semi-submerged Japanese shipping container. 'LOOK, CAPTAIN, LOOK, SIR!'

Shielding their eyes from the sun's reflective glare, the three on deck looked out squinting. 'WHAT?' the captain gasped on seeing a pair of hands appear gripping the container, Kadir's hands.

'KADIIIIIIR!' the captain screamed at the top of his voice. 'KADIR, BOY!'

The hands twitched and the half-drowned lad wrenched his exhausted body up out of the water and peered over the top.

'Dear Lord, it's the boy!' Esther gasped. 'Minnie, Minnie, it's the boy!'

Minnie clapped her hands jubilantly. 'Essy, oh Essy, he's alive, captain, captain, the boy, he's alive, oh good heavens, thank you, thank you!' she squealed, tugging at her sister's arm. 'Essy, Essy isn't it wonderful!'

'Wonderful,' Esther said, hugging her sister. 'In fact it's incredible, yes that's what it is, it's incredible!'

The captain beckoned to his first mate. 'HURRY, HURRY, BRING HIM TO ME, BRING ME THE BOY!'

Kadir had been dragged some sixty feet beneath the surface by the descending gas bottles but whilst screaming bubbles and shaking his foot violently he managed to free himself moments before his lungs filled with water at the point of no return. The young hero was helped from the bobbing container and wrapped in a heavy blanket aboard the lifeboat which was soon winched back onto the deck of the mother ship as it were. 'My boy, my boy!' Captain Kofti said, pushing his way through the gathered deck hands. 'Kadir, my boy, I thought, I mean we all thought you were dead but here you are, it's a miracle, a miracle that's what it is.' The captain crouched and hoisted the boy into his arms, brushing the dripping hair from his eyes. 'Look, look what you did,' he added, pointing out the perfectly aligned vessel. 'You saved my ship, Kadir, and more importantly you saved us all.'

'Yes, young man, you did,' Esther said, patting the boy's sodden shirt. 'In my book that makes you a hero.'

'Hero,' Kadir said before coughing up a quantity of sea water. 'Me?'

'Of course,' the captain said, setting Kadir on his feet. 'And I will see to it that you are handsomely rewarded by our illustrious owners, very handsomely indeed, think of it, Kadir,' he told the shivering boy, 'You can leave this ship and begin a new life, a better life.'

The Saudi family responsible for the Northern Star and her sister ships would indeed see to it that Kadir received more money than he'd ever dreamt of, enough in fact to ensure he never worked another day in his entire life. 'I want to stay,' Kadir said, hugging Captain Kofti whom he'd seen as a father figure of late. 'I want to stay here, with you, captain, please, please don't send me away.' Kadir then collapsed under his own weight, still weak and shaken from his hellish ordeal.

'Of course,' the captain replied, catching the breathless boy. 'Of course, Kadir, whatever you want, it would be an honour for us.'

'Ahhhh,' Minnie sighed. 'All's well that ends well, eh, dear?'

'Yes, indeed,' Esther agreed, the pair still very much on edge at having witnessed such a heart-stopping drama.

'Come,' Captain Kofti told Kadir with an arm around his shoulder. 'I will have cook fix you some soup to revive you.' He then paused beside the two anxious sisters. 'My apologies for the unfortunate events, here, take this,' he told them, removing the vending machine key which hung on a chain around his neck. 'Help yourselves to snacks with my blessing, please, take whatever you want.'

'Really?' Minnie squealed as though she'd just been handed the Hobbit's precious ring. 'Look, dear!' she said, wide-eyed and positively salivating at the merest thought of unlocking the treasure chest of tasty treats.

'Hurry, dear,' Esther said, taking her sister by the hand, 'And fetch the tote bags.'

Whilst Captain Kofti sat watching Kadir devour his soup in the galley and placing his own peaked cap on the brave boy's head, Esther and Minnie plundered the vending vault, filling their cotton tote bags to the brim and either pocket of their knitted cardigans. 'I've died and gone to heaven, dear,' Minnie said, clutching snack packets to her chest.

Leaving a solitary packet of mints in the otherwise bare vending machine, Esther slid the key across the table to the captain. 'Thank you, dear,' she said before she and her sister scurried from the galley with their hefty haul, squealing and nudging one another in the corridor just as they did when hurrying home from the corner sweet shop as bright-eyed children so long ago.

CHAPTER FOUR.

Having squirrelled away their sugary booty, Esther and Minnie packed in readiness for their arrival in Dubai that afternoon. 'Essy, dear, have you seen my taffeta scarf?' Minnie asked on all fours.

'No, dear,' her sister replied with a look of disdain. 'What would I want with that rotten old thing?'

'Oh don't be like that, Essy,' Minnie said, ducking her head under her sister's bunk. 'Granted it's a tad threadbare but it was a gift from my chiropodist, for my many years of loyal custom, and you know how I suffer with my feet, don't you, dear.'

Esther looked down at her sister's cracked heels and bulging bunions. 'Don't I just,' she joked.

'Here it is!' Minnie said, tugging her ragged ruby red scarf from behind her wicker hat box and shaking it free of the accumulated dust. 'I'm rather attached to the soppy old thing,' she added, burying her face in the warm ruffles.

'I know the feeling,' Esther said, looking at her sister with fondness.

'Ahhh thank you, dear,' Minnie said, cottoning on to the off the cuff remark. 'I love you too, dearly I do.'

The Northern Star's lost containers that had remained afloat had been rounded up and towed to the shores of Oman by a Saudi tug, so as not to add to the already overwhelming collection of litter plaguing the world's marine environment and threatening its delicate eco-structure.

Now steaming into the Gulf of Oman between Oman and Iran, the mighty freighter was an hour from the United Arab Emirates and the port of Dubai, therefore Captain Kofti gave the order to power down the engines to half speed to slow the gargantuan vessel.

Esther and Minnie's bags were taken and stowed safely back inside Vivien on the cargo deck at the request of the captain, while the sisters themselves bade farewell to their steel cabin. 'It wasn't all bad, was it, dear?' Minnie asked, closing the door with a resounding clang.

'Hmmmm,' Esther growled under her breath, choosing not to comment.

On deck the ladies leaned on the side rail and marvelled at the Iranian coastline now in close proximity with the Strait of Hormuz narrowing on the approach to Dubai and the Persian Gulf.

'Penny for your thoughts, dear?' Minnie asked her wistful sister.

'Oh don't mind me, Minnie love,' Esther said, snapping out of her daze. 'I was just thinking that Jack would have adored this experience, he always found the Emirates fascinating and pledged to visit before he....' She paused and lowered her head.

'Ohhhh, Essy,' Minnie said, wrapping an arm around her sister. 'Essy, Essy.' She kissed Esther's cheek tenderly and rubbed the back of her hand. 'I wish I could take away your pain, my darling, I truly do.'

'I'll be fine, dear,' Esther replied with a half-smile whilst wiping away a tear. 'I have you after all, don't I?'

'That you do, dear,' Minnie smiled. 'That you do.'

The Northern Star was skilfully steered between Kumzar and Suza, making a sweeping left turn towards Dubai with the world famous Palms now in sight, an ambitious series of small man-made islands in the shape of a huge palm tree and one of only a few purpose-built structures visible from space. Home to the rich and famous alike, this exclusive collection of real estate constructed from sand dredged from the Persian Gulf itself was a mammoth endeavour carried out by Dutch and Belgian contractors. Using close to 220.000.000 tons of reclaimed materials, the Palms has also attracted criticism from environmentalist groups claiming the region's wildlife had been greatly affected by the stirring up of silts, destroying established oyster beds and precious coral reefs, not to mention the coastal erosion as a result of unfamiliar wave patterns.

'Crikey!' Minnie marvelled at the renowned Dubai skyline with such prominent and princely structures as the Burj Al Arab, the Rose Tower, the Cayan Tower and the colossal Burj Khalifa, the tallest building on planet earth at a staggering 828 metres.

'Exactly,' Esther was forced to agree.

Dubai, nestled on the south east coats of the Persian Gulf with the greatest population of all the Emirates, owes the majority of its modern wealth to early oil exploration in the region and now attracts business from the far flung corners of the globe.

Learning of the Northern Star's approach, Dubai's port authorities dispatched a pilot vessel to guide her into port whilst Esther and her sister were joined on deck by the Indian military recruits in full combat fatigues, complete with backpacks and service revolvers.

'Hellooooo,' Minnie called as they approached chattering amongst themselves. 'Lovely day!' The recruits stood alongside the sisters, equally impressed at what was to be their home for the foreseeable future.

Minnie raised a hand above her eyes. 'What's that, dear?' she asked on seeing the tiny harbour vessel steaming in their direction.

'I haven't the foggiest, dear,' Esther replied. 'Perhaps it's a fishing boat, I don't know.'

Minnie turned to the soldier stood beside her. 'Excuse me, dear, what is that?' she asked again.

'Pilot boat,' the recruit informed, her gripping the rail. 'It is pilot boat, madam.'

'Pirate!' Minnie gasped. 'Did you say pirate, oh God, Essy, they're pirates.' She prodded and poked the young Indian. 'Well do something will you!' she urged. 'Shoot the blighters or something, hurry, man!'

Esther put a hand to her mouth in abject horror while the recruit attempted to explain. 'No, no, Missy, I said…'

'What do you mean no!' Minnie snapped. 'They're pirates, you fool, and they mean to board us, you'll be killed and my sister and I will be at the mercy of those bloodthirsty cutthroats, do something, man, do something!'

The soldier's apparent lack of urgency enraged Minnie further. 'Well if you won't, I jolly well will!' she blurted, wrenching his sidearm from its holster.

Before the recruit could react, and to her sister's complete amazement, Minnie aimed the pistol in the pilot boat's general direction, clenched her eyes tightly shut and let off six shots in rapid succession.

'Dear God, Minnie!' Esther cried, recoiling at the deafening sound and shoving both fingers in her ears, 'What are you doing?'

'No, no, no, no, Missy!' the recruit and his friends cried, disarming the plucky pensioner with relative ease. Somehow with her failing eyesight four of the six shots fired in anger had made contact with the Dubai pilot vessel, sending its crew of three diving for cover, two ricocheting off the steel hull and the others shattering the wheelhouse window and the brass compass glass.

'What are you doing, Missy?' the flabbergasted recruit asked with a hand to his forehead as the captain rapidly arrived at the scene.

'Defending my honour,' Minnie proudly replied. 'And that of my sister, I might add, those savages mean to have their wicked way with us and I'll not go down without a fight, I can tell you that for nothing!'

'Ladies, ladies!' Captain Kofti, cried rushing to the rail. 'What are you doing, what are you doing?'

'Seeing off that blasted pirate boat,' Minnie confessed. 'As I seem to be the only person aboard this ship with a perishing backbone!'

'Pirate boat?' the captain asked, peering over the side as the shell-shocked pilot skipper sheepishly emerged clutching a bloodied arm. 'Pirate boat, madam, that is a pilot boat, pilot, not pirate.'

The penny dropped with Esther before her bemused sister. 'Minnie, you fool!' she said, shoving her shoulder. 'What have you gone and done?'

'Pilot?' Minnie said, dumbstruck for a moment. 'Pilot boat, oh heavens I am sorry, silly me.' She leaned over the side, giving the injured skipper a nonchalant wave.

'Sorryyyyyy!' she called with a smile, shrugging her shoulders as though to excuse her reckless behaviour. 'I thought he said pirate!' She turned to receive the coldest of looks from her red-faced sister. 'What?' she asked, unable to grasp the severity. 'The young man clearly has a problem with his pronunciation, pilot, dear,' she told the recruit, apportioning blame in his direction. 'It's pilot.'

The wounded pilot skipper spun the wheel of his vessel and steamed wide-eyed back toward port, leaving the Northern Star to take her chances in the rapidly shallowing waters of Dubai harbour. 'WAIT, WAIT!' Captain Kofti called, waving his arms above his head. 'COME BACK, PLEASE!'

'Dear Lord, Minnie,' Esther said shaking her head. 'For once, just once could we please have a single day without an almighty calamity on your behalf, could we, I mean is that really too much to ask, is it?'

'Oh come now, Essy,' Minnie replied flippantly. 'Can't you see it was a genuine mistake, dear?'

'A mistake!' Esther cried, flushed with embarrassment. 'Dropping a crochet stich, that's a mistake, or laddering your nylons, that's a mistake too, but that Minnie, THAT!' she pointed a rigid finger out to sea, 'THAT WAS A MONUMENTAL CATASTROPHY!'

'Essy, dear,' Minnie said, unfazed. 'Will you please calm down, remember what Doctor Kumali said about your blood pressure.'

'To hell with Doctor Kumali!' Esther raged. 'Sometimes, Minnie, sometimes I really do despair of you, I really do, honestly!' With that she stormed off, muttering under her breath, leaving Minnie to face the captain.

'Lovely day,' Minnie chirped.

'Madam,' Captain Kofti growled, but his first mate then called from the wheelhouse, sparing Minnie momentarily.

'CAPTAIN, COME QUICK!' The Northern Star had strayed from her usual approach into port and was in danger of running aground. The captain raced back to his post to avert a second impending disaster.

'I sayyyyy?' Minnie then called to the Indian recruits still reeling from the embarrassing incident in which a proud member of the Indian armed forces was so easily disarmed by a frail member of the Mecca bingo club. 'You know you really should keep those dreadful things out of reach of the general public, heaven only knows what could happen should they fall in to the wrong hands, good day to you.' Minnie shuffled off to find her sister who was seeking solitude at the sharp end as she so called it. 'Are you still cross with me, Essy dear?' Minnie foolishly asked, having tracked Esther down. 'I'd hate for us to fall out over something so…' She was about to say trivial and thought better of it. 'Well you know what I mean.' She then staged a theatrical coughing fit in an attempt to gain some sympathy.

'Are you alright, dear?' Esther asked, hoodwinked once again by her cunning sister. 'Would you like me to fetch you a glass of water?' Minnie's health and well-being was first and foremost a priority for her elder sister, despite her calamitous tendencies.

'No, no, I'll be fine, dear,' Minnie replied, clutching her chest and coughing some more. 'It's just the salt breeze irritating my angina, ooh look, dear, a camel!' she added, pointing out to the far horizon. 'How lovely.'

'Ohhhh yes,' Esther said, shielding her eyes once again and falling for Minnie's diversionary tactics. The silhouette snaking across the sand dunes was their first taste of Saudi culture and the flavour of things to come. Minnie tugged the tablet from her bag. 'Let's have a selfie, dear,' she said, turning her back and thrusting the device out in front.

Esther stood hesitantly. 'I don't know that I should after the trouble you've caused,' she told her sister disapprovingly, 'To say, dear, that I am a tad concerned for your mental welfare would be an understatement.'

'Ohhh nonsense, dear,' Minnie laughed, lowering the tablet. 'What are you trying to say, that I'm losing my marbles or maybe going completely gaga like dear sweet Uncle Reg, God rest his soul?'

'Heaven forbid,' Esther remarked. 'Although I'd be lying if it hadn't crossed my mind on occasion.'

The sisters' Uncle Reginald who passed away in the summer of 2000 had tragically succumbed to the mentally debilitating condition known the world over as Alzheimer's several years earlier, and like over a million other British citizens his quality of life diminished along with his recognition for his close family and eventually his wife. Prior to the first of countless episodes as his loving wife called them, Reg ran a humble hardware store off London's Petticoat Lane, but his increasing forgetfulness and lack of coordination meant that at the behest of his children he was forced to close and retire after some fifty years in the business. In poor health herself Enid, his wife, cared for him religiously but after he repeatedly strayed from their family home sparking frantic police searches of the surrounding area, a joint painful decision was made to put the sisters' uncle in a secure home, or so they thought. The former Royal Marine hoodwinked the staff and slipped out one evening and was missing for a full eighteen hours wearing nothing but a light sweater, flannel trousers and backless house slippers. A concerned local resident alerted the authorities on discovering Reg sitting shivering and unresponsive in his garden shed a mile and a half from the secure unit. Sadly the lifelong devoted family man contracted pneumonia from prolonged exposure and slipped away in his sleep a week later.

'My dear,' Minnie said confidently. 'You have absolutely nothing to worry about, I assure you I am as sharp as a razor, always have been, always will be, now where did I put my spectacles?'

Esther raised her eyebrows at the spectacles hanging on a chain around her sister's neck. 'As a razor, you say,' she said, unconvinced.

Captain Kofti skilfully steered the Northern Star towards port, narrowly avoiding the treacherous sand banks on occasion and breathed a huge sigh of relief when she eventually docked.

'Oh look, dear,' Minnie said, clinging to Esther's arm. 'We have a welcoming committee, I must say the Saudis do go all out, don't they.'

'Yes,' Esther agreed, glancing down at the heavy police presence. 'It does appear that way, dear.' The sisters watched as Vivien was raised from the cargo hold and lowered gracefully onto the quayside as was the passenger gangway.

'Well thank you, captain,' Minnie said when he emerged red-faced to see them off. 'I must say it's been most enjoyable, most enjoyable indeed.'

The captain bypassed Minnie's hand and shook that of her sister. 'Goodbye, madam, and good luck.' He looked down at Minnie, wanting desperately to offer Esther his condolences at having to endure her sister as it were.

'Thank you, dearie,' Esther replied, donning her driving gloves in the searing afternoon heat. 'I tell you if I'm completely honest,' she told the captain, 'I was against this trip from the offset, totally against it I might add, but it hasn't been half bad, aside from our earlier close call of course, such a remarkable boy, young Kadir.'

'Yes, yes, quite remarkable,' the captain replied proudly whilst Minnie made her way down the gangway towards the waiting authorities.

'Helloooooo!' Minnie called, waving regally and forgetting her firearms faux pas, 'lovely day!'

'Madam,' the Dubai chief of police said, approaching with three of his officers, 'You are to come with us.'

Minnie was fast growing into her life of celebrity and merely assumed she and her sister were to be whisked through passport control without the usual tiresome formalities that the less accomplished members of the public were forced to endure. 'Oh that's awfully kind of you, dear,' she told the solemn chief. 'But my sister and I would hate to put you to any trouble, we are British after all and queuing is what we do best, do you know I once waited a full forty minutes at the post office because Mrs Thomson from the tower block at the end of our street wanted to pay her Council Tax, and renew her TV licence, and pay thirty-five pounds in loose change into her savings account, oh I didn't mind at all you see because I read my *Woman's Weekly* from cover to cover in the queue and completed the word search for a chance to with fifty thousand pounds a year for life and a beach house in the Maldives, wherever that is.'

The chief of police was momentarily distracted from his duties by Minnie's rambling tale.

'Although I was a tad peeved,' Minnie confessed, 'Because by the time I'd gotten to the counter they'd completely sold out of second class stamps and brown paper envelopes.'

Having heard enough, the chief gestured to his men who spun Minnie round and proceeded to cuff her hands behind her back.

'Ohhhhh,' Minnie cried, having been caught off guard. 'Oh dear, Essyyyyy!'

Esther looked down whilst still chatting to the captain, to see her sister shackled and being led toward a waiting police van. 'What, Minnie, Minnie, dear!' She hurried down the gangway as best she could, waving her hand in the air. 'Cooeeeee!' she cried. 'Wait, wait please, what's going on here?'

Minnie was helped into the van and sat flanked by two armed officers. 'Essyyyyyyy!' she called from the open door. 'Essyyyy what are they doing?'

'I say, excuse me!' Esther again called. 'Hellooooo, I sayyyy!' She was halted on the quayside by the chief of police, a bloated and heavily bearded Arab wearing a pristine but undersized khaki uniform.

'I'm afraid, madam, your friend is under arrest,' the chief told Esther, barring her way.

'My friend?' Esther replied, looking over his shoulder. 'That's not my friend, that's my sister for Pete's sake, now release her at once.'

'That is not possible, madam,' the chief replied with his hands wedged on his hips. 'She fired upon an unarmed harbour employee and must answer for her crimes.' The van door was slammed shut and Minnie was swiftly driven with sirens screaming from the quay.

'Wait, wait, where are you taking her?' Esther pleaded. 'It was a mistake, I tell you, a mistake, a foolish one at that I'll grant you but a mistake nevertheless!'

'I'm sorry, madam,' the chief told her, turning for his car. 'This mistake as you call it is a very serious offence in our country and must be processed accordingly, good day to you.'

'But but…' Esther stammered, starting after him. 'Where the devil are you taking her, where, she's eighty-four years of age damn it.'

'To the station,' the chief said, clambering into the back of his lavish chauffeur-driven Mercedes. 'You are welcome to follow if you so wish,' he added, slamming his door.

'Oh yes, yes of course,' Esther said, hurrying back to Vivien and frantically jiggling the key in the ignition. She'd learnt from the heavily biased media of possible lashings and even stonings being meted out for crimes committed in the Emirates, and feared for her frail sister. 'Ohhhh, Minnie,' she moaned, accelerating sharply to catch the chief's sleek car and the police van which turned every head on approach with its rooftop lights flashing and deafening siren.

Minnie rocked against the flanking stone-faced officers at every corner. 'Oh I am sorry, dear,' she regularly said, unable to steady herself. 'Are these restraints really necessary?' she also asked the officer to her left whilst again colliding with his colleague. 'I mean I'm hardly Lizzie Borden now, am I?' The mention of the infamous Massachusetts-born daughter of Aby and Andrew Borden who on August 4th 1892 was arrested for their gruesome double murders using an axe of all things, flew way over the officers' heads. Lizzie was acquitted of her parents' slayings but many historians remain sceptical. 'Lizzie Borden!' Minnie reiterated on seeing their blank expressions, then recited the popular children's rhyme of that era. 'You know, *Lizzie Borden took an axe and gave her mother forty whacks, when she saw what she had done she gave her father forty one.'*

Still the officers remained unflinching. 'Maybe not,' Minnie said to herself whilst swinging her legs and assuming the misunderstanding would be dealt with swiftly as soon as they reached their destination and she was able to plead her case to a higher ranking officer, preferable somebody a little more sympathetic to her advancing years.

Sweeping into the fortified compound of the city's police headquarters, the transport vehicle came to an abrupt stop, sending Minnie careering into an officer yet again. 'Oh dear, I'm awfully sorry,' she said, straightening her spectacles.

Esther drew in moments later in time to see her sister being led into a custom built detention block. 'I demand you release her at once!' she called on leaving her car and angered at her sister's apparent brutish treatment. 'Who do you think you are, treating a woman that way, are you alright my dear?' she asked Minnie before she disappeared through a heavy steel door. 'IF YOU HURT HER!' she yelled after the escorting officers, 'I SWEAR YOU'LL LIVE TO REGRET IT, YOU MARK MY WORDS!' She started after them but was once again thwarted by the panting chief.

'You cannot go there,' he told Esther, mopping his brow and ushering her to a second door. 'If you wish to wait,' he added, 'I must warn you this could take some time.'

'Well I'm not leaving without her,' Esther told him in no uncertain terms. 'Now point me in the direction of your superiors, you pompous oaf, and we'll have this unholy mess cleared up in no time.'

'My superiors?' the chief asked, puffing his chest. 'Madam, I am the superior officer here, I answer only to his Highness Sheik Mohammed, nobody else.'

'Really,' Esther said, standing her ground. 'Well I suggest you get this Mohammed fellow on the telephone and tell him to get his backside down here at once, do you hear?'

'Out of the question!' the chief barked, heading inside with Esther scurrying behind, 'his Highness is an extremely busy man, I will send word to him but I would not hold my breath if I were you, he could come today, tomorrow, a week, a month, who knows, it is his will,'

'A month!' Esther shrieked. 'That's preposterous, you can't keep my sister locked up in here for an entire month, for heaven's sake, you can't do you hear me, you just can't.'

'Madam,' the chief said, dropping into his creaking swivel chair. 'I am the chief of police, I can do whatever it is I wish, if I choose to detain your sister for one month then so be it, this is Dubai after all, not your British Islands.'

'Isles,' Esther corrected the chief smugly, 'It's British Isles, I'll have you know, and you look here,' she added leaning onto his desk. 'I've told you it was all a misunderstanding and that my sister is in her eighties and of a nervous disposition, she couldn't cope for a single night without me let alone a whole month, God damn it, now, please release her and we'll be on our way.'

The chief rose from his chair, also bearing down on his desk. 'Listen, woman!' he said in a derogatory tone, 'Your sister is charged with attempted murder, a crime punishable by death, I might add, so if I were you I would pray for his Highness's mercy instead of harassing his chief of police, which I must warn you is also a crime in Dubai.'

'Yes but, but…' Esther stammered, knowing full well that she was powerless to intervene. The chief said nothing more and merely gestured to a hard wooden bench to the side of his office. 'Right you are then,' Esther agreed, taking a seat whilst quietly seething. Removing his cap the chief went about his business, totally disregarding Esther's occasional sighs of frustration.

Minnie, in the meantime, had been housed in a cramped nine-by-six cell with two other Arab detainees, both of them male and decidedly shady. 'Lovely day,' she said sheepishly as they eyed her up and down and whispered between themselves.

A whole two hours later Esther hoisted herself to her feet having seized up somewhat and confronted the chief once again, interrupting his exchange of text messages with his young mistress. 'Excuse me I really must object!' she stormed whilst massaging her numb buttocks. 'I've been sat here for God knows how long and as far as I know no formal charges have been made against my sister, this really is intolerable, intolerable I say!'

'Charges,' the chief said, disgruntled at the interruption. 'Oh yes, the charges.' He then telephoned through to his second in command. 'Bring the woman,' he said before slamming down the receiver. 'As you wish,' he told Esther.

Minnie was retrieved from the mould-ridden cell having crammed herself tightly into a corner and not taken her eyes off her fellow prisoners, one of whom had shamelessly urinated against the opposite wall, grinning at her in the process. 'Essy, ohhh, Essy!' she blurted on seeing her sister. 'You have to get me out of here, darling, please, please do something, Essy, please.'

'Yes, yes, of course dear,' Esther replied, approaching Minnie with arms outstretched before she was wrenched toward the chief's desk. 'Don't worry, darling,' she called after her. 'We'll just clear up this nonsense and be on our way, you'll see.'

'Nonsense?' Minnie said with renewed hope. 'Oh yes, yes of course, dear, I see what you mean, nonsense, that's what it is.'

'SILENCE!' the chief suddenly bellowed, slamming the palm of his hand down firmly. 'I will decide whether this is nonsense and believe me it is not, under Saudi law, woman, you have been charged with the attempted murder of one Muktar Shaleem this very morning.'

'Attempted murder, don't be daft,' Minnie scoffed.

'QUIET, WOMAN!' the chief yelled, in no mood for her insolence. 'You are also charged with possessing a firearm in the port of Dubai, this is also strictly forbidden.'

'Now look here,' Esther interjected. 'I'm sure we can explain everything if you'll just hear us out.'

You!' the chief barked, pointing a finger in Esther's direction, 'Are trying my patience, I will have you arrested for obstruction should you continue.'

'Shhhh, Essy dear,' Minnie told her sister. 'No sense in both of us getting into hot water, is there, I'll be fine, dear, honestly.'

'I do hope so,' Esther replied, reluctantly returning to the bench, and sitting on the very edge wringing her hands while her sister was formally charged under Saudi law.

'Take her,' the chief eventually snapped at his sidekick.

'What, no wait!' Esther said as her sister was bundled by her. 'Minnie, Minnie, no!'

'Essy what's happening?' Minnie called, having paid very little attention to the allegation thrust upon her. 'Essy, do something!'

'I will, I will, dear, I promise!' Esther said, restrained from following. 'I'll go to the British Consulate at once, yes that's what I'll do, Minnie dearest, I'll go seem them right away, be brave, my darling, be brave!'

'Hurry please, Essy, hurry!' Minnie cried before disappearing out of sight. 'Please, Essyyyyyy!' En route back to the cell block, Minnie appealed to the marching officers at her side. 'I say,' she said with the merest hint of a smile. 'I wonder if I might have my own room, with a little more privacy if you get my drift.' Minnie got no reply and was bundled back inside the holding cell with the petty thief and the drug smuggler. 'Hellooooo,' she said when the door was bolted behind her. 'Just one or two formalities and I'll be on my way,' she explained to her bemused cellmates, the taller of whom cleared his throat and spat on the floor at Minnie's feet. 'Must you do that?' she asked, reeling back in disgust. 'It's awfully unhygienic I'll have you know, and not to mention socially unacceptable.'

Both men had very little to lose having been caught and tried for their crimes, and were almost acceptant of the grizzly fate that awaited them the very next day.

The chief of police rummaged and retrieved a business card from his desk drawer and tossed it in Esther's direction. 'Your consulate,' he said dismissively. 'Go now, woman, you offend me with your presence.'

'Charming,' Esther said under her breath while stooping for the card. 'You will take good care of my sister, won't you?' she asked. 'She has an occasional respiratory condition, you see.'

'GO!' the fuming chief roared, pointing to the door. 'Your sister will receive no privileges, I can assure you of that!'

'Oh hell,' Esther said in despair, hurrying from the room and out into the compound to Vivien. 'Excuse me' she asked a gentleman sweeping fallen palm leaves. 'Excuse me, I was wondering if you could point me in the right direction.' She thrust the card with the consulate's address under the Arab's nose. 'The British Consulate,' she told him. 'Which way is it, please, I am in rather a hurry I might add.' But the sweeper spoke no English and went about his business, flashing her a timid half smile.

Esther sped from the police compound toward the city centre, checking each road sign at the numerous intersections. 'Gotcha!' she eventually cried after some twenty agonising minutes, by chance stumbling across the plaza where the British Embassy was situated, a towering archaic building flying the Union Jack from a crumbling upper balcony. 'Oh thank heavens,' she told the doorman having left Vivien parked askew. 'I'm a Brit and I desperately need your help,' she added, gripping his jacket lapels. 'It's my sister, you see, she's been arrested, oh please you must help us, you simply must!'

The Saudi employee gestured to the front desk, standing rigidly to attention. 'There,' he said, straightening his attire.

'Oh right,' Esther said, shuffling by. 'Thank you so much, helloooo,' she called. 'I sayyyyy, you there!' She slapped her hand down on the desk, waking an elderly retired colonel. 'Hellooo, helloooo!' she insisted, prodding his pile of paperwork. 'I'm sorry to disturb you but this is a matter of great urgency,' she told him. 'I happen to be a British national and I'm in need of help, my sister is in need of help, should I say, right away if that's at all possible.'

'I'm sorry, madam,' the colonel pointed out. 'You will have to take a number and wait, we have strict procedures here at the consulate that must be adhered to, after all we are British, are we not.'

'What number?' Esther said breathlessly. 'What are you talking about for Pete's sake, my sister has been clamped in irons and treated like a common criminal, don't you understand?'

'Please,' the colonel replied, remaining calm and officious. 'Take a number and you will be seen in due course.'

Esther looked around at the deserted foyer. 'What on earth for?' she asked, growing increasingly frantic. 'This isn't the blasted post office after all, I demand to see the Ambassador or whoever's in charge around here, right now!'

'Not without a number, madam,' the unflinching colonel replied. 'Like I said, there are rules and procedures that must be adhered to at all times.'

'To hell with your procedures!' Esther barked across the desk. 'My sister has been arrested, arrested I say, now you get me the Ambassador at once, hurry, man!' but the colonel again gestured to the ticket dispenser at the end of his desk. 'Ohhhhh damn you!' Esther cursed, seething as she tore a ticket stub from the reel. 'There!'

she said, slamming it down in front of the colonel. 'One ticket, now what?'

'You wait,' she was told as he pressed a buzzer to alert the Ambassador upstairs, a Major Timothy Huntley-Palmer, a former ministerial advisor shipped off to Dubai when the scandal broke back home exposing his homosexual affair with a young cocky window cleaner at his Knightsbridge residence.

Esther paced the consulate foyer, regularly checking the large station clock that hung above a portrait of Queen Elizabeth, wondering just how her petrified sister must be coping.

Thirty five minutes later Major Palmer descended the panelled staircase to greet Esther. 'Ahhhhhh,' he said with a smile. 'I'm so sorry to have kept you waiting, Major Palmer, but you can call me Timothy, or Tim whichever you'd prefer, now, how may I help?'

'Well it's about time!' Esther snapped, starting towards the Major. 'It's my sister, Minnie, she's been arrested by that brute of a police chief, you have to do something right away.'

'Your sister?' Major Palmer asked, finding it hard to believe that anybody remotely close to Esther's age would find themselves on the wrong side if the law. 'Arrested, you say?'

'Yes that's what I said,' Esther replied in no mood for small talk. 'Arrested'

'Oh dear,' the major said. 'And er, what is it exactly that your sister has been charged with, may I ask?'

'It's all just a silly misunderstanding, that's what it is,' Esther explained, making light of her sister's firearms offence. 'Minnie had this gun, you see.'

'A gun!' Major Palmer gasped. 'Your sister had a gun, here, in Dubai?'

'Well not exactly,' Esther elaborated. 'It was on a ship during our approach to port, she fired several shots but like I say it was a silly misunderstanding, so if you'd kindly have a word with the chief then we'll happily be on our way.'

'She fired the gun,' the major said, struggling to piece together this outlandish tale.

'Oh yes,' Esther agreed. 'She thought we were about to be boarded by pirates you see.'

'Pirates!' the major remarked. 'But, but there are no pirates in these waters.'

'Yes I know that,' Esther scoffed. 'But try telling that to Minnie, she shoots from the hip if you'll pardon the pun, now look here, Major,' she added, lowering her tone. 'My sister may be a fool but she's no criminal, that I do know, now you must see to it that she merely receives a jolly good ticking off before being released, after all,' she gestured to the portrait, 'We are Her Majesty's subjects.'

'Well I'll certainly try,' the major replied, sceptical to say the least but not wishing to alarm Esther. 'Come along to my office and fill me in on all the relevant facts so I know how best to approach the chief of police.' He ushered Esther upstairs to his spacious office. 'Please take a seat,' he told her, slipping behind his desk. 'Riiight, now where were we, you say you were aboard a ship at the time of the alleged offence.'

'Yes, yes, the Northern Star,' Esther replied rocking impatiently. 'You see we left Mumbai three days ago you see, we're here to see the pyramids.'

'Yes, you and half the world at the moment,' Major Palmer relied, taking notes. 'If you don't mind me asking,' he probed a little further, 'What exactly were you doing in Mumbai?'

'Well, Minnie and I…' Esther began to explain.

'Wait, wait!' the major said, interrupting. 'Did you say Minnie?'

'Yes of course,' Esther replied. 'She's my sister.'

'Then you…' the major said, hesitating, 'You must be Esther, my God, you're the Peshwari Nans, aren't you!'

'That we are,' Esther admitted with a hint of pride. 'So now you know who we are, you'll probably know why we were in India don't you.'

'Of course,' the major said, rocking back in his seat with a smile. 'Everybody does no doubt, crikey!' he mused. 'The Peshwari Nans, here in Dubai, who'd have thought?'

'Yes well,' Esther said, prodding his desk. 'What about my sister?

'Oh, oh yes,' the major said, springing upright. 'I'll make a call to the chief right away, don't you worry, Esther, I'll have Minnie out of there in no time, I've crossed swords with the local police on several occasions and I only have to mention my political connections and they are usually most accommodating, it's not what you know, you see.'

'Oh thank heavens,' Esther sighed, clutching her chest. 'I'm afraid she doesn't cope too well on her own so time really is of the essence.'

'I fully understand,' the Ambassador smiled, putting Esther's mind at rest somewhat. 'Please don't worry, I do this sort of thing all the time, I'll have you know the consulate commands a great deal of respect in these parts, only a fortnight ago Her Majesty the Queen visited Dubai for a state dinner with Sheik Mohammed himself so I'd say your sister's release will be a mere formality.'

'Thank you,' Esther said while the major dialled the chief's office.

'Ahhh hello, it's Major Palmer here, yes, yes, the Ambassador,' Timothy told the station sergeant. 'From the consulate, yes,' he added, giving Esther the thumbs up prematurely. 'I was wondering might I have a word with the chief?'

A moment or two later the chief of police answered. 'Yes what is it?' he asked abruptly. 'What do you want, Ambassador?'

'Oh come now, chief, we both know why I'm calling, don't we,' the major said, getting straight down to business. 'You are currently holding a British national, are you not?'

'That I am,' the chief replied with a dismissive tone. Relations between the two parties had been strained in recent times with the consulate demanding leniency and fairer treatment of its subjects after a string of high profile cases.

'OK,' the Ambassador continued. 'So I trust she'll be released with nothing more than a reprimand, as a show of good will between our great nations so to speak.'

'Good will!' the police chief, said clenching a fist. 'Ambassador, you have made a mockery of me for far too long, you should remember you are a guest in our lands and must respect our laws as well as your subjects, this woman of yours,' he explained in no uncertain terms, 'She will remain in my custody and await a formal trial.'

'Now just a minute!' the major protested, giving Esther cause for concern all of a sudden. 'May I remind you she's a senior citizen and a high profile one at that, caution her if you must, deport her even, but a formal trial would be inhumane in my opinion.'

'Esther leaned a little closer. 'What is it?' she asked. 'What's happening?'

The major raised a finger to silence her momentarily.

'Your opinion!' the police chief growled. 'Your opinion, Ambassador, means nothing, nothing, do you hear, the British woman will stand trial under Saudi law, and I don't need to remind you of the consequences if she is found guilty.'

'You can't,' the major said, wide eyed. 'You can't, you hear, I'll take this to the Sheik himself you'll see.'

'As you wish, Ambassador,' the chief said, bringing their conversation to an abrupt end. 'Good day to you.'

'Wait!' Major Palmer called, tapping at his telephone.

'What is it?' Esther again asked. 'Has he agreed to release my sister?'

'I' I'm sorry, no,' the Ambassador sadly informed her. 'No he hasn't, I I...' he stammered, lost for words. 'I though a simple call would suffice but I'm afraid to say I was wrong.'

'Wrong!' Esther exclaimed. 'What do you mean, wrong, what about Minnie, what does this mean for her, you're the British Ambassador ,you have to get her out of there.'

'Now, now, calm down, Esther, please,' the major said, raising his hands and attempted to put Esther's mind at ease. 'Granted the chief can be a difficult fellow, he's a stickler for tradition you see when it comes to the judicial system, but he'll come around you'll see, I'll make a few more calls to friends in high places and see if we can't apply a little more diplomatic pressure, my advice to you,' he told her, 'Is to sit tight and be patient, oh and do try not to worry yourself, the wheels for your sister's release are in motion, you have my word.'

'Yes but how long?' Esther asked. 'How long will it take, I mean God only knows what she's going through in there.'

Minnie, although confined to a dark dimly lit cell with a pair of career criminals, had swiftly gained control of her desperate situation in her own sweet inimitable way, charming her co-detainees with tales plucked from her archive of distant memories, much of which they understood nothing of but were intrigued nevertheless. 'Well,' she said, beckoning the unsavoury characters closer. 'To say that my first boyfriend was inexperienced would be an understatement, and a gross one at that, the poor chap was so nervous he stumbled after lowering his trousers, struck his head on the gramophone and scratched Father's favourite seventy-eight, a rare recording of the Drifters *Save the Last Dance for Me,* needless to say Father wasn't best pleased and told the poor boy never to darken our door again.' Her cellmates found her yarns highly amusing whilst they awaited their own fates, a ray of sunshine in fact during their darkest hours.

'Seventy-eight?' one of them asked. 'What is seventy-eight?'

'It's a vinyl record, dear,' Minnie informed him, 'oh, you poor dear you really have led a sheltered life, haven't you, you'll be telling me next you've never heard of Royal Albert chinaware and toasted crumpets, for Pete's sake.'

The two looked at one another with blank expressions.

'Good grief,' Minnie remarked, 'Well allow me to explain.' She sat beside the two criminals imparting in elaborate detail the finer things in life in her opinion. 'And rose hip tea,' she added. 'Does wonders for an irritable bowel, you know, and not to mention flatulence.'

Esther had left the British Embassy deeply concerned for her sister's wellbeing, leaving the Ambassador thumbing through his little black book of influential friends and associates, the Prime Minister being at the top of his list but a last resort if all else failed.

The chief of police as well as the Sheik soon received calls pleading for Minnie's swift release and subsequent pardon, but the Saudis remained adamant that the gun-toting pensioner would stand trial regardless of her social standing and political pressure.

At the Ambassador's recommendation Esther checked into a nearby apartment block taking a room on the ground floor; there she sat by the telephone toying with her pearls and fretting with a deeply furrowed brow. Periodically she would call the Embassy for news but each time the major's office would inform her that everything humanly possible was being done and for her to be patient, but patience was a rare commodity where Esther was concerned, evident by the tapping of her feet and the strumming of her fingers.

Then following morning Esther woke sharply, fully clothed on the couch. 'Damn, damn, damn!' she cursed herself for falling asleep amidst the crisis and snatching the telephone. 'Hello!' she said, wiping the sleep from her eyes. 'Hello yes, it's Esther Reynolds again, my sister Minnie, has she been released yet?'

'Ahhh, Mrs Reynolds,' another of the Ambassador's assistants said hesitantly. 'Errrm, no, I'm afraid she has not, it appears the Saudis are wanting to make an example of her.'

'What!' Esther gasped, clambering from the stiff camel hair couch. 'What do you mean, make an example, it was a mistake for heaven's sake and one which the two of us are extremely sorry for.'

'Yes, yes, I'm sure you are, Mrs Reynolds,' the assistant replied. 'But…'

'Don't tell me but!' Esther stormed, pacing her room. 'You are the British representatives here in Dubai are you not?'

'Of course,' the girl replied. 'But relations at the moment aren't what they were before Her Majesty's visit.'

'Relations?' Esther blurted. 'Whatever's wrong with our relations?'

'Well I shouldn't really say,' the Embassy assistant and confirmed gossip replied, lowering her voice a tad. 'But, a certain elderly Royal has put his foot in it yet again, insulting his Highness's eldest daughter.'

'You mean the Duke?' Esther asked, incensed that an off the cuff remark with someone with a proven track record for faux pas had led to her sister's present incarceration, that and the attempted murder of a harbour official of course. 'What has that fool gone and done now?' she asked.

'I'm afraid I'm not at liberty to say,' the girl said, itching to spill the beans. 'But the girl in question suffers from a glandular condition and has ballooned in appearance of late, but you never heard that from me, do you hear?'

'Good grief!' Esther said, guessing quite rightly that the insensitive royal in question had drawn attention to the girl's bloated stature and deeply offending her father Sheik Mohammed in the process. 'So what does that mean for Minnie?' she asked. 'What of my sister?'

'I've spoken to Minnie personally,' the assistant informed Esther, 'And for someone in her position she seems in surprisingly high spirits, almost jovial I'd say.'

'Don't be ridiculous,' Esther scoffed. 'How could she possibly be in high spirits, she's locked up alone in that hell hole, God damn it.' Esther slammed down the phone and hurriedly washed and changed her clothes before driving at the breakneck speed of forty miles per hour to police headquarters. 'I'm here to see the chief,' she told the clerk in no uncertain terms. 'And my sister of course, where is she, where's Minnie?'

The clerk ignored Esther whilst polishing the buttons on his tunic.

'Hey, hey!' Esther snapped, prodding at the desk. 'Did you hear me, I said I'm here to see the chief, hellooooo.'

'Madam,' the clerk said, peering over his mirrored aviator glasses. 'The chief does not wish to be disturbed and if you are talking about the English woman I'm afraid she is no longer here.'

'What?' 'Esther said, mortified. 'No longer here, what do you mean no longer here, where the devil is she, what have you done with her damn you?'

'She has been taken from here,' Esther was told. 'To our central prison, to await her trial.'

'Prison!' Esther gasped, gripping the desk anxiously. 'My sister, prison, but, but why?' She left the desk immediately and stormed toward the chief's office.

'Madam, madam where are you going?' the clerk called after her. 'Madam, come back at once!'

But Esther pounded on the chief's door over and over before turning the handle and barging straight in, catching the police chief in an intimate clinch with his young mistress.

'WHAT?' the chief cried, pushing the girl aside and tugging at his trousers. 'What is the meaning of this, woman, were you not told I was not to be disturbed!'

'It's about my sister,' Esther snarled, marching in and taking very little notice of the half-dressed girl. 'Your, your minion out there informs me she has been taken to prison, prison for heaven's sake, tell me why, I demand to know.'

'I have no time for this,' the chief stormed. 'Your sister is gone and that is that, now get out or you will soon be joining her.'

'But why?' Esther repeatedly asked whilst the girl scurried from the office straightening her tangled hair. 'Tell me why my aged sister has been taken to a prison of all places, I demand an answer!'

'Procedure,' the chief merely said whilst buttoning his shirt.

'It is a simple matter of procedure, she has been formally charged and awaits a trial, which I would estimate will take place in two days.'

'Two days!' Esther said, growing ever anxious. 'You mean, you mean you are going to keep Minnie locked up for a further two days, this is preposterous, it's inhumane that's what it is.'

'Madam!' the chief barked, raising a hand. 'Your sister broke the law, did she not?'

'Well, well…' Esther stammered.

'Did she not?' the chief asked aggressively.

'Yes but as I explained earlier…' Esther struggled to be heard, 'it was just a misunderstanding, that's all, nobody got hurt, did they?'

'Of course,' the chief informed her. 'The pilot captain is seeking damages for his vessel and the injury to his person, from what I hear he may never work again.'

The wily pilot skipper, hearing of Minnie's notoriety, had chosen to milk his flesh wound for all it was worth and take the British pensioner for a tidy sum, enough maybe to retire.

'Oh,' Esther said, taken aback, 'I had no idea, please offer the poor fellow my sincere apologies, echoed I'm sure by my sister.'

'That is all well and good, but,' the chief replied, rocking back in his chair, 'There is still the matter of a trial, the outcome of which could be very grave indeed for this Minnie of yours, very grave indeed.'

'Oh dear, what do you mean?' Esther asked, massaging her sweaty palms. 'Whatever will become of my sister?'

'You mean if she is found guilty?' the chief asked, consulting the papers strewn across his desk and tucking a pair of his girlfriend' panties hastily into his top drawer. 'You are aware we have the death penalty here in this region?'

'Death penalty!' Esther gasped, dropping into the chair opposite the chief 'Dear Lord no, not for my Minnie, surely not.' She rifled in her handbag and produced her ruffled cheque book. 'Look if it's a question of payment,' she added assuming most law enforcement officials in foreign parts were on the take as it were, 'I think you'll find we can be very generous indeed.' She leaned a little closer. 'Maybe generous enough to take that lady friend of yours on a romantic holiday.'

'You attempt to bribe me!' the chief stormed, sitting bolt upright.

'No, no, no, no, no, no!' Esther said hastily. 'I, I was simply enquiring as to the customary procedure in these parts, that's all, I promise I meant no offence, please, I just want my sister back.'

'You ask of procedure,' the chief growled, swiping the papers from his desk. 'A trial, a trial is the customary procedure, and I must warn you if the sentence is death, then so be it, now leave me I am a very busy man, LEAVE ME!' he yelled, pounding his desk.

'Oh, oh dear,' Esther said, pushing herself up from the chair. 'Yes, yes of course, one last thing,' she added, raising a finger. 'Could I possibly visit her, please, pleaaase.'

'As you wish,' the chief replied, tossing Minnie's transfer papers across his desk. 'She is here, NOW GO!'

Esther grappled with the papers with a shaking hand and scurried from the chief's office. 'Excuse me,' she asked the clerk in the lobby. 'Could you please direct me to…' she paused, checking the transfer documents, 'Dubai central prison please.'

Whilst the police clerk explained to Esther the shortest route through the city of Dubai, Minnie was sat bleary-eyed on the edge of her tiny bunk, having had a sleepless night surrounded by pickpockets, prostitutes and political prisoners housed in an all-female wing, with much of her present company waiting on death row with very little to lose. 'YOU!' one particularly aggressive Arabian woman snarled, approaching with a swagger. 'English?'

'I'm sorry?' Minnie said sheepishly.

The cocky Arab inmate turned to her fellow prisoners, joking in a language Minnie could not decipher, coaxing a ripple of laughter. 'I said, ENGLISH?' she snapped, bending to glare into Minnie's eyes.

'Oh yes, yes, yes I am,' Minnie hastily replied, inching away. 'From London in fact, Whitechapel, do you know it?'

'Looondon!' the Arab said, mocking Minnie. 'She is from London' She turned back to confront the pensioner again. 'What you do?' she asked, picking at Minnie's neatly pressed blouse dismissively.

'Sorry, what?' Minnie asked, unnerved to say the least. 'What do you mean, do?'

Again the Arab ridiculed Minnie in her native tongue, calling her an imbecile amongst other more derogatory things. 'Yes do!' she snapped 'You smuggle drugs?'

'Drugs, oh good heavens no,' Minnie said with a hand on her heart. 'Me, drugs, oh no, no, no, no, no, I'd never, I meant I wouldn't.'

'So!' the Arab inmate barked. 'What you do, you are no prostitute that is for sure.' Her fellow prisoners fell about laughing.

'No of course not,' Minnie smirked, mildly amused. 'I had a gun, you see.'

At the mention of the 'g' word those around immediately silenced their idle chatter. 'A gun!' Minnie's aggressor gasped. 'You?'

'Oh yes,' Minnie confessed, sensing a shift in their perception of her and elaborated, but applying the truth economically in her favour. 'I stole it from a member of the armed forces you see, and shot up a pilot boat in the harbour.'

The Arab prisoner looked Minnie up and down, wondering if maybe she'd been a little hasty in her condemnation; had she inadvertently misjudged this dated book by its shabby cover and possibly enraged a psychopathic killer? 'My apologies,' she said, dropping beside Minnie on her bunk. 'I meant not to offend you, Sasha,' she said, offering a hand.

'Minnie,' Minnie replied whilst the others gathered around. To survive amongst this band of renegades and cutthroats, she thought to herself, she would need to perpetuate this elaborate myth. 'Minnie Kray,' he added. 'Perhaps you've heard of my brothers, Ronnie and Reggie?'

'The Arab woman thought for a moment. 'Ronnie, Reggie, and Minnie?' she asked quizzically.

'Precisely,' Minnie chirped, puffing her chest. 'Sadly my brothers are no longer with us so the family business is now in my capable hands, the firm I mean.'

The surrounding prisoners huddled together discussing the global notoriety of the infamous twins and the possibility of a sister now heading their criminal organisation. 'London,' one of them said, peering over her shoulder at the unassuming old woman.

'Minnie Kray!' another gasped, buying into the ruse hook line and ridiculous sinker.

Soon Minnie had quite an entourage eager to hear of her underworld exploits and of course she obliged them in spades, dropping such infamous names as Mad Frankie, Jack the Hat and a scattering of imaginary rogues. 'I remember crossing swords with Mac the Knife,' she said, spinning a lengthy yarn. 'He and his band of bloodthirsty hoodlums attempted to muscle in on our patch but my brothers and I were having none of it, well Mac soon realised he'd bitten off more than he could chew when I paid him a little visit at his bookies on the Old Kent Road.'

'What did you do, what did you do?' an inmate asked, all ears. 'Tell us, tell us, sorry, could you tell us please, Minnie?'

'That's quite alright, dear,' Minnie said, forgiving the lack of apparent respect. 'Well I gave Mac the Knife an ultimatum you see,' she continued whilst all around listened intently. 'Skip town before nightfall or I'd personally fit him with a concrete overcoat, well needless to say the spineless fool shut up shop and left with his reputation in tatters and his right arm in a sling.'

A resounding gasp rang out around Minnie in the cell block; was there a crouching tiger lurking beneath her demure exterior, they thought, a raging bull perhaps?

Of course nothing could be further from the truth but Minnie poured on the pretence until rumours spread throughout the jail of a category A high profile fellow inmate in their midst.

Instead of the hellish nightmare that her sister had imagined, Minnie's incarceration suddenly took a bizarre turn for the better with many fellow prisoners sharing their limited possessions with her, extra pillows, blankets and toiletries for instance. 'Oh really you're too kind,' she said, taking delivery of a selection of Saudi sweets. 'How lovely,' she added when a silk scarf was draped around her neck.

Meanwhile Esther negotiated the busy Dubai main streets, disregarding the stunning state of the art tower blocks, hotels and corporate buildings on either side that made this glamorous city a jewel of the United Arab Emirates. 'Get out of my waaaay!' she cried, eager to comfort her distraught sister, or so she thought.

On arrival Esther was forced to wait an agonising forty minutes while her papers were meticulously scrutinized and her background thoroughly checked for the slightest of misdemeanours. 'OK,' a stone-faced prison officer eventually said, handing Esther her documents. 'This way.'

Esther hurried after the guard, desperate for a glimpse of her sister, fully expecting to find her quivering in a corner petrified of her hellish surroundings.

'COOOOOEEEEEEE!' a familiar voice then called out. 'Essy, Essy darling, over here!'

Esther first noticed a waving hand amid a crowd of prisoners, but the attire was unfamiliar. 'Minnie?' she asked. 'Minnie, is that you?'

'Essyyyyyyy,' Minnie squealed with a beaming smile and wearing a full length prison issue robe and traditional headscarf. 'Everybody!' she told her newfound friends. 'This is my…' she hesitated to hastily falsify their relationship, 'My associate, we er, we work together if you get my drift.' Many of Minnie's cellmates rose to greet Esther as a mark of respect, assuming she too had criminal connections.

'Work together?' Esther asked her sister.

Minnie swiftly escorted her sister to one side. 'Essy, shhhhh,' she whispered. 'You must follow my lead, dear, you understand, or believe me I'm as good as dead.'

'Dead!' Esther gasped. 'Minnie, what on earth's going on?'

'Never mind!' Minnie said in haste. 'As far as this lot know, my name is Minnie Kray with obvious gangland connections.'

'Minnie Kray!' Esther laughed. 'Minnie, have you lost your mind, gangland connections, I've never heard anything so ridiculous in all my days.'

'Just do it, Essy!' Minnie insisted. 'Please, for my sake.'

'Alright, alright,' Esther relented, suddenly seeing genuine fear in her sister's eyes. 'But I'm no good at this sort of thing, you know that, so yes I'll follow your lead.' Hesitantly Esther accompanied her sister to the dining hall table where several women moved aside to allow her to sit.

'Ladies,' Minnie said, patting her sister's back. 'Allow me to introduce you to Essy, or Essy the Axe as she is better known, isn't that right, dear?' she asked.

'Essy the Axe?' Esther mouthed. 'Oh, oh yes, yes that's right, the Axe,' she informed those around them, who inched away a tad when she made several chopping motions with her right hand. 'Essy the Axe, that's me.'

'Ooooh very good, dear,' Minnie remarked proudly. 'Perhaps you're a natural after all.'

'I doubt that very much,' Esther replied out of earshot of the others. 'To be honest I'm bloomin' petrified.'

'Essy and I,' Minnie told the gathering, 'We've been through some scrapes, I can tell you.'

'Tell us please, Minnie, tell us,' the prisoners asked. 'Yes please.'

'Well,' Minnie said, leaning closer and lowering her voice for greater dramatic effect. 'There was this one time back in the 60's around the time of the Great Train Robbery, I take it you've all heard about the mail train heist, have you?' Many around her nodded in agreement. 'Well,' Minnie continued, 'You may also be aware that the villains responsible were all eventually apprehended and ultimately held accountable for their actions, but during the media storm that surrounded the high profile case my associates and I, Essy included, pulled off the caper of the century.'

Esther's eyes grew wider and wider at her sister's elaborate tale.

'What did you do?' many around Minnie asked.

'The Royal Mint,' Minnie confessed. 'We meticulously planned and executed the biggest robbery to date anywhere in the western world, and we got away with it too, the then government were so embarrassed by the train robbery that they ordered a complete media blackout of our blag as it were, and therefore not a single word of it was ever publicised.' All around there were louder gasps and nods of recognition and respect.

'And the money?' Minnie was asked, 'What of the money?'

'Buried,' Minnie replied. 'Millions upon millions in white five pound notes under the asparagus bed at our allotment, Essy here held the guards at bay with her hatchet while myself, Neville Knuckles, One-punch Wilf and Cyril the safe went to work on the vault.'

'You used explosives?' another curious prisoner asked.

'Barrels of the stuff,' Minnie explained. 'So much in fact that the tremors were felt way up in the Yorkshire Dales, I believe.' Minnie had by now successfully cemented her reputation as a criminal hard case and earned her rightful place at the very top of Dubai prison's pecking order.

Esther rose and took her sister's arm. 'Do excuse us,' she told the predominantly Arab gathering. 'Minnie, can I have a word, dear?' she asked, whisking her sister to one side.

'You were wonderful, dear,' Minnie said enthusiastically.

'Yes, yes, yes,' Esther replied with more important things on her mind. 'Now look here, I've been to the British Embassy here in Dubai,' she explained, 'And I've spoken with the Ambassador, a Major Timothy something or other.'

'Oh wonderful!' Minnie chirped. 'So you've come to get me out of here, have you?'

'Errrr not exactly,' Esther replied hesitantly. 'It appears the chief of police and the Sheik of Dubai himself are hell bent on making an example of you.'

'Me?' Minnie gasped. 'But, but, Essy why me?'

'Well let's just say,' Esther informed her, 'You are to be made a scapegoat for a recent royal rumpus that occurred here recently.'

'A rumpus?' Minnie asked. 'What do you mean a rumpus, dear, what's going on, for Pete's sake?'

Esther pondered how best to explain the predicament to her sister. 'It seems a verbal blunder was made by an aged member of our own Royal family during a visit.'

'Philip!' Minnie snapped. 'You mean Philip, don't you, he's gone and put his blasted foot in it again, hasn't he!'

'It does appear so, my darling,' Esther agreed. 'This time it was the Sheik's daughter on the receiving end, I'm afraid, and as they couldn't possibly detain the Duke, you, my dear, are a British citizen and the next best thing I'm afraid.'

'The blighters!' Minnie growled. 'So, so what happens now, dear?'

'A trial, dear,' Esther informed her. 'The Ambassador seems to think as early as two days.'

'You mean…' Minnie said, looking around her. 'I've to stay in here for another two days?

'I'm so sorry, darling, but yes,' Esther said, rubbing her sister's arm under the watchful eye of the prison guards. 'As much as it pains me to say.'

Seeing the distress etched on her sister's face, Minnie swiftly decided to make light of the whole sorry affair. 'Weeeeell, I suppose it could be worse, dear,' she said nonchalantly.

'Worse!' Esther remarked. 'Are you out of your mind, Minnie, if you are found guilty God only knows what they'll do to you.'

Minnie took her sister by the hand. 'Well, dear I suggest you rally support from our friends in the internet,' she suggested. 'Start up a campaign or something along those lines.'

'Yes, yes I will,' Esther chirped. 'That's exactly what I'll do, heaven knows we have enough friends in high places, I'll badger them all, you'll see.' A bell then sounded, signalling the end of visiting time. 'Oh, my darling,' Esther said, flinging her arms around Minnie's neck before the two were torn apart by guards. 'Be strong, won't you, be strong!'

'You too, dear!' Minnie called after blowing a parting kiss.

Esther left Dubai central prison heartbroken but determined to defend her sister at all costs, and if that meant beseeching each and every one of their tens of thousands of followers then so be it.

The campaign 'JUSTICE FOR MINNIE' began that very afternoon with instant messages of support from well-wishers the world over flooding in. Esther sat in their hotel room late into the night putting her newfound skills to good use, firing off emails one after the other to London, Australia, India, Paris and the United States to name but a few. Enraged followers who had taken both of the sisters to their hearts during their recent travels began to spread the word on the web and lobby their political leaders and presidents to drum up support for the aged inmate. 'My word,' Esther gasped at one point when a heartfelt message of solidarity came from Raj Govinda and his entire Bollywood organisation, and soon these were echoed by the British Prime Minister and his opposition, the

Obamas in the White House, a string of European leaders, Oscar-winning actors and chart-topping recording artists from the world of music including master Bieber who halted his sell out gig in Tokyo midway through his latest number one smash hit to announce his support and implore his global army of fans to do the same. Even the cast of Disney's *Frozen* recorded an adapted version of their globally known anthem *LET IT GO* accompanied by a host of international artists, *LET HER GO* thundered up the download charts within hours of its release as Esther continued her mission late into the following afternoon. Buoyant builders back home belted out the instant hit from scaffolds and rooftops. 'LET HER GOOOOOOOO, LET HER GOOOOOO, LET HER GOOOOOOO!' but even with unprecedented and mounting pressure from all walks of life his Highness Sheik Mohammed remained adamant, Minnie would stand trial no matter what.

Minnie paced her cell, picking at the peeling paint with her plastic spoon at times contemplating escape, although the prison walls were some three feet thick and any attempt with the woefully inadequate cutlery would see her long dead before making a dent. Her stay at the prison, although, was unlike that of many of the ill-fated inmates, her legion of admirers saw to it that she was kept from harm's way and made more than comfortable. 'Thank you, my dears,' she said, accepting another parcel of treats smuggled in by her minions' relatives. 'You're too kind, really you are.'

Esther meanwhile had made the British Ambassador's life a misery, telephoning repeatedly, turning up at his office first thing the very next morning, and refusing to leave until he had fulfilled his official obligations and explored every avenue to secure her sister's release, but still Minnie would stand trial that very afternoon with grave consequences hanging over them if she were to be found guilty.

An embassy official was charged with representing the pensioner, who arrived at the courthouse in an armoured truck flanked by motorcycle outriders such was the celebrity that had rapidly surrounded this case.

The Sheik himself would sit alongside the judge as a show of defiance to the bank of foreign media cameras he'd allowed within the room.

'Essy, oh Essy!' Minnie cried on seeing her sister when brought from below.

'Minnie, my darling!' Esther replied, leaving her seat to hug her handcuffed sibling. 'Good God, is this really necessary?' she asked the two guards either side of her. 'She's my sister I'll have you know, not Myra bloody Hindley!' Her reference to the evil moors murderess jailed for life in 1966 fell on deaf ears, but Minnie's cuffs were eventually removed. 'It'll be alright, dear,' Esther said, returning to her seat. 'I've been on the web thingy and we have a wealth of support, Richie Branson sends his best wishes and so does the Duchess of York.'

'Ahhhhh, how kind,' Minnie said, standing in the dock at this point.

Firstly Major Timothy Huntley-Palmer spoke as a representative of Her Majesty the Queen and Great Britain appealing for leniency and mercy for the aged defendant, but the Sheik looked decidedly unimpressed, occasionally leaning to whisper in the judge's ear to sway his opinion.

Next it was the prosecution's turn and the Saudi-born barrister presented a damning case against Minnie spouting Islamic law and the country's constitution during his eloquent opening speech. Minnie's embassy lawyer floundered hopelessly during his defence of her and looked positively amateurish at times, much to Esther's dismay.

Eventually came the summing up and after some three and a half bottom-numbing hours, the judge cleared his throat. 'Regardless of your age,' he said, looking over the rim of his glasses at Minnie, 'You have broken the law of this land with your reckless disregard for life whilst in our waters, therefore you must be punished for your heinous crimes.'

Esther dragged herself to her feet. 'Heinous crimes!' she yelled. 'It was a mistake, damn it, a mistake I tell you!

'Madam!' the judge warned her. 'Be silent or I will hold you in contempt and have you arrested, do I make myself clear?'

'Esther, please,' the Ambassador beside her said, helping her back to her seat, 'We cannot interfere during the judge's deliberation, that in itself carries a hefty penalty, believe me.'

'Well the man's a fool,' Esther said under her breath.

Again millions watched the live feed on tenterhooks, praying for a favourable outcome and the release of their beloved Minnie.

'It is the ruling of this court,' the judged eventually said after again consulting with the Sheik, 'That you be imprisoned here in Dubai for a period of thirty years,' as a huge gasp rang out around the courtroom.

'NO!' Esther shrieked. 'NO, NO, DEAR GOD, NO!'

The Ambassador raised his hand. 'Thirty years, your honour, that's life for this woman, she's eighty-four now.'

Minnie raised a hand of her own in the dock. 'Soon to be eighty-five,' she informed the court, 'And fit as a flea, I'll have you know.'

Suddenly there was pandemonium in the courtroom with camera crews and supporters alike voicing their disgust and the lengthy sentence handed to Minnie, meaning that she would undoubtedly die in prison in this foreign land.

One of the Sheik's closest advisors approached his Excellency. 'Your Highness, your Highness is this wise?' he asked. 'It appears the British woman has unprecedented international support, like nothing I have ever seen in fact.'

The Sheik looked across at Minnie, who was idly twisting a loose thread of cotton between her crooked fingers amid the uproar, and he and his official began a lengthy discussion as to the future political ramifications should Minnie perish in the Arab Emirates. 'Silence!' the Sheik then barked, raising a hand bejewelled with emerald encrusted rings. 'It is the will of your Sheik!' he informed the courtroom in an attempt to appear benevolent, 'That this woman receive a lesser sentence.' This cleverly orchestrated move would propel his status amongst his people to one of a strong but compassionate ruler, something that had been clearly lacking in former leaders. 'I will spare her the thirty years,' he added to rapturous applause. 'But instead!' he added, silencing them immediately, 'The woman will receive sixty lashes, publicly.'

'WHAT?' Esther gasped with her hand to her head. 'What, no, no, not that, not my Minnie, you can't, I won't let you!'

'Lashes?' Minnie said amid the melee. 'Me?'

At that precise moment the world was on its feet angrily voicing its objections to the barbaric sentence. 'But your Highness,' the Sheik's advisor said, shocked himself. 'You, you can't.'

'CAN'T!' the Sheik stormed. 'You dare to tell me I can't!'

'I'm sorry, your Highness but...' his official stammered sheepishly as his mobile phone began to ring in his pocket. 'Your Highness, your Highness, it is the American President, sir.'

But the ruler dismissed the call with a wave of his hand. 'My decision is final!' he growled when further foreign leaders called to beseech him on Minnie's behalf. No amount of political weight would dissuade him until a certain call came through. 'Paul O'Grady?' he asked, 'are you sure?'

'Yes, your Highness,' his advisor assured him. 'Paul O'Grady.'

'SILENCE!' the Sheik bellowed before accepting the call from the UK's number one chat show host and housewives' favourite. 'Mister, Mister O'Grady' the Sheik said, star-struck momentarily. 'It is an honour and a pleasure to speak with you, a pleasure, sir.' The Sheik himself had closely followed his television career and was a huge fan. The pair spoke briefly while Esther sat with her head in her hands sobbing, whilst her sister now trembled in the dock.

'Of course,' the Sheik eventually said. 'I am a merciful man, Mister O'Grady, and a compassionate man.' Whatever the television personality said to soften the Sheik's steely exterior obviously worked. 'Goodbye, Mister O'Grady,' he added. 'And please feel free to visit whenever you wish, in fact I would consider it an honour.' The Sheik then again raised his hand. 'After further consultation!' he said above the din, 'I have decided to reduce the number of lashes for the woman to just three, my decision is final and will remain unchanged, good day to you all,' and with this he rose and left with his vast entourage trailing behind him, leaving a stunned courthouse.

Esther again wrenched herself to her feet. 'You can't!' she begged the judge. 'Please, you can't do this to her, you can't, I won't let you hurt her, you hear!'

Again the Ambassador attempted to calm her, but Esther along with seven billion viewers was riled and incensed. 'Esther, please,' he said, patting her hand.

'Get off of me, you fool!' Esther raged, snatching her hand away and approaching the dock. 'Oh, Minnie darling, I'm so sorry,' she sobbed. 'I tried, I really tried, I swear I did, but don't worry, I won't let them touch you, I won't, I won't.'

'It's alright, my dear,' Minnie said, putting on the bravest of faces for her sister's sake but positively quaking inside. 'I brought this on myself after all.'

'No, Minnie, it was a mistake,' Esther replied, reaching to hug her sister. 'A silly, silly mistake, that's all.'

'Essy, please,' Minnie said, cupping Esther's face. 'Let's just get this over with and be on our way, I'll be fine, honestly.'

Esther kissed Minnie repeatedly about the face. 'Oh, you dear sweet thing,' she said, smearing her tears onto her sister's cheeks. 'I love you, do you know that, I love you so much.'

'And I love you too, Essy' Minnie replied as two officers arrived to escort her back to prison.

'Wait, please wait!' Esther begged, grappling with her sister to prolong their embrace. 'I'm here, darling, and I'm not going anywhere do you hear?' she told her sister. 'Do you hear?'

'Thank you, dear,' Minnie said, raising a smile. 'That's a great comfort.'

Minnie's punishment was set for nine-thirty the following morning, giving her supporters just eighteen hours to increase their online petition and hopefully overturn the Sheik's decision. *Let Her Go* was now fast approaching record sales figures, outselling every boy and girl band combined and played on loud speakers outside Arab embassies around the world as a sign of protest.

T-shirts with Minnie's face emblazoned on them were worn in their millions by well-wishers who planned to hold a candlelit vigil through the night praying for a pardon for this loveable lady.

That evening Esther sat at the hotel bar rolling a glass of gin and bitter lemon from hand to hand and staring into space, petrified for her younger sister. 'Damn them,' she cursed several times. Crying into her pillow later that night Esther eventually fell asleep a short while before sunrise, mentally and physically exhausted.

Minnie, on the other hand, had been treated like a queen by her fellow inmates who had nothing but respect for her dismissive attitude to her sentencing. Two Saudi women bathed Minnie's feet while the others gathered around offering words of comfort and wisdom, several of them having been lashed by the authorities for past offences. 'Take your mind to another place, Minnie,' one of them suggested. 'Picture your family, your friends, your home.'

'Be strong, Minnie,' another told her. 'And you will get through this, I promise you.'

'Thank you,' Minnie said, choking back a tear. 'All of you,' and she then enjoyed a banquet in her cell of olives, vine leaves, dates and bananas, along with humus and flatbreads, all of which served to distract her from her impending public lashing.

Esther was up, washed and dressed by seven a.m. although having had very little in the way of sleep. The lashing was to take place in the central square, a stone's throw from the prison itself, the approach to which was already lined with military police to prevent any surging rescue attempts by Minnie's fanatical supporters.

Major Timothy arrived at Esther's hotel to personally escort her to the proceedings. 'Any news?' Esther asked without hesitation.

'I'm afraid not, my dear,' the Ambassador replied solemnly. 'I've been in regular contact with the PM and he assures me every political angle is being explored and a mountain of pressure heaped on the Sheik and his regime, there are even talks of sanctions if the lashing was to go ahead, so I am quietly confident, shall we say.'

'Oh, I do hope you're right,' Esther said, donning her straw hat.

A huge crowd had gathered for this high profile spectacle, many carrying placards condemning the archaic practice. 'Dear Lord,' Esther gasped when first setting eyes on the post to which her sister would be shackled. 'They can't do this.'

A full media ban had been imposed but many onlookers covertly recorded the scene on mobile devices, risking a similar fate as Minnie or worse if discovered.

A tall shirtless Arab stood without expression beside the post with a coiled bull whip hanging from his right hand, beads of perspiration trickling down his muscular chest as morning temperatures in Dubai began to soar.

Soon the prison cavalcade came into sight and the pensive crowd surged behind the police ranks whilst Esther, the Ambassador and his wife were afforded a private viewing in a cordoned area.

Minnie was removed from the lead truck, squinting and unable to shield her eyes with her hands once again fastened behind her back.

'MINNIE!' Esther called, attempting to run to her, but she was restrained from doing so by numerous prison guards and the Ambassador himself. 'She's my sister!' Esther barked, struggling hopelessly. 'Minniiiiie, Miniiiiiiie!'

'Essy, Essyyyyy!' Minnie too called out, overjoyed to see a familiar face amongst the crowd. 'Lovely day!' she added gesturing to the clear blue sky above them.

Esther's heart sank. 'Minnie, you dear sweet fool,' she replied, feeling absolutely powerless to intervene and drained at this point; having skipped breakfast she'd expelled what little energy she had struggling with the burly guards and now hung limp between them. 'Please,' she begged. 'Please don't do this, pleaaaaaaaase.'

Oddly enough Minnie appeared in reasonably high spirits, nodding and smiling to many of the bewildered onlookers. 'Helloooooo,' she said chirpily, 'Lovely day!'

Esther meanwhile was having to be supported by the British Ambassador and comforted by his doting wife. 'What is she doing?' the major asked, watching Minnie trotting toward the post without a care.

Minnie's friends within Dubai's central prison had given her a parting gift as it were, a hefty quantity of amphetamine to help curb her anxiety, but Minnie not being an habitual user all but overdosed on the contraband, losing all sense of reality and disregarding completely the torture she would soon endure.

'Minniiiiie!' Esther again called, but her sister's vision was blurring rapidly with the powerful drug coursing through her aged veins, relaxing every sinew and fibre.

'I can hear you, Essy dear!' she called back. 'But I'm damned if I can see you, why are we here, Essy?'

'Oh the poor thing,' Esther whimpered. 'She's out of her mind.'

The strapping Arab entrusted with the task of meting out the Sheik's bidding grabbed Minnie by the wrists and released her shackles, tossing them to the ground before tugging her arms forcefully either side of the post and binding them with a cord.

'Oooh, Cyril,' Minnie said, hallucinating by now. 'You know I like it when you take control.'

The Sheik then arrived in his polished white Bentley, stepping out into the shade of his bodyguard's umbrella. Esther made a desperate break for him but was held back with ease by Diana, the Ambassador's flame-haired wife. 'No, Esther,' Diana told her. 'Believe me, you'll only make matters worse, I promise you.'

Minnie squealed when her prison robe was torn in two, exposing her wrinkled back to the light of day, several moles could also be seen and a scar from a childhood accident she'd received when falling from the bountiful limbs of a Victoria plum tree in their neighbour's garden.

Looking to his ruler the henchman readied his whip and the crowd fell eerily silent, save for Minnie's distraught sister. 'No, no, no, no, no, no,' she said, shaking her head when the Sheik nodded his. 'NO, PLEASE DON'T!'

The Arab took three paces back from the post and let the coil of black leather whip fall to the floor while he grasped the handle.

'Please be gentle, Cyril,' Minnie said over her shoulder.

Raising the whip, the muted man grimaced and suddenly time seemed to slow as the world held its breath, many averting their eyes in floods of tears 'NOOOOOOOOO!' Esther pleaded, bent double in the Ambassador's arms. 'No, no, MINNIIIIIIIIIIIE!'

Three time the Sheik's henchman circled the whip above his head, building momentum before letting fly with a resounding 'CRACK!'

Minnie suddenly came to and screamed a bloodcurdling scream like nothing Esther had ever heard during their entire lives together, a scream that broke her heart immediately.

'ESSYYYYYYY!' Minnie called to her elder sister as she slumped against the post whilst the whip was raised once more.

A little of Esther died that very moment, Minnie was family, she was her blood and the love between them knew no bounds. 'No, no, dear God no!' she cried, screwing her hat in her hands, as weak as a kitten and unable to break free.

'ESSYYYY, PLEASE, HELP ME!' Minnie begged, tugging at her restraints. 'ESSY, WHY, WHY ARE THEY DOING THIS, HELP ME, ESSY!' but a second crack of the whip all but broke her in two, drawing blood and a spluttering gargling cry as she slipped further down the post, sick to the pit of her stomach, reeling and arching her flayed back. 'Essy, why?' she slurred, delirious.

Esther clenched her fist. 'NO MORE!' she screamed toward the Sheik. 'NO MORE!'

'Enough please, your Highness,' the Ambassador echoed whilst many of the onlookers who'd originally relished the spectacle turned away upon hearing Minnie's pitiful cries. 'I beg of you, enough!'

The Sheik raised a hand to halt his henchman momentarily whilst Minnie wept and the sun baked her open wounds. 'Please,' Major Timothy asked once again. 'She has been punished enough, have mercy your Highness, have mercy.'

The Sheik's bloated young son tugged at his father's robes, demanding his attention which reignited his rage at his recent royal ridiculing, therefore with a single swift downward swipe of his hand he signalled with gritted teeth the final lash to be administered.

'God no!' Esther said, shaking her head. 'No, don't do it, don't do it, DON'T YOU DARE, NOT MY MINNIE!' Esther fell to her knees, attempting to crawl to her sister. 'NO, PLEASE NO, NOOOOOOOOO!'

In an unprecedented move the crowd surged to halt the final punishing blow but it was too late, the crack which shattered the sound barrier opened another lengthy swath of Minnie's aged back, causing her to cry piercingly to the heavens before collapsing in a dishevelled heap at the foot of the post.

'Dear Lord,' the Ambassador said, bowing his head with a trembling lip as his wife wept openly on his shoulder, 'Forgive us.'

Esther dragged herself to her feet, her face sodden and make-up streaming. 'Minnie, Minnie, my darling Minnie,' she said, her heart bleeding for her sister 'Minnie.' She ran for several yards with aching bones shoving onlookers aside. 'Get out of my damned way!' she cursed.

Minnie lay slumped at the post with her face in the dirt, unconscious and broken. 'My darling, my darling,' Esther cried, falling beside her, petrified at first to lay a hand on her sibling. Gently she lifted Minnie's face to her lap and wiped away the grit and tears from her eyes. 'Minnie dearest, Minnie, I'm sorry, darling, I'm sorry, I couldn't make them stop, Minnie, believe me I tried.'

'Essy,' Minnie moaned, wincing, 'Help me, Essy.'

Esther turned to glare at the henchman, a cold hard glare of pure hatred. 'Set her free,' she growled. 'Set her free right now or so help me I'll, I'll kill you.'

The Sheik's will had been done therefore Minnie was now a free woman. 'Release her!' he called with a dismissive wave.

Minnie's clenched fists full of dirt were untethered as much of the surrounding crowd dispersed, unnerved at what they had just witnessed. Major Timothy approached the sisters, his wife having fled to their car overcome with emotion. 'Let me help you,' he said stooping at Esther's side. 'God, I'm sorry, Esther,' he confessed. 'I truly am.'

A Saudi woman rushed to the sisters with water, kneeling and ever so gently sponging the dripping blood from Minnie's heavily marked back. 'Thank you,' Esther said with a breaking voice. 'Thank you, my dear.' Another Saudi wrenched the robe from his own back to cover her while a third offered shade from the now searing sun.

Esther looked up at the grief-stricken Ambassador. 'Help me,' she asked pitifully. 'Please.'

'Yes, yes of course,' he replied, kneeling to gather Minnie into his arms. 'Step aside please!' he told the remaining gathering hurrying toward his car. 'Quickly, step aside!'

'My God, Tim,' his wife said caressing Minnie's hair. 'Let's get her home. Come, Esther, we'll take care of the both of you.' Esther and Diana sat with the trembling Minnie in the back of the Ambassador's car whilst he swiftly left the square and drove toward his home in the suburbs; there she was carried inside and

276

laid on the spare room bed on her side. Diana rushed to fetch warm water towels and bandaging whilst Esther lay alongside her sister with her forehead on hers. 'I'm here, darling, I'm here,' she softly said repeatedly. Diana gestured for her husband to leave the room, his white cotton shirt smeared with Minnie's blood. Together she and Esther carefully removed Minnie shredded blouse whilst she moaned and writhed in agony. 'Shh, shh, I know, my darling,' Esther said, caressing her hair. 'I know.'

Minnie's tender aged skin was raised, blistered and beyond recognition in shades of pink, purples and black, unable to withstand such trauma. 'Ess,' she croaked, reaching out a frail hand.

'Lie still, my love,' Esther told her. 'It's over now, you're free, do you hear me, you're free.'

At home in the UK Esther's grandson sat bawling into his hand having witnessed the shared footage; suddenly he lashed out, tossing the coffee table into the air, screaming and cursing at the top of his voice and pounding the sofa over and over with every ounce of venom he could muster. Luckily his mother Elizabeth had been spared the hideous spectacle, recovering from another of her episodes as it were in a secure unit, as had she been privy to the punishment it would surely have enraged her own demons and set her rehabilitation back many months.

Both tributes and condemnation began pouring onto the sisters' social media pages with offers from several billionaires for Minnie to convalesce on their private yachts, Caribbean islands or sprawling Texas ranches. 'Look, dear,' Esther said at her sister's bedside. 'We have an invite to the White House, how thoughtful don't you think?' but Esther's attempts at conversation fell on deaf ears as Minnie lay in a tight ball staring blankly at a vase of gardenias, gripped in a state of severe shock. 'Also, dear, look here,' Esther added. 'Her Majesty the Queen would like us to join her at Balmoral for a spot of tea.'

This outlandish offer and more would, on any other occasion, have Minnie squealing with excitement and rushing to the bathroom to pee, but she remained unflinching, pale in complexion.

'You're more than welcome to stay,' Diana told Esther. 'We have another room.'

'I'll stay here if it's all the same to you,' Esther replied, refusing to leave Minnie. 'We'll be fine, thank you, Diana dear, thank you.'

Diana bent and kissed the pair of them, brushing the hair from Minnie's face. 'I'll pray for you,' she said, clutching the tiny cross which hung around her neck.

Esther joined Diana in the kitchen the following morning. 'I'm worried sick about her,' she told the middle-aged Ambassador's wife. 'She hasn't moved or made a sound the entire night, even at the mention of breakfast, and Minnie never misses breakfast, ever.'

'Oh dear,' Diana said, offering Esther a cup of English tea. 'I hardly slept a wink myself, the poor dear,' and the pair sat and sipped looking equally haggard. 'I've followed your progress with great enthusiasm,' Diana told Esther. 'From your run in with the Russian President, I must say I thought you were both done for, you must be incredibly brave.'

The sisters' previous escapade in the former Soviet Union had landed them in the hottest of waters. 'Oh I don't know about that, my dear,' Esther said modestly whilst examining the quality of the Ambassador's chinaware.

'It's Wedgewood, in case you were wondering,' Diana informed her. 'A wedding gift from Timothy's mother.'

'I'm not brave at all,' Esther confessed. 'My sister, on the other hand, she's a lioness at times I tell you, she has defended me on more occasions than I'd care to remember, but to see her like this, well it breaks my heart, truly it does.'

Diana placed a hand on Esther's. 'She'll bounce back,' she said softly. 'From what I've seen of that formidable woman I'm absolutely certain of it, only the other night Tim and I saw her high board dive on the internet and I'm telling you I felt my head spin just watching her, Tim said you wouldn't get him up there for love nor money.'

Minnie's Belgian board leap from a towering height into a shallow communal pool was still attracting thousands of viewers daily, and the attention of global advertising corporations eager for her to model and of course endorse everything from one-piece bathing costumes to waterproof timepieces, and even skimpy bikinis usually worn by stick thin catwalk queens. 'I tried to stop her,' Esther said, taking a bourbon biscuit and dipping it in her tea.

'Oh thank heavens, you're a dunker,' Diana sighed, observing Esther's ritual and hastily following suit. 'I can't tell you how many dinner parties I've hosted here for our Saudi neighbours and each time I've had to curb my desire to dunk after one incensed woman stormed from the house in disgust accusing me of being in cahoots with the devil and cursing my entire family line.'

'For dipping a biscuit?' Esther said, dunking again. 'If you ask me the woman's a fool, a damned fool.'

'Ohhhh wow' Diana said, biting into her soggy biscuit with a look of sheer bliss on her face. 'I tell you, Esther, there is nothing on God's green earth quite like it, nothing.'

'I quite agree,' Esther replied, reaching for another bourbon.

Minnie remained in a near catatonic state for a further two days with her sister and their hosts growing increasingly concerned for her wellbeing. 'Minnie, love,' Esther said, offering a breakfast tray at her bedside. 'You must eat, my dear, it's for your own good, please, Minnie.' The bruising on her back was in full bloom and would take some time to dissipate as would the mental scars from such a harrowing ordeal. 'Please,' Esther begged, setting the tray down.

Diana appeared with a family friend. 'Esther, I hope you don't mind,' she said, approaching, 'I asked a doctor Tim and I know and asked if he'd take a look at Minnie, he's very good, believe me.'

'Oh, morning, Diana,' Esther said, rising from the bed. 'Yes, yes that's quite alright, good morning, doctor.'

'Good morning, madam,' the doctor replied removing his hat and setting down his bag. 'So this is Minnie?' he added, donning his stethoscope. 'I heard of her punishment and I have to say it mortified me, you have my condolences.'

'Thank you,' Esther said, stepping aside while he bent to examine the motionless Minnie.

'Minnie, my dear,' he said softly. 'I'm just going to place this on your chest if that is OK,' and receiving no reply he proceeded whilst checking her wrist for a faint pulse. 'How long has she been like this?' he asked Esther and Diana.

'Since the…' Esther said, pausing. 'Well you know.'

'The lashes,' the doctor added. 'I see, this is not good, not good at all, we must get your sister to a hospital at once.'

'Hospital!' Esther exclaimed, clinging to Diana's arm. 'Oh no, what is it, doctor?'

'Your sister is sick.'

The doctor replied in no uncertain terms, 'And it is a matter of some urgency so please, Diana, if you would telephone for an ambulance right away, now please, Diana, quickly.'

'Oh heavens yes, yes of course,' Diana said, scurrying from the bedroom leaving Esther wringing her hands at the doctor's side.

'Please, doctor, what's wrong with her?' Esther asked, fussing nervously with the bed sheet. 'What's wrong with my sister?'

'It is too early for an accurate diagnosis, madam,' the doctor replied, packing away his stethoscope. 'But I believe the trauma has weakened her severely, she is not a young woman as you are aware and a shock of this magnitude can put an enormous strain on an elderly body, madam, I believe your sister is losing the will to live, literally.'

'Don't be ridiculous!' Esther blurted. 'My Minnie, losing the will, out of the question, she has more life in her than all of us put together.'

'She did have,' the doctor replied. 'But now look at her, she is withering, her pulse is dangerously low and her pupils are not reacting to my light, in short, madam, there is no more fight in your sister, none whatsoever.'

'Oh God, surely not,' Esther said with a hand to her trembling lips. 'No, no way, doctor I'm telling you she is a fighter, a real fighter, Minnie, Minnie dearest,' she said, stooping to gently nudge her sibling. 'Don't do this darling, please don't do this, it's me, Essy, please, Minnie don't do this not now.' Her heartfelt pleas had no effect on her ailing sister, who appeared more and more withdrawn as time went by.

Soon the ambulance arrived and Minnie was carefully wrapped in her bed sheets and transferred outside by trolley. Diana did her level best to comfort Esther, who had no idea which way to turn, her head a bucket of mixed emotions. 'I'll drive you, Esther,' Diana told her. 'You're in no fit state, my dear.' The two ladies followed closely behind the Saudi ambulance en route to the Mediclinic Dubai hospital and remained close at her side when she was wheeled inside and rushed to a private ward, where a doctor and psychiatrist were waiting to evaluate her; the pair spent some time behind the green curtain surrounding Minnie's bed whilst Esther and Diana paced the ward in opposite directions.

'Oh what are they doing?' Esther asked impatiently. 'Diana dear, what are they doing in there?'

'Please try not to worry, Esther,' Diana told her. 'Minnie is in good hands, I promise you, Timothy was once admitted here with a ruptured appendix that could have quite easily killed him so we were told, but he was home the very next day and eager to return to work, it was nothing short of a miracle, I tell you.'

'A miracle,' Esther mouthed, longing for her sister by her side. 'Do you know, Diana dear,' she said wistfully. 'That fool in there has been a thorn in my side for as long as I'd care to remember but do you know what, I wouldn't trade her for the world or all of the tea in China.'

'I know that,' Diana said with an arm around Esther's shoulder.

The curtain was eventually drawn back and the doctor and psychiatrist stood conferring in a hushed tone. 'Well?' Esther asked, a little irate at being left out of the loop so to speak. 'Are you going to tell me what's wrong with my sister or not?'

'My apologies, madam,' the doctor replied whilst his associate left the room. 'The deep lacerations to your sister's back of course will heal eventually.'

'Well I jolly well hope so!' Esther said, feeling her blood beginning to boil. 'It's nothing short of barbaric, barbaric I tell you, look at her, she's an old woman for God's sake!'

Diana did her level best to restrain Esther. 'Please, Esther,' she said. 'I know you're upset but….'

'Upset!' Esther scoffed. 'Upset, I'm telling you, you don't know the half of it, upset, I'm bloomin' livid that's what I am, livid!'

The doctor attempted to continue. 'As I was saying, madam,' he said respectfully, 'The scars will heal, but as my learned colleague confirmed there has been a great deal of emotional distress, depression even, leading to a sense of hopelessness, in short, madam, it is our opinion that your sister..' he paused to examine his notes, 'Minnie here believes it is her time.'

'Time?' Esther snapped. 'What do you mean, her time, Diana, what's he talking about, what do you mean, doctor, her time?'

'Madam,' the doctor said, approaching. 'In order for the body to fully heal there must first be the will to do so, to go on so to speak, if there is not, then we truly believe that somebody of your sister's age can literally choose when it is their time to die.'

'Die!' Esther shrieked. 'Die, no, no, no, no, no, you're wrong, you're wrong, I tell you, she doesn't want to die, God damn it, examine her again, examine her I say, it's probably influenza or, or..' she said, clutching at straws, 'I said, examine my sister again, her time, I've never heard anything so preposterous in all my life, my Minnie, wanting to die, out of the question, out of the question I tell you, Minnie wouldn't, she, she just wouldn't.'

'Madam,' the doctor again said, resting his hands on Esther's shoulders. 'I will instruct my nurses to take the very best of care of your sister but I must warn you I am sceptical she will respond to our treatment, I have seen this before, several times, and the outcome was always the same.'

'The same?' Esther asked, looking over at her wilting sister. 'Oh dear God, no.'

'Trust me when I say this,' the doctor promised Esther, 'We will do all we can and use everything at our disposal to revive Minnie, that I promise you, now if you'll please excuse me I must go but I will return periodically, I assure you,' and the doctor left the two ladies at Minnie's bedside.

'She can't,' Esther said in despair, 'Diana, she can't, she can't do this.'

Minnie was given a mild sedative and her wounds thoroughly tended whilst her sister refused to leave her side. 'Esther, you need to rest yourself,' Diana told her, equally concerned for her wellbeing. 'And you must eat, you must, you need to remain strong for Minnie's sake, let me take you home I promise I'll bring you back first thing in the morning, first thing, Esther, you have my word.'

'I, I know, Diana,' Esther sobbed. 'I do but, I hate to leave her, my darling, my darling Minnie.'

Whilst Minnie slept soundly and motionlessly, Diana ushered her exhausted sister from the ward and back to her home where she toyed with a bowl of soup in tears until her eyes grew heavy at the dining table. 'Come, my dear,' Diana said, escorting her to bed. 'We mustn't give up hope, I will personally pray for Minnie as I'm sure will Timothy.'

That night Esther cried herself to sleep stroking the spare pillow beside her, even conversing with it as though it were her sister. The following morning Esther rose at the crack of dawn and threw back the sheets with renewed vigour and gritted teeth. 'Ohhhh no, Minnie,' she said, swinging her legs from the bed.

'You're not doing this to me, not yet, not now, not like this I tell you.'

Hurriedly washing, she threw on a change of clothes and scribbled a thank-you note to the Huntley-Palmers and left quietly, clambering behind Vivien's wheel and setting off toward the rising morning sun back in the direction of the hospital. Marching into the foyer having formulated a plan, Esther snatched a vacant wheelchair and made for the elevators. 'Come on, come on!' she cursed, stabbing at the buttons and ascending to the third floor and her sister's ward. 'Right!' she said, throwing back the green curtain around Minnie's bed. 'Enough is enough, Minnie, do you hear me?'

Minnie hadn't moved the entire night and looked every inch a hopeless bundle of rags, her face withered and dark around the eyes.

'You're going to listen to me,' Esther added, prodding at the mattress at Minnie's feet. 'And you're going to listen good, this, this giving up nonsense is going to stop, right now I tell you, right now, I simply will not have it, I won't!' She gently turned down the sheets and brushed the lank hair from Minnie's face. 'I know exactly what you need and believe me this isn't it,' she told her in no uncertain terms. Puffing, blowing and grunting, Esther slipped an arm beneath her sister's neck and behind her knees and proceeded to hoist her from the bed and into the wheelchair.

'Madam!' an approaching nurse said, setting down her medicine tray. 'Madam, what are you doing?'

'What I should have done at the very beginning,' Esther replied, lifting each of her sister's feet onto the rests.

'You cannot, madam,' the nurse protested. 'You cannot take this woman at this precise moment.'

'I can and I will!' Esther growled. 'This woman happens to be my sister and I know what's best for her, me, not you or anybody else in this place for that matter, now get out of my way, we're leaving, right now!'

'But, but madam,' the nurse said, barring her way. 'It is not permitted.'

'Permitted!' Esther said, grimacing. 'Young lady, I'll tell you what's not permitted shall I, it's not permitted for my sister to die that's not what's permitted, now I'm taking her out of here whether you like it or not, do you hear me, I said do you hear me?'

Seeing the whites of Esther's eyes, the student nurse stepped aside as Esther wheeled Minnie out of the ward and along the corridor. 'Trust me, Minnie,' she told her sister, 'I know what's best for you, I always have done, and it's not this, not these meddling fools with their drips and their drugs.' With very few nurses on shift at that hour, Esther encountered very little resistance as she pushed her sister from the hospital and out toward Vivien.

'ESTHER!' a voice suddenly called out. 'Esther, where are you going?' It was Diana and her husband who had raced to the hospital on discovering her note.

'We're leaving,' Esther replied sharply. 'Don't try to stop me, Diana, please don't, I know I'm right, and I know my sister, please, Diana, just help me, will you.'

The Huntley-Palmers looked at one another momentarily before assisting Esther in hoisting Minnie aboard. 'Esther, are you sure?' Diana asked.

'A thousand percent,' Esther replied, fastening her sister's seat belt whilst Minnie stared blankly ahead. 'A thousand percent, Diana, she may be ready to die but I'm not ready to lose her, not now, not while I have a breath in my body.'

'Alright,' Diana said, sensing any attempt at reasoning would be futile. 'Alright, Esther, just promise me you'll take care that's all.' She had grown close to Esther having talked long into the Arab night on occasion, over tea and biscuits, the pair of them dunking shamelessly.

'I will,' Esther replied, wrapping her arms around the Ambassador's wife. 'Thank you, Diana, thank you.'

'Esther, look,' Major Timothy said, producing an envelope from his jacket pocket. 'I received this this morning from the Sheik himself.'

'Really,' Esther sneered at the very mention of the Arab ruler. 'If it's an apology you can send it straight back with a word or two from me.'

'That's exactly what it is,' the Ambassador informed her. 'On reflection his Highness is wracked with remorse.'

'Oh he is, is he?" Esther intervened with venom.

'Yes, yes he is,' the major added. 'He offers safe passage throughout his lands for the both of you should you leave us, he has decreed that none of his subjects should oppose you and even offer assistance where needed. This landmark decision goes against much of Saudi tradition where it is frowned upon for females to sit behind the wheel of a car let alone embark on such lengthy travels. Esther you have his Highness's blessing,' Timothy added. 'I can't tell you how important this is, it means you'll be safe, anywhere within the Arab Emirates.'

'Oh wow, Esther!' Diana said, having faced fierce criticism and an angry mob or two in the past, and the family car stoned on occasion too. 'That's a huge weight off my mind, Esther, I can tell you, when you told me you were crossing to Medina and then on to the Red sea I'll admit I had grave concerns.'

'Hmmm,' Esther merely growled. 'Well if he thinks he's getting any thanks from me,' she told the Huntley-Palmers, 'He's got another think coming,' and she climbed in beside her sister and fastened her own belt.

'Good luck,' Diana said, leaning in to kiss Esther's cheek. 'Goodbye, Minnie my dear.'

Minnie said nothing as Esther waved goodbye and started Vivien. 'Riiiight,' she sighed, settling in her seat. 'Off we go, dear.' She looked across at her sister's solemn face as they left. 'Trust me, big sis knows best,' she told her, although deeply concerned.

The Sheik's royal decree had reverberated far across his lands from the towering heights of the magnificent Burj Al Arab hotel to the humblest of desert hovels. Esther and Minnie in their classic Morris Traveller would be permitted to pass unhindered through towns and cities some eighteen hundred miles across the deserts of Saudi Arabia, watched over as newly-appointed guests of the remorseful Sheik.

'Look, dear!' Esther said pointing out the iconic Jumeirah beach resort and the vast Mall of the Emirates containing of all things a ski centre; she then rummaged behind her whilst slowing for a traffic signal, producing a packet of their treasured pink wafers. 'Wafer, dear?'

she asked. 'OK,' she added, setting them down on the dashboard in front of her sister when receiving no reply, 'I'll just leave them there if it's all the same to you.' Esther's heart sank a little at her sister's refusal of a firm family favourite, perhaps she had regressed too far, what if those heady days of confrontational banter they'd enjoyed were indeed over? But then pulling herself together she flatly refused to throw in the towel 'Didn't Cyril once visit Dubai, dear?' she asked, hoping the mention of her former lover's name would ignite a spark within her. 'You remember, Cyril, don't you darling?' Still nothing. 'Damn you, Minnie, don't you dare do this!' she cursed, growing increasingly anxious. 'Just, just don't do you hear?'

Esther drove for a further hour and a half, attempting occasional conversation before a flash of pure genius crossed her mind, she would play her trump card, the ace in the pack as it were. Rooting inside the glove compartment, she fished out a CD and slipped it into the player, turning up the volume to its maximum and sitting back whilst the all too familiar opening bars of their National Anthem raised the hairs on the back of her neck. Puffing her chest and straightening her back, Esther began to belt out the rousing patriotic song of songs.

'GOD SAAAAVE OUUUR GRAAAAACIOUS
QUEEN
LOOONG LIIIIIVE OUUUR NOOOOBLE
QUEEN
GOD SAAAAVE THE QUEEEEEEN,

Peshwari Nans Part II

'SEEEEEND HER VIICTOOOORIOUS
HAAAAPPY AND GLOOOORIOUS
LONG TOOOO REIIIIGN OVER US
GOD SAAAAAVE THE QUEEEEEEEN!'

Leaving the city and cruising the now empty motorway,
Esther put her foot to the floor, opened her window
and poured every ounce of her being into the anthem.

'HAAAAAAAAPY AND GLOOOOORIOUS!'

Remarkably Minnie's foot twitched as a powerful dose
of national pride was injected directly into her heart.
Esther continued, now in floods of tears, partly for her
beloved country but mostly for her beloved sister she
longed to have back.

'LOOOOONG TOOOO REIIIIGN OVER US
GOD SAAAAAAAVE THE QUEEEEEN!'

'YES, MINNIE, YES!' she then yelled on seeing
Minnie's lips move in time and then the faintest of
audible words. 'Yes, Minnie, you can do it, you can do it
my love, HAAAAPY AAAAAND GLOOOORIOUS!'
Croakily Minnie could barely be heard at first. 'God
saaaave the queeen.'
'YEEEEEEEEEES!' Esther screamed, punching the
air and Vivien's wheel. 'OH GOD, MINNIE,
YEEEEES!' She took her sister's hand and raised it to
the roof.
'GOD SAAAVE OUR GRAAAACIOUS QUEEN!'

291

she sang with her sister now accompanying with increasing vigour.

'LOOOONG LIIIVE OUR NOOOBLE QUEEEN!'

Soon the colour began to return to Minnie's cheeks. 'Essy?' she said, turning her head for the first time that day.

'Yes, my darling, yes it's me,' Esther replied whilst the military drums rolled thunderously and her sister squeezed her hand, attempting a smile. 'Your Essy.'

Minnie cleared her throat in preparation as did Esther when the band reached a deafening crescendo.

'Ready, dear?' Esther asked.

'Of course,' Minnie replied, the two of them tilting their heads back and singing for queen, and country, and above all, family.

'GOD SAAAVE OUR GRAAACIOUS QUEEN
LOOOONG LIIIVE OUR NOOOBLE QUEEN
GOD SAAAVE THE QUEEEEEN,

'SEEEEEND HER VICTOOOORIOUS
HAAAPPY AAAND GLOOOORIOUS
LOOOONG TOOO REIIIIGN OOOVER US
GOD SAAAAAAAVE THE QUEEEEEEEEEEEN!'

'Oh, Minnie my darling!' Esther cried, overcome with raw emotion. 'Minnie, Minnie, my beautiful Minnie.'

Minnie smiled lovingly before catching sight of the pink wafers. 'Oooh!' she chirped, 'for me?'

'Of course,' Esther laughed. 'Every last one of them, dear, every last one.'

Minnie reached, a little stiff at first, but no sooner had she grasped the pink packet than it was second nature for her to tear open one end and remove the wafers two by two. 'Mmmmm, happy and glorious,' she said with sheer delight.

Esther rejoiced in watching her sister devour three quarters of the packet in no time at all before offering them across. 'Oh no,' she said, raising a hand. 'You have them, dear, please, you need them more than I do.'

'You're quite sure?' Minnie asked without pausing to ask again. Soon the entire packet of wafer biscuits had been eaten, leaving a scattering of pink crumbs on Minnie's lap, and she looked across at to Esther.

'Go ahead, dear,' Esther said, letting her standards drop and allowing her sister this single opportunity to brush the crumbs from her knees onto Vivien's carpet. 'Just this once.'

Having expelled more energy than she'd done in previous days, Minnie reclined in her seat, resting her head on Esther's shoulder. 'If you don't mind, Essy dear,' she said, closing her eyes. 'I'm awfully tired.'

'You go right ahead, my dear,' her big sister agreed with the broadest of smiles. 'Take as long as you like.'

CHAPTER FIVE.

Whilst Minnie slept the world was still reeling from her public humiliation and corporal punishment. The subject had seen unprecedented air time with the footage repeated over and over on chat shows from continent to continent. The image of Minnie bent and broken on her knees clutching the post was being shared on social networks at a phenomenal rate. T-shirts, tote bags and billboards served as a visual reminder with women's groups rallying in vast numbers in support of her, and had she perished that very day Minnie would have undoubtedly been hailed a modern day martyr, although having unwittingly brought the whole sorry affair onto herself.

Snoring and turning restlessly, Minnie was unaware of her soaring public profile, In a world where ever-increasing terrorist activity and a devastating war in Syria had dominated the newspapers and airwaves in recent times, planet Earth's populus yearned for a hero or heroine, a rock to cling to in troubled times, and Minnie's willingness to accept her punishment, although under the influence of prison contraband, gave them just that. Minnie in effect had single-handedly boosted the cause for women's rights and equality, causing a surge of feminine pride the world over. Emmeline Pankhurst of the suffragette movement, the charitable Mother Teresa, civil rights activist Rosa Parks and young Joan of Arc, the Maid of Orleans and heroine of France, would have surely wholeheartedly approved of her steadfast defiance, and maybe, just maybe one day after her own eventual demise a sainthood might come Minnie's way, just maybe.

'Darling,' Esther said, nudging her sister to rouse her having driven some two hundred and forty miles, passing through the metropolis of Abu Dabi en route with its ever prominent Ethiad Towers dominating the skyline. Instead of the usual abuse and confrontation suffered by the majority of women drivers in the region, Esther and Minnie had been waved on by smiling Arab men mile after mile, several even rushing to their aid when Vivien laboured on a steep sandy incline. 'Thank youuuuu!' Esther had called, poking a thumb from her window. 'Minnie dearest,' she again said, patting Minnie's knee, 'Hey, sleepy head.'

'Mmmmmmm, Essy, I'm parched, dear,' Minnie said croakily. 'Do you think I could have some water?'

'Of course, dear,' Esther replied with a smile. 'Whatever you want, my darling, I could stop and get us some tea if you'd prefer.'

'No, no, dear, water's fine,' Minnie replied, taking a bottle from her sister. 'I wouldn't want to put you to any trouble, not after what I've already put you through of late.'

'Nonsense, dear,' Esther scoffed. 'That's all forgotten now, besides nobody deserves to be treated in the manner that you were, nobody.'

Minnie sat reflecting on the previous days' harrowing events. 'Sooooo,' she pondered. 'Does that mean I'm forgiven, Essy?' she asked sheepishly.

Esther did no more than pull to the side of the road, tug on the handbrake and turn to confront her sister. 'Minnie,' she said, looking deep into her eyes, 'My darling, there was never anything to forgive, you are my sister and I love you with every bone in my aged body, granted at times you've tested my patience and rattled my cage but we are family, dear, family, so no matter what you do, legal or otherwise I will always be there for you.'

'Always?' Minnie asked, welling up when feeling the warmth of her sister's affection. 'No matter what?' she again asked to clarify the point as though seeking absolution for past misdemeanours.

'Yes, that's what I said,' Esther said, pulling away. 'Why, what have you done?'

'Done?' Minnie asked. 'Oh, oh nothing,' and she turned from her sister to gaze out of the window at the distant rippled dunes.

'Minniiiiie,' Esther probed. 'Come on, out with it, I know you what have you done now?'

'It was merely to pass the time of day, dear,' Minnie confessed, skirting around the subject. 'Nothing more.'

'What was?' Esther pressed, looking down her nose now. 'What was just to pass the time of day, Minnie?'

'The hashish, dear,' Minnie said, wracked with guilt. 'I'm sorry, I knew it was wrong but the other girls they all did it and I foolishly told them I'd tried it all before and that I preferred the harder stuff.'

Esther suddenly burst out laughing. 'And it backfired on you, didn't it?' she chuckled.

'Yes, dear, yes it did,' Minnie replied with an anguished look. 'They came by my cell one evening with a hoard of elicit contraband and even a homemade bubbly hubbly, hubbly bubbly pipe thingy, well by the time they'd left I was as high as a kite, Essy, I can tell you, I'm ever so sorry, dear, and ashamed of myself too.' Minnie's drugs binge with her Saudi cell mates had been as debauched and depraved as ever could be imagined. Having paid off the corrupt night shift guards, the ladies partied in Minnie's cell listening to a pirate rock radio station on a transistor, whilst popping brightly coloured pills and filling the air with a thick smog-like smoke which enveloped the prisoners, turning their legs to jelly and banishing any inhibitions they may have had. Soon Minnie succumbed to the munchies as it were, a hunger like no other, compelling her to plunder the pill tray. 'Well I thought they were jelly beans, didn't I,' she told her sister. Pretty soon Minnie was slumped in a hallucinogenic state with a rigid smile etched on her face, waving at a flying pink unicorn circling the ceiling whilst her acquaintances cavorted semi naked around her, several of them having been handed the death sentence by their ruler therefore living out the remainder of their days as they themselves saw fit and totally disregarding the strict social norm. 'Are you mad at me, dear?' Minnie asked, dropping her head.

'Of course not, darling,' Esther joked, finding the whole thing hilarious. 'You simply weren't yourself at that particular moment in time, and had I been in your shoes I might have done the same.'

Minnie looked at her devoutly conservative sister and the pair both said in unison, 'Maybe not.'

That evening the sisters pulled in alongside a roadside restaurant on the outskirts of Riyadh, the capital and the largest city in Saudi Arabia where a group of cigar-toting Arab men stood brooding in the doorway. Ordinarily at this establishment the women would be expected to use a smaller door to the side but on seeing the sisters approaching the men parted rapidly, stubbing out their cigars and fanning the smoke from harm's way. 'Good evening,' one English speaking gentleman said, bowing courteously before his friends hastily followed suit.

'Good evening,' the sisters each replied, heading inside and turning heads in doing so.

'Table for two please,' Esther asked the maître d', who looked around the restaurant for a fitting table. Suddenly as many as eight tables became available with families finishing their meals on the hoof as it were, only too happy to accommodate the sisters.

'Oh no, that's quite alright,' Esther at first told a couple giving up their seats. 'Please, we insist,' the husband replied. 'We were just leaving anyway.'

'Are you sure?' Esther asked, eyeing the half bottle of champagne remaining in the ice bucket and their barely bitten desserts.

'Quite sure, madam,' the Arab said clutching his stomach. 'We are full, quite full.'

Minnie, still marginally malnourished, immediately took the couple up on their kind offer, lowering herself into the wife's seat and plucking a strawberry from the top of her tartlet. 'Waste not want not,' she said, tucking in greedily.

'Minnie!' Esther remarked, aghast.

'Oh I am sorry, Essy my love,' Minnie said, offering her sister the second strawberry. 'Where are my manners?'

'Where indeed,' Esther sneered.

Minnie devoured the tartlet unhindered. 'It really is rather good, dear,' she told her astounded sister, 'And such a shame to see it go to waste.'

'For heaven's sake put it down!' Esther insisted as two waiters rushed to clear the table for their esteemed guests, having to wrestle the tartlet plate from Minnie's grasp.

'Champagne, dear?' Minnie asked, plucking the dripping bottle from the bucket and filling two glasses.

'Not for me, dear,' Esther replied, vexed but finally allowing her sister an eccentricity or two. 'Can I have the wild mushroom soup to start,' she then told the attentive waiter beside her.

'Mmmmm, me too,' Minnie added, quaffing the free champagne.

'And for your main course?' the waiter asked, bent with pen and pad in hand.

'Ooh look, dear!' Minnie squealed with excitement. 'They have tofu, I'll have the brazed tofu with avocado please, young man,' she told the handsome waiter. 'With sundried tomatoes and pine nuts.'

'I tell you what,' Esther said, humouring her sister for once. 'Make that two of those if you would please.'

'Very good, madams,' the waiter said, turning to leave.

'Oh and errrrrr…' Minnie said, raising a spoon. 'Two more of these delicious tarts, each of course.'

'As you wish, madam,' the waiter nodded.

Minnie polished off the champagne during their starters and ordered another bottle to accompany their main course.

'Not for me, dear,' Esther again refused. 'Could I just have a cup of coffee,' she asked. 'Black please, and in a china cup if you have it.'

During dinner all eyes within the restaurant were on Esther and Minnie and the tongues were well and truly wagging; it was frowned upon for a lady unaccompanied by a man to consume alcohol, but the Sheik had spoken, they were not to be challenged in any way and his word was law above all others. Suddenly though one seated male guest leapt to his feet cursing in Arabic and gesturing wildly toward the sisters, obviously unaware of his Highness's decree. The slathering gentleman in a rage called on his fellow diners to condemn Minnie's abhorrent behaviour, but instead of rallying support amongst his countrymen the aggressor was immediately set upon and bundled outside bodily and informed in no uncertain terms of the error of his ways. He returned moments later, approaching the sisters sheepishly and a tad bruised with his hands clasped together in prayer. 'Please, please forgive,' he begged, fearing the wrath of his ruler. Dropping to his knees, he stooped and grasped Minnie's right foot and repeatedly kissed her patent leather shoe.

'That's quite alright, dear,' Minnie said, finding his behaviour bizarre.

'What's he doing, Minnie dearest?' Esther asked, leaning to one side.

'Taking the shine off of my blasted shoes,' Minnie said, tugging her foot free, 'That's what he's doing!'

'A thousand apologies,' the Arab said, grovelling at her side before removing his own shoe and gesturing for Minnie to beat him about the head.

'Oh no, no, no, no,' Minnie recoiled. 'I couldn't possibly, now please get up you're making a damned fool of yourself, now if you don't mind we'd like a little privacy.'

'That means go away,' Esther reiterated dismissively.

'Of course, of course,' the penitent man said, backing all the way to the door, hurling a fistful of notes at the counter and leaving hastily having narrowly escaped a trip to prison and quite possibly death row.

'Odd fellow,' Minnie remarked.

The main course duly arrived and Esther sat staring down at her plate whilst Minnie tucked in. 'So,' she said, stabbing a morsel with her fork and examining it closely, 'This is tofu, is it?'

'Yes, dear,' Minnie mumbled, enjoying her meat alternative. 'It's packed with protein, gluten free and contains absolutely no cholesterol.'

'No cholesterol, you say!' Esther added, having been warned of her escalating levels by their family doctor. 'Mmmm and tasty too,' she admitted, trying it for the very first time.

'Does that mean you are a convert, dear?' Minnie asked with a wry smile and a diminishing plate.

'Well, I'll take a little more convincing,' Esther replied, remaining ever sceptical. 'But that's not to say I'm not impressed by what I've seen so far.'

Minnie took heart in her sister's decision to not completely dismiss a meat-free existence.

Clearing their plates, Esther and Minnie relaxed amid the busy Arab bustle. 'Dear Lord!' Esther then gasped, sampling her black coffee made with a generous handful of Arabica beans and spiced with cardamom, the mud-like mix clinging to the sides of her cup and providing an instant rush of adrenalin when consumed.

'Are you alright, dear?' Minnie asked, seeing her sister's cheeks flushed, her aging organs suddenly wired to the National Grid as it were.

Esther's dentures rattled in her mouth as she struggled at first to reply. 'I'm, I'm not entirely sure,' she said, dropping several cubes of brown sugar into the brew in an attempt to dull the caffeine overload.

Minnie consumed a further three pounds of assorted fruits whilst her sister looked on, still tingling from her punch-packing beverage and the ever jovial management busily scrubbed their starters, deserts and drinks from the sisters' bill. 'My word, Minnie darling,' said Esther when handing over just a few Saudi riyal for their entire meal. 'The exchange rate is better than I'd expected.'

'Well if I'd have known that, Essy,' Minnie said, slipping her hat on and tying the ribbon beneath her chin, 'I'd have had the raspberry sorbet and melon balls, just to cleanse the palate you understand.'

Esther rolled her eyes, despairing of her sister's perpetual gluttony.

'I, I wonder,' Minnie asked the waiter, 'If I might have that to go?'

'No!' Esther snapped, tugging Minnie to the door which was held open by the smiling manager.

'I trust everything was to your liking?' he asked with a bow.

'Oh yes,' Esther said courteously with Minnie in tow. 'Most agreeable, most agreeable indeed, wasn't it, Minnie dear, Minnie?' She turned to see her sister gratefully accepting a foil wrapped package from the restaurant chef.

'Just a few kitchen scraps, dear,' Minnie informed her with a glint in her eye, 'You know I could never resist a doggy bag.' Back home Minnie's one woman war on waste was near legendary, ever since she was a small child attending the jelly and ice cream parties of her peers she hardly ever left an event empty handed, wrapping remains in paper towels. Minnie often lectured those around on the plight of famine ravaged countries such as Ethiopia and the Sudan having been horrified by news footage showing the skeletal African populous unable to feed their children after yet another failed harvest and little or no prospect of life-giving rains for the foreseeable future.

Esther raised a hand. 'I know what you're going to say,' she said whilst Minnie drew a breath in readiness. 'I am well aware there are those in dire straits at this very moment thank you, I make my donations in the high street and I have the stickers to prove it.' Esther loved her stickers and made a beeline for just about anybody rattling a tin from the cats' home to the badgers' trust; if they were dishing out freebies of any kind she was there popping a few coins in and wearing their badge, sticker or pin with pride before squirrelling them away along with the seven hundred or so others in the top draw of her linen press.

The sisters, now revitalised, travelled the motorways and dusty tracks for almost a thousand kilometres towards Riyadh, stopping on occasion to wonder at the breathtaking desert landscape and capture a photograph or two for posterity, and for their fans around the globe of course who followed their progress in their droves.

One such devoted fan and follower was of course Karl Bodene the now multi-millionaire playboy games developer responsible for the record breaking Gran Thrift Auto designed around the loveable sisters, their classic automobile and their love of tat, trinkets and thrift shops. Relaxing in his giant Jacuzzi along with half of the Miami Dolphins cheerleaders, Karl suddenly leapt to his feet, toppling his expensive champagne into the water. 'THE NANS NEED AN APP!' he shrieked, slapping his own forehead at the onset of yet another eureka moment.

'A nap?' one leggy brunette said at his side, assuming Esther and Minnie were fatigued and road weary.

'No not a nap, AN APP!' Karl replied, wading from the Jacuzzi and snatching his tablet computer from his lounger. 'You heard of Pokémon, right?' he asked the girls.

'Of course!' many of them replied, brandishing their cell phones having downloaded the ground-breaking game. 'Who hasn't?' one of them added.

Karl's mind began to work overtime as he scribbled and sketched. 'Yes, yes, of course!' he said excitedly. 'That's it!' He literally fizzed with excitement. 'We'll have access to the Nans twenty-four-seven with cameras in the car, their hotels and about their persons, users will be able to log in any time day or night for their Nan fix, forget Big Brother, this is bigger, this is NanCam and it's going to rock this world, believe me!' Karl left his California rooftop penthouse and drove his canary yellow Lamborghini at breakneck speed to the seventy-storey hub of Bodene enterprises to call an emergency meeting with his army of software developers, ordering them to drop everything and concentrate solely on NanCam, and after a brief and frantic conversation with Minnie in which she dropped her own tablet twice while her sister was cornering and stuck a toffee wrapper to the screen, he ascertained that they were bound for Cairo and arranged to meet them and install the necessary surveillance equipment.

'What was that all about, dear?' Esther asked when Karl signed off with a hearty wave,

'Something about a Pokeymon,' Minnie replied. 'Whatever that is when it's at home.'

'Pokeymon!' Esther exclaimed. 'Has the boy lost his mind?'

'Quite possibly, dear,' Minnie agreed, getting into an unholy mess with the cellophane sweet wrapper.

They entered Riyadh that evening with the iconic Kingdom centre dominating the rapidly expanding skyline. 'You choose, dear,' Esther told her sister, passing countless opulent hotels, each several floors higher than its neighbour as they headed toward the city centre along the grid-like series of highways and streets. Esther bent to her sisters every whim, still deeply relieved to have her back as close to normal as humanly possible considering her recent traumatic experience, the bruises from which would eventually fade but she would undoubtedly take the emotional suffering with her to the grave.

'Essy,' Minnie said, looking toward the heavens from her window at the hotel's heady heights. 'Would you mind awfully if we found somewhere a little closer to home as it were?'

'Closer to home?' Esther asked. 'Well, well yes of course, dear, if that's what you really want.'

'I do,' Minnie confessed, yearning for the cramped confines of their homely East London tenement. 'It's just…' Minnie stammered, unable to put into words her need to feel grounded and safe, with her sister close at hand and four walls in close proximity.

'I know, dear, I know,' Esther smiled, patting Minnie's knee, having craved the simple things herself on many occasions. 'What I wouldn't give myself,' she added fondly, 'For a pot of tea, a jigsaw and my wingback chair.'

The sisters began extolling the virtues of their hometown and the rooms they shared above the pharmacist that was once Reynolds Greengrocers. 'I miss the rattle of the market traders' trolleys at five in the morning,' Minnie mused having lain in bed listening to the multicultural market come to life. 'Don't you, dear?' On the market there were no ethnic differences, Pakistanis traded alongside Afro Caribbeans and Eastern Europeans, a brotherhood grinding out a living penny by penny and pound by pound.

'Oddly enough I do,' Esther confessed. 'And the tubes on the Met line at the bottom of the garden.' Every five minutes a tube train would arrive or depart from Whitechapel Station and rumble by, rattling the sisters' countless ornaments and tipping their picture frames askew. The trains ferried the lifeblood of the city to and from work, a relentless tube of tired commuters, each and every one of them vying for a precious seat but much of the time clinging to the overhead rail swaying like hanging carcases of meat, nodding to the monotonous beat in their headphones, and in stark contrast from the bubbly market traders outside, these weary travellers barely acknowledged the like-minded human beings beside them.

Choosing to skirt the heart of the Saudi city, the nostalgic sisters ventured further toward the suburbs, finding it difficult if not impossible to decipher the Arab signage on the adjacent businesses. Further and further away from the blinding city neons and accumulated wealth, Esther and Minnie soon found themselves amid the ancient remnants of the real Riyadh with echoes of a bygone era evident at every turn.

'Perhaps we should turn back, dear,' Esther said as the tarmac turned to desert dust beneath Vivien's wheels.

'No, no, this is fine,' Minnie assured her, waving to a small snot-nosed boy at the roadside before his frantic mother ran to retrieve him, giving the Morris a disapproving glare. 'These are our kind of people, dear,' Minnie added.

'Are you quite sure?' Esther asked, unwilling to make eye contact with the loitering locals, in fact she felt quite intimidated when they whispered amongst themselves, pointing in their direction. 'Minnie, please,' she urged. 'Let's go back, there was a perfectly charming tower block in town.'

'Have faith, Essy,' Minnie said, at ease and untroubled.

'Faith!' Esther sneered. 'A fat lot of good that'll do when you're having your throat slit by these, these…'

'Stop the car!' Minnie said, having heard enough of her sister's protestations. 'Essy, stop the car!'

'Here?' Esther said, slowing alongside a crowd of serious looking individuals. 'Are you out of your mind?'

'No, dear,' Minnie replied, flinging open her door forcing Esther to slam on the brakes.

'Minnie, what in God's name are you doing?' Esther said angrily.

But Minnie was out of the car and approaching the Arab gathering in no time.

'Minnie!' Esther barked, leaning across her sister's seat. 'Minnie, will you please get back in the car at once, Minnie, what are you doing?'

'Cooeeeeee!' Minnie chirped confidently. 'Lovely day!'

Esther once again rolled her eyes, her heart pounding in her chest.

'I say!' Minnie smiled. 'I was wondering if any of you kind gentlemen could point my sister and me in the direction of a suitable boarding house?'

The Arabs, predominantly men with the exception of a scattering of children and assorted livestock roaming free and untethered, at first said nothing.

'Oh helloooo,' Minnie said to an inquisitive goat that gently butted her bottom.

'Minnie, for Pete's sake!' Esther called, not daring to leave Vivien.

'Come away!'

'Boarding house?' Minnie reiterated to the non-English-speaking gents who murmured amongst themselves, looking Minnie up and down and over her shoulder at Esther, who quickly sat bolt upright averting her eyes. 'We are wanting a bed for the night you see,' Minnie explained. 'Nothing too fancy mind, a simple B&B will suffice.'

The Arabs picked inquisitively at Minnie's floral clothing, causing her sister's heart to skip a beat or two. 'Oh God!' she gasped, fearing for Minnie's life yet again, but as always Minnie remained unfazed.

'Hello, my darling,' she said, ruffling the hair of a young girl who instinctively clung to her leg. 'My word look at you,' she added, bending to swipe her fringe from her hazel eyes. 'Aren't you beautiful, like an angel, yes, that's it you're an angel, my dear.'

Esther clasped a hand to her mouth. 'Dear Lord, what is she doing?' she asked, stealing a sideways glance. 'The dammed fool.'

'Now where was I?' Minnie said, straightening her back with a groan. 'Oh yes, we'd like a bed for the night,' and she clasped both hands to the side of her head to indicate sleep.

'Ahhhhhhh,' several of the Arabs said with a smile and began pointing along the dirt road to a simple dwelling with a crudely painted white post hammered into the ground outside.

'There?' Minnie asked 'That's a boarding house it is?'

The men rambled in Arabic, pointing and patting Minnie's back while the child toyed with her bracelets. 'Oh OK, thanks awfully,' Minnie smiled, slipping a rubber band from her wrist. 'Here you are, my darling,' she said, handing it to the girl. 'That's for Barnardo's, wear it with pride, won't you.'

309

The girl ran to her elder sibling to show off her gift with the children's charity motto, 'Believe in children' stamped on either side. 'What a charming bunch, dear,' Minnie said, climbing back in alongside her shell-shocked sister and waving goodbye to the village folk.

Esther hastily reached across and tugged Minnie's door closed, locking it in the process, still very much unconvinced.

'Right then, dear,' Minnie said, directing her sister some fifty yards toward the white spattered post. 'I have it on good authority that we may find suitable board and lodgings here, Essy.'

'Here?' Esther again asked, stopping to peer beneath Vivien's sun visor. 'You've got to be kidding, Minnie dearest.'

'Yes, dear, here,' Minnie replied as confident as ever. 'Oh come now, Essy,' she added, taking her sister's wrist. 'Whenever did you become such a snob, didn't we once share a room with four cousins and our great grandparents?'

'Well, well, yes but,' Esther was forced to agree, 'That was before we were evacuated, dear, a long, long time ago.'

During late spring of 1940 it was deemed necessary under the codename of Operation Pied Piper to remove the sisters, their friends and their classmates from their homes and families and transport them, many by steam locomotive, to safer pastures far away in rural England for their own protection and to safeguard future generations whilst London was being heavily pounded by the German Luftwaffe during the Blitz as it was called.

Esther at the time went with minimal fuss, but Minnie being terribly close to her father kicked up a riot at King's Cross railway station on the morning of their departure, and she tore the gas mask from her side and threw it to the floor, stamping her feet with reddened cheeks and floods of tears. 'It's alright, my darling,' her father said, scooping her up into his arms. 'Essy will take good care of you, won't you, Essy?'

'Yes, Father,' Esther agreed, rolling her eyes at her blubbering sister.

Minnie's father hugged her tight. 'It won't be for too long, I promise,' he assured her.

'No, no, I won't go!' Minnie said, kicking out. 'I want to stay with you, Father, please,' and she flung her arms around his neck and clung as tightly as she could. 'Please, please, Father!'

'ALL ABOAAAAAAAARD!' was the station master's cry signalling their impending departure, followed by his shrill whistle.

'Minnie Moo, you have to go, darling,' her father said, choked up himself while their mother buttoned Esther's coat.

'Now you take real good care of Minnie, won't you,' she said, mopping her own tears with a red spotted handkerchief. 'Don't forget to read her her story every night, please, Essy, there's a good girl.'

'I will, I promise, Mummy,' Esther said, tugging at her sister's foot. 'Come, Minnie,' she urged, 'It'll be a grand adventure, just like Father said.'

Their father wrenched the reluctant Minnie free and kissed either cheek. 'I promise, darling,' he told her, choking back a tear himself. 'I promise you'll be home real soon, you will, Minnie Mooo, you will.'

Mrs Harrogate the class tutor began gathering the children together. 'Esther, Minnie!' she called. 'Come now, children!'

Their mother pulled her girls back to her breast and pressed a lingering kiss to their foreheads before their hands were taken by Mrs Harrogate. 'We must stay together, girls' she told them, nodding politely to the parents and heading her brood to the train with Minnie still screaming her objections.

'NOOOOOO, I DON'T WANT TO, I DON'T WANT TO!' she cried, stretching out a hand toward her waving father, 'DADDYYYYY, DADDYYYYY!'

Their parents clung to one another as did dozens of others lining the platform, their hearts breaking watching their children leave, their life blood. Hanging from the open windows upwards of a hundred children waved excitedly to their parents and older siblings, except Minnie, that is, who bawled constantly as the iron wheels began to turn, slowly at first whilst anxious parents filed to the very end of the platform waving handkerchiefs, hats and newspapers.

During these troubled times a staggering three and a half million children were shipped out of the war-torn capital to pastures new. Esther eventually dragged her sobbing sister from the window and coaxed her to sit with a packet of aniseed twists. 'Take two, Min,' she urged with her sister's eager hand fishing inside the paper bag. 'Here,' she then said, thrusting Minnie's gas mask back onto her lap. 'Remember what Father said, we must carry these at all times, all times, Minnie, do you hear?'

Minnie peered once again from the window, sucking her boiled sweet noisily. 'But why?' she asked, tugging the mask from its box and pulling it over her face and checking her reflection. 'Are the Germans coming?' She'd heard the exaggerated horror stories in the school playground and often woke in the middle of the night in a sweat calling for her father.

'Yes, yes they are,' Esther informed her, strapping her own mask to her face and sitting alien-like beside her sister attempting to read her prized copy of *Swallows and Amazons* published in 1930 and written by Arthur Ransome who went on to write a series featuring a group of adventurous children indulging in outdoor pursuits during their school holidays. A gift from her mother, the book very rarely left Esther's side. She would lie awake late at night beneath the bed sheets with her father's heavy battery torch, reading the same chapter over and over, memorising it word for word.

Arriving many hours later at Kingsbridge in Devon amid a puff of steam, the awestruck children alighted, the majority of them never having further from their homes than their primary schools. There the children were met by local families and childless couples willing to take in the young refugees. Esther and Minnie were chosen to be billeted with Mr and Mrs Bramley of Netherlock Farm, a mile and a half from town.

The Bramleys, a middle-aged God-fearing couple, ran a modest small holding growing fruits and vegetables to assist with the war effort as well as their numerous livestock, many of them being household pets rather than commodities. There was Churchill the bull who stomped angrily in a field of his own, snorting and charging anyone brave enough to enter his half acre kingdom. Martha and Cedric the Muscovy ducks and their endless flocks of little ones trundled behind them, Clarence the rescued Welsh pit pony and Gwendolyn the goat, who assumed without a shadow of a doubt she was a dog, venturing inside at every opportunity to share the Bramleys' supper and curl in front of their log fire, rolling to have her tummy rubbed.

'Now, children,' Mrs Bramley said to the girls who were packed onto the back of their cart pulled by Clarence. 'Mr Bramley and I have fixed up the attic room for the pair of you so you can feel right at home. 'Peter, that's Mr Bramley, has cleverly constructed two cots from apple crates and I've stitched you a pair of polka dot curtains, you'll have the run of the farm while you're with us, but you'll also be expected to help with the chores too, mind.'

'Yes, Mrs Bramley,' Esther said as though in class.

Mrs Bramley looked down at Minnie for a similar reply but Minnie remained tight-lipped 'Do I make myself clear?' she asked, stooping to look Minnie in the eye.

Esther leaned across her sister. 'Yes, Mrs Bramley,' she said, answering for her sibling. 'She misses Father terribly, that's all,' she explained.

'Oh,' Mrs Bramley replied, sitting upright. 'I see, well that's understandable I suppose, but nevertheless you'll be expected to earn your keep.'

During their first night at Netherlock Farm Minnie refuse to unpack, assuming she would be returning home the very next day; she sat at the tiny attic window wiping away the dust and looking out across the moonlit cabbage and cauliflower fields clutching the book her sleeping sister had read to her.

Hardly eating a morsel at breakfast the following morning, Minnie sobbed again when told that she would remain with the Bramleys for the foreseeable future.

Trudging in Wellington boots around the farm behind her enthusiastic sister, the lack-lustre Minnie became increasingly withdrawn despite the Bramleys' repeated attempts to integrate her into their humble family life. Esther happily helped with the harvesting of the crops and feeding of the animals whilst her sister toyed with the ragged teddy her father had given her for her previous birthday until one afternoon Esther let out a cry, 'Minniiiiiiie!' having discovered her sister missing from the hay bale on which she usually sat. 'Minniiiiie, where are you?' Esther ran to the Bramleys' kitchen where husband and wife were sharing a pot of tea. 'Minnie's gone!' she said, bursting through the door and startling the couple. 'My sister's gone, you must come quick, I can't find her!'

'Oh don't be daft,' Mrs Bramley said, setting down her mug and peering from the window. 'She can't have gone, silly.'

The three of them searched the farmhouse from top to bottom before venturing to the farm's outbuildings calling Minnie's name, but to no avail. 'Oh dear,' Mrs Bramley eventually said after some thirty minutes. 'Darling, do you think perhaps we ought to telephone the police?' she asked her husband as he descended the hay loft ladder.

'Perhaps we should, my dear,' a red faced and wheezing Mr Bramley replied, 'I just hope she hasn't wandered down to the bottom field, that's all.'

'You mean….' his wife replied with a hand to her mouth. 'With Churchill!' The Bramleys scurried from the barn with Esther close behind, yelling at the tops of their voices, 'MINNIIIIIIIE, MINNIIIIIIIE!'

Anyone foolhardy enough to enter Churchill's paddock soon lived to regret it with the three-thousand-pound bull charging them down aggressively, intent on running them through with his blunt but menacing horns. 'MINNIIIIIIIIIE!' the Bramleys and Esther called, racing as best they could down the lane flanked with dry stone walling before rounding the bend and clutching the five-bar gate to Churchill's paddock. 'What the?' Mr Bramley said, clutching his chest as did his wife. The sight that greeted them beyond the gate positively bowled them over. 'Minnie, love!' Mr Bramley called. 'My God, girl, what are you doing in there?' Several yards on the opposite side of the gate Minnie sat in the knee-length grass happily plucking wild flowers with the hulking bull lying at her side with three daisy chains strung around his broad neck and a posy of crimson poppies platted into his forelock.

'Well I'll be blowed,' Mrs Bramley said, mopping her brow, flabbergasted to say the least. 'Girl, what on earth?'

'Minnie love, come away!' her anxious husband called. 'It's not safe in there, I tell you, Churchill's a baaad, baaad bull so he is.'

'He's not bad, Mr Bramley!' Minnie called back, completing a fourth daisy chain and setting it around the seemingly docile animal's neck. 'He's just lonely, that's all.'

'Don't be daft, girl!' Mr Bramley said, beckoning and reluctant to enter the paddock. 'Please, come away will you, he's a cantankerous old so and so, I'm telling you,' but Minnie refused to leave her newfound friend.

Minnie and Churchill both found something within one another that hazy summer's afternoon at Netherlock farm, and formed a bond that would remain unbroken for the remainder of Minnie's stay until it was deemed safe enough for the sisters to return to London and their frantic parents, and when the two finally parted there were more tears on Minnie's behalf than when she'd arrived.

'Do you remember Churchill, dear?' Minnie asked with great fondness at her sister's mention of the evacuation. 'And Mr and Mrs Bramley of course?'

'Yes, yes I do,' Esther smiled, reluctant to leave the car. 'You and that bloomin' cow were inseparable if I remember rightly.'

'He was a bull not a cow,' Minnie reminded her sister. 'Churchill was a bull and he was my friend.'

'Oh I have no doubt about that, my dear,' Esther agreed, 'as I recall you sat and read to that creature day in and day out while I worked my fingers to the bone picking those damned cabbages.'

Before her unlikely encounter with the Bramleys' bull Minnie's reading had been poor to say the least, but she'd memorized much of *Swallows and Amazons* from her parents' countless bedtime tales and sat with Churchill amid those wild flowers for days and weeks reciting the story, struggling at first with the long words but eventually cracking the code to fluent recital. Churchill listened intently watching his young friend's lips moving, sometimes sleeping at her side with her head resting on his neck as she rambled on, oblivious to the war raging in her home town many miles away.

Minnie stepped from Vivien. 'I'll get the bags, dear,' she told her sister.

'Oh, darling,' Esther said, leaning across her seat. 'Do we have to?'

'Essy!' Minnie snapped, looking back inside. 'We're stopping here and that's that, so I suggest you get a move on before all the best rooms are taken.'

Esther looked around for the hordes of holiday makers beating a path to the lowly guesthouse, but of course there were none. 'Best rooms!' she sneered, eyeing the tattered hessian drapes billowing through the open window. 'Minnie, please, darling, let's try a little further down the road.'

Minnie merely turned, nudged open the creaking and crudely crafted gate and tottered toward the door.

'Minniiiiie' Esther moaned, wrenching at Vivien's handbrake and stepping from the car. 'Ohhhh alright, have it your way,' she added, stomping after her sister.

'Helloooooooo!' Minnie said when an elderly Arab woman, possibly ten years their junior, answered her repeated knocking. 'Oh hello,' she added with a smile. 'My sister and I would like a room for the night if at all possible please, have you anything available?'

Esther crossed her fingers behind her back hoping for a negative response, but the shabbily dressed proprietor of the humble boarding house recognised the sisters immediately, and clasped her hands to her head and let out a harrowing cry.

'What on earth?' Esther asked, ducking behind her sister. 'Minnie, whatever did you say to her?'

'Nothing I…..' Minnie replied as the landlady flung her arms into the air and then around her. 'I merely asked for a room, Essy' she added whilst being repeatedly kissed about the cheeks by the distraught woman. 'Whatever's wrong, my dear?' Minnie asked. 'My apologies if we've offended you in any way.'

'No, no, no, no, no, no, no!' the woman cried, shaking her head. 'No offend, no offend, I see you!'

'What is she talking about, Minnie?' Esther asked, totally bemused, finding the whole thing bizarre. 'What's the matter with her, we just want a room, my dear!' she said over the constant wailing. 'But if there's a problem we'll leave.'

'No, no, no, no, no, no, no leave!' the Arab said, sobbing now. 'I see you, I see you!' she said as she mimicked Minnie's recent corporal punishment having vehemently opposed the sentencing, considering it a shame on the Arab people as a whole. 'I sorry, I sorry!' she said, raising Minnie's hands to her lips. 'I sorry for you!'

'Shhhhhh, it's alright,' Minnie said, attempting to calm the repentant Riyadh resident. 'It's not your fault, my dear, you have nothing to be sorry for I assure you, I'm fine, honestly.' Although Minnie was still far from fine mentally and perhaps physically she couldn't bear to witness the woman's guilt-ridden grief. 'Shhh, shh, shh, honestly I'm fine,' she reiterated. 'Aren't I, Essy?'

Esther's mind had wandered momentarily as she eyed the face of a small child at the window. 'ESSY!' Minnie snapped, 'I'm fine, right?'

'What, oh, oh yes, yes of course,' Esther replied eagerly. 'Are you, dear?' she then asked her sister.

Minnie glared at Esther whilst comforting the sobbing woman. 'Now, do you have a room, my dear?' she asked, lifting the landlady's chin. 'Nothing too grand, we aren't fussy, are we, dear?"

'Grand?' Esther said under her breath, looking about the place with trepidation. 'Oh no, we're not fussy at all,' she reluctantly agreed.

'A room, yes, yes!' the owner happily replied, leading Minnie inside. 'Come, come!' she beckoned to her hesitant sister.

'Helloooo,' Esther said to the young boy inside aged between three and four when he raced to greet her, brandishing a die cast aeroplane. 'Your grandson?' she asked the landlady.

The Arab woman nodded and ushered the boy away with a cursory word.

'What a dear little thing,' Esther remarked watching the lad scurry to his room steering the aeroplane above his head.

'Please, please,' the Arab woman said, directing the sisters to a side room.

'Oh' Esther said, peering over her sister's shoulder into the bright and airy room, painted in brilliant white with one or two pieces of contemporary furniture dotted about the place with a sprawling and ever so inviting double bed in the centre. 'Wow, this'll do just fine, thank you,' she told their subservient host,

Minnie again glared at her sister for having pre-judged the place. 'In fact,' she told the owner, 'I'd go so far as to say it's gorgeous, simply gorgeous, my dear.' Minnie took great joy in watching her sister squirm and eat her words 'Essy?' she asked, coaxing a little more from Esther.

'Yes well em,' Esther eventually agreed, 'Perhaps I was a little hasty.'

'Hmmmmm!' Minnie agreed. 'I think you'll find presumptuous is a more accurate description, wouldn't you, dear?' she asked.

'Yes, yes, alright!' Esther barked, barging past her sister and setting down her case. 'Thank you, my dear,' she told the hovering owner. 'This is more than adequate.'

'Precisely,' Minnie wholeheartedly agreed as their host left the room.

Exhausted and emotional from recent events, the sisters left their cases where they were dropped and both stretched out on the bed for a cat nap, Minnie remaining on her side with tender scar tissue hampering her movements.

But merely fifteen minutes later Minnie stirred, unable to sleep fully. 'Oh hell,' she remarked, swinging her legs to the side and heaving herself upright whilst her sister slept soundly. Venturing out into the hallway, Minnie looked either way. 'I sayyyy!' she called, peering into the kitchen and finding the owner kneading dough at the table. 'I thought I might take a bath if that's alright with you, my dear,' she said politely. 'Could you please point me in the right direction?' After a blank expression in reply Minnie reiterated, 'A bath, you know, washy washy.'

'Ahhhhh,' the Arab woman said, wiping the flour from her hands onto her apron. 'Yes, yes I fix for you, I fix for you,' and with that she filled a large copper kettle at her stone sink and hoisted it up onto the hotplate of her Aga. 'Come, please,' she smiled, taking Minnie's hand and leading her to a spacious and equally white en-suite devoid of all furnishings save for a tin bath in the middle of the room.

'My word, this takes me back,' Minnie confessed, kicking off her shoes and running a hand along the turned galvanised rim. Whilst Minnie undressed the woman ferried urns of cold water from the kitchen and the occasional copper kettle, gradually filling the tub. Minnie stood covering her privates whilst Dead Sea salts and minerals were added to the water along with a scattering of garlic and lavender flowers picked from her sparse garden. 'How lovely,' Minnie remarked, lifting a leg into the tub. After another pitcher of cold water was added, Minnie gingerly lowered herself down into the steaming tin tub. 'Ahhhhhhh,' she sighed with a look of ecstasy on her face. 'Now that, my dear,' she told their host, 'Is sheer heaven.'

The landlady then clasped her hands to her mouth upon seeing the lengthy lash marks across Minnie's back. 'No, no, nooooo,' she said reaching with a gossamer touch, then as Minnie's mother had done countless times the woman knelt beside the tub, reached for the sponge and a block of soap and proceeded to ever so gently wash her.

'Oh, thank you,' Minnie said, taken aback. 'But I assure you, my darling, that really isn't necessary.'

'Please,' the woman replied remorsefully. 'Please, I do,' as though to atone for her leader's wrongdoings she begged to attend to her cherished guest. 'Please.'

'Very well,' Minnie said, closing her eyes and freeing her mind whilst her heartbroken host worked the sponge into a lather and squeezed a cascade of water down her back, weeping silently to herself with the bitter memories of her late abusive father prevalent in her mind and the strap he took to her own back as a young girl for the most innocent of misdemeanours leaving clear evidence even to that day. 'Hey, hey, hey,' Minnie said taking her hand. 'What's wrong, my dear, you really don't have to do this, I'm fine, honestly, it's not your fault, my darling, really it isn't,' but the scars of domestic violence ran deep within the hostel owner. 'I tell you what,' Minnie added, attempting to lighten the sombre mood. 'Why don't you fix us both a nice cup of tea, you do have tea, don't you, I'm sorry I didn't catch your name, my dear, your name?'

'Samir,' her host replied, 'I am Samir.'

'Samir,' Minnie echoed. 'How lovely, well, Samir,' she added, offering a dripping hand, 'I'm Minnie, and sleeping beauty in the other room is Esther.'

'Esther,' Samir replied. 'And Minnie.'

'Yes, that's right,' Minnie smiled. 'Now, how about that tea?'

'Tea, tea yes, yes,' Samir said, clambering to her feet. 'I make for you tea.'

Whilst Minnie relaxed although unable to fully recline, Esther slept like a queen emotionally fatigued at having stood by and watched her sibling's gruesome torture, an image burnt deep into her subconscious and one that would haunt her for years to come. In fact Esther slept the entire evening and night while her sister and Samir sat at the kitchen table, sharing pot after pot of hot sweet tea and tales of their respective homelands as Samir's boisterous grandson, orphaned when her only son and his wife were killed when a flight they were taking from Dubai to Bahrain suffered a critical engine failure and came down in the desert killing all one hundred and eighty people on board. 'Oh, I'm so terribly sorry, Samir,' Minnie said on hearing of the tragedy, as she reached across and took the woman's trembling hands in her own. 'And your husband?' she asked.

'Husband has gone,' Samir said, gesturing to the door.

'Gone?' Minnie asked. 'You mean he left you?'

'Husband gone,' Samir again said, refusing to elaborate; in fact her husband of some fifty years had been dogged by the mentally crippling condition of dementia, and as is common the world over in poorer parts his ailment went untreated and worsened rapidly until one late afternoon during the festival of Eid, which marks the end of a month of fasting for Ramadan, he left the family home and wandered aimlessly for hours and hours eventually straying into open desert calling for his mother and father who had both been dead for more than twenty years. A search party of concerned friends and neighbours was hastily mobilised but returned dejected after a full day and much of the night. Samir's husband was never found; disorientated, delusional and dehydrated he'd collapsed a staggering fifteen miles from home and his body was engulfed by the shifting sands.

Minnie later returned to bed and slipped in beside her contented sister, the pair waking the following morning a little after seven-thirty. 'Morning, dear,' Minnie said, stretching out her arms having changed into her pyjamas.

'Morning?' Esther exclaimed, looking over her shoulder. 'What do you mean, morning?' She eyed her sister's attire and then her own.

'Morning!' Minnie reiterated, swinging her legs clear of the bed once again and standing to open the timber shutters to greet the rising sun. 'Rise and shine, sleepy-head.'

'But, but…' Esther said, bewildered and rubbing her eyes. 'It can't be morning, surely not.'

'Yes, dear, it is,' Minnie informed her. 'Now shall I ask Samir to run you a hot bath to get those old bones of yours going, I can highly recommend it.'

'I'll give you old bones, you cheeky mare,' Esther growled attempting to rise. 'Ooooh, actually,' she added, rubbing her back, 'That wouldn't be such a bad idea after all, would you mind, Minnie?'

'Not at all, Essy,' Minnie replied, having sampled the healing properties of the Dead Sea salts herself.

Leaving Esther to fully regain consciousness, Minnie joined Samir in the kitchen again where she was preparing breakfast for her grandson. 'Morning!' she chirped, ruffling the boy's hair and still wearing the brightly coloured pyjamas she'd purchased at a Mumbai street market.

'Good morning, Minnie,' Samir replied whilst stirring a pot of porridge oats, 'I fix for you breakfast.'

'Oooh, just a little toast for me please, Samir,' Minnie replied eyeing her host's selection of potted preserves perched precariously upon a crooked shelf. 'I wonder, do you have greengage by any chance?' She was unable to decipher the Arab labelling.

'Greengage?' Samir said quizzically.

'Yes, greengage, my dear,' Minnie replied, plucking a random pot. 'It's a fruit, my dear, Aunt Maud used to grow them in a butler's sink beside the outside lavatory.'

'No, no, no,' Samir said, setting the boy's breakfast before him 'Is mango, pineapple and orange.'

'Orange, you say?' Minnie said, swapping pots. 'Like marmalade, you mean?'

'Is orange,' Samir once again said, having never heard of the classic British breakfast spread.

'Oh and might I trouble you, Samir,' Minnie added, wrestling with the lid. 'To fix my sister a bath, the poor dear's as stiff as a board at this hour of the day.'

Esther trudged into the kitchen, bleary-eyed 'Mmmmorning,' she said with a lengthy yawn. 'Good morning, little man.'

During her own spell in Samir's tin tub, Esther moaned and groaned with sheer delight sinking to submerge her shoulders as the soothing salts freed her crotchety muscles and joints. 'My word, Minnie, that was divine, dear,' she eventually said, emerging with a towel wrapped around her torso and another tied turban-like about her head.

'Isn't it just,' Minnie agreed. 'And Samir here has very kindly given us a box of her salts to take with us, isn't she the sweetest?'

'Indeed she is,' Esther said, stooping to pluck the boy's plane from the floor and setting it beside him.

'Look, dear, marmalade,' Minnie informed her sister, biting into her slice of toast.

'Is orange,' Samir said, slipping another plate of golden brown toast across the table toward Esther. 'Please, sit,' she added.

'Ooooh, thank you,' Esther said, wide-eyed. 'I'll be honest, Samir,' she confessed. 'I had my doubts about this place, but that just goes to show appearances can be deceiving, by the way,' she added, looking about the place, 'Where are your other guests, this place is charming you must be inundated with reservations.'

'Guests?' Samir replied, having struggled of late to make ends meet. 'Is no business.'

'Ohhh no,' Minnie sighed, glancing across at the boy's tattered and dated Ninja Turtles T-shirt. 'That's such a shame, this place is a positive oasis, isn't it, Essy dear?'

'Yes, yes it is, an oasis,' Esther agreed. 'It's quite heavenly.'

Packing to leave, the sisters looked at one another and smiled in agreeance before leaving a more than generous tip and a packet of Parma Violets on the bedside table. 'Thank you again, my darling,' Minnie told Samir at the door. 'Now please don't worry, I've had a word with Mister Google and recommended your charming rest house, so pretty soon I have no doubt you'll be inundated, dearie.'

'Yes thank you, Samir,' Esther echoed. 'And the very best of luck to you, goodbye, my sweet,' she added, stooping to kiss the boy's head at her side.

Peshwari Nans Part II

Waving theatrically the sisters stowed their bags and boarded Vivien. 'BYYYYYYE!' they called whilst Esther turned the key. 'THANK YOUUUUU!'

Leaving Riyadh and starting out on the desert road, Esther and Minnie settled in their seats. 'I don't mind saying, dear,' Esther told her sister while wriggling her shoulders. 'I feel bloomin' marvellous.'

Minnie's travel advisory report on Samir's guest house was already attracting attention as by now an endorsement from the Peshwari Nans meant big business for those concerned, and as she had quite rightly informed the grandmother, tourists would be hot-footing it to her door eager to retrace the Nans' steps. Already savvy travel companies had put together 'The Peshwari Package' tracking Minnie and Esther's route from London to Raipur and beyond, with wealthy retirees clambering over their walking frames to emulate the efforts of the gutsy sisters, albeit from the relative comfort of an air-conditioned tour bus with eager guides narrating the tale at each and every stop along the way, from the French male lavatory where Minnie had become trapped with chanting footie fans, to Germany's Nurburgring race track where the two had wandered through the night lost in the surrounding woodland following Minnie's hapless orienteering. The Belgian municipal baths were now also a popular tourist hotspot with very few, if any daring to repeat Minnie's now legendary high board dive. Monique and her lusty father Ludvik had also benefitted from having encountered the sisters at their Polish chateau, escorting paying guests to the secret garden where Esther had painted the nude portrait of her sister which had been replicated and sold as postcards along with Monique's homemade spirit in their hastily constructed gift shop.

All in all the tour was a resounding success with pre-bookings stretching several months into the future and one day soon Samir would receive her very own slice of the lucrative pile.

Instead of waning, the media interest surrounding the Peshwari Nans thundered on like an unstoppable freight train obliterating any supposed ground-breaking scoop that dare to oppose them and vie for the coveted from pages.

The sisters' onward journey would take them a blistering 860 kilometres across the Saudi heartlands, diverting to several much needed watering holes en-route and again receiving willing assistance from the Sheik's subservient subjects, two camel herders helping to reattach Vivien's rear chrome bumper which rattled loose over a period of time on the punishing desert roads.

Situated to the east, a mere 120 kilometres from the coast and the Red Sea beyond lay Medina, or the Radiant City as it is also known and famously containing the Prophet's mosque, the place where Muhammad was laid to rest, a city second only in religious terms to Mecca itself. Housing some one and a half million inhabitants with perhaps its most famous landmark being the green dome beneath which Muhammad was buried, Medina was originally a walled fortress surrounded by high towers and gates to guard against the warring Meccan forces who'd sought to overrun the city on several occasions in such skirmishes as the famous Battle of the Trench in the year 627.

As with Mecca it was strictly forbidden for non-Muslims to enter the sacred city core and the sisters would do well to remember that having already felt the wrath of the Saudi Sheik.

'Pickle, dear?' Minnie asked, fishing their jar of preserved shallots from behind her seat and prodding at the bobbing onions with her bony fingers. 'Oh blast!' she cursed when their mother's wedding ring slipped from her finger and sank to the bottom of the pickle jar. 'Damn it!' she added, holding the jar aloft to locate the treasured possession which had been the sorest of sore points between her and Esther for many years.

'What have you done now?' Esther asked. 'It's the ring isn't it?'

'No, no, no, no,' Minnie said, concealing the jar whilst rummaging through the tight glass neck.

'Yes it is!' Esther insisted. 'I told Mother, I told her, don't give it to Minnie she'll only lose it, and you have on several occasions, haven't you, if my memory serves me right, I should have been given it instead of you.'

'Well Mother gave it to me,' Minnie said smugly whilst unable to reach the pickled ring. 'And you've always resented me for it, haven't you, Essy.'

'Yes!' Esther blurted. 'Yes I have, because, Minnie, you being the absent-minded fool that you are have managed to lose our mother's wedding ring a grand total of five times, haven't you, haven't you?'

'Well,' Minnie said, with very little to offer in the way of defence, 'Yes but....'

'Yes!' Esther snapped. 'Mother would turn in her grave if she only knew, five time, Minnie, five times for heaven's sake!'

'It's never five times,' Minnie protested, licking the vinegar from her fingers and wincing. 'Are you sure you wouldn't like a shallot, dear?' she added, attempting to change the subject.

'Five, Minnie, five!' Esther raged, refusing to be swayed. 'Would you like me to remind you, well I'm going to anyway, once down the back of the sofa, another time down the back seat of your boyfriend's Triumph Herald, what you were doing at that time I shudder to think.'

Minnie raised a finger to explain but Esther was having none of it. 'Then!' she remarked, 'Then you dropped it down the drain after a night at the Red Lion and woke half the street singing *Cockles and Muscles alive alive oh.*'

'Oh yes,' Minnie laughed, recalling her drunken revelry at the expense of their neighbours. 'But the nice man from the council retrieved it for me if you recall.'

'Yes, three days later!' Esher reminded her sister with a wrinkled glare. 'And then!' she continued. 'You fed the damn thing to a New Forest pony of all things!'

'It wasn't my fault,' Minnie whined. 'Cyril and I were off to a bowls tournament in Bournemouth and stopped at the roadside to feed the darlings some sugar cubes, well one little chap sucked the ring right off my finger it did and swallowed it, but Cyril being the gentleman that he was followed that pony for five hours until nature finally took its course and after delving in the dung as it were he emerged victorious, mind you we were late for the tournament and disqualified before we'd even bowled a jack.'

'Well that serves you right,' Esther scoffed, 'As I said, that ring should have rightfully passed to me.'

'But it was my birthday,' Minnie reminded her sister. 'And I'd just recovered from the measles if you recall.'

'Yes I do!' Esther replied, raising her eyebrows. 'And boy, did you milk it, so much in fact that you worried Mother half to death and she gave you the ring when the vicar was called to read you the last rites.'

'But, Essy, I was sick,' Minnie pleaded. 'Honestly I was.'

'Sick!' Esther laughed. 'Sick, how many sick people do you know, Minnie, that climb out of bed and out of the window for a spot of heavy petting on the street corner, I saw you, Minnie, with Teddy Pierce, so don't you dare deny it.'

'I, I needed some air,' Minnie stammered. 'To help with the fever.'

'Ohhhh you had a fever, did you?' Esther said, mocking Minnie. 'A fever, well that didn't stop you returning an hour later with a bite on your neck as big as a billiard ball did it, what was it I heard one young lady on the bus call it, oh yes, a shag badge.'

'Esther!' Minnie exclaimed, horrified at the insinuation but knowing full well it was true, every word of it. 'Anyway that's only four times I've lost it,' she reminded her sister. 'Not five.'

'Are you serious?' Esther asked, raising her eyebrows yet again in disbelief. 'You mean to tell me you've forgotten the cupcake incident?'

'Oh,' Minnie said sheepishly. 'That.'

'Yes that!' Esther replied sharply. 'Mrs Fenton has never fully recovered, I'll have you know.'

Minnie had been given the responsibility of baking a batch of twenty-four cupcakes for the church bazar, and it was whilst mixing the wet ingredients in her enamel pudding bowl she inadvertently dropped the diamond and sapphire ring into the dough and turned it in before baking in a hot oven for the required fifteen minutes. Mrs Fenton, the church organist along with several peckish parishioners purchased the cakes and ate them there and then with a cup of rosehip tea from Esther's urn. An ambulance was swiftly called when the organist began coughing and spluttering when the gleaming gemstones tore at her innards. Later surgeons worked for six hours removing part of her stomach lining in the process and eventually retrieving the seemingly cursed wedding ring and returned it to the red-faced Minnie and her glaring sister.

'Five, Minnie!' Esther raged. 'Five times you've lost our mother's treasured wedding ring, five, and now, now to add insult to injury you drop the darn thing into a pickle jar, give it here will you.' She reached across whilst steering round a rocky bend.

'No, no, no, it's mine!' Minnie said, cradling the jar like the deranged Gollum from Tolkien's *Lord of the Rings*. 'Mine!'

'Give it here, you fool!' Esther growled, veering towards the uneven verge.

'Careful, Essy!' Minnie cried, swatting her sister's hand.

'Ouch!' Esther cursed, correcting her steering but over-compensating and leaving the road only to plough into a desert dune.

'Arrrrrgh!' the sisters both shrieked, clutching their hats and lunging forward, the pickle jar slipping from Minnie's fingers and tumbling to the floor spilling the remaining shallots and vinegar onto Vivien's floor pan carpet which Esther had replaced using remnants from the floral Wilton weave she had fitted in their lounge.

'Damn it, damn it!' Minnie cried, releasing her belt hastily and fishing at her feet. 'Yes!' she then said, triumphantly rising with the ring. 'Got it!' and with a smile she turned to face her sister whose expression was one of the complete opposite. 'What?' Minnie asked before peering from the window at the heaped sand around them. 'Ah,' she said, sucking the vinegar from the ring and slipping it back onto her finger. 'Essy?' she then asked. 'Why on earth are we….?'

'Not a word!' Esther warned her sister. 'I mean it, not, a, word.'

Prising the door open, Esther clambered out allowing a quantity of sand to tumble into the car. 'Ohhhh hell,' she cursed, trudging to Minnie's side of the car, her feet sinking to her ankles in doing so. 'This is all your fault,' she snarled, directing her wrath once again at her sister who had just retrieved an onion and was sitting plucking off the fluff.

'I'm sorry, dear, what did you say?' Minnie asked, rolling down her window. 'Pickle?' she added, offering the shallot.

'No I do not!' Esther stormed, batting the pickle from Minnie's hand. 'Look at what you've done!'

'Me?' Minnie exclaimed, opening her own door and rummaging in the sand for the pickle. 'Now look,' she moaned, 'I've gone and lost it now.'

Esther threw her hands into the air whilst Minnie climbed clear of the car and dropped to all fours digging in the sand with her bare hands. 'I knew it, I knew it!' Esther cried, looking to the heavens. 'We should have turned back at Raipur, that's what we should have done, I'd be home right now listening to the wireless with tea and biscuits but instead I'm stuck out here in the middle of God knows where with a bumbling fool!'

'Oh thank heavens,' Minnie said, oblivious, locating the wayward pickle and painstakingly removing the grains of sand before popping it into her mouth. 'Essy!' she then said sharply whilst climbing up Vivien's door to her feet and removing the ring from her finger. 'Look, if it means that much to you, you have it.'

'No, no,' Esther said defiantly with her nose in the air. 'Mother gave it to you remember, albeit under fraudulent circumstances.'

'Essy, I really was sick,' Minnie said pleading her case. 'I had spots on my tongue and everything.'

'Spots, you say,' Esther scoffed. 'You probably got those from Teddy Pierce too no doubt.'

'Estherrrrrr,' Minnie moaned, offering the ring. 'Let's bury the hatchet shall we, here, I want you to have it, it's only right, as you say you are the eldest so therefore it rightly belongs to you.'

'I said no!' Esther snapped, shoving Minnie's hand once again. 'I wouldn't take it from you now for all the tea in China, I said NO!'

The pair shoved the ring back and forth until between their awkward fumblings it dropped at their feet.

'OH GOD!' Minnie cried. 'ESSY, THE RING!'

The pair immediately clung to their spectacles scanning the desert floor but their mother's precious wedding ring had been swallowed by the hourglass-dry sand.

'Minnie, you fool!' Esther cried with her hands to her head. 'Right, don't move, don't move a muscle, Minnie, do you hear?'

The two sisters stood motionless, straining their eyes. 'Where is it, Essy?' Minnie asked, panic-stricken. 'Where is it?'

'QUIET!' Esther barked, tugging her sister's sleeve sharply. 'Now it's important we remain calm, any sudden movement could bury it deeper and we'll never find it.'

'Never find it,' Minnie gasped. 'Oh dear Lord, no.' She dropped immediately to her knees again and began digging like a deranged dog, sending a shower of sand across Vivien's bonnet. 'I can't find it, Essy!' she shrieked, plunging her arthritic hands into the warm desert floor.

'MINNIE, STOOOOOP!' Esther yelled, seeing no sense at all in her sister's crazed excavations. 'STOP, MINNIE, STOP FOR PETE'S SAKE STOOOOOP!' She then caught sight of a glinting diamond in the deepening hole Minnie had dug. 'THERE!' she cried, lunging. 'There, Minnie, there it is!' but once again the almost molten sand poured down and devoured the ring. 'NO, NO, NO, NO!' Esther begged, digging frenziedly at Minnie's side, herself ejecting sand in the opposite direction until the pair were waist deep in a creation of their own making, sifting for their mother's prized possession.

In the sisters' heightened panic they failed to notice a motorcade of thirteen dazzling yellow American Hummer vehicles approach, slow and stop beside them.

'I saw it, I know I did!' Esther puffed, red-faced. 'Minnie, dig for Christ's sake, dig will you!'

The smoked glass passenger window of the lead vehicle lowered and a manicured olive-skinned hand extended a 24-carat mobile phone in the sisters' direction to capture the ridiculous scene.

'Oh,' Esther finally said, catching sight of the gaudy vehicles. 'Hellooooo!'

The Hummer door opened and a slender leg emerged complete with designer shoe and extravagant ankle bracelet; suddenly the doors of the remaining twelve cars sprang open and upwards of thirty heavily armed bodyguards in black fatigues clambered out and stood in tinted aviator glasses scanning the surrounding countryside. 'Mistress, please!' one of them said, rushing to greet the Arabian beauty as she ventured from the protection of her armoured car. 'What are you doing, it is not safe?'

The mistress in question was the twenty-four-year-old daughter of a prominent Meccan Sheik and a multi-millionairess in her own right, having launched a range of dazzling Arab robes designed to flatter the previously hidden female form, consequently the gutsy girl had enraged the majority of her country's old guard as they were known. 'Get away, I am fine!' the young Arab socialite said, dismissing her chief of security in the employ of her overbearing father. 'I said I am fine!'

The dapper henchman retreated several yards and stood rigid and chisel jawed, eyeing her every move.

'Hello to you!' the girl called through her thinly laced veil. 'Please tell me, what are you doing?'

'Oh hello,' Minnie replied mopping her brow. 'We've lost our mother's wedding ring!'

'We!' Esther said with her hands on her hips. 'What's this we, you lost the ring, yet again I might add!'

'Oh come now, Essy,' Minnie said, sitting back against the sand bank and removing her hat to fan her face. 'If I'm big enough to accept responsibility then I believe you should too.'

'Me!' Esther gasped, outraged by her sister's attempt to apportion blame. 'Over my dead body, you lost it, Minnie, and I for one will never forgive you for it.'

'Errr helloooo,' the girl called while the sisters sat bickering in their hole. 'Perhaps I could be of some assistance!'

Minnie wagged a finger at her sister. 'I distinctly remember handing it to you, Essy,' she said, 'And you dropped it, admit it, Essy, go on.'

'Never!' Esther replied defiantly.

'Hellooooo!' the girl called waving a hand above her head to attract the squabbling sisters' attention. 'Would you like some help?'

'Help?' Esther asked, clearly flushed and fatigued. 'Oh, oh yes, yes please my dear.' Esther hastily dusted her dress and replaced her hat. 'That's awfully kind of you, but we'd hate to put you to any inconvenience.'

'Nonsense,' the girl said, clicking her fingers and summoning her guards to her side. 'Your ring, you say?' she asked the sisters.

'Yes, yes that's right,' Esther replied. 'As my sister said it was our mother's, you see, so it has enormous sentimental value.'

'Yes, enormous,' Minnie agreed.

'Be quiet!' Esther snapped. 'How on earth can it be sentimental to you, you've misplaced the damn thing countless times.'

'Ohhh, Essy, that's not fair,' Minnie said, shaking her own ankle-length dress.

The two sisters attempted to scramble from their pit of despair as it were but the crumbling sand hampered them. The girl again clicked her fingers and several of her burly men hoisted the sisters out with ease.

'My, my,' Minnie squealed in the meaty arms of a former member of the Arab secret service, 'I haven't been manhandled like that since Cyril took advantage of me in Morrisons, I was reaching for a gypsy tart on the top shelf you see and I must have aroused his bed snake as we used to call it.'

'Minnie!' Esther barked, tugging her sister clear of the hefty hunk. 'This isn't the time and it certainly isn't the place for such vulgarity.'

'Well that's what I told Cyril, dear,' Minnie explained, dusting her dress once again. 'But it happened again in frozen foods, I was bent double delving for a packet of potato waffles when I felt it again.'

'Felt it?' the now inquisitive girl asked.

'Bertie,' Minnie innocently informed her. 'The bed snake.'

'Minnie, please!' Esther said, beside herself at this point and blushing in front of their new acquaintances.

'What, dear?' Minnie asked. 'Oh, oh yes I do apologise, but Cyril was always one for spontaneity, you know I was once in the fitting room at Debenhams when Cyril popped in and dropped his…'

'Dear God, woman!' Esther screeched. 'Will you please stop!'

'I was about to say, dear,' Minnie continued adamantly. 'He dropped his sherbet lemons, mind you that's not to say we didn't have fun on the floor ferreting about for the perishing things.'

'I do apologise for my sister,' Esther told the bewildered girl. 'Unreservedly.'

'Come,' the girl said, ushering the sisters to her car. 'I have lemonade, you must be thirsty.'

'I'll say,' Esther agreed, grappling with the huge door to clamber inside.

'Help me, dear,' Minnie asked behind her, having difficulty raising her right leg to the running board.

'I'd rather not actually,' Esther smirked.

'What was that, dear?' Minnie asked heaving herself onto the seat beside her sister.

'Nothing, dear,' Esther replied, admiring their spacious and sumptuous surroundings. 'My God, it's like a cathedral on wheels,' she remarked, stretching out both arms unable to touch either side.

Aliya the Arab girl reached into a refrigerator and poured two glasses of ice cold lemonade.

'Oh you're too kind, my dear,' Esther said with a smile whilst Minnie hesitated.

'I, I couldn't trouble you for a cocktail cherry, could I?' she asked, having caught sight of the jar. 'Or two perhaps?'

'Yes, yes of course,' Aliya obliged. 'Cherry, dear?' Minnie asked her sister who returned the proposition with a disapproving glare.

The three ladies watched from the air-conditioned comfort of the huge car as several guards stripped to the waist and leapt into the sisters' previously dug pit and began sifting for the precious ring. 'Well I never,' Minnie said, looking over the rim of her spectacles at their tensile torsos. Even Esther cast an admiring eye down toward the bobbing buttocks outside, but her sisters constant slurping of the cherries soon drove her to distraction. 'Really?' she simply said, leaning back to observe the grotesque spectacle as Minnie fished for another then another.

'Sorry, dear, I don't follow,' Minnie confessed, oblivious to her actions.

Aliya found the sisters' constant bickering hilarious, having yearned of late for scintillating company. 'Have dinner with me,' she suddenly blurted. 'At my palace, please?'

'Dinner?' Minnie slurped, averting her gaze from the guards and popping another three cherries into her mouth. 'Did you say dinner, my dear?'

'Yes I did,' Aliya smiled. 'I have more than I need and would consider it a great honour, Minnie and Esther, yes I know who you are.'

'Oh,' Esther replied, assuming they'd slipped beneath the celebrity radar. 'Well I suppose, but, but what about Vivien?'

'Vivien?' Aliya asked in return whilst looking around for a third travelling companion.

'Yes, Vivien,' Esther informed her, gesturing to their stricken car just as a triumphant guard held their mother's ring aloft.

'I HAVE IT!' he yelled. 'I HAVE IT!'

'Oooooh splendid!' Minnie squealed, bobbing in her seat. 'See, Essy!' she told her sister. 'I didn't lose it after all.'

'Hmmmmm,' Esther groaned under her breath whilst Aliya exchanged several words in Arabic with her guards.

'They will bring your Vivien,' she told the sisters before waving her driver on.

'Thank youuuuuuuu!' Minnie called whilst slipping the ring back onto her finger. 'There,' she told Esther, stretching out her hand to admire the heirloom. 'Back safely where it belongs.'

She turned to smile at her sister but thought better of it on seeing Esther's scathing glare.

'Safe!' Esther grimaced. 'Safe, ha, the Artful Dodger himself would have taken better care of it, of that I'm sure,' and she pursed her lips referring to Oliver Twist's poverty-stricken pilfering pal.

'Oh come now, Essy,' Minnie replied, plucking out another cherry. 'Must you be so melodramatic?' She turned to Aliya. 'My sister does have a tendency to overreact,' she told her, patting the Arab princess's hand; she then glanced down at her ring finger which was ring-less once again. 'Oh,' she remarked, looking down between her knees and fumbling beneath her frock.

'What is it?' Esther asked abruptly. 'What have you done, Minnie?'

'Nothing!' Minnie said in a bid to conceal her carelessness. 'Just massaging my corns, dear, that's all.'

Esther bent forward and snatched the ring at Minnie's feet. 'That's it!' she said angrily. 'That is it, Minnie, and you say I'm melodramatic, ha, you, my dear, are a clumsy buffoon who never should have been entrusted with such a keepsake in the first place.'

'Oh but, Essy,' Minnie moaned, righting herself a little too sharply and going a little giddy. 'It's mine, Mother gave it to me remember.'

Aliya couldn't help but laugh at this point. 'You two are adorable,' she said, throwing back her head.

Vivien was soon rescued from the sand pit with the help of a heavy steel cable and winch attached to the bumper of one of Aliya's support vehicles. Two hulking guards crammed themselves inside and chuckled when following behind the convoy, honking Vivien's pathetic horn occasionally and grimacing when sharing a packet of the sisters' scented Parma Violet sweets.

Aliya's walled palace nestled among the relentless Saudi dunes on the edge of Medina city, rising from the desert, white, resplendent and without a doubt magnificent, its central pearl-like dome towering some seventy metres, dwarfing its neighbours and casting a long creeping shadow for much of the day.

'You live here?' Esther asked as the motorcade swept through the fortified steel gates opened by an aged groundsman.

'Yes,' Aliya replied, waving courteously to the crooked figure bowing at the gate.

'With your family?' Minnie asked, craning her neck to glance up at the dome.

'No, no, no, I live alone,' Aliya informed them. 'My father's house is several kilometres from here.'

'Alone!' Minnie pondered, awestruck at the vastness of her estate, with servants' quarters, twin pools and guest accommodation in the east and west wings fit for royalty.

'Yes, I prefer it this way,' Aliya said, taking a guard's hand to alight from her car. 'Please,' she told the emerging sisters. 'My home is your home, relax, enjoy and stay as long as you wish.'

'Oh look, Essy,' Minnie said when Vivien arrived moments later. 'It's our Vivien.'

'So it is,' Esther said, clasping her hands together and smiling on hearing her unmistakable horn once again. 'Yes, yes, dear, I hear you.' she added affectionately. 'I've missed you too my darling.'

With their luggage unloaded and carried inside, the sisters shuffled behind Aliya hastily seeking shelter from the sun's searing rays. 'Ohhhh how lovely,' Minnie said, removing her hat in the entrance hall to feel the cooling turbulent breeze whipped from the overhead fans.

Esther slipped her silk scarf from her neck, dabbing her perspiring upper lip. 'Mmmm yes, dear, lovely' she agreed.

'Come, come,' Aliya urged beckoning, and kicking off her elaborately decorated moccasins, 'Join me for tea.'

'Did you say tea, dear?' Minnie asked, starting after her. 'Essy, my love,' she said tea,' she said.

Esther fanned her flushed cheeks with her hat and eagerly tagged along.

'Essy, look!' Minnie gasped again on entering Aliya's palatial kitchen, a vast expanse of gleaming stainless steel, seamless granite and polished copper cookware, a culinary haven putting most Michelin Star establishments to shame, not to mention Esther and Minnie's own galley kitchen where their bottoms would regularly become wedged against the peeling Formica when passing one another leading to frequent flustered bickering over possession of the biscuit barrel and the garibaldis therein.

'However do you keep it clean?' was Esther's overriding thought, having spent no more than a minute or two dragging a J-cloth across her laminated replica redwood surfaces and running a finger across Aliya's spotless natural stone imported from a quarry in the north of England no less.

Aliya provided the answer when clapping her henna-tattooed hands to summon six willing maids, each of then barely adolescent, fresh-faced and doe-eyed. 'Tea for my guests,' she told them before stopping one girl in her tracks to straighten her bejewelled hair piece. 'Confidence, my dear,' she said, lifting the girl's chin with a finger. 'What have I told you, confidence is the key.' The girl nodded while blushing in the strangers' company then hurried about her business.

The girls numbering eleven in total within Aliya's residence had been snatched from abusive and forced marriages by the princess, further angering the archaic establishment, but Aliya championed the cause of women's liberation, courageously defying threats from the great and powerful who enforced the law of the land with a rod of iron so to speak.

'I say!' Minnie piped up. 'Could I trouble you for a china cup?' she asked their host. 'For the tea, I mean, it really does make a world of difference you know.'

'But of course,' Aliya said, sliding a sleek slab of American Walnut aside to reveal her true hidden gems, something that had the sisters riveted to the spot momentarily.

'Oh my word!' Esther gasped, positively green with envy as was her transfixed sister beside her.

'You are quite right, Minnie dear,' Aliya said, revealing her simply stunning collection of English fine bone china amassed during her frequent visits to Britain's pottery towns whilst sourcing fabrics for her daring designs. 'It does make a world of difference.'

'Look, dear!' Minnie said with a trembling hand. 'She, she, she has the Crown Derby.'

'Do you like it?' Aliya asked proudly, removing three cups from her gilt-edged set.

'Like it?' Esther gushed. 'I love!'

Royal Crown Derby as it is known is professed to be the very pinnacle of pottery perfection having been fired in the Derbyshire kilns since the 1750's.

Esther and Minnie were drawn hypnotically toward it, drooling almost, their hands outstretched whilst the tea was poured by the bashful maids and offered. 'Why thank you,' Esther told one fifteen-year-old who had previously been savagely beaten by her father for daring to voice her objections to an arranged marriage to an aging business associate. The girl remained, head bowed, so as not to reveal the true extent of her facial disfigurement, the cold steel buckle of his leather belt having fractured her tender cheekbone and nearly blinded her left eye.

'Thank you,' Aliya told the girls. 'Please return to your studies.' Under Aliya's guidance and home tuition each of her rescuees had excelled in their chosen educational subjects, an advantage formerly denied to them. One of her girls had gone on to achieve a master's degree in criminal law and had consequently been offered a position in a prestigious overseas firm with a tempting six figure salary attached.

'Oh wow,' Minnie said, sipping her steaming brew, 'That is delightful, dearie, what is it if you don't mind me asking?'

'I thought you would like it,' Aliya smiled, blowing across the surface of her own china cup. 'It is a centuries old blend of Arabian herbs and Assam tea, Sahib my gardener he makes it for me, but only when the leaves have been drying in our desert sun for a year and a half, he is very particular that way.'

'And quite right too,' Esther agreed whilst her sister was more a fan of the instant bagged variety.

'A year and a half!' Minnie protested. 'I'm sorry, my dear, but in the time it takes your Sahib to produce a pound of tea I've had a hip replacement, a new set of dentures, three pairs of glasses and a water infection.'

Esther once again glared at Minnie. 'Do excuse my sister,' she told Aliya. 'She's a philistine when it comes to the finer things in life.'

'I am not!' Minnie moaned, then with a furrowed brow added, 'I'm sorry, dear, what's a philistine?'

'Exactly,' Esther scoffed.

The sisters were then treated to a tour of the palace which simply wowed them at every twist and turn. 'Is that, is that a Steinway?' Esther asked catching sight of a polished grand piano in the drawing room,

'Yes, yes it is,' Aliya replied. 'Do you play?'

'Does the Pope wear a bloomin' daft hat,' Minnie replied, superseding her sister.

Again Esther gave her sister the look. 'On occasion,' she told Aliya dismissively, 'I find sheet music fascinating, you see.'

Minnie raised her eyebrows, glancing at the precious piano. 'I could never make head nor tail of it myself,' she confessed. 'Crochets and quavers, it's all gibberish to me, now the penny whistle, there's an instrument that takes skill and dexterity, I was something of a prodigy with mine, wasn't I, dear?'

Esther ignored her sister's witterings.

'I said I was quite the child prodigy with my penny whistle, dear,' Minnie insisted proudly.

'Prodigy!' Esther laughed. 'You played *Three Blind Mice* morning noon and night, driving our parents and me for that matter to the brink of insanity, and you say that makes you a prodigy.'

'Well, well yes,' Minnie said confidently. 'Do you remember Father sent me to evening classes?'

'Yes for the peace and quiet,' Esther confessed. 'As I recall him saying it was worth the ten shillings just to be rid of you and that woeful whistle of yours.'

'He did not!' Minnie remarked, stiffening her back. 'Father would never say a thing like that, not about his little Minnie Moo.'

Aliya stood in the hallway revelling in the sisters' frequent squabbling, evoking memories of her own now deceased elderly relatives.

'Don't you believe it,' Esther informed her sister. 'He said at one point if he could afford the air fare he'd have sent you to Timbuktu with the perishing thing.'

'Daddy?' Minnie said in abject disbelief. 'I doubt that very much, you know I was the apple of his eye.'

Aliya began to tap her toes impatiently. 'Shall we?' she said, eager to show the rest of her glorious home to her new guests.

'I was his baby as he always said,' Minnie continued. 'Right up until the day he....' She hesitated unable to say the word. 'Well, you know.'

'Well sometimes,' Esther said smugly. 'The truth hurts, my dear.'

Minnie's relationship with her father, as Esther knew full well, was as close as close could be after a complication with her birth in which the umbilical cord became entwined around her neck; she was eventually born whilst he paced the hospital hallway wringing his hands and begging the Almighty for a miracle. Consequently from birth Minnie was spoilt rotten at each and every opportunity, showered with infinitely more gifts than her elder sibling which surprisingly hadn't fazed Esther at all. But despite his endearing love for his little Minnie Moo as he called her, the aforementioned penny whistle and her piercing rendition of *Three Blind Mice* was enough to have him questioning his devotion and at times, namely six-thirty on a Sunday morning when she'd march around the house with it jammed between her lips tormenting her father's very soul and have him tightening his house coat cord in his hands mimicking the deadly umbilical.

Aliya raised a hand to her mouth. 'Ahem!' she said, smiling politely. 'Ladies.'

'Oh,' Minnie remarked, looking round, having lost herself in conversation. 'Aliya, I am sorry, my dear, where were we?'

'Timbuktu,' Esther sneered, leaving Minnie standing.

'What was that, dear?' Minnie asked.

Esther took Aliya by the arm. 'Lead on, my darling,' she said, dismissing her sister as she was ushered into Aliya's workshop, a festival of coloured fabrics hanging around the vast machine-filled room.

'And this,' Aliya said proudly, 'This is where I spend much of my time.'

'Ohhhh wow,' Esther gushed in awe at the dazzling rainbow draped on heavy wooden dowels some thirty metres in length. To one side a row of exquisite mannequins in female form stood modelling her lurid creations, garments fit to grace the catwalks of Paris, New York, London and Milan, anywhere in fact than the Arab Emirates.

Much of Aliya's collection was specifically tailored for women in the throes of youth with a daring cut designed to accentuate and reveal rather more flesh than the Arab hierarchy would otherwise allow, but one or two more lengthier garments caught the sisters' eye, one in cotton candy pink and the other a dazzling shade of tangerine.

'You like it?' Aliya asked when Esther thumbed the cloth. 'It's yours.'

'Oh no, I couldn't possibly,' Esther replied, having dressed conservatively for many years whilst Minnie released the tangerine toga from its hanger.

'Oh, Essy, isn't this just adorable,' Minnie said, raising a leg and eyeing the elaborate pleating.

'Yes, yes, I totally agree but…' Esther said, rather taken with her own choice. 'You really must allow us to pay for them, Aliya,' she insisted, taking her bag from her arm and delving for her purse.

'No, no, no,' Aliya insisted. 'Consider it a gift, please.'

'Ooooh thank you,' Minnie said, accepting without hesitation whilst her elder sister at first refused the charitable gesture, offering a fistful of her recently acquired Emirati Dirham to their gracious host who merely pushed her hand back towards her purse.

'Please,' Aliya insisted. 'Let me do this.'

'Well,' Esther said reluctantly. 'Well if you're quite sure, I mean we'd hate to take advantage, dear,' but then Minnie's huffing and puffing distracted her as she turned to see her sister in a state of undress tugging the toga over her head. 'Minnie!' she barked. 'Have you no shame, woman?'

'Sorry, dear,' Minnie said in her bra and bloomers with her head concealed. 'I wonder, would you give me a hand, I appear to be stuck somewhat.'

Esther looked at Aliya in despair. 'I am so, so sorry, my dear,' she said, red-faced and shielding her unabashed sister. 'Minnie, get dressed at once!' she snarled, tugging the toga down around her sister's neck and over her shoulders. 'What on earth were you thinking?'

'Oh, Essy,' Minnie smiled, letting the sister dress her as her unofficial valet. 'We're all girls together, aren't we, Aliya darling?'

'But of course,' the princess agreed, although in a state of mild shock at the bizarre spectacle before her. 'In fact,' she added, 'I find it quite refreshing that you are so comfortable with your body, Minnie.'

'Comfortable,' Esther sneered, wrenching the toga down around her sister's knees. 'I've never been so embarrassed, Aliya, really I haven't, I must apologise once again.'

'Oh I'm sure you have, Essy dear,' Minnie smirked, tossing Aliya a cheeky wink. 'There was that time you saw a cockroach in the changing room of Dorothy Perkins and ran screaming headlong and half naked into a party of snap happy South Koreans, oh you should have been there, Aliya dear,' she told their host. 'It was hilarious, amid the blinding frenzy of flash bulbs one poor premature darling suffered a seizure when he shot his entire load of Fuji film before he had a chance to remove his lens cap.'

'Minnie, please!' Esther said in an attempt to silence her mocking sister. 'There are times in one's life that are best left forgotten, do you hear?'

'I doubt he's ever forgotten it, dear,' Minnie said, tongue-in-cheek. 'If I hadn't have administered CPR I doubt he'd have made it out of women's lingerie alive, quite what they were doing in there in the first place is beyond me, but I must say that was half a crown well spent.'

'Half a crown?' Esther asked, straightening her back having concealed the majority of her shameless sister's flesh. 'What do you mean, half a crown?'

By now Aliya was intrigued too as were most whenever within earshot of Minnie's ramblings.

'The cockroach,' Minnie chuckled, 'I bought it at the joke shop and lowered it over the rim of your cubicle on a piece of Father's fishing wire.'

Esther's eyes were immediately out on stalks. 'YOU DID WHAT?' she screeched, recalling the anguished shame and ridicule she endured on that fateful bustling Saturday afternoon. Minnie's timing was quite superb to say the least, the leading clothing chain had recently announced a half-price sale on everything in store causing a stampede amongst their loyal and discerning customers. Esther later had her own loyalty card confiscated and cut in two by the irate floor manager and told in no uncertain terms never to darken their doors again. 'Why, youuuuuuuuu!' she growled while Aliya clasped her hands to her stomach in a midst of a fit of the giggles as Minnie backed slowly to a safe distance.

'I'm sorry, dear,' Minnie said, unable to control the mischievous smile on her face. 'I simply couldn't resist it, you know I used that cockroach again and again, once on the terraces at West Ham United.' She drew another breath. 'The lady beside me screamed, threw her cocoa and her hands into the air and inadvertently started a Mexican wave.'

Aliya was now bent double. 'Stop, stop, please stop!' she laughed whilst Esther remained tight-lipped.

'Minnie, I fail to see the hilarity in your childish shenanigans,' she said, wagging a finger. 'One of these days, young lady, you'll land yourself in hot water, you mark my words.'

'Ladies, ladies,' Aliya said, almost blue in the face and cross-legged. 'You must excuse me, I really need to pee, I have this almighty bladder weakness, you see and just being in your company stirs my waters if you know what I mean.'

'Don't worry, dear,' Esther said sympathetically. 'You go right ahead, don't mind us.'

'Cooeee! Minnie said, stopping Aliya. 'If you don't mind me saying, dear, you should get yourself a bag, Ida at the Co-op has one fitted to the inside of her right leg, she swears by it she does, well she's behind that counter for hours on end, the poor dear.'

Aliya backed away, unable to stem the flow a moment longer. 'I'm sorry, I really must,' she said in a strained tone.

'Her bag for life, she calls it,' Minnie continued. 'I must say though it comes in awfully handy when sneaking a litre and a half of Pinot Grigio into the Mecca Bingo, every so often I'd drop my dobber between her legs and top my hip flask up from her tap.'

Well this was more than Aliya's bloated bladder could withstand. 'Oh no!' she shrieked. 'No, no, no, no, no!' and she hurried away as best she could, leaving a spattered trail in her wake desperate for the bathroom and a change of linen.

Minnie twirled in her tangerine toga. 'What do you think, dear?' she asked, marvelling at the lavishly embroidered hemming. 'Essy dear?' she asked again, seeing her sister with a hand to her mouth and her complexion a whiter shade of pale, the grotesque picture of her Minnie decanting warm Pinot from her friend Ida's colostomy bag foremost in her mind. 'Was it something I said?' Minnie added, characteristically oblivious. 'Here, dear,' she said throwing the second toga into Esther's arms. 'Try yours on for size, the feeling of freedom is simply divine, dear, simply divine.' Having spent years restrained beneath robust layers of fortified and figure clenching garments of gabardine, Harris tweed, flannel and fleece, the loose cooling cotton toga came as a welcome relief.

'Certainly not,' Esther said abruptly. 'Not here anyway, you, Minnie may be a shameless exhibitionist but I for one am not.'

'Oh don't be such a prude, dear,' Minnie smirked, stooping to scoop the hem of her sister's skirt up around her hips. 'Come on, let's get you into something more fitting for the current climate.'

'Get off of me, what are you doing!' Esther protested, wrestling with her insistent sister. 'Minnie, Minnie, I said no!

'Oh don't be daft, dear,' Minnie replied. 'There isn't a soul around, now come on quickly, you'll thank me for it, I promise you.'

Esther had indeed been feeling the heat of late, perspiring more than she liked. 'Ohhhh damn you, Minnie,' she said, conceding. 'Unhand me, will you, I can do it myself!'

Minnie continued to assist Esther, hoisting her dress up over her breasts and onto her head.

'Let go, will you!' Esther again snapped at her willing sister, then glancing to her left she suddenly caught sight of Aliya's elderly gardener and all round hired help Sahib, leering at her through an open window whilst he hoed the bordering rose beds. 'ARRRRRGH!' she squealed, clutching the candy pink toga to her chest. 'GO AWAY!' she yelled toward the amorous Arab who hadn't laid eyes on an undressed female in a very long time.

'Cooeeeeee!' Minnie called with a courteous wave while her sister dropped to the floor and hurriedly tugged on the toga.

'Thank you for it!' Esther cursed her sister. 'I'll bloomin' swing for you, Minnie, so help me I will, now close the damned window, will you!'

'I'm sorry, dear, what was that?' Minnie asked, swishing the hem of her own toga seductively while the gardener stumbled hypnotically outside.

'I said, oh never mind!' Esther said angrily. 'Come away, will you, he's nothing but a peeping Thomas.'

'Oh I think he's rather sweet, dear,' Minnie replied heading to the window to retrieve a plump rose bloom Sahib had hand-picked for her. 'Why thank you, my dear,' she told him, lifting the heavenly scented canary yellow flower to her nose. 'Mmmm, gorgeous,' she added, leaning out of the window to survey his neatly cultivated plot of pristine bushes. 'I say if you don't mind me asking,' she pondered, 'How do you keep them so lush and vibrant, I mean they are absolutely beautiful, I swear you could show them at Chelsea.'

Sahib did nothing more than point across the courtyard at a steaming heap of freshly turned camel dung.

'Ohhhh of course,' Minnie smiled. 'My sister and I,' she confessed, 'Used to have the unenviable job of pursuing the milkman and his trusty nag around the estate with a bucket and spade waiting for nature to take its course.'

'Minnie, come away, I said!' Esther called, beckoning and ducking out of sight.

'Ohhh alright,' Minnie moaned. 'Goodbye, my dear,' she told Sahib, flashing her dentures before closing the window.

Aliya then reappeared wearing another freshly laundered robe. 'I do apologise,' she said, blushing somewhat. 'Shall I show you to your rooms?'

'Rooms?' Minnie asked, having gotten used to sharing with her sister in recent times. 'But…'

'That would be lovely, dear,' Esther quickly interjected. 'Thank you.'

Aliya led the way to a central lengthy corridor and gestured in either direction. 'Now, Esther I've put you in the east wing with views of the minarets above Medina and, Minnie, you are to the west where I'm sure the desert sunset will enchant you.'

'The west, but I thought…' Minnie said, looking almost lost.

'Marvellous!' Esther smiled, leaving her sister standing.

'Dinner is served at eight,' Aliya informed the sisters before taking Minnie's arm and leading her in the opposite direction.

'Yes but I thought…' Minnie again said, looking over her shoulder at her departing sister. 'I, I mean we've gotten into the habit of sharing, you see, Aliya dear, back home we cuddle up in our bed socks listening to the wireless with a water bottle.'

'Miss Minnie, you do paint a charming picture,' said Aliya, feeling nothing but affection for the British pensioners. 'But I assure you your rooms are all you could wish for, and much more.'

Esther's monogrammed luggage had been left at her door, as had Minnie's.

'Ahhh here you are,' Aliya said, pushing open the bleached oak door to reveal a glamorous suite fit for a queen.

'Oh my,' Minnie said, completely taken aback. 'All of this, for me?' Her and her sister's entire Whitechapel flat could have quite easily fitted two or possibly three times within the west wing suite.

'Yes of course,' Aliya replied, handing Minnie a key and marching to the floor-length curtains to sweep them aside and reveal a towering wall of plate glass with as promised breath-taking views across the Saudi desert.

'Oh wow!' Minnie said, quite simply stunned by the inspiring panorama. 'I see what you mean, dear,' she said as she ran a hand over the hand-carved Japanese bedstead. 'I, I suppose it wouldn't hurt to give it a try,' she said with an immediate change of heart.

'I'll have you know,' Aliya informed Minnie, who pressed her nose to the triple glazed window, 'Your Paul O'Grady once stayed in this very room.'

Minnie immediately spun from the window, almost dislocating her hip in doing so. 'He never did!' she exclaimed wide-eyed.

'Of course,' Aliya reiterated. 'Sahib is a huge fan so I had Mr O'Grady fly in as guest of honour at his birthday party, you should have seen his face, Minnie, it was a picture.'

'Saints preserve us,' Minnie said, clutching her chest and eyeing the bed where her idol had once rested his head and where she too would sleep. She remained clutching the bedpost and her chest, overcome with emotion.

'Here,' Aliya said, filling a glass with water. 'You're obviously unaccustomed to the heat.'

'Oh I can handle the heat, dearie,' Minnie replied, trembling as she sipped and picturing Paul O'Grady possibly unclothed purring beneath those silken sheets. 'Lord have mercy,' she begged for forgiveness for the sinful thoughts now racing through her mischievous mind. 'I must tell Essy at once,' she added starting for the door, unable to contain her enthusiasm and at the same time with a squeal relishing the look on her sister's face when revealing her earth-shattering news. The competitive nature of their affection for Mr O'Grady had seen them on the verge of several violent altercations in the past, like the time the chat show host arrived in their home town to officially open the flagship store of 'Betta Bargains', yet another hulking premises piled high with tacky foreign imports. Thousands upon thousands of products from skincare containing radioactive isotopes to a range of replica toy dolls reportedly resembling A-list celebrities; this of course would have been true had the stars undergone reconstructive surgery or treatment for a crystal meth addiction. During the attempted cutting of the red ribbon with several pairs of Betta Bargains faulty scissors, the pushing, shoving and cat calling amongst the amassed senior citizens reached fever pitch with Minnie stepping on her sister's toe in an attempt to gain a better vantage point. Lashing out in retaliation, Esther pushed her sister into a head-high stack of dented rice pudding tins, sending the teetering tower and Minnie for that matter tumbling with a cacophonous din into the aisle, further upsetting a display of dehydrated cup noodles and flavourless pyramid tea bags.

Paul's patience with the cut price cutting implements soon diminished and he enlisted the help of the pampered pooch tucked beneath his arm, a snorting squat-nosed pug answering to the name of Elvis, who eagerly gnawed through the entrance ribbon in record time receiving a round of applause from the store manager, the mayor, the pensioners and paparazzi alike. 'ESSYYYYYY!' Minnie called, shuffling along the corridor. 'COOEEEEE, ESSYYYYYY!' and without knocking Minnie barged into her sister's equally elegant suite. 'Essy, Essy, I simply must tell you…' but Esther was nowhere to be seen. 'Essy, where the devil are you?'

The French doors leading to the balcony were wide open and a cool early evening breeze toyed with the muslin drapes. 'Essy my love, oh there you are dear,' Minnie said excitedly when finding her sister lounging on a bed chair with her spectacles teetering precariously on the end of her nose and the tablet computer on her lap.

'Apparently, dear,' Esther said before Minnie could break the news. 'The Americans have begun investigating the great pyramid of Giza believing there to be a thus far undiscovered chamber within.'

'Yes dear but…' Minnie said, almost breathless. 'I have something more important to tell you!'

'More important!' Esther remarked, glaring at her sister over the rim of her glasses. 'More important, Minnie, do you realise they could be on the verge of the most significant archaeological discovery since the boy king Tutankhamun himself was found?'

'Yes, yes, yes,' Minnie said dismissively. 'Never mind all that, what I wanted to say was….'

'Minnie!' Esther barked, sitting upright and removing her spectacles, a sure sign she meant business, as Minnie had learnt on numerous occasions. 'Rumours are circulating that it could be the long lost tomb of..'

she hesitated 'Dare I say it, Cleopatra herself, Cleopatra, Minnie, do you understand what that means?'

Minnie stood fizzing like a magnum of champagne about to burst. 'But, Essy I must tell you about my room!' she begged, bobbing up and down.

'Nonsense!' Esther insisted. 'Minnie, archaeologists have been searching for the burial place of the former queen of Egypt for centuries, and now, now, Minnie, they could be within striking distance, and…' She clutched her chest 'God I can't breathe, I'm so excited,' she added, struggling to catch her breath.

Minnie thought for a moment. 'Did you say Cleopatra, dear?' she asked, assuming her hearing had failed her once again.

'Yeeeees!' Esther said, rolling her eyes. 'Cleopatra, and who knows maybe her Roman consort Mark Anthony, it was first suspected the two were entombed somewhere in Alexandria but an inscription found on the great pyramid suggests otherwise!'

'My word,' Minnie gasped, dropping onto the bed chair beside her sister. 'Cleopatra.'

'Isn't it wonderful,' Esther said, patting Minnie's hand. 'And we'll be there, dear, to see history in the making, it's estimated it will take workers at least a week to penetrate the hidden room leaving us ample time to get there, oh Minnie, I shan't sleep a wink tonight, not a wink I tell you.'

'Cleopatra!' Minnie marvelled. 'Cleopatra, Essy.'

'Yes, dear,' Esther agreed. 'Now, dear, what was it you wanted to tell me?'

'Do you know, darling?' Minnie said, thinking long and hard, 'I haven't the foggiest.' The archaeological revelation had completely thrown Minnie, knocking her off kilter so to speak. 'Now, dear,' she said, shuffling closer and completely forgetting Mr O'Grady and her many desires. 'Tell me more about the Americans and the pyramid?'

That evening the sisters dined with Aliya with Esther wittering nonstop about the possible impending discovery of one of Egypt's most iconic historical figures whilst her sister ate, and ate, and ate, only coming up for air occasionally. 'Oh I simply loved *Carry On Cleo*,' she mused, referring to the 1960's comedy classic, part of the now treasured Carry On series making household names of the likes of Sid James, Kenneth Williams, Hattie Jacques, Barbra Windsor and Amanda Bourne who played the gorgeous Cleopatra to Sid James's Mark Anthony. Charles Hawtrey, Kenneth Connor, Jim Dale and Joan Sims added to the line-up of possibly one of the greatest of Carry Ons.

'Carry On?' Aliya asked 'What is this Carry On?'

'What is this Carry On!' Esther and Minnie both said, spinning their heads to glare wide eyed at their host. 'What is Carry On?' Esther said, flabbergasted. 'You mean, you mean you don't know!'

'No,' Aliya confessed, shrugging her shoulders. 'I do not.'

'Oh, you poor sweet thing,' Minnie said, patting the back of her hand. 'You simply haven't lived, have you.'

The sisters went on to describe in great detail the series of hilarious capers that made up the fine comedy compendium. Minnie clumsily re-enacted Julius Cesar's memorable scene played by Kenneth Williams and those ridiculous immortal words, 'Infamy, infamy, they've all got it in for me!'

Aliya found the whole thing peculiar and sat listening intently to quotes and anecdotes from *Carry on Camping, Carry On up the Khyber, Carry On Doctor* and several more. Soon the Arab princess was in fits of hysterical laughter at the sisters' theatrical mimicking, each of them attempting the inimitable laugh of Sid James, the nasal tones of Kenneth Williams and the scathing scowl of Hattie Jacques's matron.

'I have to see this,' Aliya chuckled. 'Come, come to my private room.' Aliya led the bubbly sisters to her home cinema complex, yet another cavernous room lined with plush crimson velvet with row after row of sumptuous cushioned seating facing a big screen, the likes of which the Odeon and Top Rank cinemas would be proud of. Aliya summoned her personal cinematographer and insisted he locate the entire back catalogue of Carry On movies via the internet and play them immediately back to back.

Popcorn was hurriedly prepared by the young housemaids, who joined their mistress and her guests for what was to be a cultural comedic experience like no other.

Esther and Minnie roared with laughter at the clips they'd seen countless times before. 'Wait for it, wait for iiiiiit!' Minnie shrieked, moments before Barbra Windsor's bra famously pinged from her breasts during a morning exercise routine in *Carry On Camping*.

Tears of laughter also soon flowed down Aliya's cheeks as she rocked in her seat, tossing popcorn playfully at those around her while Sid James played the highwayman Dick Turpin pursued by Captain Fancy and Sargent Jock Strap in the 1974 addition to the series which spanned several decades.

After four more movies and three boxes of tissues the Princess could take no more. 'I will diiiiiiie!' she cried, covering her eyes. 'I swear I will die if I watch another moment of this delightful madness!'

The lights were raised as the credits rolled on *Carry On Doctor.* 'I swear,' Esther said, drying her own eyes. 'I never ever tire of watching those.'

'Me neither,' Minnie agreed wholeheartedly.

Generation of Brits had been weaned on the innocently provocative pictures crammed full of double entendres, sending up some of history's most prominent heroes, heroines and villains.

'Good grief, look at the time!' Esther remarked, raising her toga sleeve. It was approaching two-thirty a.m. and way, way beyond the sisters' bedtime. 'If you'll excuse us,' she told Aliya, who sat red-faced having had another bladder malfunction brought on by the evening's viewing, 'We simply must retire,' she added, patting Aliya's hand. 'A young dove like you, my dear ,has no need of beauty sleep but Minnie and I, well as you can see we need all the help we can get.'

Minnie looked mortified at her sister's acceptance of their waning years and appearance. 'You speak for yourself, Essy dear,' she said abruptly. 'I for one am planning to turn back the hands of time, with the help of an artificial procedure or two that is.'

'You are not!' Esther gasped. 'At your age, Minnie, don't be ridiculous!'

'And why ever not?' Minnie asked, having given the subject a great deal of thought of late. 'Apparently,' she told her sister, 'So I've heard on the world web a trout pout is a must have for any self-respecting selfie aficionado.'

'Minnie!' Esther remarked, tugging her sister from her seat, 'Did you just use the words trout pout and self-respecting in the same sentence?' She failed to see the connection. 'Anyway, what is a trout pout?' she asked.

Minnie pursed and puckered up her craggy lips.

'And?' Esther said, folding her arms across her chest. 'That's a trout pout is it?'

'Yes, dear,' Minnie said enthusiastically. 'It's all the rage nowadays, just like nylons and Bobby socks were when we were young.'

'Exactly!' Esther snapped. 'We were young, Minnie, a long, long time ago, but not anymore.'

While the sisters got into another heated debate, Aliya sloped away to change yet again.

'So, Minnie my dear,' Esther continued. 'You can just forget any ridiculous notions you may have of cosmetic surgery right this minute, trout pout indeed, you look like a demented duck, now off to bed with you.'

'Oh but, Essy,' Minnie moaned as the two of them left the auditorium. 'A nip and a tuck here and there could take years off a person so I'm told.'

'I'll give you a nip and tuck,' Esther cursed.

The sisters tottered to their respective suits at either end of the corridor. Minnie waving to her stone-faced sister before Esther slammed her door shut.

Esther had very little trouble getting off to sleep, finding her solitary accommodation a welcome break and a peaceful one at that. Minnie, on the other hand, stood in her room like a little lost lamb staring at the huge gaping expanse that was her bed, one that she was to occupy alone. Dropping the tangerine toga to the floor, she slipped apprehensively between the sheets where she tossed and turned for several minutes before hugging the spare pillow tightly as though it was her sister, or the afore mentioned Mr O'Grady.

Minnie slept eventually but uneasily, waking regularly to peer bleary-eyed over the duvet at her shadowy surroundings. 'Ohhhh, Essy,' she croaked, pulling the pillow closer still. Minnie later rolled onto her back making the nasal gargling that her sister was so pleased to be rid of, albeit for one night only.

Aliya slept with her bedroom door heavily bolted and her father's service revolver beneath her pillow, the threats on her life having escalated of late. That night one such threat was to be exacted by a pair of radical brothers, Zafir and Waseem, sworn in blood to defend the ways of their forefathers and the Prophets they were prepared to die for their strongly held beliefs, and to kill for that matter.

Approaching cloaked in darkness in black robes from the desert dunes, the stealthy brothers scaled the palace walls and dropped silently into the compound within, ducking behind the heap of dung when Sahib emerged from his quarters to light a cigarette and admire the pearlescent moon. Leaning from his veranda to catch the heady scent of his cherished roses, Sahib failed to notice Zafir rapidly approaching from his rear until it was too late. Raising a rock above his head, the would-be assassin bludgeoned the aging gardener's head before he could raise the alarm. Sahib groaned and slumped to the floor, clinging to the rail at first before collapsing, losing consciousness and a large quantity of blood.

Trampling the roses with complete disregard, the vengeful Zafir and Waseem tugged at several doors and windows but the princess had taken her security very seriously indeed following a previous failed attempt on her life. 'Here!' Wasaam told his brother, the pair drawing their daggers at a patio window. Cautiously sliding the glass door open the two shadowy figures squeezed through and stood concealed by the drapes, peering to see a motionless body beneath the bed sheets before them.

Kissing their glinting blades, the murderous pair emerged bare-footed and approached ghost-like, but the desert breeze that accompanied them caressed Minnie's cheek and she stirred. 'Mmmm, Essy,' she groaned under her breath. 'Essy, is that you?'

A hand tattooed with ancient scriptures clawed at Minnie's sheet as she in turn reached for the bedside lamp. 'Oh, Essy, I'm so glad you came,' she said, unable to focus, at the precise moment Zafir wrenched the sheets down to Minnie's feet, revealing her near naked aged body with her bloomers wrenched up around her naval and her loose fitting bra twisted and sagging.

The sight immediately mortified the fanatical brothers who'd imagined the youthful princess in couture lingerie.

'Essy?' Minnie said, rubbing her eyes and donning her spectacles before screaming on seeing the two blackened figure looming over her. Her cries were stifled by those of the brothers, whose horror at the sight before them was compounded tenfold by the addition of Minnie's teeth submerged and magnified in a glass of water beside her.

'ARRRRRRGGHHH, ESSYYYYYYYY!' Minnie screeched, shielding her face from the raised daggers. 'ESSYYYYYYYY!'

Esther and Aliya both woke and sat bolt upright in bed. 'Minnie?' Esther said, half asleep and fumbling for her toga. 'Minnie, what is it?'

Aliya reached for her revolver, leapt from her bed and raced from her room in her underwear.

Now as callous and cold hearted as the assassins were they would never harm a hair on the head of an elder.

'GET AWAY!' Minnie screamed, tossing the spare pillow toward the startled brothers. 'GET AWAY WITH YOU, GET AWAY I SAID!'

Hearing Aliya's pounding footsteps racing toward them along the corridor and a shot she fired into the ceiling, Zafir and Waseem fled the room and out across the courtyard, the heavily thorned roses tearing at their lower legs.

'MINNIE!' Aliya yelled, bursting into the room brandishing the firearm. 'WHAT IS IT?'

'Men!' Minnie said, wrenching her duvet back up under her nose. 'Two of the blighters!' she added, trembling and pointing toward the open terrace door.

Aliya cocked her weapon once again and sprinted outside, firing several shots toward the departing figures winging Zafir on his right shoulder before the pair clambered back over the wall and out into the desert scrub. 'SAHIB!' Aliya then cried on seeing her gardener-cum-confidant slumped and bleeding on his veranda. 'SAHIB!'

Esther shuffled as hastily as she could, rattled by the shots fired, joining Minnie moments later. 'Minnie!' she said breathlessly. 'Minnie, whatever's the matter, darling?'

'Oh, Essy,' Minnie sobbed with arms outstretched, beckoning to her sister. 'Essy, Essy, I was so frightened.'

'What?' Esther said, looking across the room at the open door and the muslin drapes billowing inside. 'What on earth's happened here?'

'Intruders, dear,' Minnie croaked, reaching for her sister's hand.

'Stay there,' Esther told her distraught sister, making for the door herself.

'No, Essy!' Minnie cried. 'Don't go out there!'

'Quiet, dear!' Esther replied, grabbing at the drapes and peering cautiously outside. 'Aliya?' she called. 'Aliya is that you, dear?'

'ESTHER!' Aliya called back at Sahib's side. 'ESTHER, HELP ME PLEASE!'

'Oh, oh yes,' Esther replied, turning to her sister who cowered in her bed. 'Stay right there, Minnie, do you hear!' she told her in no uncertain terms. 'I'll be right back, I promise.'

'Essy, no, please!' Minnie begged, reaching again. 'Please, it's not safe!'

'Shhhhhh,' Esther replied reassuringly. 'Please, Minnie, you must do as I say and stay put.' She ventured outside and hurried to Sahib's veranda. 'Oh dear Lord!' she cried with a hand to her mouth. 'What's happened, oh sweet Mary, look at the blood, Aliya, is he?'

Sahib let out a pitiful groan.

'Help me,' Aliya asked again. 'Please, Esther, help me.' She heaved Sahib up into a sitting position. 'It's me, Sahib, Aliya,' she told him. 'It's alright, I'm here.'

Between the two of them Esther and Aliya helped the battered Sahib inside and onto his single bed. 'Please stay with him, Esther,' Aliya said, 'please, I'll fetch water and towels.'

'Yes, yes of course, dear,' Esther replied, having fully woken now to this hellish nightmare.

'Essyyyyy!' a voice then called from the veranda. 'Essy, where are you?' Minnie had ventured from her bed and was stood trembling beside the spattered blood. 'ESSYYYYYYYYY!' she then cried, panic stricken.

'IN HERE!' Esther called back, clutching the moaning Sahib's hand and a pillow to his head wound. 'Minnie, I thought I told you to stay put!' she snapped when her sister appeared.

'Oh good heavens!' Minnie shrieked. 'Essy, Essy, is he?'

'No, dear,' Esther hurriedly replied, sitting at Sahib's side. 'But somebody's beaten the poor soul pretty badly indeed.'

Aliya returned moments later having donned her own toga in haste. 'My poor Sahib,' she said, setting down a bowl of warm water beside the bed and submerging a white hand towel before wringing it and mopping her battered friend's seeping wound. 'We must stitch this,' she told the sisters, producing a first aid tin. 'But, but I cannot.'

'Give it here, dearie,' Minnie said, approaching the bed still visibly shaken but eager to help. 'I once stitched Essy's knee when she came a cropper from a motorcycle I'd borrowed, you were riding pillion, weren't you, dear.'

'Not for long,' Esther replied, scowling. 'I'd have been fine if you hadn't accelerated at breakneck speed like a woman possessed, oh and while we're on the subject you specifically told me Father had given you permission to take his bike, and he clearly did not, I was grounded for a fortnight along with you when the police brought his mangled wreck home.'

Aliya handed Minnie the tin. 'Will you, Minnie, please' she asked.

'Yes of course,' Minnie replied, rounding the bed on the opposite side of her sister for fear of antagonising her further. 'Hold him, Essy,' she told Esther whilst threading the needle up to the light.

With Aliya and Esther grappling with the writhing patient, Minnie skilfully and delicately stitched the two lesions on his scalp tightly closed. 'Ooooh I'm sorry, darling,' she said when he winced as she tugged the thread for the last time and snipped off the remainder. 'Bandages, dear,' she told Aliya, taking complete charge of the situation considering her recent fright. 'Essy, lift his head, please,' she asked, reaching to bind the victim several times.

'Thank you, Minnie,' Aliya said, rubbing Minnie's back. 'Thank you so much, and I am sorry for this, I should have told you there are those in my country who wish to do me harm.'

'But why, dear?' Esther asked, finding the situation unfathomable. 'Why would they do this, it's despicable, utterly despicable.'

'Fear,' Aliya told the sisters. 'Fear of change and what it may bring to our lands, but I say change is good, and the people, the people they want it too but our leaders, they say we must follow the ways of our ancestors.'

'Dear Lord,' Esther remarked. 'Can't they see change is inevitable, it's a fact of life, just like evolution.'

'Quite right, dear,' Minnie agreed. 'If not we'd still be running around in bear skins, pig ignorant and uncivilised.'

'Exactly,' Esther nodded. 'Although in my sister's case,' she told Aliya, 'There is always an exception.'

Minnie thought for a moment, not knowing whether she'd just been complimented or degraded, then smiled assuming it was the former, but of course she was wrong. 'Why thank you, dear,' she said mopping the last of the blood from Sahib's face. 'As they say,' she added proudly and quoting her primary school head mistress, 'The cream always rises to the top.'

'No, dear,' Esther said in a bid to clarify things. 'You don't understand,' but then seeing the look of gratitude on Aliya's face for her sister's selfless bedside manner she declined to elaborate. 'Well done, dear,' she opted to say instead.

'Yes indeed,' Aliya agreed. 'I cannot thank you enough, both of you, Sahib has been with me many years and quite frankly I don't know what I'd do without him.'

'Essy,' Minnie asked, doe-eyed. 'Can I, can I stay with you for the rest of the night, pleaaaase?'

'But of course, dear,' Esther said without hesitation this time around. 'After all, those men may return, perhaps, Aliya, we should telephone for the police, dear.'

'No need,' Aliya replied, clinging to Sahib's hand. 'My father's men have returned and are on guard around the palace, they will not leave their positions until I give the order so you will be quite safe now, I assure you.'

'Oh right,' Esther said, turning to her sister to take back her offer of a shared bed but Minnie had already left the room and was safely tucked between her sister's sheets. 'Ohhh alright,' she soon told her sister, having left Aliya to sit with Sahib for the remainder of the night. 'But I don't want to hear a peep out of you, Minnie, do you hear, Minnie, Minnie, I said do you hear me?'

Minnie's rude awakening and near death experience as she saw it had rattled her to the point of exasperation, sapping what little strength she may have had at such an ungodly hour, therefore once reclined her faltering resilience gave way to sweet unbridled slumber with the break of dawn soon to be upon them.

During Minnie's conscious hours, more often than not she would try her sister's patience and test her to the point of breaking, but it was only when she slept, be it a cat nap in her threadbare wingback chair or snoring thunderously beside her in bed, that Esther could look upon her for what she truly was, a kind considerate warm hearted individual capable of selfless acts of kindness and compassion, the likes of which she had shown Sahib that very evening and many before him.

Emotionally charged with sibling pride, Esther drew the sheets up onto her gargling sister's chest. 'Night, night, darling,' she softly said, settling beside her, reaching to turn out the bedside lamp. Despite the horrific events of that night Esther lay awake staring at Minnie, even raising a smile, but her contentment was short-lived when her sister stretched out a flaying arm in her sleep and struck her square on the nose. 'Ooooh, you cow!' she cried, flinging Minnie's arm back across the bed and immediately switching her opinion toward her from one of deep devotion to that of seething resentment, and so the circle of life encompassing these extraordinary British pensioners turned another revolution, drawing the inevitable and their unspeakable end another day closer. Both sisters were fast approaching an age surpassing their parents, whose funerals they had solemnly attended, wept at and fought as they so often did to blot out all thoughts of either sibling's eventual demise.

CHAPTER SIX.

The following morning while the sisters slept soundly, news of Zafir and Waseem's capture and detainment filtered back to Aliya's palace. Learning of their plot to murder his daughter, her furious father had immediately offered a colossal reward for information, enough in fact to change the lives of an entire village let alone a single informant. The fleeing brothers had been cornered in a goat shed and handed over bound and gagged within hours of the generous offer being made public. Local authorities too had been paid to turn a blind eye while the matter was dealt with in house as it were.

Aliya's father, an influential man and distantly related to royalty, was intent on nipping any further attempts on his daughter's life in the bud by making an example of his two captives. After a brief kangaroo court hearing by family and peers, sentencing was merely a formality. The pair were to be stripped naked and driven a hundred or so miles out into the Saudi desert and cut loose to wander without water beneath the scorching sun, a slow and agonising death and stark warning to others. Many had called for the brothers' heads on a block as was customary, although a swift end may have appeared more favourable to them when their skin began to peel reptilian-like from their reddened backs with no shade or sanctuary in sight.

Esther stirred around ten a.m. and instantly felt restrained; opening an eye she gave her sister a sideways glance, Minnie having clung tightly to her sister whilst sleeping and nuzzled her nose into her ear. 'Get off of me,' she said, wriggling and tugging at her sister's arms.

'Mmmmm morning, Georgie,' Minnie said dreamily. 'Shall we try that again?'

'Georgie!' Esther exclaimed, pushing her sister's face away and wriggling from her grasp. 'Minnie, wake up, you fool!'

'What, what?' Minnie mumbled, rubbing her eyes. 'Oh, oh it's you, Essy,' she said, disgruntled somewhat.

'Of course it's me,' Esther replied. 'Who else would it be, and who the devil's Georgie for Pete's sake?'

'Georgie Clooney,' Minnie replied reaching for her teeth. 'I was in the midst of the most realistic dream, dear,' she continued. 'Georgie and I had just spent the most amazing night in a Bedouin tent beneath the stars making mad passionate love and whipping up a sandstorm if you get my drift, I managed to hold my own of course but the poor dear tired after round three.'

A shudder ran the length of Esther's spine at Minnie's graphic revelation. 'Do you mind!' she asked abruptly, clambering from the bed to distance herself from her debauched sister.

'Well I did at the time, dear,' Minnie confessed. 'I was just getting into my stride as it were.'

'Dear Lord preserve us,' Esther groaned, donning her toga and shuddering. 'And you were clinging to me like a damned limpet, I need to take a shower,' she added, feeling decidedly grubby all of a sudden.

'Well,' Minnie said with a mischievous grin. 'If you hadn't have woken me, dear, I was about to give Georgie the best....'

'Not another word, Minnie!' Esther insisted, raising a hand to silence her sister. 'Not another word, I haven't eaten yet and the thought of you pleasuring this Georgie Clooney of yours without your teeth in is making me feel quite bilious, quite bilious indeed, now if you'll excuse me I need the bathroom then I'm going to look in on poor Sahib, I do hope he's alright.'

'Right you are, Essy dear,' Minnie chirped, sitting up content at having bedded the A-list celebrity of her dreams, albeit from the confines of her sordid imagination.

Esther met Aliya in the corridor. 'Oh good morning, my sweet,' she said, tugging at her tangled hair. 'How's Sahib, I hardly slept worrying about the poor darling.'

'He is badly shaken,' Aliya replied, returning from his room with a breakfast tray. 'Our family physician has seen him this morning and assures us there is no internal bleeding which was a great concern.'

Esther rubbed the girl's arm. 'Oh I'm so glad, dear,' she said sympathetically. 'I can see you're very fond of him.'

'Yes I am,' Aliya said, managing a smile. 'He has served me well and I will see to it that he has the very best of care, the very best, Esther.'

'Cooeeee!' Minnie then called from Esther's room with a rolled towel under her arm. 'How's the patient this morning, my dear?' she asked in passing.

'Much better, thank you,' Aliya replied. 'And how are you, Minnie?'

'Oh I'm fine,' Minnie said nonchalantly. 'The bathroom, it's this way is it?'

'Yes, yes,' Aliya called after her. 'The last door on the left!'

'Hey, hey!' Esther called too. 'I was about to…!' but her hapless sister disappeared out of sight, bolting the bathroom door behind her.

'I'll, I'll bloomin'!' Esther raged.

'It's alright, Esther,' Aliya laughed. 'I have another seven bathrooms, please I will show you.'

Esther was led to Aliya's private en-suite, the finest in the palace in fact, surpassing Minnie's in size and grandeur by a mile. 'Ohhhhh,' Esther said at the doorway, dazzled by the presence of so much gold. 'Please tell me that's brass,' she said in awe. Aliya simply shook her head confirming the authenticity of her fixtures and fittings. 'Noooo,' Esther gasped running a hand along the free standing slipper bath compete with twenty four carat ball and claw feet.

'Please, enjoy,' Aliya said, heading for the kitchen. 'And take your time.'

Esther did so, as did Minnie, the pair later joining their host at the breakfast table. 'English tea,' Aliya informed them turning the Wedgewood pot three times. 'And of course in the Royal Albert,' she added.

'Quite right too, my dear,' Esther agreed with a grin, whilst tucking a linen napkin into the neck of her blouse and plucking a slice of toast from the rack.

Minnie took Aliya's hand. 'Will you be alright, dear?' she asked with a mouthful of muesli. 'I mean the two of us must be on our way soon but we are reluctant to leave, with those bad men at large and all.'

'There are no more bad men,' Aliya informed the sisters. 'My father has seen to that, of course I would love you to stay but you fine ladies must follow your heats and your dreams wherever they may take you, but know this, there will always be a place for you in my home, always.'

'Thank you, dearie,' Esther said, sipping at her tea. 'Oooh and you're right,' she exclaimed. 'This is English tea, where on earth did you get it. Aliya?'

'Your Fortnum and Mason,' Aliya replied. 'I have a shipment every month, my father is a fan also you see.'

Following a hearty breakfast and with midday fast approaching, Esther and Minnie ventured to Sahib's room. 'Hellooooo,' Minnie said peering around his door. 'How are you, dear?'

Sahib beckoned from his bed, now in a more coherent state. Grabbing at Minnie's hand, he pulled her close and in Arabic thanked her from the bottom of his heart for her medical assistance.

'Oh that's quite alright, my lovely,' Minnie replied, getting the gist of his foreign tone. 'I'm sure you'd have done the same for my sister and me.'

Reaching to fumble in his bedside drawer, Sahib retrieved a tiny golden camel and thrust it into Minnie's hand.

'For me?' Minnie asked. 'Are you, are you sure?'

Sahib nodded and closed her hand around the centuries old relic before gripping Esther's hand in thanks too, saddened that they must eventually leave.

Esther plumped Sahib's pillow and straightened the creases in his bed sheets. 'You be sure and get plenty of rest, dearie,' she told him. 'I do hope we have the pleasure of meeting you again some day.'

After exchanging kisses with Sahib the sisters retrieved their bags and left the palace to find Aliya admiring Vivien. 'She is beautiful,' the princess told them.

'Yes, yes, she is, isn't she,' Esther agreed, opening the rear doors. 'I wouldn't trade her for the world, you know.'

'One moment, dear,' Minnie said, retrieving the tablet. 'Have we time for a selfie?'

'But of course,' Esther said, slipping an arm around Aliya's waist and posing with her radiant palace as a stunning backdrop whilst her fumbling sister extended her arms.

'I will miss you,' Aliya confessed, having like so many before her warmed to the sisters during their brief encounter.

Minnie angled the tablet screen a tad to capture Sahib's smiling face at his window, helped by the housemaids, his head still bandaged but his spirit unbroken.

Esther hugged the girl. 'Now are you sure you're going to be alright, my darling?' she said, concerned to say the least. 'Safe I mean?'

'Oh yes, yes, yes,' Aliya smiled, brushing her robe aside to reveal the revolver tucked into her bodice. 'Quite sure.' With a hug and a kiss the sisters boarded Vivien, Aliya closing Esther's door behind her. 'You take with you my love and admiration,' she told the two travellers. 'You are indeed an inspiration to women the world over, and for that I thank you.'

'Oh I don't know about that, dearie,' Esther said humbly. 'If you ask me we're just a couple of dotty old fools that don't know when to call it a day, aren't we, dear?' She turned to see her sister bent over scooping up strewn olives from the foot well. 'I rest my case,' Esther added, tapping Aliya's hand and starting off out of the gate.

'Oh, oh byeeeeeee!' Minnie called, straightening her back and waving with three pitted green olives in her mouth. 'Goodbyyyyyye!' she gurgled, retrieving another of the escapees and picking off a clump of Vivien's carpet fluff. 'Olive, dear?' she asked her sister.

Without uttering a word Esther gave Minnie her reply by means of a disapproving glare whilst turning onto the desert road once again.

'Essyyyy?' Minnie said probing a short while later. 'Who's Wilfred?'

Esther immediately stiffened at the wheel. 'What?' she swiftly replied 'I, I, who?'

'Wilfred,' Minnie reiterated. 'You mentioned him in your sleep, my dear, I woke to check the windows and you were muttering.'

'Was I?' Esther replied, unable to look her sister in the face. 'You must've been mistaken, dear, you were shaken after your experience don't forget, maybe even a little delirious.'

'No, no, I distinctly heard you,' Minnie said pressing the point. 'Quite clearly, and what's more…'

'More!' Esther blurted over her sister. 'What do you mean more, Minnie, I'm telling you, you are mistaken, I don't know any Wilfred and never have so can we kindly leave it there thank you,' and she gripped the wheel tightly looking straight ahead, her pupils dilated.

'You could have fooled me, dear,' Minnie insisted, popping another olive into her mouth before coughing and spluttering into her hand.

'Are you alright, dear?' Esther asked slapping her sister's back as she turned a little red in the face.

Minnie soon regurgitated an olive stone into the palm of her hand. 'Pitted, my backside!' she cursed, scrutinizing the jar, 'Remind me, Essy,' she added, tossing the stone from the window, 'To draft a strongly worded letter to these blighters, and if I don't receive a handful of free coupons for my troubles I'll be decidedly miffed I tell you.' The sisters in the past had mastered the art of the free coupon, meticulously checking labels for minor defects that may somehow infringe upon their statutory rights, then winging off letters penned on scented note paper willy-nilly to all and sundry like many of their retired counterparts do with unlimited time at their disposal. One by one like a lottery windfall the free vouchers, coupon and bleating apologies would land on their doormat. Amongst their most prized freebies was a tour of the Cadbury's chocolate factory after Esther's scathing review of a broken finger of fudge, a set of Tetley tea mugs after Minnie's eagle-eyed reporting of a labelling blunder, a mountain of Mint Imperials hand delivered by the company's vice president when the sisters threatened legal action over a weight issue, their packets clearly stated weight of 43 grams coming up short by a gram and a half, and the crème de la crème of freebies, an all-expenses-paid week for two at the Pontins holiday resort at Camber Sands. This generous summer vacation was by a well-known soap powder manufacturer when their new and improved formula disintegrated the sisters' delicate net curtains at the recommended thirty degrees.

Esther and Minnie saw themselves as champions of consumerism, taking on global corporations from their fireside and only accepting an apology if it were accompanied by a customary sweetener of sorts.

'Well?' Minnie continued to plague Esther. 'Come on, out with it?'

'Out with what?' Esther asked, skirting the subject, 'Honestly, Minnie, I don't know what you're talking about.'

'Wilfred,' Minnie said, screwing the lid back on her olive jar. 'I can always tell when you're lying, Essy,' she added, peering over the rim of her spectacles. 'Your nose twitches and you do that knee trembly thing.'

'I do not!' Esther said, trying desperately to still her pulsating left leg. 'It's, it's just a touch of cramp that's all.'

'Essyyyyyy?' Minnie dogged her sister for an answer. 'I clearly heard you, something about Wilfred and his liquorice pipe.'

'Ohhhh,' Esther cursed, having been backed into a corner. 'Well if you must know.'

'Yes, yes I must,' Minnie chirped, all ears.

'Wilfred is my friend and nothing more,' Esther explained. 'He runs the pick and mix sweetie stall on the market outside the dental practice.'

'Yes, yes, I know the fellow,' Minnie interjected before lunging forward as Esther braked sharply to avoid an emaciated dog.

'I call by once in a while,' Esther continued whilst eyeing the dig in her mirror. 'For a quarter of aniseed twists and a Curly Wurly.'

'I must say, Essy,' Minnie smiled, 'He's quite the looker, I can see why you would be attracted to him.'

'I am not attracted to him!' Esther informed her sister sharply. 'He's just a friend, that's all, he's been very kind since Jack passed away.'

'I bet he has,' Minnie said, tongue-in-cheek, 'You lucky minx, you, he must be all of seventy-five and not a day older, a toy boy in fact, Essy.'

'What are you insinuating?' Esther asked angrily. 'You know how I loved my Jack, I would never...'

'I never said you did, dear,' Minnie said in her defence. 'But he's clearly smitten with you, and you him no doubt, I've seen you sucking on that liquorice pipe with a twinkle in your eye.'

'What, no, don't be ridiculous!' Esther stormed, keen to defend her honour. 'I, I mean,' she stammered. 'Well yes Wilfred is rather handsome, and generous too when weighing out my aniseed twists but that's as far as it goes, I promise you.'

'That's a shame,' Minnie said, deflated somewhat. 'I was rather hoping you might pander to his affections as it were, and in doing so procure a little discount on a regular order of peanut brittle and Pontefract cakes, you know how I like my Pontefract cakes.'

'Minnie, are you suggesting?' Esther asked, aghast. 'That I, I prostitute myself for a measly bag of Pontefract cakes!'

'Oh no, dear, of course not,' Minnie smirked. 'Nothing of the sort, but if you could possibly return his flirtatious gestures on the odd occasion, or maybe dress a little more provocatively I'd be more than grateful, and so would Wilfred no doubt.'

'I'll do nothing of the sort!' Esther said in retort. 'I've had more than my share of admiring glances of late so there is nothing at all wrong with my attire.'

Minnie looked her sister up and down. 'Oh come now, dear,' she said, mocking her. 'Look at you, I dare say Queen Victoria revealed more flesh than you ever did, have you ever considered a halter neck, I hear they're all the rage with these young teeny types.'

'A halter neck!' Esther said, bemused. 'What do you think I am, Minnie, a ruddy shire horse, and anyway those teeny types as you call them ought to cover up and leave a little more to the imagination, my Jack certainly preferred it that way.'

'That was Jack, dear,' Minnie reminded her. 'But if you want to woo Wilfred you'll need to think outside the cardboard box as they say.'

'Minnie,' Esther said, having left Medina far behind by now. 'I do not want to woo Wilfred, not now and not ever, he is merely a friend, nothing more.'

'But, but, Essy,' Minnie pleaded. 'What about my Pontefract cakes?'

Esther refused point blank to be drawn on her supposed friendship with the over-affectionate confectioner, even if she had allowed herself an occasional fleeting fanciful thought or two, or possibly three.

The sisters' next destination was to be the small town of Duba on the northern banks of the Red Sea, a distance as the crow flies of three hundred and fifteen miles, but by desert road probably a great deal further, although with Minnie's constant wittering and Esther's speed increasing at time to fifty miles per hour the pair made gradual progress.

Duba would be their crossing point by ferry to Safaga and the start of the sisters' Egyptian leg of their journey. It has been said on numerous occasions that it is unadvisable for Western women to travel unaccompanied through vast swathes of Saudi Arabia, especially when entrusted to operate an automobile, but with the royal decree still very much in place Esther and Minnie encountered very little resistance. The odd stone was hurled in their direction by those foolish enough to flout the law but all in all the sisters had gotten off lightly.

'AND TO YOU, SIR!' Minnie yelled in reply, mistaking a gentleman's angry rantings for familiarity. 'LOVELY DAY!'

Esther wrenched her sister away from the window on seeing the street vendors shaking fists in her rear view mirror. 'Come away, dear!' she warned her. 'By the looks of things not everyone is a fan of ours.'

'Ohhh nonsense, dear,' Minnie smirked, seeing only good in most people. 'I usually find a wave and a friendly smile sways most opinions,' and at that precise moment a hail of coarse gravel showered Vivien, startling the sisters. 'WHY YOU!' Minnie growled, looking over her shoulder to see a taxi driver standing beside his rusting car, screaming at the heavens to send down a thunderbolt to smite the Western whores. 'Pull over, dear!' Minnie barked. 'I'll give that blighter a piece of my mind, so help me I will.'

'I'll do nothing of the sort,' Esther replied, accelerating further still while her sister rolled up her sleeves spoiling for a fight.

'I'll not be humiliated, dear,' Minnie told Esther defiantly, and she then sank low in her seat as the same taxi driver sped by barracking them from his window and leaving Vivien in a cloud of desert dust.

'Has he gone?' Minnie asked, peering sheepishly over the dashboard.

'Yes and good riddance,' Esther replied, winding up her window and wiping her spectacles clean.

Entering Duba, Esther stopped for fuel and in stark contrast received the warmest of welcomes from the willing pump attendant. 'No, no I insist,' she told him, thrusting the correct amount of Riyal into his hand, 'There's no such thing as a free ride you know.'

The subservient attendant insisted though on topping up Vivien's oil and water and thoroughly cleaning her windows to send them on their way in ship shape fashion, albeit with several tiny stone chips, a small price to pay for passing unscathed through the Saudi heartlands.

'Now, dear,' Minnie said, consulting the tablet once again. 'By my reckoning we are to catch the ferry to Safaga from the port ahead, oooh, Essy!' she added excitedly. 'We're going to cross the Red Sea, can you believe it?'

'Hmmm,' Esther merely mumbled, having had her fill of all things nautical aboard the Northern Star from Mumbai. 'If we really must,' she told her enthusiastic sister, 'But I'm warning you, Minnie, if you…..'

'I promise, dear,' Minnie said, interrupting.

'I promise you it'll be smooth sailing and hassle free, you have my word as a former Brownie on it.'

Esther gave her sister another of her sideways glances whilst navigating the poorly maintained back roads of Duba, a town described fondly by its people as the Pear of the Red Sea, but more importantly it provided a vital link between Saudi Arabia, Jordan and Egypt used by tens of thousands during the annual pilgrimage to Mecca, of Hajj as it is known.

'Brownie, my foot,' Esther scoffed. 'If my memory serves me right you were expelled during summer camp, were you not?'

'Well, well yes,' Minnie confessed. 'But, but it wasn't my fault, Suzie Watkins put me up to it.'

'Yes I know,' Esther replied, recalling the sorry tale when Minnie was goaded by her peers to stuff nettles into Miss Baxter's sleeping bag. The furious leader, or Brown Owl as she preferred, bolted from her tent wearing nothing but her cotton bloomers, her screams piercing the night air penetrating deep into the ancient forest of Sherwood. The following morning whilst scratching fiercely she launched a formal enquiry, that's when Suzie Watkins buckled under interrogation and snitched on Minnie, turning her supposed friend in and in doing so earning herself a commendation and a silver ribbon for her uniform. Minnie, on the other hand, received the sharp end of Miss Baxter's tongue and was stripped of her previous accolades, including her fire lighter's badge, orienteering and needlecraft ribbons and her prized neck scarf before being shamefully and ceremoniously drummed out of the all-girl group.

Esther shook her head. 'Three shillings a week Mother paid for that uniform,' she reminded her sister. 'And you lasted a month.'

Minnie lowered her head in shame, knowing full well her parents often went without to give their girls the very best their meagre salaries could afford.

'And I wouldn't have minded,' Esther continued her berating, 'But you had already received a written warning for fetching a stray dog into the church hall.'

'Oh but, darling,' Minnie replied hastily. 'It was the dead of winter with a foot of snow on the ground, what else was I supposed to do?'

'Well for once,' Esther explained, 'Mother commended your actions but I doubt the vicar has ever forgiven you after the flea-bitten beast ran amok in his church sinking its canines into his candles, peeing in the pews and defecating on the organist's stool.'

'Me neither,' Minnie agreed, having given the vicar a wide berth until his eventual demise, he himself taking his wrath and resentment toward her and the hound to the grave.

Esther parked Vivien adjacent to the bustling ferry terminal and the two alighted, once again groaning as they straightened. 'I SAY!' Esther called to a gentleman in boating attire, 'WE'D LIKE TO TAKE THE FERRY TO…'

She paused and turned to Minnie who had stooped to coax a feral kitten from an abandoned tea chest. 'Minnie!' Esther said, tapping her sister's plump bottom. 'Minnie, where is it we wish to sail to, Minnie, leave it will you,' she insisted. 'It's probably riddled with mange.'

'I'm sorry, dear,' Minnie said, straightening yet again with a pained expression. 'What was that?'

'The ferry,' Esther grimaced irritably beneath the burning sun. 'Where is it we are headed, oh do pay attention, dear!'

'Safaga, my love,' Minnie said, addressing the ferryman who spoke only Arabic and looked right through the elderly sisters. 'Cooeeeee!' Minnie said, snapping her fingers. 'We wish to take the ferry to Safaga, could you please tell us where we may purchase a ticket for the said crossing!' but again a blank expression was received.

Suddenly a tall tanned travelling gent stepped between them, complete with backpack, beard, boots and a B.A. in foreign languages. 'Please allow me, ladies,' he said in a broad Aussie brogue, further addressing the ferryman in fluent Arabic, much to Minnie and Esther's surprise. 'Ya got a couple of hours before the next boat leaves,' he told them, 'And it's twenty Riyal each and another fifty for the station wagon.'

'Station wagon!' Esther said, defending Vivien's honour. 'I'll have you know Vivien here is a vintage Morris not some mass-produced mechanical monstrosity.'

'Vivien?' the Aussie replied. 'So the car's a Sheila?'

'Oooh, an Australian,' Minnie chirped. 'How delightful, thank you kindly, sir,' she said over her sister's shoulder, 'For your assistance that is.'

'No worries, Missy,' the Australian national replied, swinging his backpack over his shoulder. 'Listen,' he added, 'I'm headin' over to Safaga meself, why don't I buy you Sheilas a cold one while we wait, wodaya say?'

'A what, sorry?' Esther, asked bewildered.

'A tinny,' the backpacker replied. 'A tube, a beer.'

'Beer!' Esther remarked, wrinkling her nose. 'Oh no, no, no, no, no, we're quite alright, thank you.'

'We?' Minnie said, stepping forward. 'Essy, I'm as parched as parched can be so a cold tinny tube sounds positively heavenly right now.'

'No beer!' Esther said with conviction. 'Now if it was a lemon tea you were offering then we may be persuaded, but only after formal introductions have been made, you can never be too careful, you understand.'

Minnie barged past her sister. 'Ohhh nonsense, dear,' she said. 'I'd love a tinny beer,' she told the traveller. 'Hello, I'm Minnie and the frosty mare behind me is my elder sister Essy, shall we go?'

'G'day,' the Aussie said, tipping his typically Australian hat. 'The name's Lawrence, Lawrence Matherson, pleased to meetcha.'

'Of Arabia,' Minnie said, looking back across Duba and the distant desert horizon. 'Oh how wonderful, Essy, Essy, dear take a look!' She pointed to the Australian's chiselled jaw. 'He even has the look of Peter O'Toole about him, don't you think?' She of course referred to the Irish born actor nominated for an Oscar for his part in the 1962 epic Arabian drama depicting the life of T.E. Lawrence and his hard fought exploits during World War One.

'What was that, dear?' Esther asked, paying very little attention.

'Ohh never mind,' Minnie said, taking Lawrence's arm. 'Right, young man,' she said with pursed lips. 'Let's see about that tinny tube beer, shall we.'

'Minniiiie,' Esther said, scurrying behind them. 'It's a lemon tea or nothing, do you hear!'

Lawrence stooped and lowered his voice. 'Hey, Minnie love?' he asked. 'What's eatin' ya, sis?'

'Ohhh don't mind Essy,' Minnie replied, tickled pink at strolling arm in arm with one so dashing. 'It's the heat, dear, it causes her to perspire in the most private of places and fattens her ankles too.'

'Minnie!' Esther barked, appalled at her sister's blatant revelation. 'Do you mind!' She looked around swiftly for anybody within earshot of her less than sensitive sister. 'I'll thank you to keep such personal matters to yourself, besides it's not the heat that swells my ankles it's these damned crimplene tights, I bought them in Mumbai and they're playing havoc with my circulation.'

'You're wearing tights?' Minnie asked, astounded given their current climate.

'But of course,' Esther confessed. 'A lady cannot travel without all her bits and pieces stowed securely.'

'Bits and pieces,' Minnie smirked, 'Essy, it's eighty-five degrees, my darling, I for one have gone commando today.'

Lawrence roared with laughter with an arm around Minnie's shoulder, pulling her tightly to him. 'Jeepers, Minnie love,' he said striding with her in tow. 'You're a spirited Sheila, aren't ya?

'Oooooh,' Minnie squealed, turning to her sister. 'Did you hear that, Essy, I'm a spirited Sheila.'

Esther followed with a quizzical look on her face. 'What do you mean, commando?' she asked, never having come across the modern term,

Minnie did nothing more than lift the side of her flowing skirt to reveal a partial bare buttock.

'MINNIE!' Esther shrieked, mortified to say the least. 'Have you completely lost your mind, girl?'

'Not at all, dear,' Minnie said with a spring in her step, 'You really should try it, Essy, I find it quite liberating.'

'Liberating!' Esther cursed, 'I'll give you liberating, you, you floozie you!' Esther then wrenched at the crotch of her tights having felt some discomfort for the past hour or so and suffered from a severe bout of feminine perspiration, but persevered with her robust regulation crimplene tights.

Lawrence led the ladies to a tiny back street café containing just four dust-covered tables, one of them occupied by three domino-clattering locals 'Mustafa, me old mate!' Lawrence called to the heavily bearded proprietor who sat slumped across his sagging counter top.

'Ahhhhhh, Mister Lawrence!' he replied, sitting upright with a beaming smile of familiarity. 'It is so good to see you again,' and stubbing out his bitten cigarette he dragged the heavily stained cloth from his shoulder and smeared the counter in readiness.

Lawrence gestured to the sisters. 'Mustafa I'd like ya to meet a coupla friends of mine,' he said, having frequented the café on numerous occasions during his stay in Duba. 'This here's Minnie and her sister with the starched drawers there is Essy.'

'Oh really,' Esther frowned, unimpressed.

Lawrence slammed his hand down on the crooked counter. 'Give us three tinnies will ya, mate,' he said confidently.

Esther raised a hand in objection. 'Oh no, no not for me,' she insisted. 'Just a lemon tea or a cordial will suffice, my good man.'

'OK, two tinnies and a juice,' Lawrence added. 'Me and the Sheilas have got a mighty thirst on so look lively will ya, me old mate.'

'I'm sorry, sir,' Mustafa said, wary of the strangers that accompanied him. 'I do not have these tinnies you request, may I remind you it is forbidden in these parts.'

'Forbidden my arse,' Lawrence scoffed. 'Come on, Mustafa, you know me,' he joked. 'I was in here last night and I left here shit-faced.'

'You are mistaken, Mister Lawrence,' Mustafa said, looking the sisters up and down. 'I run a respectable establishment here.'

'Look, Mustafa!' Lawrence said, leaning across the counter. 'If ya worried about the Sheilas they're kosher, mate, just a coupla regular Poms.'

'I beg your pardon?' Esther objected to his terminology.

'Ohhhh,' Mustafa replied, tipping Lawrence a playful wink. 'I see, Mister Lawrence, you are wanting the coconut milk are you not?'

'That's the one, Mustafa,' Lawrence smiled, leaving Minnie and Esther bewildered. 'Coconut milk.'

'Coconut milk?' the sisters mouthed while Mustafa stooped below his counter to retrieve two tins of Australian beer crudely whitewashed with the word 'Cokonut' scrawled across them.

'And one juice,' Mustafa said, filling a filthy glass with warm grapefruit extract.

'Cheers, mate,' Lawrence smiled handing Minnie her tin. 'There ya go, me darlin',' he added, cracking open his own tin and downing half in no time at all.

Esther first examined her less than hygienic glass before taking a tentative sip. 'Good grief!' she exclaimed. 'I say do you have any alternative?' she asked the owner, who again disappeared beneath his counter and produced another tin this time having been haphazardly hand-painted red with the word 'Cokacolla' written on it.

'Coke?' Mustafa offering it to Esther. 'It is a big hit with our regular customers.' Esther looked around at the three smiling domino players who barely had a tooth between them. Mustafa's homemade take on the popular soda drink contained a whopping seventy percent raw sugar, date pulp and a mystery ingredient derived from the droppings left on the Red Sea sands by visiting turtles, and as far removed from any thirst-quenching beverage as humanly possible, but with very little in the way of alternatives the devout tea total locals had grown accustomed to its acidic aroma and palate-punishing taste.

'Oh, errr thank you,' Esther said, wary to say the least.

'If you wish,' Mustafa said, peering over the counter at Esther's swollen ankles, 'I have it in diet too.'

'Oooh, you cheeky blighter,' Esther remarked, sipping her regular Cokacolla defiantly but then suddenly retching uncontrollably. 'Oh dear Lord!' she croaked.

'Essy?' Minnie asked, enjoying her Aussie brew. 'Essy, are you alright, dear?'

Esther's cheeks began to turn a sickly shade of blue and her eyes filled with water. 'Lawrence!' Minnie cried. 'Lawrence, please help her!'

Brushing Minnie aside, the burly Australian stooped to comfort her convulsing sister. 'What's up, love' he asked, rubbing her back vigorously.

Gasping, Esther gestured to her throat. 'Jesus, mate,' Lawrence said, having had little or no medical training but possessing a cool head in a crisis. 'I gotcha,' he added, wrapping his arms around her waist from behind and attempting the Heimlich manoeuvre, thrusting and gyrating whilst Esther clawed at her neck.

'Oh dear,' Minnie winced while the gathered locals and Mustafa looked on, finding the proceedings entertaining and a welcome relief from their otherwise tedious and tiresome existence.

Lawrence's manly arms hoisted Esther several inches from the floor with every thrust of his buttocks.

'Oh dear, dear, dear,' Minnie cried, clutching her tin to her chest, 'Dear, dear Essy!'

Esther groaned and gargled until violently vomiting an undissolved pellet of turtle poo from her mouth at breakneck speed to a cheer and a round of applause from the eager onlookers,

'There ya go, me darlin',' Lawrence said proudly, having inflicted heavy bruising to Esther's midriff but possibly saving her life in doing so.

Esther mad a grab for her sister's tin taking a huge greedy gulp to dilute the taste from her mouth. 'Cola!' she eventually screeched. 'More like caustic bloomin' soda if you ask me!'

The domino crew hoisted their own tins in the air in salute having learnt over time to chew any residual turtle debris with what little teeth they possessed.

'Come, Minnie!' Esther said, grabbing her sister by the hand. 'We're leaving.'

'Leaving?' Minnie replied, retrieving her tin. 'But, but Essy.'

'No buts, Minnie,' Esther warned, wrenching open the door and hoisting her sister out into the street.

Lawrence waved whilst tugging on the ring pull of another beer. 'Seeya, ladies!' he called after the departing sisters.

'Goodbye, my dear!' Minnie called back, still supping at her tin. 'Essy, Essy?' she added with her feet hardly touching the ground. 'Aren't you going to say goodbye, the man saved your life after all.'

'Saved my life!' Esther stormed. 'The fool almost snapped me in two for Pete's sake.' Esther chose to wait out the remaining ninety minutes behind Vivien's wheel with her protesting sister at her side, disgruntled at having unceremoniously left Mustafa's café-cum-covert bar, Lawrence and the tasty Aussie brew.

'Will you be quiet!' Esther eventually blurted, having heard quite enough. 'I swear, Minnie, you're becoming quite the drinker of late and I for one am not impressed in the least, in the least do you hear?'

'That's a lie,' Minnie replied, giving very little thought to her recent escalating alcohol consumption. 'I agree I may have had the odd social tipple but that hardly makes me a roaring drunk, now does it?'

'Hmmmm,' Esther growled under her breath. 'All I'm saying, Minnie dear,' she added in an authoritative tone, 'Is that it's a very slippery slope you are embarking on so I suggest you nip it in the bud while you still can.'

The sisters bickered to and fro, which while raising their blood pressures to a level that would give their family physician cause for concern also served to pass the time of day. 'And another thing,' Esther said above her sister, but suddenly the queue of vehicles ahead of them fired up their engines and filed toward the departure gate.

'Essy!' remarked Minnie, prodding her sister's knee. 'Pay attention, will you!'

'What, what oh yes,' Esther replied, desperate to get her point across, but the honking horns behind them stifled her burgeoning wrath. 'Ohhhh alright,' she snarled with a reluctant wave.

Purchasing their tickets from her window, Minnie complimented the salesman on his eye-catching floral neck tie then on the other hand chastised him for running a minute and a half behind their scheduled departure time. 'Punctuality, my good man,' she called back as Esther steered Vivien up the rickety loading ramp. 'Without it the world would descend into complete and utter chaos!' She looked across at Esther for moral support but received the cold shoulder instead. 'Father always said,' Minnie added insistently, 'Punctuality and politeness are the cornerstone of any business, do you remember, dear?'

Esther sat high in her seat, guided into position by a flag-waving deck hand. 'Essy, do you remember?' Minnie asked again, labouring the point. 'What Father used to say?'

'What?' Esther asked, applying the handbrake and switching off the engine. 'What are you wittering on about, what did Father say?'

Minnie raised a finger to enlighten her sister and then paused. 'He used to say, erm,' she pondered with her sister all ears now.

'What?' Esther asked impatiently.

'Do you know, Essy,' Minnie confessed, 'I haven't the foggiest,' and she strummed her fingers on her lap, frustrated at her absentmindedness. 'Oh wait, yes that's it,' she said, raising the finger again. 'Coughs and sneezes spread diseases, that's what he used to say, do you remember, dear?'

'Yes, yes I do,' Esther replied quizzically. 'But somehow, Minnie, I fail to see the relevance.'

'Relevance?' Minnie asked, pondering the point again.

Esther climbed from the car. 'I swear, Minnie,' she warned her sister once again. 'If you lose your mind I will abandon you in a heartbeat, young lady, in a heartbeat.'

The two sisters stood at the side of the Saudi ferry, looking back at the Arabian coastline with mixed emotions. Esther soon simmered down and raised a hand to stroke her sister's back, feeling the raised scar tissue from her public thrashing through her flimsy summer dress.

'I'll be alright, dear,' Minnie reassured her, having quite accurately read her sister's mind and eyeing the glint of a solitary tear. 'Please don't cry for me, Essy,' she said patting her sister's hand reassuringly. 'I'm not worth it.'

Minnie's blatant confession wrenched at Esther's heart strings. 'Come here, you silly old fool,' she said, throwing open her arms and embracing Minnie tightly. 'Of course you're worth it, my darling, and I'm sorry,

I'd never abandon you, I might gag you and sedate you on occasion but I'd never abandon you.'

'Ahhhh,' Minnie sighed, clinging to her hat and pecking her sister's cheek, 'That's nice, dear.'

Ahead of the Peshwari Nans lay the Egyptian coast and the wonders of the ancient world beyond. No other country on earth conjured such mystery and intrigue as Egypt with its iconic pyramids being possibly the greatest conundrum ever built by an ancient civilization, of extra-terrestrial beings as many broader thinking theorists believe, nevertheless the perplexity remained to this day fuelled by speculation and quite possibly the Egyptian tourist board who stood to benefit from the vast hordes of inquisitive tourists following in the footsteps of ancient Pharaohs.

Letting her guard down for a moment, Minnie released her grip on her hat to retrieve her handkerchief from her sleeve, and in an instant a gust of warm desert wind snatched it from her head. 'OH, oh, oh no, no, no, no, no!' she shrieked, wrenching herself from her sister and reaching out in vain as her beloved and slightly wrinkled straw hat danced on the breeze out across the open water before descending daintily. 'Oh, Essy, oh blast, dear!' she cried. 'Look for Pete's sake, look, what am I to do?'

'I told you, didn't I,' Esther said, having warned her sister several times with her own hat tied securely beneath her chin with her silk headscarf. 'I told you this would happen, Minnie, didn't I, but ohhhhh no you wouldn't listen, would you.'

Minnie's hat had accompanied her for a dozen or so years with its pale blue ribbon around it first used to decorate their mother s wedding cake. Peering over the side at the Red Sea some twenty meters below Minnie once again threw caution to the wind and grappled with the rail, hoisting one wrinkled leg up revealing more of her upper thigh than her horrified sister would like to have seen.

'Minnie!' Esther screamed. 'Minnie, what the, what the devil d'you think you're doing get down, get down at once!'

'It's alright, dear,' Minnie groaned, straddling the handrail red-faced and in some discomfort. 'I'll be back before you know it.'

'Back!' Esther cried. 'What do you mean back, you're not going anywhere, now get down this instant!'

'But, Essy, Essy, Mother's ribbon,' Minnie exclaimed. 'I promised.' At the age of five Minnie was gifted the keepsake to wear in her hair for the Queen's birthday celebrations and had sworn, although an infant, to hold it dear throughout her entire life.

Minnie's own daughter Sophia had also worn the ribbon for a friend's tea party shortly before she passed away.

'Get down, I say!' Esther barked, tugging at her sister's arm. 'Don't be ridiculous, I simply won't allow it, get down, will you!'

'NO, ESSY!' Minnie screamed in reply, wrestling to free herself. 'You don't understand, you don't, Essy, the ribbon, the ribbon, Essy!'

'Leave it, Minnie, please!' Esther begged, attracting some attention by now. 'Let it go, Minnie, you have to let it go!'

The hat bobbed and swirled in the Red Sea current, ebbing further and further from the ferry. 'Essy, pleaaaaaaaaaase!' Minnie cried, reaching out desperately with thoughts of her darling Sophia skipping gaily around their garden with the ribbon tied in the neatly plaited hair bouncing behind her. 'Pleaaaaaaase!' but Esther would not relinquish her grip on her sister, not for the ribbon, not for all the gold and silver in the world.

Suddenly a familiar voice called out to them. 'Minnie darling, wocha doin, girl?' It was Lawrence who had hitched a ride with a Saudi sandal trader.

'Lawrence!' Esther called in despair. 'Lawrence, please help me, help me, will you!' The Australian backpacker raced between the parked cars and trucks to lift Minnie clear of the rail.

'No, no, no, no, no!' Minnie protested, beating his chest. 'You don't understand!'

'What is it?' 'Lawrence asked, ducking a flailing fist before setting her down. 'What's the matter?'

'My hat!' Minnie informed him, 'I must have my hat!'

'Ya hat?' Lawrence said, looking over the side. 'Crikey, Minnie, what were ya thinkin'?'

'She doesn't,' Esther added, raising her eyebrows. 'She never does.'

Minnie made another lunge for the rail. 'The ribbon, Essyyyyyy!' she cried, distraught by now. 'Let me go!'

'Not likely,' Lawrence replied, barring her way. 'Look,' he added, unbuttoning his khaki shirt. 'If it means that much to ya, I'll get it meself.'

'Would you?' Minnie said, stopping in her tracks. 'Would you really, Mister Lawrence, would you please?'

Esther then intervened. 'No, Lawrence, it's far too dangerous,' she said, ever being the voice of common sense. 'Minnie darling, you must let it go, dear,' she told her sister, maintaining her grip on her wrist.

Lawrence stripped to the waist, dropped his shoulder bag and kicked off his boots. 'It's alright, Esther love,' he reassured her. 'I did cliff diving in California, believe me this is a piece of cake.'

'Oh thank you, dear,' Minnie gushed. 'Thank you, thank you.'

Lawrence hopped athletically up onto the rail, stood for a moment with his arms outstretched then leapt thrusting his hands over his head, piercing the Red Sea surface like a dart and disappeared momentarily leaving only ripples and a trail of bubbles.

Esther gripped the rail. 'Oh I do hope he's alright,' she said, before he broke the surface taking in a lungful of air and shaking the water from his sun-bleached hair.

'There he is!' Minnie squealed. 'Behind you, my darling!' she called.

Lawrence turned, kicked and swam towards Minnie's bobbing hat.

'Yes, yes!' Minnie mouthed at her sister's side. 'Please yes!' Another twenty meters and Lawrence finally snatched at the drifting straw hat and popped it onto his own head before turning back for the slow-moving ferry. 'Ohhhh, how wonderful,' Minnie shrieked, clapping her hands repeatedly. 'Look, dear, he's got it, he's got it!'

'Yes I can see that,' Esther said, shrugging off her jubilant sister who shook her violently. 'Unhand me, you fool,' she barked, concerned for their Australian friend. 'He's not out of the water yet, I'll have you know.' The pair watched with an ever increasing crowd as Lawrence battled the swell created by the ferry's huge turbines, making slow progress and tiring somewhat and choking intermittently after swallowing a quantity of sea water.

'LAWRENCE!' Minnie yelled, beckoning, 'SWIM, LAWRENCE, SWIM, MY DARLING!'

'YES, YOU CAN DO IT!' Esther urged. 'THAT'S IT, THAT'S IT!'

Breathless, Lawrence reached for a life ring tossed overboard by a crewman who pulled the orange rope with the help of his colleagues with the Aussie attached. 'Quickly, dear,' Esther told her sister, hurrying to help. Soon she, her sister and several bystanders dragged Lawrence the final few meters back toward the ferry and helped him aboard.

'Well done, well done, you,' Minnie said, helping him over the rail and safely on deck where he handed her back her beloved hat whilst bent double wheezing and spitting water.

'There ya go, me darlin,' he said, brushing his sodden hair back over his head and wiping the water from his face.

'Are you alright, dear?' Esther asked with one hand on his back. 'Can I help you in any way?'

'No, no I'm fine,' Lawrence said, raising a hand. 'Just give me a minute will ya.'

'Minnie caressed the dripping silk ribbon with an overwhelming sense of relief. 'Thank you,' she told Lawrence softly. 'Thank you ever so much, you don't know what this means to me.'

'No worries, Min,' Lawrence replied, straightening to wring the water from is hair. 'I just got into a spot of bother with the rip tide, that's all, I once got dragged a mile and a half away from Bondi beach before the coast guard picked me up, best days surfin' I ever had though.'

'Well I for one,' Esther told him, 'Think you're incredibly brave, incredibly brave indeed.'

'A hero in fact,' Minnie added, 'Yes that's it, you are a hero, Lawrence darling, and I for one will never forget what you have done, never.'

The crowd eventually dispersed and Lawrence sat drying in the late afternoon sun with Esther and Minnie and her hat tied firmly on her head with her own shimmering silk scarf.

Docking later at the Egyptian port of Safaga, Lawrence and the sisters reluctantly said their goodbyes. 'Are you sure you won't join us?' Esther asked from within Vivien. 'We're headed north to Cairo.'

'I'd love to, ladies,' Lawrence replied, stooping at the door. 'But I got a bitta business at Aswan, six months surveying cracks in the dam.'

Esther let out a gasp. 'Cracks in the dam!' she exclaimed, knowing full well, as many of her generation did the significance of the dam. 'In the Aswan dam?'

'Yeah,' Lawrence said nonchalantly. 'Nothin to write home about though, just routine maintenance, ya know what I mean.'

'Oh, oh I see,' Esther said relaxing in her seat.

The Aswan high dam, built between 1960 and 1970 to control fertile flood waters to the Nile delta was once described as the eighth wonder of the world, towering at a colossal 111 meters high and close to 400 meters in length, and just as the Great Wall of China, clearly visible from space.

Lawrence swung his pack over his shoulder. 'The pay's bloody great too,' he added. 'Should set me up for another coupla years travellin'.'

Minnie leaned across her sister. 'Well, Lawrence my darling,' she said, resting a hand on Esther's lap. 'My sister and I are travelling too so I sincerely hope our paths cross again some day, I really do.'

'Yes, me too,' Esther agreed, patting the Aussie's hand. 'You, sir, are a gentleman in every sense of the word, a rarity in this day and age sadly.'

'Well thank you, me darlins',' Lawrence said, tipping his hat. 'It's been a pleasure meetin' ya, I mean that, and yeah I hope we meet again, till then, ladies, I'll love ya and leave ya, stay safe and happy trails, yeah.'

'You too, dear,' Esther replied. 'You too.'

Again Minnie's emotions got the better of her. 'Wait!' she said, throwing open her door, heaving herself out of her seat and rounding the car. 'Come here, you,' she said with open arms. 'I want to thank you again.'

'No need, love,' Lawrence said, hoisting Minnie up onto the tip of her toes.

'Listen,' he told her, 'I'm a bloody good judge of character, me, and I reckon you two ladies are proper people if you get me drift and I'd do it again truly I would.'

Minnie turned to her sister. 'Did you hear that, Essy?' she said, dropping to her heels. 'Apparently we are proper people.'

'Yeah, proper,' Lawrence reiterated.

'Thank you, dear,' Esther said, leaning from her window. 'And do you know I'm a firm believer in fate and that some people are just destined to meet, a firm believer.'

'I think ya right,' Lawrence agreed. 'Listen, I gotta run,' he told them as the ferry docked and the ramp was lowered onto the jetty. 'I got a taxi waitin', be lucky, ladies, see you again sometime maybe,' and with that he tipped his hat once again and left in haste dodging in and out of the waiting vehicles, down the rickety ramp and hopped into a taxi cab at the quayside.

Minnie stood and waved until he disappeared out of sight. 'I do hate goodbyes,' she told her sister, climbing back in alongside her. 'And for some unknown reason that was particularly wrenching, funny isn't it?' she confessed. 'We hardly know the chap.'

'I know what you mean,' Esther agreed, proceeding slowly in line to the ramp. 'There was definitely something about Lawrence, wasn't there?'

'Hmmm,' Minnie said wistfully. 'Something indeed.'

They were clear of the ferry and border officials, some of whom insisted on posing for photographs beside the now iconic Trafalgar blue Morris, its reputation and that of its occupants unprecedented at this stage. 'Thank youuuuu,' Minnie called, waving the bottle of mineral water and freshly baked bread she had been given in return. 'Goodbyyyyyyye.' Grinning, she stowed their provisions and slapped her knees in anticipation of their onward journey. 'Riiiight,' she said, 'Cairo here we come, right, dear?'

'Sorry, what was that, dear?' Esther asked, paying close attention to the garbled road signs.

'Cairo!' Minnie said again. 'The pyramids, you remember.'

'Yes, yes, I know that,' Esther said, a little tetchy at having negotiated the same junction for a third time. 'Switch on the thingy will you, Minnie, please' she told her sister, gesturing to the tablet at her feet. 'And get us out of here before I lose my mind, they may as well have written these damned signs in hieroglyphics, I can't make head nor tale of them' One sign in particular would surely confuse the most travel-savvy of Egyptian native, a mish-mash of vague symbols hand painted on plywood with more arrows than there were directions.

'Right you are, dear,' Minnie said, stooping. After several minutes of tapping and searching for internet connectivity, during which Esther became increasingly frenzied, Minnie eventually located their global position. 'Ahhh her we are, dear,' she chirped confidently. 'That's us, the little blue dot.'

'Yes, yes, get on with it!' Esther groaned. 'Which way, damn it?'

'Oh yes, yes of course,' Minnie replied, having become distracted by the search engine's new customary advertisements. 'Ooooh look, dear,' she mused. 'Apparently if you are over seventy you can save ten percent on your car insurance, ten percent, Essy, and you get a free fountain pen if you apply today.'

'Minnie!' Esther growled, waving to the same traffic marshal yet again in passing, 'Which way?'

'Left, dear,' Minnie informed her. 'You have to make a left towards Qena, oh and they have a two for one offer on flights to the Maldives with British Airways too, dear, I've always wanted to see the Maldives.'

'Which left?' Esther asked, circling the roundabout and growing ever exasperated, 'Minnie, which left for Pete's sake?'

'Sorry, dear, what?' Minnie asked, distracted once again by news of the impending Harrods sale. 'Oh blast!' she cursed, slapping her thigh. 'We're going to miss the sale, dear.'

'Sale?' Esther said, none the wiser and hot under the collar. 'What are you talking about you, fool?'

'Harrods, dear,' Minnie reminded her. 'You know how we love to browse.' The sisters had indeed regularly attended the historic Knightsbridge store's annual sale to browse, or nose as some would say. Seldom purchasing more than a hat pin because even at a reduced rate much of the glitzy stock was well beyond their meagre means, but perhaps not now with their handsome monthly allowance from Karl Bodine.

'To hell with the blasted sale!' Esther stormed. 'Just get us out of here!'

'I told you to make a left, dear,' Minnie said, looking over her shoulder. 'But you seem to have missed it a second time, dear, never mind you'll just have to go around again.'

'Oh good heavens, this is intolerable,' Esther moaned, slapping the wheel before waving to the bemused traffic official. 'Sorryyyyyyy!' she called, 'It's my sister, you see!'

'Me?' Minnie said with a hand to her chest. 'Aren't you forgetting, dear,' she added, holding the tablet aloft, 'I'm the one with the satellite navigation.'

'Ohhhh well that's alright then,' Esther replied sarcastically. 'If we want a fountain pen and a flight to the blasted Maldives!'

'Well really!' Minnie exclaimed, her nose having been put out of joint so to speak. 'I don't know why I bother sometimes, Essy, I really don't, oh and by the way,' she added, 'You need to take the next left.'

'At last,' Esther sighed, turning onto the road to Qena, a city on the eastern banks of the Nile and a mere eighty six miles from the port of Safaga, a stone's throw in comparison to many of their previous jaunts.

Tinkering with the tablet and refusing to talk to her sister, Minnie's eyes suddenly lit up. 'Oooooh!' she couldn't help but say, and then said no more.

'What?' Esther asked. 'What is it?'

Minnie remained tight-lipped, having been scolded by her sister once too often for her liking.

'Minnie?' Esther urged brimming with curiosity. 'What is it?'

Minnie eventually turned the screen away from her sister, whose eyes flitted back and forth from the road to the tablet. 'Well?' Esther asked, craning her neck.

'You wouldn't be interested,' Minnie said smugly.

'Interested?' Esther asked. 'Interested in what exactly?'

'Ohhh nothing,' Minnie replied, paying close attention to the completely free gift offered by a well-known insurance broker.

'Nothing, my foot!' Esther scoffed. 'Out with it, Minnie, or so help me I'll, I'll, I'll take back my Betty Boop bed socks.'

'You wouldn't dare!' Minnie exclaimed, horrified at the suggestion. 'You said they were a gift, you wouldn't dare go back on your word, would you?'

'I might,' Esther said with her nose in the air, having gifted her sister the souvenir socks after she repeatedly borrowed them without prior consent. 'After all,' Esther continued, 'It was only a verbal agreement, you have nothing in writing to prove ownership, do you?' Esther had once again backed her sister into a corner, safe in the knowledge that Minnie simply adored those socks and would never part with them.

'Plates,' Minnie reluctantly informed her sister. 'Commemorative plates, if you must know, to mark Her Majesty's ninetieth birthday,' she read the brief description out loud. 'According to this they are a limited edition set of six hand painted by the Duke himself.'

'Nooooooo,' Esther grimaced in disbelief. 'Hand painted you say?'

'By the Duke,' Minnie reiterated. The aging Royal had indeed daubed a series of crude likenesses of his dear wife, but needless to say art was not his forte. Some critics although had been kind considering his royal lineage, other foreign journalists though with absolutely no allegiance to crown or country had openly mocked his infantile images which accentuated the features his good lady wife would have rather concealed. All in all sales of the souvenirs had been poor with the vast majority of purchase being made by patriotic pensioners just like Esther and Minnie, whose extensive collection of Royal memorabilia extended to Jubilee mugs, coronation calendars, first edition stamps and Royal Mint coins with some items a tad tackier than others, such as the Charles and Camilla dustpan and brush and the Windsor Castle wall clock, which chimed a muffled Rule Britannia at ten past the hour for reasons unbeknown to the sisters.

'We must have them,' Esther said without hesitation. 'Marjorie would be positively green with envy, Minnie.' Again Esther's competitive streak emerged when considering her neighbour and rival collector. 'I can't wait to see her face,' she added, bobbing in her seat. 'Sign me up, Minnie,' she told her sister adamantly. 'I don't care what it is, we must have those plates, we simply must, do you hear.'

'Life insurance, dear,' Minnie informed her. 'And wait for it, for another twenty pounds per month they will insure our home contents too, if we sign today of course.'

'A bargain!' Esther scoffed. 'And a small price to pay for peace of mind too, I might add, after all once word gets around that we are in possession of the Duke's hand painted porcelain God only knows what unsavoury attention it might attract.'

'Quite right, dear,' Minnie agreed. 'I suggest we remove the spare key from under the mat from now on too.' The bygone custom of leaving a key to your door under the mat or adjacent plant pot was sadly frowned upon in these days of rising opportunist crimes, although the Duke's poorly painted portraits would be safe if the doors and windows were left wide open twenty-four hours per day.

'Sign us up at once, Minnie!' Esther urged. 'Sign us up before it's too late, good God, if Marjorie gets them and I don't I'll be devastated, Minnie, simply devastated.'

'Right you are, dear,' Minnie said, tapping at the screen to cover the remainder of their days and more importantly secure the introductory free gift.

Peshwari Nans Part II

The following two hours to Qena were more jubilant between the sisters, pleasantly passing the locally baked bread between them and occasionally breaking into a chorus of *Daisy, Daisy* and *Knees Up Mother Brown* to pass the time of day.

Approaching Qena, Esther covered her mouth to yawn. 'Ohhh, darling,' Minnie said sympathetically. 'You must be exhausted, you poor thing.'

'Hmmm, yes,' Esther replied, wriggling in her seat. 'I'm quite pooped actually, perhaps we should find lodgings and bed down early, what do you say?'

'Marvellous idea,' Minnie agreed, eyeing the simple roadside houses and apartment blocks and feeling a rumbling in the pit of her stomach as was common around that hour, and not uncommon at any other hour. 'Perhaps a spot of dinner before we turn in too, dear, and dare I say it a sweet sherry by way of a nightcap.'

'Hmmmm,' Esther mused again. 'Personally I'd rather a cup of cocoa and a ginger biscuit, I find the combination a sure-fire relaxant.'

'Ooooh yes, ginger biscuits,' Minnie said eagerly. 'My dear friend Eveline has a Cavalier King Charles that simply adores them, do you know the dear little thing would sit with a biscuit balanced on the tip of his nose for upwards of half an hour without flinching until Eveline clicked her fingers.'

Esther eyed her sister's nose. 'Without flinching, you say?' she asked, plotting human trials of the obedience task in an attempt to silence her sister.

Esther drove toward the centre of Qena with its rows upon rows of distinctive palms, distant mosque minarets and the ever present street vendors hawking everything from fresh dates to Nile cruise tickets promising, as they all did, the trip of a lifetime aboard modern air conditioned vessels, although modern was a term that was used very loosely when describing several of the cramped and creaking crafts serving up fly-infested food and cold coffee. Noticing Vivien's western-style plates many sandal-wearing salesmen dashed into her path to flag the sisters down, waving their glossy printed flyers with evocative images of tomb treasures, the weathered Sphinx and the enigmatic pyramids silhouetted against a full Egyptian moon. 'Get out of the way!' Esther called, honking Vivien's horn and waving an arm from the window, but in an instant a dozen or more advertising leaflets were tossed into the car accompanied by chants of, 'You come cruise, good price, you come cruise!'

'Not today, thank you,' Esther replied, dabbing the brake pedal to avoid a manslaughter charge. 'For heaven's sake get out of the way!' she cursed, accelerating when the coast was clear, leaving the group dejected and turning to confront another foreign vehicle.

Esther tossed the litter from her lap across to her sister, who eyed the thought-provoking images intensely. 'Look, dear!' Minnie said, wide-eyed at King Tut's burial chamber. 'In just a day or so we'll be there in person, gosh, I'm so excited I could pee, dear!'

'Please don't,' Esther replied, straight-faced. 'But you're right, Min, I think I've longed to see the pyramids and such like my entire life.'

'Well, dear,' Minnie said, patting her sister's lap, 'We'll see them together, won't we.'

'Quite right,' Esther agreed whilst dodging a stray cat, and then another, and another.

'There, dear!' Minnie shrieked a short while later, startling her sister when pointing out a three-storey hotel. 'There, look.'

Esther pulled to the side of the road but kept Vivien's engine running. 'Would you enquire, dear?' she asked. 'We'd like a twin room with air conditioning, an en-suite and breakfast if at all possible.'

'Leave it to me, Essy dearest,' Minnie confidently replied, opening her door and tossing out a leg.

'I have a general understanding of the language, Mister Farook my dentist used to put me at ease before an extraction by reciting Egyptian poetry, I swear, Essy,' she informed her sister, whose grip once again tightened on the wheel. 'That man,' Minnie continued halfway out of the car, 'That man could charm the birds from the trees I tell you.'

'Minnie!' Esther barked, tired and decidedly irritable. 'The room?'

'Oh, oh yes,' Minnie said, gripping Vivien's roof rack to hoist herself upright with a groan. 'I'll tell you another thing,' she then confessed. 'I don't miss my molars half as much as I miss Mister Farook, I would stare deep into his hazel eyes while he tugged out my teeth one by one.'

Esther merely lowered her spectacles to the end of her nose and glared at her sister, which was enough to send her hastily tottering off toward the modest hotel entrance, turning to give her sister the thumbs up.

415

'Hurry, you fool!' Esther called, shaking her head.

Knocking three times on the bolted door, Minnie stood rocking back and forth from her toes to her heels with her hands clasped behind her back. 'Ahhh good evening, kind sir,' she then told the middle-aged balding proprietor who seemed surprised to see her, catering mainly for his fellow countrymen whilst westerners usually preferred the tourist traps a little further along the sparsely paved highway. 'I'm sorry,' Minnie added when receiving no reply. 'Do you speak English by any chance?'

The Egyptian hotelier shrugged his shoulders and pointed along the street before grabbing at the door.

'Wait!' Minnie said as her curious sister looked on from the car. 'Wait one moment, please, errrrm.' She thought long and hard having memorised much of her dashing dentist's dialogue. 'Yes, yes that's it,' she said, leaning a little closer. 'I have it.' Minnie successfully strung an Egyptian sentence together and waited proudly for an answer, but the hotelier immediately flew into a rage, yelling and cursing at the top of his voice, which alarmed Minnie and her sister several yards away.

'What the devil?' Esther said, unbuckling her safety belt and preparing to leave the car.

'No, no wait!' Minnie told the Egyptian, raising a hand. 'You don't understand!'

But the disgruntled owner understood only too well after Minnie had inadvertently insulted his entire family line, likening them in fact to rancid sewer rats, it seemed her pronunciation left a little to be desired.

'MINNIE!' Esther yelled from her seat. 'DOES HE HAVE A ROOM OR NOT?'

The fuming hotelier reached wild-eyed for a broomstick and raised it above his head whilst Minnie turned tail and hot-footed it back toward the gate.

'Well?' Esther asked.

'Not without a prior reservation, it seems,' Minnie said, lying through her dentures, winding up her window and locking the door. 'Drive on, dear,' she told her sister. 'Hurry, dear, drive on.'

Seeing the angry owner starting down the path toward them, Esther stepped on the accelerator. 'Reservation?' she asked, speeding away. 'Are you sure?'

Minnie cowered in her seat, peering over her shoulder once or twice at the hopping mad Egyptian.

At their next port of call Esther insisted on making the necessary enquiries herself and braced for a similar reception. 'Oh,' she said when greeted favourably, 'You do!' The English-speaking receptionist confirmed the availability of a suitable twin room with an en-suite fitted with state of the art mobility aids for the physically impaired.

On inspection both sisters were absolutely delighted with their second choice of accommodation. 'Oh look, Essy how wonderful,' Minnie marvelled at the motorized sling designed to lower the infirm into the bath tub. 'I can't wait to try it,' and she kicked off her shoes and began removing her clothing.

Esther left her sister to bathe and retired to the lounge to rest her weary feet; moment later shrieks of laughter could be heard from the bathroom as Minnie lowered and raised herself over and over, dipping her bottom like the dunking of a biscuit into the foaming water. 'Damn fool,' Esther said disapprovingly while letting her shoes slip from her feet. 'Mmmmm,' she sighed, watching the evening sky darken to a burnt umber. Suddenly there was a screech, a splash and a resounding clang as the hoist Minnie was riding could withstand no more and the silicone sheet on which she sat tore from its mounts and dumped her unceremoniously from a height into the ivory white enamelled bath.

Minnie emerged moments later looking decidedly unimpressed in her flannelette housecoat, rubbing her bruised bottom. 'I'd give the ducking stool a miss if I were you, Essy,' she said, rounding the sofa still dripping to find her sister sound asleep. 'Essy?' she said, nudging Esther's knee. 'Oh, Essy, how many more times have I told you,' she added with a, 'Tut, tut, you really shouldn't sleep with your teeth in.'

But Esther had gone to the place beyond sleep where the physically and mentally exhausted go to reboot and recharge as it were, and nothing on earth would rouse her until she was good and ready. 'Essy, love,' Minnie urged, reaching for her sister's open mouth, 'Essyyyyyy,' but on gripping her slumbering sibling's dentures Minnie took a step forward to gain greater leverage and in doing so stomped squarely on Esther's big toe, and more importantly the troublesome blister she had been nursing for the previous two days.

The aforementioned statement, nothing on earth would rouse her of course hadn't accounted for Esther's hapless sister, and the searing pain woke her like a powerful dose of smelling salts, sending an electrifying spasm through her entire body causing her to grimace and clench her false teeth down hard onto the mindless Minnie's fingers.

Minnie in return immediately let out a deafening high pitched squeal, a screech and a cry which roused her sister further.

Esther opened her eyes wide at her sister's siren-like screams and recoiled in horror herself at the wriggling hand in her mouth. The pair of them raised the roof at eighty decibels, disturbing guests on the upper and lower floors. 'MINNIE!' a semi-conscious Esther snarled.

'What the, get away from me, get away, what on earth do you think you're doing?'

Minnie tucked her severely bitten digits beneath her arm and rocked back and forth with her face contorted. 'You bit me!' she cursed. 'Essy, you bit me!'

Esther sat bolt upright rubbing her eyes. 'Bit you!' she said, shoving her sister away. 'Of course I bit you, you imbecile, what did you think you were playing at?'

'Ow, ow, ow it hurts, Essy!' Minnie moaned, shaking her hand limply. 'I was only trying to help and you bit me, Essy, owwwwwww!'

'Oh be quiet, will you,' Esther snapped. 'Of course I bit you, you fool your hand was in my blasted mouth was it not?'

'I was trying to help, Essy,' Minnie moaned, wincing constantly. 'Everyone knows it's not advisable to sleep with your teeth in.'

'My teeth?' Esther remarked. 'Yes but,' she added, piecing the puzzle together 'of course I know that but…'

'But you bit me!' Minnie complained, examining her chomped finger and again attempting to shake the pain away.

'Yes well,' Esther said. 'You might have woken me first.'

'But, Essy, I tried to,' Minnie explained, making her way hastily back to the bathroom to run her hand under the cold water tap.

Esther settled her nerves momentarily before joining her sister. 'Minnie, I'm sorry, dear,' she confessed. 'Of course you're quite right, you were only trying to help, I shouldn't have shouted at you, please forgive me.'

'No!' Minnie barked from the pedestal sink. 'No I won't, you really hurt me, Essy.'

Esther's repeated apologies fell on deaf ears, until that is she ventured to the bedroom returning moments later brandishing another pair of her elaborately embroidered bed socks featuring a childhood favourite of theirs, Rupert the Bear. 'Ahem!' she said at the bathroom door with the socks dangling from her hand, resplendent in red and yellow check, Rupert's trademark colours. 'Would these go some way to healing the rift between us?' she asked expectantly.

Minnie turned from the basin, her eyes immediately widening on seeing her sister's olive branch. 'For me?' she asked, wiping her hands on the hem of her housecoat and instantly dismissing the dull throbbing.

'Yes, yes,' Esther agreed. 'That is if you'll forgive and forget my finger-biting faux pas.'

'But of course, dear,' Minnie said without hesitation and holding up her bitten hand. 'Look, there's hardly a scratch,' and she then snatched the bed socks from her sister's hand and held them to her face. 'I shall wear them tonight, Essy darling,' she told her relieved sister.

'As you wish, dear,' Esther replied, watching Minnie totter on one leg in an attempt to don the socks. 'Sit down, you silly old fool,' she added, directing Minnie to the lavatory and taking charge of the Rupert replicas.

'Thank you, dear,' Minnie said, grinning with one foot on her sister's knee. 'I do hope you don't think I was feigning injury for my own personal gain.'

The thought hadn't crossed Esther's mind, until in fact her sister had mentioned it. 'Hmmmm,' she pondered.

Minnie had on several occasions hoodwinked her sister out of items of clothing, perfume and even jewellery by apportioning blame and guilt in her direction and soon those occasions sprang to mind. Like the infamous red stiletto incident when Esther falsely accused her sister of borrowing and losing the sapphire pendant she'd worn during her first date with her late husband Jack. Minnie had stomped and sulked for days, even after the pendant was returned to Esther by an eagle-eyed usherette at the cinema where she herself had mislaid it. Minnie flatly refused all attempts at reconciliation by her sister until Esther offered the patent shoes on loan to ease the tension between them, but once in her possession Minnie refused to return them claiming damages for stress and anxiety.

'There,' Esther said, wrenching herself to her feet using the bath tub and choosing not to broach the subject at that time. 'Now let that be an end to it.'

'Thank you, dear,' Minnie said, rising to parade in her new bed socks. 'Essyyyy?' she then asked sheepishly. 'I don't suppose I could trouble you for the matching slippers?'

Esther glared at her sister, amazed at her seemingly limitless audacity. 'Oh but of course, my dear,' she said with a wry smile. 'But' she added, baring her teeth. 'I'm afraid I'd have to bite you again.'

Minnie immediately snatched her throbbing fingers behind her back. 'On second thoughts, Essy my love,' she said, cowering, 'I'd really hate to deprive you of them, really I would.' Minnie nervously side-stepped her sister and shuffled through to the bedroom, shining the teak flooring in the process with her newly acquired socks and her sister in hot pursuit.

'Just a little nip,' Esther said, chomping her dentures together and chasing her sister around the bed.

'No, no, go away!' Minnie cried, leaping beneath the sheets and tucking both hands beneath her bottom. 'I don't want your blasted slippers, Essy!'

'Are you sure?' Esther asked whilst stripping for bed, and as earlier advised removing her dentures. The pair slept soundly beside one another with Esther even reaching to hug her sister during the night whilst dreaming of her beloved Jack.

The sisters woke the following morning and stood sipping hot sweet black coffee on the balcony with a clear view of the Nile delta and the flotilla of fishing and trade vessels already navigating the winding river. Also charter cruises were preparing for the day's sailing, swabbing the decks at the harbour. 'Essy, shall we?' Minnie asked, lowering her cup.

'No!' Esther said before her sister could finish. 'No, Minnie, I know exactly what you're going to say and the answer is a resounding no, I've had my fill of boats recently so if it's all the same to you I'd like to remain on terra firma for the foreseeable future.'

'Oh,' Minnie said, having had the wind sucked from her sails. 'I see, yes but, Essy,' she added, 'We could…'

'No, Minnie!' Esther replied, turning back inside. 'You can bleat all you like but I won't be swayed, now hurry and pack your things, and stop sulking, dear, it really doesn't become you.'

Minnie trudged into the bathroom whining under her breath; somehow a visit to Egypt seemed incomplete without the obligatory Nile cruise, but then again, she thought looking down at her feet, she was up one pair of Rupert Bear bed socks so perhaps it was best she didn't push her luck. 'Ready when you are, dear,' she later said waiting at the door, suitcase in hand.

'Yes, yes, one moment,' Esther said scanning the room intensely. 'Where the devil?' she asked, lifting the sofa cushions. 'Minnie, dear, have you seen my sunnies?'

'Your what, dear?' Minnie asked, turning away and removing her sister's sunglasses.

'Oooooh, you minx!' Esther cursed, catching sight of her favourite shades before Minnie could conceal them.

'I, I,' Minnie stammered, compounding her guilt and wracking her brain for a plausible excuse. 'Oh how silly of me,' she chuckled nervously, 'I thought they were mine, dear, you know my eyes aren't what they used to be.'

'Give me those!' Esther snapped, snatching back her stolen sunglasses. 'You just can't help yourself, can you?'

'No, no I…' Minnie blurted. 'I swear it was a genuine mistake, Essy.'

'Genuine!' Esther sneered. 'Minnie, I doubt you have a genuine bone in your body, you knew these were mine because you lost yours, remember?'

'I didn't lose them,' Minnie confessed. 'They were stolen.'

'Exactly!' Esther replied, flinging open the door. 'You left them unattended at that roadside bazar in Medina didn't you, and that, that creature made off with them.' Whilst the sisters were perusing the souvenirs and fresh produce of Medina's central market a mischievous marmoset monkey, recently escaped from its exploitative handler took a shine to Minnie's mother of pearl Polaroids, another of her astute acquisitions having saved a dozen coupons from the rear of their TV guide leaving only the postage and packing to pay.

'Oh but, Essy,' Minnie said, following her sister out of the room. 'You have to admit he did look simply adorable in them, I took a photograph,' and she fumbled in her shoulder bag for the tablet as they descended the hotel stairs displaying the image in the lobby. 'You see, dear,' she added, enlarging the snap of the monkey sat astride an adjacent roof ridge posing like a pro in the designer shades and mocking the sisters below.

The image once uploaded to their social media platforms had received a whopping seventeen million views in the first twenty-four hours alone, making the pesky primate one of the fasted overnight sensations of all time, and again advertising agencies realising the global appeal and marketability of such a captivating creature clamoured for the rights to this single fantastic frame, desperate for the artful thief to be the face of their lucrative campaigns.

Richard, Esther's grandson, had recently agreed to handle all incoming electronic mail and negotiations on their behalf whilst his mother convalesced following a series of unfortunate episodes brought on of course by her mother's absence and more importantly her narrow escapes with her younger sister.

Elizabeth had been transferred to a rest home in Whitstable Bay where it was thought a complete change of scenery may aid her recovery, but on hearing the conversation of a group of rowdy road workers outside her window, each of them wagering on the date of the, 'Old dears' demise as they called them, with odds on favourite that the sisters would not see the end of the month in light of recent experiences, she suffered a severe relapse trashing yet another room and taking a member of staff hostage until police and trained negotiators were able to subdue and section her once again.

Following a fortifying breakfast of toast, beans and yet more dates washed down with a potent pot of sweet coffee, the sisters stepped from the foyer to survey the road ahead of them, a battlefield or so it seemed of bicycles, motorcycles, heavy goods wagons and livestock-drawn carts, each of them enduring the age old ritual of attempting to stay alive amid the motoring madness between Qena and Cairo.

The roadside was littered the length of the highway with the mangled remains of those less fortunate. 'Good heavens!' Esther said, letting her case slip from her fingers, 'Minnie, if you think for one moment

I'm…' She looked around but her sister was already sat buckled in Vivien braced for adventure and buzzing from her caffeine boost.

'Ahem!' Minnie called to her shell-shocked sister. 'I appear to be minus a driver!'

The cacophonous din of honking horn and screaming Egyptian obscenities filled the air from the seemingly everyday occurrence. There were no rules to the road, no highway code so to speak, merely survival by any means possible.

Esther glanced across at the meandering Nile, weighing up the lesser of either evil. 'Dear Lord, deliver us,' she said to the heavens whilst opting for dry land having felt decidedly nauseous the last time afloat.

'Right, dear,' Minnie said when Esther eventually buckled in beside her filled with anxiety and trepidation. 'Well?' she then asked with her sister, hesitant to insert the key. 'What are we waiting for?'

The highway traffic hurtled by at break-neck speed, bumper to bumper, or ox tail at times. Esther attempted to enter the furore on several occasions but each time her nerves got the better of her. 'Oh this is ridiculous!' she cursed concentrating on her rear view mirror until Minnie turned it in her direction to apply a little rouge to her cheeks. 'What are you doing, you fool!' Esther cried, snatching back the mirror and hastily adjusting it to its former position whilst a queue formed behind her. 'YES, YES ALRIGHT!' she yelled from her open window. 'I'M TRYING, GOD DAMN IT!'

Minnie sat impatiently strumming her fingers on the tablet. 'Er helloooo,' she said, rolling her eyes at her sister.

'Yes, yes be quiet!' Esther again growled with her foot hovering over the accelerator. 'Oh damn, here goes,' she said, wincing when rapidly speeding onto the harrowing highway. 'ARRRRRGGHH!' she immediately screamed when a honking truck roared by within inches of her door, leaving a shower of grain tumbling from its rear in its wake, pelting all in its immediate vicinity. The choking dust cloud whipped up from the passing wheels and drawn into the aging Morris had the sisters coughing and spluttering and covering their mouths with their cotton handkerchiefs.

What was to follow for a full nerve-wracking ninety minutes could only be described as pure unadulterated motoring mayhem, with Esther eventually losing her voice following more close calls than she'd care to remember whilst her thrill-seeking sister relished every nail-biting moment.

Having witnessed at close hand some fourteen minor collisions and the varying degrees of carnage caused, Esther was soon a jabbering bag of nerves concentrating so intensely on remaining unscathed she barely had time to take in the breathtaking delta astride the Nile.

Minnie, on the other hand, hung the tablet from her window snapping and savouring every moment. 'Smile, dear!' she said attempting a high octane selfie. 'Essy, Essy smile, dear!' she insisted, but her sister remained rigidly focussed, her heart pounding and her palms moistening the wheel.

'WHAT?' Esther yelled, taking her eyes off the road for a split second to berate her sister. 'In case you hadn't noticed, Minnie!' she cursed. 'I am driving!' A motorcycle suddenly swerved across two lanes into their path. 'CHRIST!' Esther screamed, taking evasive action at the risk of running aground on the steep embankment to her left, Vivien's nearside wheels kicking up the loose gravel at the roadside.

'Steady, dear,' Minnie said, apportioning blame her sister's way and cowering away from her window.

Esther gave her sister a lightning look of pure hatred whilst silently praying to the Almighty for salvation. 'SORRYYYYYY!' she then called having inadvertently strayed across the weathered lane markings, causing a cursing cabbie to break violently and his untethered passengers to tumble forwards and face plant the front seats. 'Sorryyyyyyy.'

Rounding a hairpin bend, the sisters both gasped on seeing the grain transporter that had earlier passed them laid on its side with its load of some thirty tons spewed out across the hard shoulder, with the driver sat bewildered at the roadside nursing a bloodied head. 'Dear Lord!' Esther said in passing,

'Dear Lord indeed,' Minnie agreed, waving courteously to the concussed trucker. 'MORNING!' she called. 'LOVELY DAY!' Minnie later sat toying with a blouse button, bored and restless. 'I spy!' she suddenly blurted, 'With my little eye, something beginning wiiiiiith P!' She nudged her sister's leg, urging her to participate in the childish game. 'Essy, P dear?'

But Esther sat grinding her dentures at the sheer lack of respect shown by her fellow road users. 'AND YOU!'

she replied, raising two fingers to a manic moped rider vexed at her failure to give way.

'Essyyyyyy, something beginning with P dear?' Minnie again asked, bubbling with enthusiasm.

'What?' Esther asked, unable to avert her eyes from the death race she found herself involved in.

'P dear, P?' Minnie insisted. 'It's I spy, remember, Essy?'

Esther's blood pressure, already having spiked, raised another notch.

'Essy?' Minnie continued to press. 'Any ideas, Essy, Essy, Essy, dear?'

'PALM TREE!' Esther eventually roared at the very end of her tether and observing the sea of palm trees now flanking the highway. 'IT'S PALM TREE, you know it and I know it now, let that be the end of it, please!'

Minnie sat rigid and quietly cursing under her breath at the speedy conclusion to her puzzle, which considering their surroundings was blatantly obvious. 'No it's not,' she said lying and plucking a morsel of bread from the dashboard. 'It's pitta bread, dear, my turn again.'

'Don't you dare,' Esther grimaced, in no mood for parlour games, or pleasantries for that matter.

'I spy,' Minnie said, characteristically unfazed. 'With my little eye.'

'Minnie, I'm warning you!' Esther said, flustered and rattled to near breaking point and longing to be out of the whacky races.

'Something beginniiiiiiiiing,' Minnie continued, sitting perfectly at ease. 'With P again!' she chirped. 'Essy?'

Esther zigged and zagged from lane to lane, their lives at times hanging in the balance by a silken thread.

'P, Essy dear?' Minnie probed further, wincing only when a tin of soda was tossed at Vivien by a passing bus driver angered at having sat behind the Morris for a mile and a half.

'What the?' Esther screeched, starting the wipers to clear the cola from the screen. 'DAMN YOU, SIR!' she yelled. 'DAMN YOU TO HELL AND BACK!'

'Essy dear?' Minnie asked, stroking her sister's thigh to sooth her temper.

'Essyyyyyy?'

'WHAT?' Esther yelled, pounding her sodden wheel. 'What Minnie, WHAT?'

'P,' Minnie simply said. 'I spy, remember, oh and before you ask,' she added brushing the crumbs from her lap, 'It's not pitta bread, I ate that,' and she then sat eagerly awaiting her sister's participation.

Seething Esther pondered her limited options, whether to throw her galactically annoying sister from the moving vehicle or guess correctly and put an end to this foolishness once and for all. 'Palm tree,' she reluctantly said, this time with confidence. 'There, now please, Minnie, put an end to this tomfoolery and leave me be.' She then braked suddenly when another ox-drawn cart surged into her lane.

Minnie meanwhile shook her head with her nose in the air. 'Nnnnnope,' she replied to rain on her sister's parade as it were.

Esther leaned on Vivien's horn but neither farmer nor ox batted an eye. 'No?' she remarked, wide-eyed. 'What do you mean no, it has to be.'

'Nnnnnope,' Minnie again scoffed, clicking her heels in anticipation and overly confident at having outwitted her big sister.

'Good Lord!' Esther suddenly exclaimed, looking beyond the sea of palms to the horizon. 'Pyramids!'

'What?' Minnie cursed with a clenched fist. 'Oh blast!'

Sure enough, approximately twenty miles off to the east beyond the bustling Nile delta and silhouetted against the glaring mid-morning sun were the unmistakable angular outlines of the Great Pyramids of Giza.

'Ohhhh wow,' Esther said, awestruck immediately at the magnificent wonder of the ancient world, an expression echoed by the tens, if not hundreds of thousands of annual visitor to the region. 'Minnie, look,' she added, slowing while mesmerised. 'Look, Minnie.'

'Yes, yes, alright,' Minnie replied calmly, although vexed at her sister. 'I couldn't have made it any easier for you if I'd tried.'

'Oh never mind all that,' Esther said dismissively. 'It's the Pyramids, Minnie, for Pete's sake.' Slowing further still to the sound of irate honking, Esther managed to break from the fearsome flow of traffic and pull to the side of the road.

'Why are we stopping, dear?' Minnie asked.

'Minnie!' Esther said, pointing toward the iconic burial tombs. 'The Pyramids,' and she pushed open her door and stepped out to wander a while.

'Yes, yes, but it's your turn, dear,' Minnie called after her. 'Essy, Essy, Essyyyy!'

But Esther stood with her hands shielding her eyes fixated on the horizon; she'd of course been taught about the pyramids during her formative years in school, read about them in her weekly glossies and watched countless documentaries on the subject from her sagging wingback chair, but nothing, nothing could have prepared her for being there with the river Nile flowing literally at her feet. 'My God,' she quietly gasped, catching the scent of eucalyptus in the air and the sound of braying camels carried on the warm desert wind, a sensual overload from a land mostly unchanged since the very dawn of time.

Rooted to the spot, Esther simply oozed appreciation for her surroundings, letting out a contented sigh with her heart rate slowly returning to normal.

'Essy!' Minnie suddenly said at her side, tugging at her sleeve and shattering the tranquil moment. 'Essy, it's your turn!'

'I'm sorry, what?' Esther replied without averting her eyes from the Giza Pyramids.

'I spy!' Minnie tiresomely reiterated. 'You must take your turn, dear, it's the rules.'

Esther snatched at her sister's arm, put a finger to her lips to silence her jabbering and pointed. 'Look,' she simply said. 'Just, look.'

Although anxious and pensive Minnie did as she was asked. 'Oh,' she eventually said when it hit her. 'Oh, yes I see what you mean, dear, I do.'

'Fiiinally,' Esther sighed, releasing Minnie.

Whilst the highway traffic thundered by behind them Esther and Minnie marvelled at the living tapestry before them, the lush green delta palms, the golden papyrus swaying at the banks of the mighty river now a foaming cocktail of the blue and white Nile tributaries which are believed to have begun their journeys in the countries of Burundi and Ethiopia flowing some 4800 miles through Khartoum where the two Niles converge, then on through Aswan, Luxor and Cairo before spilling into the Mediterranean sea.

Esther climbed back behind Vivien and hastily bolted Minnie's door from the inside before she could join her. 'What are you doing, dear?' Minnie asked, tugging at the chrome handle. 'Essy, Essy what are you doing?'

'Giving you an ultimatum,' Esther replied, winding down the window a tad. 'Either you sit quietly whilst we continue on our way and stop bothering me with your senseless gibberish or, I'm leaving you here, It's your choice, Minnie, what's it to be?'

'Leaving me?' Minnie asked, astounded. 'Essy, you wouldn't, surely not?'

Esther started Vivien and gripped the handbrake in readiness. 'Try me,' she said in reply.

'But, but I'm your sister,' Minnie said with a trembling lip. 'Essy, you wouldn't leave me.'

'I want your word, Minnie,' Esther said with sincerity. 'You must solemnly swear to curb your enthusiasm as it were, the choice is yours.' Esther turned her face away, leaving her sister to contemplate her limited options.

'Ohhhhh,' Minnie said, bobbing beside the car. 'Essyyyyyy, this is silly, let me in, pleaaaaaase.'

But Esther remained adamant, eyeing her frantic sister fleetingly. Of course Esther would never leave her but considering her fretting Minnie was unaware of this.

'Ohhhh,' she moaned again. 'Alright, alright, Essy,' she blurted, tugging at the door once again. 'I promise now let me in please, Essy, Essy, don't leave me!'

Esther couldn't help but smile as she reached to unlock the door, and quick as a flash Minnie leapt in and buckled her belt. 'Thank you,' Minnie said, slamming her door. 'Thank you, dear, you have my word, Essy darling, you have my word,' she told her sister, wriggling in her seat to find the divots her backside had moulded during the previous weeks. 'From now on, dear, I'm going to be the model sister, you'll see.'

'Hmmmmm,' Esther mumbled, doubting her sister's sincerity when pulling back into dense traffic to a barrage of sounding horns once again. 'Oh be quiet!' she snapped dismissively.

Oddly enough over the course of the following forty-five minutes Minnie never uttered a solitary word, pleasing her sister greatly, but bemusing her also at the same time. 'Ahem!' Esther said, clearing her throat and thus breaking the silence between them.

Minnie merely smiled politely and sat with her hands neatly positioned on her lap.

'Lovely day,' Esther added a short while later when lowering her window in thinning traffic and loosening the scarf around her neck. 'Phew!'

Again Minnie smiled and nodded whilst uncharacteristically silent.

Esther glanced across occasionally while trundling on towards the ancient and much documented city of Cairo, the Mecca for any self-respecting Egyptologist. 'Five more kilometres, Minnie dear,' she said, brimming with excitement. 'Can you believe it?'

A distant smile was her sister's only reply which tore at Esther's innards; Minnie's jabbering was indeed insufferable but the silence, the silence was somehow worse, eerie almost. 'Ohhhhhhhh,' she groaned with her steely exterior crumbling. 'Alright, alright!' she blurted reluctantly. 'I Spy!'

Minnie immediately sat bolt upright, rubbing her hands together with the broadest of smiles. 'Thaaaaat's the spirit!' she squealed, bobbing once again. 'Go ahead, dear,' she added triumphantly. 'I'm all ears.'

CHAPTER SEVEN.

Spluttering at the brow of a hill, Vivien gifted Esther and Minnie their first glimpse of the sprawling city of Cairo, a city of myths, legends and earth-shattering discovery and wonder nestled in the Nile valley.

The city of a thousand minarets as it has been called, dating back to around 960AD and of course the capital of Egypt. 'Cairo,' Esther said in awe. 'Minnie dear, we made it.'

'Sorry?' Minnie replied, tugging and tearing open a packet of popcorn and in time-honoured fashion depositing much of it onto the floor. 'Ohhhh hell,' she cursed, kicking it into as neat a pile as she could and in doing so discovering the pearl earring she'd misplaced several days earlier. 'Oh how wonderful!' she cried, stooping to pluck it from the accumulated debris at her feet, yet another sore point between her and her fastidious sister.

'Isn't it just?' Esther remarked, referring of course to the riveting region before them, both ancient and modern and a vital trade route steeped in history with as rich a cultural heritage as any other place on earth.

Buffing her pearl on the sleeve of her cardigan, Minnie slipped it back into her ear and eyed the matching pair in the mirror. 'There,' she said, contented. 'That's better.' Minnie still hadn't acknowledged the cityscape ahead of them. 'Do you know I thought I'd eaten it, dear,' she told her sister. 'If you recall I was shelling hazelnuts whilst we crossed the Saudi desert.'

'Yes, yes, I do,' a disgruntled Esther replied, peering down at the scattered remains at her sister's feet. 'It's a wonder we're not running alive with mice you know.'

'Ohhh don't be daft, dear,' Minnie laughed whilst glancing down herself for any signs of rodent infestation, gingerly kicking at the empty biscuit wrappers and Styrofoam coffee cups. 'I suppose I really should make more of an effort.'

'Oh you suppose, do you!' Esther sneered, disassociating herself from her slovenly sister. 'Why break the habit of a lifetime, dear, you were a messy little moo as a child and you still are to this very day, look at you, you're not happy unless you're knee deep in your own detritus.'

'That's a lie!' Minnie replied robustly whilst attempting to sweep her clutter beneath her seat unseen. 'Unlike you, Essy,' she added, 'I have chosen to spend what little time I may have left on God's green earth engaging in more meaningful and rewarding pastimes instead of faffing around as you insist on doing with that blasted dustpan and brush of yours, I swear, Essy you are obsessed, woman, obsessed.'

Back home it was true that Esther routinely followed her sister around their tiny flat on bended knees sweeping up her freshly deposited crumbs, boiled sweet wrappers and curled coloured pencil shavings, one of Minnie's meaningful pastimes as she called them being her addiction to colouring books designed primarily for the under-fives. She'd sit for hours with her tongue clamped between her dentures oblivious to all else whilst attempting to scribble within those darned lines; more often than not she would stray when her arthritis

locked the ligaments in her withered wrist causing her
to curse out of the blue and startle her dozing sister,
Minnie would then tear the pages from the book and
toss the screwed balls between their dented wicker
basket with one in ten hitting its mark, and the
remainder were hastily scooped from the carpet by her
disgruntled sister who in turn would curse the day she'd
agreed to once again cohabit with her unkempt kin
having endured many years top to tail with her in the
bedroom of their parents' two-up-two-down.

'Oh look, dear!' Minnie piped up in an attempt to steer
the conversation in a more favourable direction. 'Shall
we?'

'Oh,' Esther said, eyeing the adjacent market, or souk as
they are known locally. Dozens upon dozens, if not
hundreds of jabbering vendors plying their trade
throughout the network of narrow dimly lit cobbled
streets and alleyways, the vast majority thrusting
identical wares under the noses of the endless
procession of inquisitive tourists. 'I er, I don't see why
not,' she added when a particularly handsome hearth
rug caught her eye.

'Now, Essy,' Minnie said raising a finger, 'I am well
aware of your lifelong reluctance to barter, or haggle as
it were but I have it on good authority that the good
people of this fair city expect a little persuasive
purchasing, why it's positively encouraged, my dear.'

'Yes, yes but…' Esther sneered, 'I just can't be
bothered with it all.'

'Bothered!' Minnie remarked, turning in her seat to face
her sister. 'Bothered, my darling Essy,' she added raising
her eyebrows. 'You simply haven't lived, have you, I tell

you I find it thoroughly exhilarating, like picking the winning tombola ticket at the church bazar, do you remember, dear, I chose the mango chutney as my prize, and very nice it was too, mind you, Muriel from the WI was furious, she had to make do with the pickled beetroot, the look on her face, Essy. Oh it was priceless, absolutely priceless.'

Esther of course had switched off, hearing only a monotonous drone from her sister's direction. Wrenching on Vivien's handbrake at the side of the road, Esher flung open her door on seeing a party of Canadian ladies caressing the very rug she'd set her heart on. 'I sayyyy!' she called, swinging her legs and tugging herself to her feet. 'I sayyyyy!'

'Essy, what are you doing?' Minnie asked following suit.

'The rug, Minnie, the rug!' Esther squealed, reaching for her purse. 'I must have it!'

'No wait, dear!' Minnie protested a yard or so behind her. 'If you appear to keen, dear, they'll undoubtedly up the ante!'

'I don't care!' Esther said fixated with the hand woven heart rug, each fibre lovingly stitched by village elders in the foothills to the west of the city. 'Ahem, I sayyy!' she again called, approaching the party and nudging her way through. 'I believe I saw it first,' and she placed a hand on the rolled rug alongside that of a fearsome and rather robust looking gym mistress by the name of Prudence.

'Like hell you did!' the Canadian replied, looking Esther square in the eye. 'I saw it and it's mine.'

Sensing a confrontation the stallholder raised a hand. 'I have many rug,' he told them, gesturing to his mountainous stock pile, none of which matched the fine specimen between Esther and Prudence. 'How much?' Prudence asked, slapping the rug heartily. 'Name your price, buddy.'

Minnie craned her neck at the rear of the jostling crowd. 'Essyyy,' she called bobbing on the tip of her toes. 'Essy, haggle, dear, haggle!'

The Egyptian trader produced a battered calculator from his back pocket and prodded repeatedly. 'This particular fine carpet,' he told them, beginning his pitch perfected over many years, 'Was once owned by Queen Nefertiti herself, yes, yes, Nefertiti I tell you, so I cannot let you have it for less than two hundred of our Egyptian pounds.'

Prudence produced her own purse. 'No problem, buddy,' she told him, 'I'll take it.'

Esther wrenched a fistful of notes from her purse. 'Wait, wait!' she said, thumbing the local currency. 'I'll give you two fifty for the rug!'

Try as she may, Minnie could not break through the enthusiastic gathering. 'How much, Essy?' she called over their heads.

'Two fifty!' her sister called back. 'It's a bargain, dear!'

'No, no, no!' Minnie yelled in reply. 'Play the game, dear, remember to play the game, tell him you'll give him thirty and not a penny more!'

Prudence produced another note from her Christian Dior purse. 'Get outta here,' she told Esther whilst waving another fifty. 'Hey, pal, I'll give you three hundred,' she told the vendor. 'Now wrap the damn rug, will ya.'

'Three fifty!' Esther blurted much to her sister's horror.

'Three fifty?' Minnie gasped. 'Essy, no, for Pete's sake, offer thirty-five and not another penny!'

'Four hundred!' Prudence said adamantly whilst toe to toe with Esther, battle lines had been drawn and principles were now heavily at stake.

With a fierce bidding war ensuing, the stallholder's eyes were a dazzle. 'Tutankhamen himself played on this very carpet as a child,' he told the opponents, hoping further false provenance would increase the cheap replica's value. 'Yes the boy king himself, on this very carpet I tell you!'

With Prudence looking down her nose at her, Esther dug in her heels and stiffened her back. 'Fiiiive hundred!' she said with a smirk, assuming wrongly that she'd frightened off her opposition.

'Fifteen!' was Minnie's call from the back of the crowd. 'Fifteen is our final offer, take it or leave it, Mister!'

Prudence pursed her lips at Esther with sheer and utter contempt but Esther merely glanced over the crowds heads at her sister. 'Minnie, you are not helping in the slightest,' she told her. 'Now will you please be quiet and let me handle this!'

There was a sudden gasp from within the gathering before the whispers began. 'Minnie, Minnie, Minnie, it is I tell you, it's her,' and one by one they each turned from the stall to face Minnie, their faces aglow at being in the presence of a much admired Peshwari Nan.

'Damn it, Esther!' Minnie called over them. 'Haggle, dear, haggle!' and she then acknowledged the sea of faces before her. 'Hellooooo,' she said politely. 'Lovely day.'

The whispers then echoed Esther's name too and one or two of Prudence's party tugged at her tasselled sleeves. 'Pru, honey,' her friend said, leaning to lower her voice.

'Who?' Prudence said, snatching her head in Minnie's direction. 'You're kiddin', right?'

'No, no it is!' the friend and neighbour reiterated. 'The Peshwari Nans, God damn it.'

Prudence's eyes flitted back and forth between the two sisters before the colour slowly drained from her face. 'Sweet Jesus,' she gasped with a hand to her head. 'Forgive me please, Esther honey,' she said, eating a healthy portion of humble pie. 'I, I had no idea, darling, no idea at all.'

'Oh that's quite alright, dear,' Esther replied still gripping the souvenir tightly 'It's the rug, you see, it'll go beautifully with our Capodimonte.' The cheap chipped porcelain figure that Esther referred to which sat alongside their electric fire was in part the exact shade of maroon as the majority of the coveted rug.

'Well in that case, honey,' Prudence agreed, releasing her own grip, 'Of course you must have it.' Her sudden U-turn was a direct result of the sisters' unfaltering following throughout the United States, Canada and of course the wider world. 'Golly gee, Esther darling, if I'da known it was you,' she confessed, 'I'da never bid against ya, you have my word on that.'

'Like I said,' Esther explained, 'It's quite alright,' and she handed the ecstatic salesman her agreed five hundred Egyptian pounds, twice his usual asking price.

Minnie levered her way between the gathered tourists. 'Sorry, sorry,' she said, standing on one or two toes.

'Do excuse me,' and breaking through and nudging past Prudence she held up an Egyptian note of her own. 'We'll give you five for the rug, you rogue, or the deal is off,' she insisted, tipping her sister a wink. 'Leave this to me, dear,' she added. 'Like I said, these blighters expect to be bartered with, now do we have a deal or not?' she asked the salesman who stood thumbing her sister's payment.

'Minnie dear,' Esther said, tucking the rug beneath her arm. 'The deal is done.'

'What?' Minnie hastily replied. 'What do you mean, done, I'm about to deliver the decisive blow,' and she brandished five pounds in her clenched fist.

Several Canadians rummaged for autograph materials and waited politely in line whilst Esther obliged them.

'Essy?' Minnie asked, swatting a notebook aside. 'How much did you pay?'

'Sorry, dear, what was that?' Esther replied, returning another pad to its smiling owner.

'I said,' Minnie reiterated, completely ignoring the Canadians, 'How much did you pay for the rug?'

'Oh it was an absolute bargain, dear,' Esther replied. 'A steal even.'

'Yes, yes, but how much?' Minnie pressed.

'Oh well, Minnie, if you must know,' Esther said, signing the back of a bus ticket. 'I gave five for it.'

'Oh you did,' Minnie said, stunned somewhat by her sister's apparent astute bargaining and conceding to the surrounding autograph hunters. 'Well that's alright then.'

Prudence pressed her journal into Minnie's hand. 'Could you put to Pru with love?' she asked supplying a ballpoint pen too.

'Of course, my dear,' Minnie smiled.

The grateful stallholder handed Esther a free gift, a cheap soapstone Sphinx. 'For you, madam,' he said with a bow. 'Please enjoy your carpet with my compliments, five hundred is good price, very good price.'

Minnie suddenly stopped mid-signature. 'Sorry, did you say five hundred?' she asked with Prudence hovering behind her.

'Yes, madam,' the stallholder said, beaming from ear to ear. 'A good price for such a treasured antiquity, did I mention it was found in the tomb of Tutankhamen himself.'

Minnie eyed the label dangling from one end of the rug stating the presence of modern fire resistant fibres. 'Five hundred!' she said, staggering a step or two. 'Essy darling, Essy, please tell me you didn't.'

Esther remained chuffed with her purchase as the gathering around them increased along with the whispers.

'Essy, Essy!' Minnie cried when the two were separated by the jostling camera-wielding crowd.

Prudence again waved her notepad under Minnie's nose. 'Minnie darling, would you mind?' she asked.

'Yes, just a moment, dear,' Minnie replied brushing her pen aside.

The carpet trader then produced an identical rug from beneath his stall. 'Good price for this treasured antiquity!' he reeled off his ridiculous spiel once again whilst caressing the twenty-first century polyester parlour rug. 'Found in the tomb of Tutankhamen himself, good price, good price!'

'You, sir!' Minnie said, pointing a crooked finger, 'Are nothing but a fraudster, a racketeer, a charlatan and a....' She then paused her venomous tirade, catching sight of a tapestry depicting several of the gods worshipped by ancient Egyptians; Anubis with the head of a jackal who is thought to have watched over the dead, Osiris the ruler of the underworld, Horus with the head of a hawk, the God of the sky and Amun the most powerful of all and hailed as the king of the Gods. 'Ooooh!' she said, swatting Prudence's persistent pen aside once more, 'I say, how much for that delightful tapestry, young man?'

The eager salesman cast aside the rug and took down the tapestry. 'A wise choice, madam, a wise choice indeed,' he told her.

'Yes, yes, how much?' Minnie insisted, having already made up her mind it would hang above the mantel back home between the potpourri and the potted pelargonium, but the carpet vendor elaborated a little further.

'Madam, this exquisite example was discovered hanging in the tomb of none other than Ramesses the first himself, Ramesses, madam, Ramesses, I think you will agree that make it a rarity and one of epic proportion and significance.'

Minnie simply adored it, so much in fact that her better bargaining judgement was blurred on this occasion.

The wall hanging itself was barely a month old and produced half a world away in the Philippines using polyester and nylon. Anubis bore more of a resemblance to a lop-eared basset hound than a jackal and Horus the hawk a budgerigar. 'To you, madam,' the salesman smiled, 'Shall we say, three hundred?'

'Done!' Minnie said abruptly without the hint of a haggle.

The Canadians around her, assuming Minnie had an eye for antiquities suddenly entered into a fierce bidding war raising their hands and the price for that matter to a staggering fourteen hundred Egyptian pounds.

Even Prudence who had earlier apologised to Esther for intervening got in on the act. 'Fifteen hundred!' she called, glaring at her friends and neighbours with contempt.

Esther looked back whilst loading her purchase into the back of Vivien, alerted by the escalating commotion surrounding the carpet stall. 'What on earth?' she said on seeing her sister's hand rise triumphantly from the crowd.

'THREE THOUSAND POUNDS!' Minnie cried, brandishing her credit card in a bid to stave off any further rival bids.

Esther closed the rear doors. 'What was that?' she asked out of earshot and striding back across the street. 'Minnie dear!' she called to her sister but was unable to force her way through the crowd. 'Minniiiie!'

Minnie's extravagant shot across the bow had the desired effect, with the majority of the Canadians shaking their heads and pocketing their purses.

'Touché' Prudence too said, admitting defeat whilst Minnie was handed the spoils and the jubilant salesman's card reader.

'Minnie, there you are,' Esther eventually said as the crowd thinned, she then saw the hideous tapestry of the ridiculous replica gods draped over her sister's arm. 'Dear Lord, Minnie,' she said with a hand to her mouth. 'Your obsession with tasteless tea towels really must stop, my dear, we simply haven't the room.'

'Tasteless tea towel?' Minnie remarked, pulling her purchase closer to her chest. 'Don't be daft, dear,' she scoffed. 'This is a genuine antiquity from the tomb of, wait for it dear, Ramesses the first, Ramesses dear, I thought we could hang it over the mantelpiece.'

'Ramesses the first,' Esther chuckled, thumbing the lightweight fabric and the clown-like caricature of Osiris. 'Minnie, it's a souvenir,' she reminded her sister. 'And a dreadful one at that, I hope you didn't pay more than a pound or two for it.'

On closer inspection the penny finally dropped with Minnie, compounded by the fact that three adjacent stalls were each peddling the self-same tea towel tapestry. 'Oh er, no, dear, of course not,' she said, swiftly pocketing her credit card. 'You know me,' she added, glaring at the salesman who was busily and shamelessly for that matter peddling another of his Filipino bulk purchases to a pair of perusing Parisians.

'From the tomb of the mighty Khufu himself,' he said, falsifying yet another yarn as did his fellow peddlers who claimed the wholesale imports were the prized possessions of Egypt's all powerful ancient rulers, Seti the first, Mentuhotep and even Alexander the Great.

'How much?' Esther probed, curious as to who would buy such a thing.

'I'm sorry, dear, what?' Minnie said, hastily leaving the stall with her purchase.

'How much was it?' Esther said, badgering her sister.

'Ohhhh not much, Essy dear,' Minnie replied, tossing the tea towel into the car with complete disregard. 'A pound or two, I can't quite recall,' and she slammed the rear door and sat red-faced in her seat.

Esther leaned at her sister's window. 'I should have listened to you and haggled, dear,' she confessed. 'You always were the more astute of the two of us, quite the entrepreneur, that's what I always say.'

'Yes, ahem, quite, dear,' Minnie said, sinking in her seat. 'Shall we go?'

Esther climbed in alongside Minnie. 'I really don't know how you do it,' she continued, 'I simply haven't the nerve.'

'Hmmmm,' Minnie mumbled, reluctant to be drawn on the subject. Ordinarily Minnie could indeed charm the birds from the trees and badger a bargain from the most adamant and pushy of peddlers but on this occasion she'd been had, and it grated on her.

'I swear it's a gift,' Esther added, starting the car. 'That's what it is, a gift.'

Minnie quietly seethed for a further fifteen minutes whilst her sister continued to compliment her on occasion. 'Ooooh look,' Esther then suddenly said when passing another covered bazar. 'Shall we….'

'NO!' Minnie swiftly blurted, startling her sister somewhat and having lost the appetite to rummage. 'I er,' she added, searching for a plausible excuse, 'I'm getting one of my heads, dear, so if it's all the same to you,' she rubbed her temples with both hands, 'I'd rather not.'

'Oh!' Esther replied, craning her neck at the gaily coloured wares just ripe for the rummaging. 'Are you sure, dear?' she asked. 'I swear I see a kaftan in lilac that'll match your flip flops beautifully.'

'Sorry, dear, I really couldn't,' Minnie insisted, averting her eyes from the bustling bazar whilst the traffic slowed toward the city centre; she then sat deep in thought for a moment strumming her fingers again on the tablet. 'Did you say lilac, Essy dear?' she asked nonchalantly.

'Yes, yes I did,' Esther replied, confident in her sister's predictability. 'Worn by Cleopatra herself, no doubt.'

Minnie strummed a little harder. 'Stop the car, dear!' she suddenly yelled whilst reaching for her credit card. 'I must have it!'

'Right you are, dear,' Esther said, having hoodwinked her sister yet again.

'I sayyyy!' Minnie called whilst caressing the kaftan and summoning the stallholder who was sat shelling pistachios on a brandy barrel. 'Hellooooo!' she added with a courteous wave. 'How much please?'

The peddler sprang to life at the prospect of a sale dropping his shelled nuts in the process. 'Ahhh a wise choice, madam,' he said echoing the corrupt carpet seller and just about every vendor within a mile. 'A wise choice, a wise choice indeed.'

'Yes, yes how much?' Minnie insisted once again.

The stallholder took a deep breath in readiness to unload his well-rehearsed patter claiming as Esther quite rightly predicted that the garment in question was once worn by Egyptian nobility, and so the circle of life was complete once more.

Weary and weighed down with trinkets and souvenirs abound, the sisters later returned to Vivien. 'Can you believe it, dear?' Minnie said, brandishing a nondescript rock having been convinced it had fallen from the worn facial features of Egypt's iconic Sphinx. 'From the Sphinx!' she marvelled. 'I shall have it mounted on mahogany and show it at the next WI meeting, the ladies will be green with envy, Essy, green with envy.'

The racketeer from whom she'd purchased the suspect artefact had hand-picked the pieces on his stall from a discarded heap of builders' rubble proving once again just how gullible and blinded foreign tourists can be, letting their emotions and mystical surroundings rule their hearts and empty their pockets. Esther barely responded, having died and gone to heaven as it were when securing the steal of a lifetime as she described it, paying a mere forty pounds for Nefertiti's teapot complete with certificated authenticity from the bogus *Egyptian bureau of all thing old and ancient* emblazed with a crude crest and a woeful watermark. 'Good lord, Minnie dearest, look!' she exclaimed, lifting the lid and finding a dried and tasteless tea bag in the bottom, a pyramid bag of course, circa 2016. 'The bag itself could fetch a small fortune,' she added carefully wrapping the Taiwanese teapot in a pair of her beloved bloomers for safe keeping. 'All in all a successful day thus far, wouldn't you say, dear?' she said, closing Vivien's rear doors and patting her roof. 'I don't know about you, Min,' she added. 'But I'm a mite peckish.' She turned to see that her sister had disappeared. 'Minnie?' she called. 'Minniiiiie!'

'Here I am, dear!' Minnie replied, emerging once again from the bazar dragging a hessian sack behind her filled with a dozen or so more pieces of the hefty builder's rubble. 'Help me, will you, dear,' she wheezed, positive that the online auction rooms would be abuzz when presented with her centuries-old Sphinx chippings. 'I'm sorry but it was just too good an opportunity to pass by, you do understand, don't you?'

'Oh but of course, dear,' Esther agreed, opening the doors once again and helping heave the bag aboard. 'Far too good an opportunity indeed.'

Ecstatic, the sisters drove further toward the centre of Cairo in search of suitable accommodation, something a cut above the rest having endured the barest of necessities of late. Minnie ferreted in her numerous carrier bags between her legs whilst her sister navigated the heavy city traffic. 'Look, Essy dear,' Minnie said, brandishing a novelty scarab beetle, a little too lifelike for her sister's taste.

'Christ, Minnie, what on earth!' Esther recoiled with the battery operated beetle thrust under her nose.

'I got it for free, dear,' Minnie informed her, delighted with her childish acquisition. 'It's a torch too, dear,' she added, illuminating the crude creature's beady eyes with the push of a button and dazzling her sister with the powerful twin LED lights.

'Minnie for Pete's sake!' Esther cried swatting the tacky toy and struggling to focus. 'I can't see, damn you!' Braking sharply to avoid a collision, Esther retrieved her spectacles that had fallen into her lap and glared at

Minnie who sat switching the torch on and off repeatedly and becoming increasingly enthused by the flash of light.

'I thought it'd come in handy, Essy darling,' Minnie said, pocketing the cheap imitation. 'During power cuts.'

'Power cuts!' Esther exclaimed. 'May I remind you, sister, that we are living in the twenty-first century and that that sort of thing is now as rare as rocking horse manure as Father used to say.'

During the sisters' early years when the National Grid was in its formative stage power cuts were a regular occurrence and households the length and breadth of the country were 'cut off' as the saying goes when increased demand would overload the primitive and fledgling technology.

Minnie once again sat popping dates into her mouth and routinely spitting the pips into her paper coffee cup.

'You will live to regret that, my dear,' her sister warned when the cup was all but full. 'Haven't I told you before about the pitfall of prunes and dates, and not to mention those blasted dried apricots you insist on slurping after supper, I swear, Minnie, it drives me to distraction, it does, to distraction, but will you listen, ohhhhh no, Minnie knows best as always.'

Minnie raised her eyebrows whilst her sister dealt out yet another lengthy lecture.

'You'll be up half the night again,' Esther continued while dropping another gear in heavy traffic, 'Whining about stomach cramps and your rumbling bowel no doubt, well you best not keep me awake, my girl, or there'll be hell to pay, do you hear?'

'Essy I'll be fiiiine,' Minnie replied confidently. 'I have the constitution of an ox, I assure you.'

'Ha!' Esther scoffed, having endured her sister's woeful wailing and belly-aching from the bathroom and calls for more three-ply cushioned toilet tissue.

'Besides,' Minnie added, 'I might save the stones and start a seed bank, for future generations, you know the sort of thing, I read an article in one of my magazines about a group of girl guides in Glamorgan.'

Esther groaned under her breath and switched on the radio to drown her sister's nonsensical nattering.

'Apparently!' Minnie said over the indecipherable Egyptian local radio din, 'spitting a thousand pips apiece earned the guides two dozen brownie points and a yellow ribbon, quite admirable, I'd say.'

'I'm sorry, dear, what was that?' Esther smirked, tapping her fingers on the wheel in time to the Cairo choristers and their clanging camel bells, the very best Egypt had to offer the world musically at that moment in time. The land of the Pharaoh's may have the boy king Tutankhamen but the rest of the world had trumped them with Justin Bieber.

Minnie mouthed several more dates, again spitting the stones into her brimming cup. 'Now that's worthy of a brownie point or two, don't you think, dear?' she asked Esther. 'Essy, Essy dear?'

Esther rocked her head and hummed along to the radio.

'Essy?' Minnie urged. 'I said that's worthy of a brownie point or two, would you say, Essy, ohhhhh never mind,' and she sat with her arms folded across her chest with her cup of stones clamped between her knees.

As with their previous destinations, the sisters regularly encountered the cat calls of elderly suitors who'd gotten wind of their visit and turned out to strut like peacocks in the hopes of attracting a seemingly wealthy mate. All of which Esther and Minnie found highly amusing and rating them five stars if they were tactile and toned, or just the one for tired and toothless.

'Oh he's a four!' Minnie suddenly said, peering over her spectacles at a heavily tanned tour guide touting trips to the Valley of the Kings as were countless others. 'I said he's a four, dear!' she yelled over the monotonous choir.

'No, no, Minnie, he's a three,' Esther insisted checking her rear view mirror. 'I'm not fond of the beard and his trousers are too tight.'

'That's why I rated him a four, dear,' Minnie chuckled to herself, having eyed the tout in lengthy detail. 'He hasn't left much at all to the imagination, I'll give him that.'

'Now that!' Esther remarked, gripping the wheel and experiencing palpitations. 'Is a resounding five without a shadow of a doubt.'

Minnie was forced to agree, rising in her seat to gaze lustfully upon the shapely buttocks of a bending barista busily serving coffee and pastries outside an adjacent café. 'My word!' she said, resting a hand on her beating heart. 'Five minutes,' she said, breathlessly fantasising. 'Five minutes, dear, that's all I want and I'll blow the froth off of his latte.'

'Minnie!' Esther spluttered, wide-eyed. 'Dear Lord, he's half your age,' she reminded her sister with one eye on the crease in the rear of his taut trousers. 'Mind you,' she then said cheekily. 'I wouldn't mind a minute and a half myself.'

The sister laughed together, rating at least a dozen more waiters en route. One bare-chested bartender receiving a five and an attempted wolf whistle from Minnie with her loose denture sounding as though she were blowing a raspberry at him. 'Ohhh hell,' she cursed, mopping her chin and trying again to no avail. 'I was a dab hand at that, Essy, when I had all my own teeth.'

'Minnie dearest,' Esther chuckled, 'You haven't had your own teeth for fifteen years, I gave you a tuppence from the tooth fairy when you lost the last one to a bar of peanut brittle, and after I'd given you fair warning too.'

'Yes, yes, I know but…' Minnie replied, fishing for an excuse. 'The brittle was two for one and I had a coupon you see, a bargain is a bargain, dear, whether it's peanut brittle or sugared almonds,' two of Minnie's firm favourites and equally responsible for her present dental replacements, along of course with the Parma Violets, sherbet lemons, aniseed twists and copious amounts of cream soda.

Steering around a group of tethered camels waiting in the blistering heat to ferry overweight tourists to and from Tutankhamen's tomb, Esther glared at their keeper who was sat sipping iced tea beneath the shade of a crooked palm whilst his animals endured a life of perpetual misery to line his pockets in the name of tradition. A merciless trade seen the world over, from the elephant of Sri Lanka beaten by their mahouts to the majestic orcas of California confined to what amounts to a bath tub of water and trained through starvation to entertain the paying public. Stolen as infants from their herds and pods the elephants and orcas would otherwise roam vast distances, at times crossing continents instinctively as their predecessors had done for centuries, but confinement and communal deprivation more often than not would quite literally drive these harmless creatures insane, leading them to harm themselves and in a few isolated incidents their trainers.

Minnie tossed the camels the remainder of her dates. 'I say, Essy,' she said, scrolling the pages of her tablet in search of a bed for the night and dismissing the motels, boarding houses and B&B's in favour for the more high end hotels. 'Do you think we could be a tad pretentious and go five star?'

Ordinarily Esther being the more financially frugal of the two of them would shun such decadence, but her lower back, creaking knees and throbbing feet were screaming to be pampered, and as their bank balances were swelling beyond their wildest dreams as sales of Peshwari Nans merchandise including jigsaws, board games, monogrammed carpet slippers and chinaware had spiked at an all-time high, the odd extravagance here and there would barely dent their ever deepening pot. Although that said, Esther still insisted on darning the holes in their threadbare socks and repairing her beloved spectacles with a little household fuse wire and super-glue. 'I don't see why not,' she agreed, skilfully unravelling a boiled sweet whilst driving.

'Oooh look, dear!' Minnie chirped in time-honoured fashion. 'The Fairmont offers free canapés and rum punch on arrival.'

'Canapés, you say?' Esther marvelled. 'Well what are you waiting for, dear,' she added, prodding the tablet. 'Make a reservation at once!'

The five-star Fairmont Nile City Hotel on the banks of the mighty river itself affords distant views of the pyramids and the surrounding ancient city, the epitome of luxury, opulence and style, a jewel in a bustling oasis with some five hundred rooms spread over twenty-five floors, a champagne bar, a rooftop sky pool and Onyx lounge. The Fairmont would offer the sisters an experience an entire world away from their humble beginnings.

'Take a left, dear,' Minnie instructed her sister whilst expertly navigating with the aid of the GPS coordinates. 'Third right then left again.' Her dexterity with the tablet computer meant that a hotel reservation was now a mere trifle, a swipe of her finger, several clicks and her credit card details and bingo, she had secured them a Nile-facing room on the twenty-fourth floor with twin double beds, a whirlpool bath and as luck would have it, a pair of wingback chairs not dissimilar to theirs back home, minus Minnie's toffee wrappers and tangerine skins of course.

The road-weary sister each gasped in unison when rounding the final corner and catching their first glimpse of the Fairmont flanked by the twin Nile City complex towers. 'Good grief!' Esther said, selecting the wrong gear and grinding Vivien's dated cogs. 'Oh blast!' she added, wrestling with the stick as they shuddered to a halt, stalling the tiny but reliable 1100 engine. 'Do forgive me, Vivien dear,' she then said, stroking the dashboard and turning the key.

Minnie's details had caused quite a stir when entered into the Fairmont's booking system, sparking the highest level of protocol as it did with visiting Royalty and Presidents alike. A rapid-fire briefing was given by the hotel manager to his impeccably turned out staff, putting into place a speedy reception for the now A-list OAPs.

On approach Esther and Minnie were greeted by no less than fifty of the hotel's contingent of chambermaids, porters, bartenders and front of house staff proudly standing to attention either side of the beaming manager on his recently rolled out red carpet. 'Wait, dear!' Minnie said, taking her sister's arm and looking over her shoulder for a fleet of limousines or Ferraris perhaps, but of course it was they who were to be greeted graciously.

Esther leaned from her window whilst slowing at the foot of the steps. 'I sayyyy, should we go round back?' she asked.

The hotel manager raced to open her door. 'Of course not, madam,' he said, bending at the waist. 'Welcome to the Fairmont Cairo,' he added, clicking his fingers to warn his staff to avert their gaze for fear of unsettling his gracious guests.

A footman opened Vivien's rear doors and loaded their cases onto a gleaming brass trolley, and was soon joined by Minnie who hauled the sack of rubble free and dumped it amongst the cases. 'Sphinx,' she merely said to the bewildered footman. 'Could you please see to it that it's deposited into your safe, my good man.'

'Errrrrm, yes, madam,' the footman replied, rolling the rocks and cases up the adjacent ramp. 'Yes, yes of course, right away.'

Esther was wary of parting with her recent acquisitions and draped her replica rug over the startled manager's shoulder, tucking an Egyptian pound into his lapel pocket before leaving him standing. 'Well come along, dear!' she told him. 'I don't want the sun bleaching the delicate yarn.'

The manager looked down his nose at the tatty and tasteless souvenir but hurried along all the same. 'My apologies, madam,' he said whilst his maids curtsied and barmen bowed.

'Helloooooo,' Minnie said, pausing to exchange pleasantries as Her Majesty their Queen often did. 'Oh how lovely,' she added, accepting a posy of petunias. 'Thank you, my dear, lovely day isn't it.'

Ushered to a private side desk away from the common folk as it were, the sisters availed themselves of the hotels hospitality, rum punch, champagne, canapés and crudités. 'Mmmmm oh, darling,' Minnie said with a fistful of tender asparagus tips and a brimming glass of intoxicating punch. 'I swear I could get used to this.'

Esther on the other hand opted for a flute of cooling grapefruit juice, steering well clear of the rum punch and snatching the ladle from Minnie's reaching hand. 'That's enough, dear,' she warned her gluttonous sister who downed the potent brew before her glass too was whisked away.

'Ohhh but, Essyyyy,' Minnie moaned, nibbling her asparagus.

'I said that's enough,' Esther reiterated. 'Now come along, I'm desperate to bathe my bunions.'

'Ohhhh very well,' Minnie sulked, dipping a discreet finger into the bowl in passing. 'That is delightful,' she told the manager whilst they trudged toward the elevators. 'Have room service make me up a nightcap, will you, dear?' she whispered out of earshot of her sister.

'But of course, madam,' the manager willingly obliged.

The jaw-dropping view from the sisters' luxurious suite had the two of them mesmerised and rooted to the spot for several minutes, the late afternoon sky layered in copper tones providing an exquisite backdrop to the distant Giza pyramids and of course the shapely feline Sphinx sat facing the setting sun. Once buried to the neck beneath the desert sand, it is believed to date back to the 4th dynasty, although several theorists believe the enigmatic statute is older still but there was no clear cut evidence.

'Asparagus, dear?' Minnie asked, having pocketed a large quantity of the marinated sprouts, along with a dozen pickled walnuts.

'I'll pass if it's all the same to you,' Esther replied whilst her sister plucked the cardigan fluff from her squirrelled provisions.

'Suit yourself, dear,' Minnie said depositing her mini buffet onto the onyx coffee table.

Esther kicked off her shoes. 'Ahhhhhh, thaaaat's better,' she groaned, wriggling her toes amid the deep twisted pile of the Persian carpet.

Minnie followed suit, upsetting a crystal decanter, chipping the narrow neck in the process with a single flick of her faux leather brogue.

'Minnie, for Pete's sake!' Esther barked, rushing to right the damaged decanter and grapple beneath the table for the heavy stopper. 'Five minutes, Minnie!' she snapped. 'We've been here five minutes and you insist on wreaking havoc, don't you, don't you?'

'Well, dear,' Minnie replied, offering a paltry defence. 'If it had been full of brandy it might not have toppled, don't you think, or cognac, yes, yes, I'd prefer cognac, Cyril and I used to indulge in a box of liqueurs after a pickled egg and a port and lemon at the Plough and Anchor, you remember the Plough and Anchor don't you, dear?' she asked amid her meandering monologue. 'They had a hot pot to die for and an African Grey perched on a pint pot at the end of the bar cursing at the customers like a drunken docker, do you know, Essy dear, he once told me to go….'

'Minnie!' Esther barked, cutting her wittering sister short. 'Enough please!' She clasped a hand to her forehead. 'I swear you are driving me insane with your blasted parrots, pickled eggs and port and flaming lemon!'

'Are you alright, dear?' Minnie foolishly asked. 'You haven't been taking your vitamin supplements have you, only you seem a tad tetchy if you ask me.'

'Tetchy!' Esther raged, throwing her hands in the air, 'Tetchy, dear God, woman, if it were not for my arthritis,' she reached out her crippled fingers toward her sister's neck, 'I'd have throttled you long before now!'

Minnie took a cautionary step back. 'Oh you don't mean that, dear,' she smirked, 'You're just run down, you know you really should learn to relax, have you ever considered meditation, or Tai Chi perhaps, Nelly from the newsagents says it works wonders for her sciatica, perhaps you need a massage,' she suggested, quickly rounding her seething sister and clumsily manipulating her tired neck and shoulders. 'Ooooh yes, you're a bag of knots, my dear,' she added whilst inflicting far more tension than she'd set out to relieve.

'OW, get off of me, you foolish woman!' Esther yelled, shrugging clear of Minnie's inexperienced massaging.

'But, darling,' Minnie insisted, eager to offer her assistance. 'You really should let me take care of those knots, you'll feel a whole lot better, I assure you.'

'I'm warning you, Minnie!' Esther said, edging further away. 'If you so much as look in my direction for at least the next hour the only knot you'll have to deal with will be the slipknot around your neck, do I make myself clear?'

'Just as I thought,' Minnie scoffed, giving her sister the space she so eagerly craved. 'It's the multivitamins, you know you really should keep up with the recommended dosage, dear.'

Esther turned away to control her rocketing blood pressure and stormed into the adjacent bathroom, thrusting the door closed behind her. Once inside she let out an extended growl, gripping the towel rail in a futile attempt to tear it from the wall, such was her frustration. Splashing her face with cool water and shaking her head at her reflection in the mirror, Esther struggled at that moment to find a single discerning quality possessed by her sister, a single question tumbled over and over in her mind. Why, why was she cursed with a simpleton for a sister, why must she endure such purgatory, why, why? Locking the bathroom door as she had done at home and in countless hotels when accompanied by her sister, Esther chose to sit in tranquil silence on the lavatory seat blotting all thoughts of her sister from her mind by way of meditation, a skill she had acquired through necessity.

Minnie, on the other hand, stood at the open window humming '*Daisy, Daisy give me your answer do*' and offering a small fragment of rubble she'd plucked from her pocket to the horizon in an attempt to ascertain which particular part of the Sphinx it had fallen from, such was her blissful ignorance at having driven her sister to her present safe room as it were.

Forty-five minutes later Esther clawed herself from the lavatory, having seized up in position but reduced her stress levels to zero nevertheless. Again she doused her face with water and turned the key, insisting to herself that she was not going to let Minnie get to her, not one iota. Her near Zen state of consciousness assured she was impervious to stress and anxiety, safe on a higher plateau reached through controlled breathing and the occasional recital of the Lord's Prayer for good measure. But, and with Minnie there is always a but, even the most devout and dedicated of meditative monks may have met their match and possibly broken a lifelong vow of silence when greeted by a sister such as Minnie. 'What in God's name?' Esther then asked, finding her sister sat on the floor amid the crumpled window drapes, scattered plaster and fixings, and if that wasn't calamitous enough the Fairmont's mini bar door was no longer attached to the cooler, that too was strewn with various components across the travertine tiled floor.

'Hellooooo,' Minnie said, unravelling herself from the curtains and setting the detached pole aside. 'Now, dear, let me explain,' she hastily said.

Esther stood with her mouth gaping. 'I don't believe it,' she said at the incomprehensible picture before her. 'I just, don't believe it.'

'I assure you it was an accident, dear,' Minnie said, quick to point out. 'I stumbled you see, when my brooch became snared in the satin, I've a good mind to complain you know.'

'Complain!' Esther remarked. 'We'll be lucky if we're not kicked out on the blasted street for this, and what, dare I ask, have you done to the refrigerator?'

'Ahhh,' Minnie said, scrambling free of the drapes and heaving herself to her feet with the help of the heavy plump sofa. 'I was attempting to reverse the door you see, dear, but I seem to have misplaced one of the screws, you know how I am with small parts, all fingers, thumbs and toes.'

'Yes, yes I do!' Esther said, offering up her wrist. 'You assured me you could mend my Tiffany timepiece, you promised, Minnie, did you not, yes, yes, you did and now look at it.'

Minnie had once again meddled with her sister's belongings, this time misplacing the glass bezel, over winding the delicate instrument to the point where the hour hand rotated a full revolution every five minutes

464

and all but three of the surrounding diamonds remained. Esther then backtracked for a moment. 'And, what do you mean you were reversing the door, why on earth would you do that, why, Minnie, tell me why?'

'Well,' Minnie replied, gesturing to the remainder of the kitchen cupboard doors which were all hinged to the left. 'You know how I'm a stickler for uniformity don't you, dear, now I know it's a minor detail but believe me it would have bothered me no end until it was rectified.'

'But it isn't, is it?' Esther quite rightly pointed out. 'Rectified, I mean, look at it, it's broken, just like my blasted watch, and while we're on the subject of your malicious meddling might I remind you that we have a tumble dryer that hasn't so much as tumbled since you tinkered with it, a toaster that cremates our crumpets and ejects them at breakneck speed and a TV remote that now activates the door chime and every car alarm within a quarter mile.'

'Oh I'd hardly call it malicious, dear,' Minnie said with a blasé attitude to her former blunders. 'Anyway didn't Mother always teach us to make do and mend?'

'That's just it!' Esther replied amidst the wreckage. 'You haven't mended anything, not a single thing, have you, have you?'

Minnie paused for thought, pondering her numerous attempts at household repairs, albeit with the very best of intentions, but someone once said a little knowledge can be a dangerous thing, and Minnie had very little knowledge indeed. 'Yes but...' she said, raising a finger with very little in the way of substance to follow. But Minnie's saving grace came by way of a knock at the door. 'Ooooh I'll get it!' she said, hastily side-stepping her sister who stooped to retrieve the refrigerator door and associated fixtures and fittings.

'Good evening, madam,' a smartly dressed porter said when Minnie greeted him with a smile, he then pushed a linen-draped trolley into the suite laden with a sumptuous selection from the hotel kitchen and a freshly corked bottle of bubbly nestling in a bucket of ice. 'Compliments of the Fairmont, madams,' he informed them, draping a cloth across his forearm and pouring the champers into two glasses.

'Oh thank you, young man,' Minnie said without hesitation.

The porter then looked Esther up and down and more importantly at the mini bar door in her hand. 'Madam?' he asked bemused.

'Oh!' Esther remarked, suddenly aware of his presumption that she was somehow responsible for this wanton destruction. 'No, erm,' she stammered, hastily placing the door onto the counter top. 'I er, I see how this must appear to you but please allow me to clarify things.'

'It's OK, madam,' the porter smirked, taking her rage and lack of dexterity into account whilst Minnie remained tight-lipped behind her champagne flute. 'At the Fairmont we forgive and forget the occasional, shall we say, mishap.' He then glanced across at the crumpled satin curtains on the floor and the broken pole alongside. 'And at times the more frequent,' he added, shaking his head.

'No, wait, you don't think…' Esther blurted, red-faced.

The porter turned and made for the door. 'No need to explain, madam,' he told her. 'I will see to it that maintenance make the necessary repairs.'

'No, no you don't understand!' Esther said in pursuit. 'It wasn't me, it was…'

'There is no need to apologise,' the porter said, raising a hand at the door. 'Please enjoy the remainder of your stay at the Fairmont,' and with this he was gone leaving Esther guilt-ridden at the door.

'Champagne, dear?' Minnie asked courteously.

'What?' Esther snapped, positively fuming at being implicated in her sister's vandalism of hotel property.

'Champagne,' Minnie reiterated. 'Oh and you really should try the damson tartlets, they are to die for, dear, oooh and so is the cranberry lattice for that matter.' Minnie swiped the crumbs from her chin and paused with her sister glaring at her. 'What?' she then asked, plucking another sweet tart from the trolley. 'Oh dear, don't tell me,' she added, 'I have jam on my chin, don't I, silly me.'

Esther did nothing more than snatch the champagne bottle from the bucket and storm back into the bathroom slamming the door behind her once again; if meditation would not ease the stress, strain and even pain of life with Minnie then perhaps alcohol would.

'Essyyyy,' Minnie called after her. 'Essyyyyyyy, whatever's the matter, dear?' Minnie's complete ignorance had her sister flabbergasted and swilling champagne uncharacteristically from the neck of the bottle.

'Essyyyyy,' Minnie called again, followed by a tap on the bathroom door. 'I'm sorry to bother you but I need to use the lavatory, Essyyyyyy.'

Esther was now close to tears and breaking point for that matter. 'GOD GIVE ME STRENGTH!' she barked, pleading for salvation and wrenching open the door.

'Thank youuuuuuu,' Minnie said with a wistful smile and ducking past her sister clenching her knees. 'Oh,' she then added. 'I do apologise, dear, but I seem to have eaten all the tartlets,' and with this she closed the door in her sister's face and raised the lavatory seat.

Esther glanced across at the meagre scraps her sister had left behind on the tray, a half-eaten bun and a scattering of salad garnish, before reaching for her handbag, and more importantly her medication.

Minnie emerged a short while later to find a duvet dumped on the sofa and a *do not disturb* card hanging on the bedroom door knob. Then and only then did Minnie have the faintest inkling that her sister may be aggrieved in some way and that she should prepare for a night alone.

Whilst Esther had absolutely no trouble drifting off to sleep, having polished off the remainder of the champagne, Minnie on the other hand tossed and turned on the narrow sofa, wriggling beneath the duvet unable to settle without her sister in close proximity. 'AHEM!' she called out, hoping to attract Esther's attention, but nothing, she then faked a coughing fit gradually increasing in volume and intensity until Esther stirred, opened an eye and cocked an ear.

'Minnie?' Esther said, mildly concerned.

Hearing this Minnie upped her game as it were, adding a gargle or two.

'Minnie!' Esther called, throwing back her own duvet and wrenching herself from the bed. 'Minnie dearest!' and opening the door she shuffled to the sofa side. 'Minnie, darling what is it?' she asked. 'Whatever's wrong?'

'Oh, oh, Essy,' Minnie said, ceasing her seizure. 'Sorry, I do apologise, did I wake you?'

'Yes, yes, but not to worry,' Esther replied. 'Are you alright, I heard you coughing.'

'Did you?' Minnie asked, reeling her sister in at this point. 'I, I think it's the sofa, dear,' she added coughing again. 'It's the polyester, you see, I've inhaled so much I'm about to pass a fur ball.'

'Oh dear,' Esther said, stroking her sister's hair and buying the sorry tale hook line and pathetic sinker. 'Best you come with me then, dear,' she said, tugging the duvet from her sister.

'Oh no I'll be fine, really, dear,' Minnie feebly protested. 'I don't want to bother you, you go back to bed and don't mind me, I'm just sorry I woke you that's all,' and again she croaked and spluttered a little. 'Like I said, I'll be fine, honestly.'

'Nonsense,' Esther insisted. 'You're coming with me, now up you get.'

Minnie attempted to resist once more.

'Ah, ah,' Esther said, hoisting her sister to her feet. 'I'm sorry, it's all my fault,' she added, 'I never should have left you out here, please forgive me.

'Ohhh don't blame yourself, dear,' Minnie said croakily. 'I just need the comfort of a real bed, that's all.'

'Yes, yes, of course,' Esther replied, helping her sister into her double bed and tucking the blanket up under her chin. 'Can I get you anything?' she asked. 'A glass of water perhaps?'

'Water?' Minnie replied, stretching out her arms and legs. 'Whatever for, Essy?'

'For that horrendous cough of course, dear,' Esther said, hovering at the door.

'Cough?' Minnie asked. 'Oh, oh yes, my cough, yes, dear, that would be marvellous, thank you.'

'Anything else?' Esther asked, still concerned.

'Oooh erm,' Minnie pondered. 'I er, I left half a bun on the trolley, dear, you don't mind, do you?'

'No, no, not at all,' Esther smiled, catering to her sister's whims and fancies. 'I'll be back in a jiffy, darling.' On her return barely three minutes later Esther stood in the doorway bun and water in hand, mortified that not only was her sister spread-eagled across the bed but she was sound asleep and snoring nasally. 'Every time,' she cursed to herself for once again allowing Minnie to hoodwink her. 'Every blasted time.' Shoving Minnie bodily and inching in beside her, Esther now found herself unable to sleep amid her sister's gurgling and dragged her pillow up over her face and yelled muffled obscenities into it.

470

CHAPTER EIGHT.

Waking the following morning to the sound of voices outside the bedroom door, Esther looked around for her sister. 'Minnie?' she said with her head pounding as a result of excessive champagne consumption. 'Minnie, is that you?' she asked, clambering from the otherwise empty bed. 'Oh!' she then remarked, opening the door and discovering the hotel's maintenance man busily repairing their broken property.

'Morning, dear,' Minnie piped up, shadowing the repairman closely and unsettling him somewhat. 'I'm just assisting Kamal here, well I told him I had considerable experience with this sort of thing.' She snatched the wrench that Kamal was reaching for and handed it to him. 'There you are, dear,' she smiled. 'Now do take care not to over-tighten those fasteners, won't you.'

Kamal raised his eyebrows but continued in a professional manner.

'Oh and you might want to take a look at the television too while you're here,' Minnie informed him. 'I've taken the back off expecting to find a blown fuse but oddly enough there weren't any, no wonder I can't get the darn thing to work.' Minnie had indeed dissected the flat screen television in the corner of the room having observed her father on numerous occasions replacing the fuses and valves on their very first set, an enormous piece of furniture taking up the window bay of their humble terraced house.

Kamal looked on in despair at the stricken set with its motherboard and intricate circuitry dangling from its delicate wiring.

'I was hoping to catch Judge Judy, you see,' Minnie added, hovering over Kamal. 'Essy and I never miss an episode do we, dear, I said we never miss an episode do we, dear!' she said a little louder.

Esther struggled to disguise her embarrassment. 'I'm awfully sorry,' she told Kamal, whose limited tool kit was no match for Minnie's destructive dabbling.

'She can be such a cow,' Minnie explained. 'But I love her, Judge Judy that is, not my sister, although Essy has her moments don't you, dear, I said you have your moments, dear!' she called to Esther.

'Come away, will you!' Esther snapped, beckoning with a glare. 'And leave the young man alone, I am so sorry to have troubled you,' she again told Kamal who had reattached the mini bar door under Minnie's close supervision. 'Thaaat's better,' Minnie marvelled now that all the doors were symmetrical. 'Don't you think dear?' she asked her sister who had disappeared back into the bedroom cringing.

Minnie toyed with Kamal's measuring tape tugging a meter or so out repeatedly until it jammed and refused to recoil. 'Oh blast' she cursed, bending the now defunct tape and thrusting it back into Kamal's tool bag unseen. 'She looks as though she's been sucking lemons at times, you know,' she rambled on to the repairman. 'Judge Judy, not my sister.'

The sisters regularly delighted in watching the US reality TV star Judge Judy rule her courtroom with an acid tongue and rapier-sharp wit.

472

Kamal worked tirelessly while the sisters prepared for a voyage of discovery in the land of the Pharaoh's. 'I thought we might visit the Cairo museum first, dear,' Esther said, straightening her straw hat in the mirror whilst Kamal eventually packed away his things and coming across his tangled tape, but again said nothing. 'Good day to you, madams' he then said, forcing a smile. 'Good day.'

'Bye byyyyyyye!' Minnie replied with a wave. 'See you again!'

'Undoubtedly,' Esther smirked, popping her handbag handles onto her arm. 'Shall we go?' she asked Minnie who was opening and closing the mini bar door, giving Kamal's handiwork the once over. 'Minnie!' Esther called sharply. 'For heaven's sake leave it alone, will you, and hurry will you, woman, I'd like to beat the rush!'

The Cairo museum along with the pyramids attracted huge visitor numbers, each and every one of them desperate for a glimpse into the past and to marvel at the wondrous collection of a staggering 120,000 artefacts and treasures of phenomenal value. 'Ooooh will there be mummies?' Minnie asked, following her sister out the door,

'My darling sister,' Esther replied, striding toward the elevators. 'If there isn't I shall demand a full refund and pen a strongly worded letter to the curator, you see if I don't.'

Of course the Egyptian museum of antiquities as it is also known contains a jaw-dropping collection of mummies including King Ramesses II who still to this day has traces of hair.

The mummy room can be accessed for an additional fee which the majority are more than happy to pay to look upon the faces of the greatest leaders mankind has ever known, with the jewel in their museums crown possibly being the 11kg solid gold burial mask of the boy King Tutankhamen who was reportedly murdered at the tender age of nineteen, although many would believe otherwise, suggesting maybe a chariot ride or disease ended his short reign. This mystery only serves to enhance the young man's popularity, sealing his place in history for all eternity.

'Humbug, dear?' Minnie asked, fishing the last of her boiled sweets from the lining of her summer coat.

Esther paused before accepting it. 'Yes, dear,' she said, snatching it from her sister. 'Thank you, I think I will.'

'Oh,' Minnie replied, almost reluctant to part with it. 'You will?'

'Yes,' Esther said unravelling it before her and popping it into her mouth before unlocking Vivien. 'Mmmmm,' she then mumbled, handing her sister the empty wrapper once inside. 'Buckle up, my dear,' she gargled.

Minnie rammed the buckle into the clasp and sat rooting in her lining once again but came up empty-handed.

Since leaving Whitechapel London Vivien's mileage had more than doubled what had been amassed by the previous fifty years or so of occasional motoring, but she showed no signs of stopping, just the odd splutter here and there or a whining from the drive shaft. Vivien was a true testament to the early British motor industry and an icon that was cherished the world over.

Parking a stone's throw away from the museum, Esther groaned when alighting on seeing the already snaking queue at the main entrance. 'Oh for Pete's sake, Minnie,' she said directing the blame toward her sister. 'If you hadn't have insisted on pruning your blasted toenails this morning we'd have had a head start on half of this lot.'

Minnie pulled on her straw hat and trudged after Esther to the end of the line a full hundred meters from the museum doors. Soon the balls of their feet began to ache as did their aged spines shuffling a few inches at a time for what seemed like an absolute age. 'I can't do this anymore,' Esther said, admitting defeat. 'Shall we go?'

Minnie stood with her mouth wide open and her nose twitching before letting out a loud theatrical sneeze, startling the couple directly in front of them.

The husband and wife flinched before glancing over their shoulder, the pair gasping when instantly recognising the Peshwari Nans; immediately they patted and tapped the shoulders of those ahead of them who in turn stared wide-eyed and moved aside. The whispers began to reverberate all the way along the line to the museum entrance. 'Peshwari Nans, Peshwari Nans, Minnie, Esther, Peshwari Nans.'

'Look, Essy!' Minnie marvelled. 'How kind.'

The sisters were ushered forward flanked by smiling tourists on either side. 'Hellooooo, helloooooo,' Minnie called in passing.

'Thank you, dear, thank you,' Esther said, finally embracing the benefits of their celebrity. 'So kind, thank you, my dear,' she continued to the entrance where the line closed ranks behind them. 'Two please,' she said, insisting on paying their way just like everybody else. 'Oh my!' she then gasped on catching her first glimpse of the wonders within.

'Ohhhhhh, Essy,' Minnie gushed, shuffling to press her nose to a glass display case containing a Pharaoh's accumulated wealth once destined for the afterlife.

Esther joined her sister, pocketing their tickets. 'Now don't you be wandering off, Minnie, do you hear?' she warned her sister amid the ever-increasing crowd.

Of course Minnie paid no attention and scurried from case to case gawping at the astonishing finds within.

'Minnie, Minnie!' Esther barked, attempting to keep up. 'God, that infernal woman!' she cursed, acknowledging the lone parent of a runaway five–year-old.

'Kids, eh?' the exasperated mother said in passing.

'Hardly' Esther said making a grab for her sister and dragging her into tow 'Will you behave!' she said through gritted dentures, echoing the child's mother a yard or so away.

Entering the mummy hall, the two sisters stood in shocked silence beside the body of Ramesses II laid out in yet another glass case. 'Crikey,' Esther said under her breath when reading the brief description of his reign.

'He looks as though he's sleeping, dear,' Minnie said indiscreetly as the hall filled behind them.

'Shhhhhh!' Esther said while all around whispered respectfully amongst the dead.

The young boisterous five-year-old tapped on the glass beside Minnie. 'Is he sleeping, Mummy?' she asked her mother.

'That's what I thought, my darling,' Minnie stooped and replied.

Esther rolled her eyes at the mother, the two of them ever so slightly embarrassed whilst Minnie and the boy giggled poking fun at the mummified Pharaoh.

'I do apologise,' the child's mother told Esther. 'I thought it would be a good idea bringing him.'

'Yes I know what you mean,' Esther said wistfully before tugging her sister clear yet again; she then watched as the mother clipped the boy to a set of training reins to curb his enthusiasm. 'Hmmmmm,' she pondered, sizing up her sister.

Minnie later retrieved the tablet from her bag and insisted on photographing her sister beside King Tut's magnificent mask. 'Now do me, dear,' she asked, Esther hastily switching places. 'If only we could have one together,' she added.

'Please allow me,' a voice then said behind them.

'Oh!' Minnie said spinning, somewhat startled. 'Oh yes, would you?'

'Sure,' a tall gangly American said, taking the tablet from them. 'No problem.'

'Ooooh, you're American,' Minnie said astutely.

'Yes, ma'am,' the gent replied. 'Illinois born and raised.'

'Oh how lovely,' Minnie said with a smile whilst joining Esther beside the mask. 'We're from London,' she informed him. 'Whitechapel born and bred and bloomin' proud of it.'

'London!' the American marvelled, lining up their shot. 'Well it's a pleasure makin' your acquaintance, now smile.'

'Thank you, dear,' Esther said, relaxing. 'Illinois you say, my, you're a long way from home, are you on holiday?'

'Not exactly, ma'am,' the American said, handing Minnie back the tablet. 'I'm here with a team from the University of Chicago.'

'A team?' Minnie asked whilst uploading the snap to the delight of their fans. 'What sort of team, football, rugby, oh no, no, no, no, don't tell me!' she said excitedly. 'You're a cricketer, a batsman I bet, yes, yes I knew it, you have the legs for it, doesn't he, dear, I said he has the legs for it, dear!' she said to her confused sister.

'Actually,' the American smiled. 'I'm an archaeologist.'

'What? Minnie exclaimed, spinning to look him in the eye. 'You mean you're not a batsman?'

'No, ma'am,' the American laughed.

'Not even a wicket keeper?' Minnie asked. 'Our father was a wicket keeper, you see and he had legs just like yours, didn't he, dear, I said he had legs like this young man's, didn't he, dear!' she called to Esther.

'Who did?' her sister replied, not having been privy to the entire conversation.

'Father,' Minnie said, becoming a little irate. 'Oh, Essy dear, do pay attention, anyway,' she continued, turning back to the equally baffled American. 'Oh I'm sorry, I didn't catch your name,' she asked, offering her hand. 'I'm Minnie by the way and little Miss Snooty over there is my sister Esther, or Essy for short.'

'Mike,' the archaeologist replied. 'Mike Landon, and I'd just like to say I've never played cricket in my entire life, I played baseball in high school and I shoot a little pool but that's as far as it goes I'm afraid.'

Esther sidled over. 'An archaeologist, you say,' she said, offering her hand. 'How exciting, are you here on a dig by any chance?'

'I certainly am, ma'am,' Mike replied, 'Although personally I think we're shootin' in the dark but they're payin' me a stack of money so I guess I'll run with it.'

'Ohhhhhh the Americans,' Esther said as the penny dropped. 'You're looking for Cleopatra, aren't you, I read about it.'

'Yes, ma'am, yes we are,' Mike admitted. 'As you may know she's never been found, now some whiz kid at Harvard has this crazy notion that she's inside the great pyramid of all places.'

'The great pyramid!' Esther scoffed. 'But surely that's impossible, after all the pyramids were built long before her reign, everybody knows that.'

'I don't,' Minnie piped up.

'You're right,' Mike agreed. 'But this crazy guy has a theory that the Queen had given instructions for the great pyramid to be reopened on the event of her death and the tongues cut from the mouths of all who knew her location, I know how it sounds and I for one think it's bull, but what if it's true and Cleopatra is in there, this discovery,' he paused, 'This discovery, well it's just too fantastic to even think about, do you know what I mean?'

'Yes, yes I do,' Esther said, wide-eyed. 'I was only saying to my sister the other day how exciting that we'll be here to see it.'

'Well you come by the pyramids, you hear,' Mike told the sisters. 'I'll see you get a ringside seat.'

'Wow,' Esther gasped, 'Did you hear that, Minnie dear, a ringside seat.'

Minnie was oblivious, looking Mike up and down. 'I honestly believe you'd have had greater success as a cricketer,' she told him. 'You have excellent bone structure.'

'Minnie!' Esther snapped. 'We're talking about Cleopatra here, if this Harvard chappie is right and she has fooled grave robbers and Egyptologists alike for centuries it would truly be a momentous discovery.'

'Yes I suppose so, dear,' Minnie said with more pressing things on her mind. 'Do you think we could stop for a spot of lunch?' she asked. 'I'm famished.'

Not Cleopatra, Moses or even the discovery of alien life would detract from Minnie's rumbling stomach, she was a creature of habit and insisted on being fed and watered at regular intervals.

'Minnie,' Esther urged. 'Cleopatra for Pete's sake!'

The Harvard graduate in question had studied Egyptian hieroglyphics and even majored in the subject, particularly those in and around the great pyramids of Giza, so intensely in fact that he believed he'd stumbled upon a partial inscription thus far overlooked. His paper written on the subject was immediately dismissed by learned Egyptologists the world over, but a private consortium, seeing the possible revenue implications, had stumped up the necessary monies for the excavation and more importantly the permission of the Egyptian government. Suffice it to say the price tag ran into the tens of millions with some officials demanding extravagant sweeteners as it were to silence their objections.

Nevertheless the wider world was right to be sceptical, the young man's notion was far-fetched to say the least and never for a moment contemplated by those who had dedicated their lives to finding the most famous queen of all, Cleopatra, an Egyptian icon and a goddess to her people.

Born in Alexandria in 69 BC to a family of Macedonian Greeks, Cleopatra, named after her mother, led the most extraordinary of lives, first sharing the throne with her father Ptolemy XII, giving her her first taste of Egyptian rule. Following this she presided over her people alongside her brothers both of whom she wed as was customary at the time. She was linked with the great Julius Caesar whose power she utilized to cement her own until his death by treachery in 44BC. It was then that the fairy tale began when she met and fell in love with Mark Anthony, and the rest as they say is history.

'Yes, I know it's Cleopatra, dear,' Minnie protested. 'But I haven't eaten in what seems like an eternity and I'm getting the shakes, look at me.' She held out a trembling hand. 'I swear, Essy, I'm borderline diabetic, I'm sure of it.'

'You are not diabetic!' Esther argued. 'You're just a glutton plain and simple.'

'I am not!' Minnie objected strongly. 'I just have a high metabolism that's all, I take after our father, do you know, Mister Mike?' she said turning to the now bemused American, 'Our father could eat a double helping of pie and mash, jellied eels, countless roast potatoes and bar snacks and fourteen points of brown ale at the Flying Horse and still be up for a generous slice of Mother's home-made sticky toffee pudding when he returned home.'

'She's right,' Esther agreed. 'Our father could eat.'

Minnie tugged at her sister's sleeve. 'Yes so shall we go, pleaaaaase Essy?' she begged. 'Goodbye, Mister Mike,' she added preparing to leave.

'It's just Mike,' Mike replied stepping aside for the sisters.

'I do apologise, Mister Mike,' Esther said in passing. 'It's my sister, you see.'

'I understand,' Mike smiled. 'It's not easy being diabetic.'

'Oh she's not diabetic, dear,' Esther informed him. 'She's just a right royal pain in the backside, that's what she is, aren't you, dear!' she called after her sister. 'I said you're a pain in the backside, aren't you!' Esther may as well have been talking to herself because Minnie had switched to survival mode, craving substances to quell her raging hunger pangs. 'Good day to you, Mister Mike,' Esther said shuffling after her.

'It's just Mike!' Mike called after her. 'I'll see you ladies at the pyramids, yeah?'

'Right you are, dear,' Esther replied with a wave. 'See you at the pyramids, Mister Mike!'

Mike chuckled to himself recalling his own late grandmother's humorous eccentricities.

Esther and Minnie dined at a nearby café, or should I say Minnie dined while her sister observed, plucking the occasional grape from Minnie's towering order.

'Thaaat's better,' Minnie eventually said with a tiny burp. 'Do you know what, Essy,' she added, pushing away a near empty plate. 'I couldn't eat another thing, I really couldn't, I am stuffed to the gills I am, stuffed to the gills.'

'I'm not surprised,' Esther scoffed, watching the waitress remove her sister's three plates.

'Would you like to see out dessert menu?' the girl asked, returning with her notepad.

'Oh no, no, no, no, no,' Esther smiled, raising a hand. 'That won't be necessary, my dear.'

'Just a minute,' Minnie intervened, eyeing the adjacent table and the rich dark chocolate gateau being shared between a family of Bulgarians.

'You're not serious?' Esther asked, following her gaze. 'Surely not, Minnie, you'll make yourself sick, you will, you mark my words, young lady.'

Minnie licked her lips. 'Well perhaps just a taster, my dear,' she told the waitress. 'Nothing too extravagant, say around an inch and a half.'

'Inch and a half?' the Egyptian girl asked, bemused. 'What is this?'

'Oh I do apologise, dearie,' Minnie smirked. 'You've probably never heard of feet and inches, have you?'

'Feet?' the girl said, looking down at her ankle boots. 'What is wrong with my feet?'

'No, no, dear,' Minnie laughed. 'Your feet are adorable, I assure you, I tell you what, just bring me the cake and I'll cut it myself, alright?'

'Yes, madam, as you wish,' the confused girl said, scurrying away.

Minnie caught sight of her sister's disapproving glance. 'What?' she asked. 'Essy, believe me I know what I'm doing, trust me.'

Esther leaned across the table. 'Do you remember the last time you had chocolate cake on a full stomach, do you?' she asked in a motherly tone. 'You were bunged up for days, doubled over every five minutes whining like a sick puppy, don't you remember?'

'No,' Minnie said, blatantly lying. 'No, Essy, you must be mistaken, I'll be perfectly fine just you wait and see.'

'Alright,' Esther scoffed. 'On your head be it.'

A fresh gateau arrived and Minnie was presented with a triangular cake knife which she hovered over the chocolate dessert for a moment or two.

'Don't do it, Minnie,' Esther warned her, ever the sensible sister. 'Minniiiie.'

Minnie wrestled with her inner demons, who took complete control of her hand and the knife, carving out a huge slice and depositing it onto her plate.

'Oh really, Minnie,' Esther moaned, rocking back in her seat in disbelief. 'You, my dear, have just sealed your own fate.'

'Like I said,' Minnie replied, tucking in. 'I'll be fine, besides I have plenty of water so there really shouldn't be a problem.'

'Suit yourself,' Esther gloated. 'But don't come crying to me when the cramps set in.' Esther's warnings fell on deaf ears as her sister devoured two-thirds of her generous slice and wrapped the remainder in a napkin.

'I'll have that later,' Minnie said, tucking it into her bag alongside three small bottles of water, her tacky torch and the obligatory contents for a woman her age, scattered tissues, denture grip and an assortment of buttons.

Esther drove from the café fizzing with excitement at finally getting to see the great pyramids up close, to walk where the Pharaohs once walked and touch the mighty stones laid down by hundreds upon hundreds of their loyal subjects.

The grey hairs on the back of Esther's neck bristled and her heart rate fluttered. 'I can hardly contain myself, dear,' she told her sister, who remained unenthusiastically silent. 'I said I can hardly contain myself,' Esther said again. 'Finally we get to visit Giza and the pyramids.'

Again Minnie said nothing.

'Are you alright, dear?' Esther asked at a traffic signal.

'Me?' Minnie piped up. 'Oh, oh yes, yes of course I'm fine, dear,' but nothing could be further from the truth, she was suffering from severe bloating to the point of extreme discomfort.

'Are you sure?' Esther quizzed her sister. 'Because you don't look fine to me.'

'Quite sure, dear,' Minnie groaned, rummaging for a mint to hopefully settle her grumbling stomach.

'OK,' Esther said, setting off once again and quite rightly having her doubts. 'After all,' she added, 'The last thing we want right now is a medical emergency, not when we are so close.'

'You have nothing to worry about, dear,' Minnie reassured her sister. 'We are here to see the pyramids and see them we shall.'

Both sisters gasped a lengthy gasp when the giant peaks came into sight. 'Dear Lord,' Esther said, lowering her visor to shield her eyes from the sun.

'Exactly,' Minnie agreed, the stabbing pains in the pit of her stomach having abated ever so slightly.

'Oooooh!' Esther shrieked, tapping Minnie's knee, 'We're here, Minnie, we're finally here, my dear.'

Minnie clicked away repeatedly with the tablet from her window, capturing everything from emaciated dogs to trinket salesmen dogging the constant stream of tourists.

Parking Vivien on a steep camber, Esther climbed from her seat, and once straightened she rolled a fist-sized rock with her foot beneath Vivien's wheel as a precautionary measure. 'You can never be too careful,' she told her sister alluding to Vivien's dated and decidedly worn handbrake.

'Wow,' Minnie sighed, resting her bottom against Vivien's front wing, taking in the majesty of these colossal structures. 'Ohhh, Essy,' she added with a lump forming in her throat and an all too present rumbling tummy. 'The television just doesn't do it justice, does it, dear?'

'You're quite right, dear,' Esther said at her side, their faces illuminated by the early afternoon sun and the arid golden landscape.

'I, I don't know what to say,' Minnie confessed, taking out her handkerchief to mop the sweat from the bridge of her nose.

'Really?' Esther smirked. 'Now that truly is amazing.'

'Sorry, dear?' Minnie asked, distracted to say the least.

The American Mike Landon arrived moments late in his ex-military open top jeep, a relic of the Second World War with bullet holes to prove it. 'Ahhh, you made it,' he said, greeting the sisters and retrieving several scrolls from the rear of his vehicle. 'Listen, why don't you both go take the tour,' he told them. 'Then come see us, we're digging round back.'

The American party, closely observed by the Egyptians, were excavating the great pyramid on the opposite side of the main tourist entrance with ever increasing numbers of the world's media arriving daily. 'Ohhh hell,' Esther cursed, seeing the media hounds and lowering the brim of her hat to avoid detection. 'Come, Minnie,' she told her sister. 'Let's not draw attention to ourselves just yet, thank you, Mister Mike,' she told the archaeologist, leading her sister toward the pyramid.

Minnie suddenly stopped and clutched her stomach, leaning forward with a strained expression and letting out an agonising groan. 'Ohhhh, Essy, it hurts,' she told her sister. 'My tummy hurts.'

'I told you,' Esther said wagging a finger, 'didn't I tell you, Minnie, didn't I, I told you you'd suffer for the chocolate cake but ohhhhh no, ohhhhh no, Minnie knows best as always, you just wouldn't listen, would you?'

'Not now, Essy, pleaaaase,' Minnie moaned, desperately seeking a public convenience.

Mike had re-joined his team having clarified one or two details with the Cairo museum, he then unravelled the scrolls and instructed his Egyptian foreman to work his men a little harder with hopes of reaching the hidden chamber within a matter of days if not hours; whether it be Cleopatra's or not the chamber in itself would be a noteworthy find.

'Oooooh thank heavens, Essy,' Minnie squealed, spying a row of portable lavatories erected to serve the media circus. 'I'm sorry, dear, nature calls,' she told Esther, who sighed in reply.

'If only you'd listened to me for once,' Esther said, aggrieved at the delay, now within a hair's breadth of the pyramid entrance but restrained by her sister's present gastric predicament. 'Do hurry, dear!' she called after her, positively champing at the bit,

'Yes, yes, alright!' Minnie replied, scurrying towards the plastic toilet block.

With their cameras trained on the great pyramid itself, hardly a soul noticed the world-renowned Peshwari Nans in close proximity. 'I won't be a moment, dear!' Minnie said, ducking inside the first available cubicle and tugging the door closed. 'Oh my word!' she then shrieked, emerging with a hand covering her mouth. 'Filthy blighters,' she growled, trying the neighbouring lavatory and this time bolting the door.

A short while elapsed with Esther kicking at the dirt and looking longingly at the pyramid. 'Minnie, what are you doing in there?' she asked, rapping her knuckles on the door.

'I'm trying, Essy, honestly I am!' Minnie called from within. 'I'm having to hover, you see, and swat away the flies at the same time!'

'Well do hurry, please, for heaven's sake,' Esther moaned. 'It's positively stifling out here.' The sun had previously peaked but it still remained a blistering forty-five degrees outside.

Minnie began humming *Daisy, Daisy* again which echoed within the plastic pod.

'I'll give you Daisy, Daisy!' Esther barked, recognising the tune immediately and banging on the door once again. 'Hurry up will you!'

Minnie was more concerned though with remaining clear of the rancid public lavatory seat, that and the graffiti scrawled on the rear of the door, much of it in Egyptian but the graphic illustrations left very little to the imagination. 'Good grief!' she said, positively blushing and tilting her head to the side to fully observe the crudely daubed creation with exaggerated body parts performing a contorted act, the likes of which Minnie had never imagined let alone experienced. 'Sorry, dear!' she later said, emerging to her furious sister who stood fanning her reddened face with her hat. 'I can't say I recommend the facilities,' she warned Esther. 'But the hieroglyphics are an eye opener, that's for sure.'

'Well speaking of hieroglyphics,' Esther said, donning her hat in a huff. 'Could we please just take the tour and get out of this damned heat?'

'Right you are, dear,' Minnie replied, slipping her arm through Esther's.

'What are you doing?' Esther asked, still peeved with her sibling.

'Oh come on, Essy dear,' Minnie smirked. 'Let's just try to get along and enjoy the experience together, after all it's the pyramids, you know.'

Esther raised her eyebrows. 'That's what I've been trying to tell you all along,' she sighed. 'But you will insist on wittering on and on in your inimitable but ridiculous way, sometimes, Minnie,' she said, pausing for breath, 'I really do despair of you, I really do.'

Minnie rummaged in her over-sized bag and retrieved a bottle of spring water. 'Water, dear?' she asked, observing her sister's glistening complexion.

'Oh,' Esther said, startled and caught completely off guard. Whilst vexed, Esther had forgotten to pack refreshments and eyed the bottle longingly, her throat drying rapidly. 'Em, yes, yes please.'

'There you are,' Minnie chirped, ecstatic at having doused her sister's wrath.

'Thank you, dear,' Esther was forced to say. 'Thank you so much, that's awfully kind of you.' This time Esther took Minnie's arm. 'Shall we?' she asked, now within spitting distance of the great pyramid.

'Let's,' Minnie agreed.

Esther reached a trembling hand and touched the first of the historic stones. 'My word!' she gasped under her breath, sensing the weight of four and a half thousand years in a single fleeting moment.

'Help me, will you, dear,' Minnie asked, having trouble with the very first step, her legs having seized somewhat from a seemingly similar weight whilst hovering inside the plastic Portaloo.

'Yes of course,' Esther said, sharing a tender moment with her sister, a rarity of late with her temper fraying repeatedly, fuelled by Minnie misdemeanours. 'I've got you, dear,' she said rubbing Minnie's back. 'Are you sure you'll be alright? she asked, a tad concerned.

'Yes, yes, yes,' Minnie replied confidently. 'I didn't come all this way to be beaten by a little cramp, I assure you.'

'Thaaat's the spirit,' Esther smiled, patting Minnie once again.

The pair were overtaken by a party of boisterous Brazilians, several feisty French and a coach-load of camera clicking Canadians whilst they stood for a moment in the entrance savouring the fruits of their arduous journey. 'We've come so far, dear,' Minnie reminded Esther, and it was true, the pair had travelled close to twelve thousand miles since leaving their beloved East London home in a car half a century old.

Taking their first tentative steps inside the great pyramid, the ladies breathed a sigh of relief once out of the sun's roasting rays. Immediately they were spellbound by the colossal scale of this monumental construction, supposedly built by early man with limited technology, although there are some that would question that theory, arguing the improbability of such a feat and suggesting possible alien involvement. Either way it was magnificent and like nothing the sisters had ever experienced throughout their lengthy lives.

Esther and Minnie followed the hordes of tourists as best they could, paying close attention to their guides who paused at regular intervals to educate their clients, the regular intervals being a welcome break for the sisters who found the going exhaustive, clambering up crude timber steps, clawing hand over fist at the handrails whilst exploring the king and queen's chambers via the ascending and subterranean passageways, at times stooping through narrow low corridors with walls honed flat and precisely true and a work of phenomenal engineering.

Slowing considerably, the sisters dropped behind the multinational visitors. 'Do keep up, Minnie dear,' Esther said finding their solitude eerie.

'I'm trying, Essy, believe me,' Minnie replied, straightening her back once again. Their voices echoed within the cavernous interior of the wondrous pyramid. 'One moment, dear,' Minnie said moments later. 'I have a stone in my shoe.'

'Oh, Minnie, for heaven's sake,' Esther groaned, growing increasingly concerned at their apparent isolation. 'Can't it wait?'

'No, dear, it cannot,' Minnie protested. 'Essy, there is a stone in my shoe, do you understand?' Minnie lifted her right foot.

'Just a minute!' Esther barked. 'Those are my shoes!'

'Ah,' Minnie said, quickly lowering her foot. 'Essy, I can explain,' she added, suddenly wishing she'd hobbled on, stone and all.

'Explain!' Esther snapped, echoing a dozen times. 'Once again, Minnie, you have betrayed my trust and stolen, yes stolen my belongings.'

'Oh come now, dear,' Minnie scoffed. 'I think the word stolen is a tad strong, surely borrowed would be a more fitting analogy, don't you think?'

Esther adored those shoes and until her sister drew attention to them she hadn't noticed she'd been wearing them the whole day. 'No!' she barked. 'No I don't think, you took them without my express permission, therefore, Minnie, you stole them, just like you've stolen from me my entire life, you remember the skates I received for my eighth birthday that mysteriously vanished for several weeks and reappeared beneath your bed, your bed, Minnie, yours, you just can't help yourself can you.'

Minnie attempted to intervene and defend her actions but was shot down on opening her mouth.

'You're nothing but a common thief!' Esther continued and perhaps overreacting ever so slightly, but fear and frustration gripped her and Minnie, whether innocent or not, would find herself on the receiving end of yet another outburst.

'But, but, Essy I'm sorry,' Minnie stammered, offering her hand.

'Sorry!' Esther snarled, swatting at her sister. 'How many times, Minnie, have I heard that you're sorry, sorry I broke your glasses, Essy, sorry I borrowed your teeth, Essy, sorry I shrunk your nightie, Essy, sorry, sorry, sorry, I'm sick of it, Minnie, sick of it you hear.'

'Sorry, Essy,' Minnie said solemnly whilst hanging her head.

'There you go again!' Esther blurted. 'The problem is, Minnie, you are not sorry at all, if you were you would learn from your mistakes like any normal person would, oh but I'm forgetting you aren't normal at all, you're Minnie for Christ's sake!'

'Oh, Essy, come now, dear,' Minnie smiled in an attempt to make light of the situation. 'Let's be friends shall we, after all, look where we are.'

'I know exactly where I am,' Esther said, glancing at her surroundings. 'And if I had my way I'd seal you up in here for another four and a half thousand years.'

'Oh you don't mean that, Essy,' Minnie said with her bottom lip now quivering.

'Try me!' Esther barked, starting off along the dimly lit corridor desperate to distance herself from her sister.

'Essy, wait!' Minnie called after her, hobbling with the grit piercing the sole of her foot. 'Essy, pleaaaaase!'

But pyramid or no pyramid Esther was keen to be out of there where she could breathe and collect her thoughts.

'ESSYYYYYYY!' Minnie cried, unable to take another step. 'Oh blast,' she moaned, wincing and eyeing a stone block on which to rest and remove her sister's shoe.

What was to follow could only be described as purely remarkable, purely remarkable indeed. 'ESSY, WAIT PLEAAAAAASE!' Minnie again called on seeing her sister turn a corner with her crooked shadow diminishing. Lowering her bottom onto the stone, she was blissfully unaware that she was about to set in motion a cataclysmic chain of events that until then had never been repeated. The ingenious early Egyptian builders, or space men whichever you'd prefer, were masters of stone masonry and cryptic concealment in an attempt to fool any would-be robbers. 'Ahhhh,' Minnie sighed, sitting and slipping off the shoe to tip the offending stone out. It was then that the rock beneath her bottom shuddered suddenly. 'What the?' she shrieked in astonishment. Never before had anybody of Minnie's precise body weight of eleven stone three and a quarter pounds sat the way she did that day. 'Dear Lord!' she cried out of earshot of her sister as a half-ton slab of smooth granite beside her raised some five feet by means of shifting ballast sands deep within the ancient pyramid. 'No, no, no, no, no, no, no, ESYYYYYYYY!' she called, unable to stand before her stone stool slid inside a blackened void and the hefty granite slab plummeted to the ground with an almighty thud. 'No, no, wait, oh God, WAIT!' Minnie shrieked, slapping at the slab, unable to focus in the pitch black. 'ESSY, ESSY, WHAT'S HAPPENING?' she begged, rising from her seat and immediately striking her head on the solid stone above. 'Owwwwww!' she cried, bending and clenching her eyes tightly shut and clutching her now crumpled hat.

Concussed, dazed and completely confused Minnie grappled in the dark, feeling to her left and right, repeatedly calling for her sister who had ascended a stairway and stood amongst a party of Portuguese seething but willing to wait for Minnie to catch up.

Esther waited and she waited, and she waited, occasionally looking back along the stairway but there was no sign of her sister. 'Minnie?' she called. 'Minnie, are you there?'

'Oh Essy, Essy, where am I?' Minnie sobbed, turning full circle, disorientated and bumping the walls. 'Oh God, Essy, I don't like this, please get me out!'

'MINNIE, DEAR!' Esther called a little louder, clutching the stair rail. 'MINNIE, WHERE ARE YOU?' She was then approached by a pyramid guide who spoke excellent English.

'Madam, what is wrong?' the guide asked, leaving his group.

'I don't know,' Esther replied, growing anxious. 'It's my sister, she should be here by now.'

'Your sister,' the guide said, looking up the stairway too. 'Perhaps she is resting.'

'Not for this long,' Esther told him. 'I know my Minnie, she hates to be on her own, she always has,

MINNIIIIIE!' she called again. 'MINNIE DEAREST, I never should have left her.'

'Wait here,' the guide said, starting up the stairs. 'I will find her for you, I know this place, you see.'

'Oh would you, dear?' Esther pleaded. 'I'd be awfully grateful, her name's Minnie, did I mention she's my sister.'

'Yes, yes you did, madam,' the guard said over his shoulder. 'I will find her, please do not worry.'

'Right you are, dear,' Esther nodded. 'I expect she's sat sulking after that ticking off I gave her, she can be a frightful pain at times.' Esther remained at the foot of the stairs relieved that her sister would soon be found and that it was not she that had to climb those stairs again. But a full ten minutes elapsed and Esther's heart rate increased steadily. 'Minniiiie!' she called, hoisting herself up several steps. 'Minniiiiie!' Soon the guide appeared at the top of the steps and stood shrugging his shoulders.

'Madam, I cannot find her,' he informed a tense Esther. 'Where did you say you left your sister?'

'What?' Esther said, mounting another step. 'What do you mean you can't find her, she was right there!'

'I assure you, madam, she is not,' the Egyptian explained. 'I have been to the opposite side of the pyramid and even the queen's chamber and there is no sign of another British woman, are you sure she entered with you?'

'Am I sure?' Esther snapped. 'Of course I'm sure for heaven's sake, she was right there I tell you, with a stone in her shoe, or my shoe, please look again will you, she has a hat like mine and a blue spotted dress, she's my sister you see.'

'Yes, yes, I know,' the guide said, having scoured much of the inner labyrinth, but sensing Esther's obvious distress decided to appease her. 'OK, OK,' he said, raising a hand. 'I will look again, a blue spotted dress, you say?'

'Yes, yes her name's Minnie!' Esther told him yet again in her anguished state. 'She's my sister!'

'I will do my best,' the guide said disappearing again.

Unable to settle, Esther climbed back up the twenty-foot shaft once again, puffing and panting. 'Where the hell is that woman?' she asked herself 'Minniiiiiiie!' she yelled. 'It's alright, I'm not cross with you anymore!'

Minnie in the meantime was still turning this way and that behind the giant granite slab, unable to hear her sister's calls. 'ESSYYYYYY, HELLLLLP!' she herself called, sobbing and feeling her way along the concealed passageway, blindly stumbling on loose fallen rock. 'Oh dear, dear, dear, dear, dear,' she moaned. 'Essyyyyyyyyyy!' Bumping into yet another solid stone wall she grappled her way left and right, it was then that she remembered the tacky head torch she had purchased at the bazar and foraged in her handbag. 'Where is it, where is it?' she frantically said, never having been a lover of the dark. Fishing the fake golden headdress from her bag, Minnie groped at the intricate object, eventually locating the on-off switch. 'Oh thank you, Lord,' she said, when the LED bulbs illuminated her cramped surroundings.

Removing her hat and slipping the gadget onto her head, Minnie looked all around, slapping the smooth stone walls that encased her. 'What the?' she said, unable to fathom what had just occurred and even more disorientated than before. Should she go right or left at the intersection, and where on earth was Essy?

Esther herself had breathlessly reached the spot where she had torn her sister off a strip. 'Minniiiiii!' she puffed. 'Minnie dear!'

The guide reappeared once again, sweating profusely.

'Well?' Esther asked. 'Where is she, where's my Minnie?'

'I am sorry, madam,' the guide said, approaching and mopping his brow. 'I assure you your sister is not inside the great pyramid, madam, I have looked everywhere.'

'What do you mean she's not in here!' Esther said in an aggressive tone. 'Of course she's in here, I left her right here, right here, damn it!'

'Maybe you are mistaken, madam,' the guide suggested, assuming she may be stereotypically absent minded, or even senile perhaps.

'Mistaken!' Esther raged. 'This is my sister we're talking about, of course I'm not mistaken, she was here I tell you, now please will you find her.'

The guide had exhausted all options and avenues and himself for that matter. 'Madam,' he said in an attempt to calm Esther. 'Is it possible your sister slipped past you and left the pyramid perhaps, after all the lighting in here is very poor, very poor indeed, only last week I lost three of my German clients and found them eventually outside at the Sphinx, perhaps you too should check outside.'

Esther shook her head repeatedly. 'No, no, no, no, of course she hasn't slipped by me,' she protested. 'Why on earth would she do that, no, no, she's in here I tell you, MINNIIIIIIIE!' she called again, removing her hat and wringing it in her hands. 'MINNIE DEAREST, IT'S ESSY, WHERE ARE YOU?' She paused and listened, but nothing. 'I don't understand,' she said, looking this way and that, 'I left her right here, I know I did, I know I did, I swear my Minnie was right here, damn it.'

'Please, madam,' the guide said, offering a word of comfort and a hand on her back. 'I'm sure we will find your Minnie outside, come, I will help you.'

'But, but….' Esther stammered, reluctant to leave the narrow corridor. 'I know she's in here, I just know it.'

'It is not possible,' the guide informed her. 'I promise I have searched every corner of this place, every corner.'

'Really?' Esther asked. 'And you honestly believe she's outside?'

'I am sure of it,' the guide smiled, ushering Esther back toward the stairway. 'Come, please.'

Esther looked over her shoulder at the spot where she and Minnie parted whilst leaving. 'Ohhhh, Minnie,' she mumbled.

Hurrying as best she could, Esther followed the pyramid guide back to the entrance, shielding her eyes when emerging back outside. 'Minniiiiiiie!' she called, squinting and attempting to focus. 'Minnie dear!' she grabbed at a Latvian lady in vaguely similar attire. 'Minnie, there you are,' she said with a smile, but the returning foreign accent disheartened her once again. 'Oh dear, I am sorry,' she told the tourist before scanning the surrounding crowd and replacing her straw hat to blot out the sun. 'Excuse me?' she asked a security officer. 'Have you seen my sister, her name's Minnie?'

'Your sister,' the guard replied. 'Madam, I have seen many peoples,' he confessed. 'So many peoples.'

'Yes, yes, but I can't find her,' Esther insisted. 'She was wearing a dress similar to mine only blue, she's a little shorter than I am and several pounds heavier, although she won't thank me for telling you that.'

The guard shook his head. 'I am sorry, madam, too many peoples,' he told, her gesturing to the now bustling entrance.

Esther caught sight of the Portaloo. 'Minniiiiiie!' she called, assuming her sister had experienced another gastric movement. Approaching with the concerned guide in tow Esther repeatedly called for her sister. 'Minniiiiie, Minniiiiiiie are you in there?' Thumping a bolted door, Esther offered a grovelling apology. 'Minnie, I know you're in there and I know you're cross with me,' she said thumping again. 'But I just want to know you're alright that's all, Minniiiie.'

Suddenly the door opened and a disgruntled Texan man appeared complete with ten gallon hat and check shirt. 'What in tarnation!' he asked, wrestling with his huge cow horn belt buckle.

'Oh!' Esther said, taking a step back from the stench that followed him as did the guide. 'I, I'm sorry,' she added. 'I, I thought you were my sister you see.'

'Well I'm tellin' you this, ma'am,' the ticked-off Texan replied. 'I sure ain't no lady.'

'Yes, yes, I can see that,' Esther said, looking up at the towering American with his stomach hanging over the waistline of his blue jeans. 'I am awfully sorry, it's just that I can't find my Minnie, you see.'

Meanwhile deep within the pyramid Minnie was equally frantic having decided to proceed to the left. 'Essyyyyyyy!' she called, her voice echoing over and over and over. 'Essy can you hear me?' She barely noticed the elaborate hieroglyphs that adorned the walls of the passageway that had not seen human life or light for that matter for centuries. Down and down she staggered, then left, right and up again. 'Helloooooooo!' she cried. 'Essyyyyyy, anybodyyyyyy, hellooooooooo!' Stopping to catch her breath Minnie began to wonder if left had been a wise choice after all. 'Ohhhh hell' she cursed, retrieving a bottle of water from her handbag to sip. 'Now don't panic, Minnie,' she told herself. 'Don't panic, everything's going to be alright,' but that didn't help at all. 'ESSYYYYYYYYYYY!' she then screamed at the top of her croaky voice. 'ESSYYYYYYYYYY, HELLLLLLLLLP, ESSY PLEAAAAAAASE!' but when the very last echo had faded Minnie made a rash decision to proceed, simply because to return along her previous arduous route filled her with dread. 'Helloooooooo!' she continued to call, expecting any moment to come face to face with her fellow tourists, but the truth of the matter was there was now some ninety feet of solid rock between them and she was venturing further and further away, the bright light from her head torch flitting this way and that in sheer desperation.

Confinement and claustrophobia wasn't an issue for Minnie, as a child she would cram herself into the smallest of nooks, crannies and cupboards when hiding from her sister but nevertheless she longed to be out of there, with Essy.

Outside Esther was understandably growing increasingly frantic having been separated from her sister for forty five minutes or more by now.

'I am sorry,' the guide told her. 'I must return to my clients, I'm sure your sister will materialize, good luck to you, madam.'

'Oh but wait!' Esther said, reaching out. 'What if she doesn't, materialize that is, what if I can't find my Minnie?'

'Perhaps she has returned to your hotel!' the guide called from a distance. 'I am sorry, I must go!'

'Oh Lord,' Esther begged. 'Minnie where are you?' Esther returned to Vivien, hoping to see her sister's smiling face, but of course her hopes were dashed.

'Excuse me!' she asked a group of New Zealanders. 'Have you seen my Minnie, I mean my sister, about so tall wearing a blue dress like mine?'

'Sorry, love,' one of the departing tourists replied. 'Can't say that I have, hey I know you,' she then said, pausing. 'Yeah I'm right aren't I, you're one of those Nans aren't ya?'

'Well, well yes,' Esther groaned. 'But I really must find my sister.'

'Arthur, Arthur!' the woman called to her husband. 'Arthur, ya great dope, come 'ere will ya, it's one of them Nans I was tellin' ya about!' the woman's downtrodden husband trudged back laden with cool boxes, cameras, parasols and souvenirs. 'Yes dear,' he said, panting. 'What is it?'

'Look!' his wife pointed out. 'See for yaself, a Peshwari Nan in the flesh for Christ's sake, now do as ya told and take a picture will ya.'

'Oh no please,' Esther begged. 'I haven't got time, it's my sister you see.'

'Nonsense,' the bolshie wife insisted, slipping a bloated arm around Esther's shoulders. 'Hurry up, Arthur!' she said in a high-pitched screech. 'We haven't got all day!'

'Yes alright, dear,' Arthur replied fumbling with the three cameras around his neck.

'Arthur!' his wife moaned. 'Arthur, you've got the bloody lens cap on, ya big dope!' she cursed. 'I don't know why I married you, Arthur, I really don't.'

Esther attempted to break away. 'I really must find my sister,' she said, looking back toward the pyramid. 'Please.'

'Arthur, use the bloody tripod!' the New Zealander barked. 'Jesus, if brains were dynamite, love, you wouldn't have enough to blow ya bloody nose, now get on with it ya dope!'

Since their wedding all but a year ago Arthur had been called a dope or far worse by his newlywed wife dozens of times daily and was beginning to rue the day he ever set eyes on her at a speed dating party. 'Yes, dear,' he said subserviently whilst clattering the cumbersome tripod.

'God, he's such a dope,' his wife told Esther who was still firmly within her grasp. 'Get the car in too, Arthur, and don't you dare cut my bloody head off or I'll thump the living daylights outta ya, d'ya hear?'

The thought of decapitating his wife brought a wry smile to Arthur's face as he bent to capture the moment.

'Cheers, love,' Muriel, the aggressive New Zealander said when her husband gave her the thumbs up. 'Where's the other one?'

'I'm sorry, what?' Esther asked, confused somewhat.

'The other Nan?' Muriel asked again. 'I thought there were two of ya.'

'That's what I've been trying to say, damn you' Esther replied, growing hot under the collar. 'She's missing and I really need to find her, and you are not helping one bit, not one bit I tell you.'

'Well there's no need to be like that!' Muriel told Esther whilst Arthur wrestled with his tripod once again. 'Jeez it's true what they say about you'z celebrities ain' it, ya never the same in real life, come on, Arthur ya big dope,' she said, heading off and leaving him struggling with their equipment.

'Yes, dear,' Arthur said, hurrying behind with a clatter.

Esther wandered in a daze between the bustling visitors desperately seeking her younger sibling, every so often catching a fleeting glimpse of blue, raising her hopes before dashing them in an instant.

'Esther!' a voice then called out to her. 'Esther, over here!' and she turned to see the raised hand of the American Mike. 'How ya doin?' he asked, making his way toward her. 'What do ya think?' he added, gesturing to the great pyramid. 'Isn't it really something?'

Esther barely acknowledged him.

'Are you alright?' Mike asked on, seeing her solemn face. 'What's wrong?'

'It's Minnie,' Esther informed him with a quivering lip and the screwed hem of her cardigan in her hands. 'I, I can't find her, I can't find my Minnie.'

'What do ya mean?' Mike asked, scanning the crowd himself for another tell-tale straw hat. 'Are you sayin' ya got separated or something?'

'Yes well, sort of,' Esther confessed, 'Ohhh it's all my fault, Mister Mike,' she moaned. 'I got het up again over something so blasted trivial, I said things to her, Mister Mike, terrible things, and now, I can't find her.'

'Hey, hey, hey,' Mike said, slipping an arm around her as she burst into tears. 'Calm down, Esther, it's alright, we'll find her she can't have gone far, she's an old lady for Christ's sake, no offence, Esther,' he added.

'Do you think so, Mister Mike?' Esther said, looking up into his eyes. 'Oh I'm such a damned fool at times, a damned fool, she's all I have you see, oh I have my daughter and Richard my grandson but Minnie well, she's my Minnie, my soul mate if you like, oh Mister Mike, where is she?' The two of them circled the pyramid calling occasionally over the course of the next hour or so, meeting up with the pyramid guide again who was known to Mike.

'Yousef, my friend,' Mike said, grasping his hand. 'Esther here tells me you looked for her sister.'

'Yes, Mike, I looked everywhere,' Yousef replied. 'And my associates, they are keeping a close eye out for her.'

'Thank you, dear,' Esther said, her options rapidly depleting. 'Wherever can she be?'

'ESSYYYYYYYYY!' Minnie cried, nearing the pyramid's core having trudged some five hundred meters through twisting passageways leaving her shuffled footprints in the dry sand floor as Egyptian builders and slaves had previously done many years before. She stooped to retrieve the neck of an ancient urn used to carry water or wine for the parched builders, but the fragile antiquity was of little interest to Minnie as she discarded it flippantly and continued in the hopes of a swift end to this nightmare, one that she and Esther would laugh about over another of the hotel's rum punch cocktails that very evening no doubt, the thought of which spurred her on. But several more left turns through corridors decreasing in height soon disheartened her once again, until she was eventually forced to lower herself onto her hands and knees and crawl beneath a mighty slab of stone, dragging her hat and handbag behind her. 'Please, please, please, please,' she begged, approaching yet another turn hoping for an illuminated exit sign perhaps, as though this were some elaborate tourist attraction; either way she wanted out, and fast.

Of course there was no exit sign, only hieroglyphics and the earliest forms of graffiti mocking the slave masters of old. Clambering back onto her feet, Minnie slumped against the wall momentarily, wincing and probing her aching back. This feat of endurance was fast depleting her limited energy levels, but still she pressed on calling for her sister and her soul mate too, cursing herself on occasion for being the ever present thorn in her Esther's side. 'Ohhhh no,' Minnie then remarked, turning into an open room and the end of the subterranean track. 'No, no, no, no, no, no, no!' There was no exit, no way out, and no salvation.

Distraught and with just a narrow beam of light Minnie barely noticed the huge stone sarcophagus in the centre of a scattering of precious artefacts around. 'No, no, no, please no!' she cried, feeling her way amongst a group of crouching jackal statues, still very much oblivious to the priceless hoard at her feet. 'Dear God, Essy where am I?' she asked in despair whilst resting a hand on the granite sarcophagus and clutching her chest with the other, her breathing now heavy and rasping. Not even the flash of gold from an elaborate throne could lift her spirits and the thought of making such a monumental discovery barely entered her mind.

Minnie turned with the heaviest of hearts to leave before a shooting pain in her chest stopped her in her tracks. 'Oh please no!' she said, doubling over unable to catch her breath. 'Essy, Essy help me!' she croaked before the dizziness set in and her knees buckled beneath her. Minnie clawed at the sarcophagus, letting her handbag slip from her shoulder, her heart beating irregularly and her eyes now glazed. 'Essy,' she said one last time before another searing spasm dropped her like a stone to the dirt floor where she lay twitching for a moment or two and then, stopped.

'MINNIIIIIIIE!' Esther and Mike called, cupping their hands to their mouths outside, turning heads as far as the eye could see. 'MINNIIIIIIIE!' The two of them approached every tourist within striking distance asking if they'd seen a short plump pensioner in a blue spotted dress and a straw hat and of course received the same reply every time. 'Wherever can she have gotten to?' Esther asked, beside herself with worry at this point. 'Where is she, Mister Mike, where's Minnie?'

'Esther, love,' Mike said with the hours of daylight ebbing away. 'Is there any chance she may have gone back to your hotel, any chance at all, you said you had an argument, right?'

'Yes, yes but…' Esther said, having entirely dismissed such a thought. 'She wouldn't, Mister Mike, I know my Minnie, she just wouldn't.'

'But it is possible,' Mike assured her. 'She could have taken one of those taxis back into town, you'll see, Esther, I bet she's sitting by the pool right now with a gin and tonic and her feet up.'

'I don't know,' Esther replied, wrestling with conscience. 'I, I, I suppose it is plausible.'

'Of course it is,' Mike smiled, escorting Esther back toward Vivien. 'Come on, I'll follow you back and join you both for a drink, what do ya say?'

'Yes, yes you're right,' Esther, her spirits lifted somewhat. 'Silly me, what was I thinking, that's just the sort of thing my Minnie would do, head to the bar in times of crisis, dear God, she's so predictable.' Climbing into her car Esther hastily reversed narrowly missing a group of Germans. 'Sorryyyyyyy!' she called out the open window when they scattered yelling obscenities.

Leaving the Giza Pyramids and unbeknown to her, her sister, Esther drove back to central Cairo with butterflies in the pit of her stomach. 'I'll buy her a large rum punch,' she said to herself with a smile. 'And a new pair of shoes, two new pairs of shoes, yes two pairs.'

Leaving Vivien outside the hotel foyer, Esther hurried inside followed by the American archaeologist. 'Minniiiiiie!' she called making her way through the restaurant to the sun deck. 'Cooeeeee, Minnie love!' All but two of the sun loungers were occupied, mostly by a party of Irish stag revellers, the majority of them passed out from an afternoon's heavy drinking. 'Excuse me!' Esther asked the stag himself. 'I don't suppose you've seen my sister, have you, a little like me only shorter and slightly more rotund, in a blue dress, answers to the name of Minnie?'

The slurring groom-to-be tipped his green leprechaun hat politely before slumping back in an inebriated stupor.

'Oh dear,' Esther said, looking amongst the collection of floating inflatables in the pool, three crocodiles, a walrus and a killer whale but still no sign of Minnie.

'Let's check your room,' Mike suggested, growing a little concerned now himself. The pair took the elevator and after yet another fruitless search stood on the balcony overlooking the city.

'We should go back,' Esther said, turning for the door. 'Back to where I left her, oh why, oh why did I leave her, she must be petrified wherever the poor dear is.'

'Esther, wait!' Mike said observing her fatigue. 'Look, Yousef and his guides have promised to keep an eye out for Minnie but personally I think she's around town somewhere, maybe at the bazar.'

'Yes, yes that; it the bazar!' Esther said, her eyes lighting up. 'Of course, Mister Mike, she's at the bazar, oh why didn't I think of that, I'll go look right away.'

'Hold on there, Esther,' Mike said, taking her arm. 'Why don't you rest up a while, she'll be back when she's good and ready, you both need time by yourselves by the sound of things anyway.'

'You're so right, Mister Mike,' Esther agreed, removing her bag from her arm. 'Thank you ever so much, thank you, you mustn't let me keep you any longer from your work, how are things going at the pyramid anyway?'

'Yeah we're making progress,' Mike informed her. 'We have guys working three shifts around the clock and I feel we're getting close, but hey this is the great pyramid so anything's possible, who knows we could dig for months and not find a darn thing.' This of course was true, the chances of them striking the mystery tomb were slim at best.

'Well I wish you luck, Mister Mike,' Esther said, shaking his hand before lowering herself into an easy chair and kicking off her shoes. 'Whoever's in there,' she added, taking off her hat, 'Is long dead so I'd say you have all the time in the world, dear, wouldn't you agree?'

'Quite frankly yeah,' Mike concurred. 'Although the guys footin' the bill for this venture might have other ideas, they've been chewin' my tail for results.'

'Oh dear,' Esther sympathised. 'Well you'll just have to tell them that some things are worth the wait, dear, take my Jack for instance.'

'Jack?' Mike asked.

'My husband,' Esther informed him. 'My late husband.'

'Oh I'm sorry,' the intrepid archaeologist said, lowering his tone. 'Sorry to hear that, Esther.'

'Thank you but as I was saying,' Esther continued. 'I had my eye on Jack Reynolds for quite some time you see, but he was spoken for and it simply wasn't the done thing in those days to come between a courting couple, so I waited you see, for their relationship to run its course and fizzle out as it were, so you and those merry men of yours will have to learn to be patient and in time you will reap the rewards of your labour, just as I did with my Jack.'

Although the precious time Esther spoke of equated to dollars and cents to Mike's financial backers it meant a whole lot more to Minnie, who at that precise moment lay barely breathing beside the very granite sarcophagus and riches that Mike and his team sought, and while his fears of miscalculating the dig, even by a few degrees would spell disaster for the expedition, Minnie's own fate hung by a slender thread.

The gang of forty labourers were some sixty feet from the tomb and veering precariously to one side, hampered by faulty global positioning equipment. 'Will you be OK, Esther?' Mike asked, closing her balcony doors as a sand storm loomed on the horizon.

'Yes, yes, I'll be fine' Esther replied, settling into her chair. 'I'll sit and wait for that...' she was about to mock her sister but their agonising time apart forced a change of heart, 'That darling sister of mine,' she swiftly added. 'No doubt she'll be half starved when she returns, desperate for a drink and weighed down with as much woeful tat as she can possibly carry, do you know we once spent a weekend in Walton-on–the-Naze and I left her to her own devices, just for an hour mind you, and in that time she'd spent half of her savings on chips, candy floss, ice cream, a kiss-me-quick hat, not one but two inflatable rings, a bucket and three spades, a replica ship's wheel and a collection of driftwood carvings, she had a whale of a time, the dear sweet thing,' Esther recalled their brief vacation with upmost fondness.

'Walton on the what?' Mike asked, unfamiliar with the British seaside resort.

'The Naze dear,' Esther explained. 'Oh you poor thing, you Americans with your California and your Hollywood, you really haven't lived, have you.'

'I guess not, maan,' Mike replied, assuming the quintessentially British seaside town may somehow rival the likes of Vegas, Niagara or possibly Palm Beach Florida, home to millionaires and playboys alike. 'Look, Esther, take my number,' he suggested, taking a creased business card from his wallet. 'Call me in the morning and I'll be happy to meet with the two of you again.'

'Why thank you, Mister Mike,' Esther smiled. 'That would be lovely.'

'Oh and it's just Mike,' Mike reminded her yet again.

'Of course it is, dear,' Esther agreed then yawned a long tired yawn. 'Oooh excuse me,' she said, attempting to rise from her chair.

'No, no, don't get up, Esther,' Mike insisted. 'I'll see myself out, you take it easy, and call me, you hear.'

'Thank you, I will,' Esther replied, relaxing as Mike left the room. 'Bye, bye, Mister Mike!' she called after him. 'Bye, bye!'

Mike smiled to himself strolling toward the elevator. 'Bye, bye, Esther,' he laughed under his breath.

Mike left Esther reclining, watching and waiting for her sister's return until her eyes grew heavy and her head began to nod. Fighting fatigue, Esther slapped her cheeks and wriggled in her seat, eyeing the door, but soon she could fight no more or keep her eyes from closing. Moments later Esther was purring like a comfortable kitten slumped in her easy chair facing the door in readiness to greet her wayward sister.

Deep within the largest of the Giza pyramids Minnie fluttered an eye, groaned and attempted to focus. 'Ohhh what, what?' she croaked, startled to be in such close proximity with the stone foot of Anuket, the goddess of the Nile. Reaching a shaky hand she felt the foot, unfamiliar at first with her surroundings. Then on closer inspection it dawned on her. 'Essy?' she said, heaving herself up onto her bottom, brushing the sand from her cheek and looking frantically for her sister. 'Oh no, please no,' she added when the lack of reply confirmed her fears; this was no dream, this was a living nightmare of galactic proportion.

Weak now from her partial seizure brought on by severe stress and physical exertion, it was all that Minnie could do to crawl and drag herself up the central sarcophagus where she slumped resting on her forearms, surveying the tomb with her crooked headlight illuminating the trappings of Egyptian nobility.

Whilst any would-be explorer, archaeologist of historian at this point would be utterly euphoric and screaming their discovery from the rooftops, Minnie on the other hand, in her lack of infinite wisdom quite wrongly assumed that the find was merely an extension of the pyramids previously unearthed exhibits and whilst mildly impressed, her present perilous predicament took president. 'Right, don't panic, old girl,' she told herself, straightening her back and deciding to retrace her steps in the hopes of a reversal of fortune. 'Whatever you do don't panic.' Straightening her mock golden crown, Minnie took several tentative steps toward the cramped corridor, faltering at the tomb entrance and grabbing at the occupant's elaborate throne, weak at the knees with a stiffness in her spine. 'Damn you, Minnie,' she cursed every aspect of her present life, her stupidity, her lack of judgement, her age-ravaged body and her undeniable ability to upset her one true friend, her sister, her Essy. 'Damn, damn, damn, you.'

Wheezing, Minnie dropped onto the throne to rest a while, taking a bottle of water from her bag and dousing a handkerchief to cool her face and the back of her neck. 'Helloooooooo!' she called out in vain. 'Hellooooooooo, anybodyyyyyyyy!'

The two sisters sat in very dissimilar circumstances, both longing for one another, Esther in a reproduction faux leather lounger with a half-smile on her face having pictured her sister haplessly haggling for worthless trinkets and tat amid the souks and bazars of Cairo, and Minnie slumped on a priceless hand-carved antiquity staring into space and the chiselled face of Anubis, her thoughts racing from a dozen or so destinations she and her beloved sister had experienced together; their stay at the Mumbai Taj Mahal Palace hotel entertaining the guests on the piano, albeit alcohol-fuelled, their brush with death with the ferocious Bengal tiger and their now legendary parade around Germany's Nurburgring racetrack flanked by Hells Angels, to name but a few. Each one a precious memory, more precious perhaps than the material possessions surrounding her, an inanimate hoard without feeling, incalculable in wealth but worthless now to their former owners.

Minnie soon began to tire once again, so very weak and fragile. Back home either sister would take regular cat naps as it were, routinely having to explain the beginning, middle or end of a movie to the other.

Yawning, Minnie nestled as best she could into the rigid back of the gilded throne, her pale drawn complexion almost mummified in appearance. She slept under the assumption she would be discovered by pyramid officials or like-minded tourists taking the self-same subterranean tour that she had inadvertently taken.

Esther woke suddenly to a knock at her hotel room door. 'What, who, what?' she said, coming to. 'Minnie, Minnie is that you, dear?'

There was a second knock and then a third whilst Esther clambered stiffly from her chair. 'Yes, yes, yes, dear!' she called in reply. 'I told you, Minnie, to take your key but ohhhhh no, as always Minnie knows best,' and straightening her aching back Esther reached for the door. 'Oh!' she exclaimed, opening it, 'I, I, I thought you were my sister.'

'Good morning, madam,' the hotel porter said, pushing yet another heavily laden trolley into the room. 'Your breakfast, Miss Minnie ordered it.'

'Breakfast!' Esther said, bemused to say the least. 'What do you mean, breakfast?'

'Yes, breakfast,' the porter said, unveiling a mountain of Minnie's favourites. 'Your sister ordered breakfast for eleven o'clock sharp.'

Esther struggled with reality for a moment. 'But, but surely breakfast should be served in the morning, should it not?' she asked.

'Madam, it is the morning,' the porter replied, pouring two cups of coffee. 'Eleven o'clock sharp,' and he rolled back his starched white sleeve to display his wristwatch. 'You see?'

'Morning?' Esther said with a hand to her forehead. 'But where's Minnie?' She hurried to the bedroom but found only a neatly made bed. 'Minnie,' she called, rushing to swipe open the curtains to reveal the sun's glare. 'Dear God, you're right!' she gasped. 'It's morning!' Examining the bathroom, Esther rushed around the suite in a flap. 'Where is she, where is she?' she asked as the bemused porter looked on. 'Have you seen her?' she asked.

'Seen her?' the porter asked,

'Yes!' Esther snapped. 'My Minnie, for Pete's sake, she's not here, have you seen her, have you?'

'No, madam,' the porter replied, setting down the coffee pot. 'Perhaps she left early for the bazar.'

'No, no, no,' Esther said, turning this way and that, 'she hasn't returned since yesterday, I know that because my Minnie never makes the bed, ever, oh where is she?' Esther shuffled to the balcony and peered down into the street below and then off to the distant pyramids. 'Minniiiiiie!' she called in vain.

'Your sister, madam?' the porter asked. 'She is missing?'

'Yes, yes, of course she's missing!' Esther barked.

'Soooo shall I serve breakfast, madam?' the hovering porter asked, unable to grasp the sense of urgency.

'What?' Esther replied abruptly, desperately looking below for her sister's tell-tale blue dress.

'Breakfast, madam?' the porter reiterated. 'Would you like me to serve?'

'No!' Esther cursed. 'Why on earth would I want breakfast at a time like this, take it away, take it away, you foolish little man, and get me the police right away, right away, you hear!'

'The police, madam?' the porter asked naively.

Esther glared at him. 'Yes the police, damn you,' she snarled. 'I told you, my sister is missing, now go, hurry, go, go, GO NOW!'

'Yes, yes, yes, madam, the police,' the half-witted porter eventually said. 'Shall I, shall I leave your breakfast?'

'Get out of my way!' Esther stormed, barging past him to gather fresh clothes before disappearing into the bathroom, leaving the porter decidedly confused but removing the breakfast trolley all the same and returning to the lobby to report the incident.

Several miles away within the giant pyramid of Giza, Minnie later stirred, startled once again to be sat on a firm golden throne. 'Dear Lord,' she groaned, unable to move momentarily. Focussing, she looked back along the blackened corridor, her torch lighting the first of many twists and turns. 'Dear, dear Lord,' she echoed as the grim reality slowly set in, she was alone and could be for some time. Minnie's mouth was dry and unlike her sister she always had an appetite for breakfast and no amount of barracking from Esther would deter her, no matter how late they were running, once missing a flight to Benidorm Spain because she insisted on toasting a third slice of granary and pouring the last of their tea from their Wedgewood pot. 'Waste not, want not, dear,' she said whilst the frustrated taxi driver outside leaned on his horn.

'Cake, cake, cake,' Minnie suddenly said, foraging on the floor beside the throne for her bag, thankful for the slice of chocolate cake she had stowed that previous afternoon. Minnie devoured every last crumb, sipping water intermittently to conserve her limited supply, she also thought of the tiny lithium battery powering her head torch but after sitting in complete darkness for all of thirty seconds she had an immediate change of heart, imagining all sorts currying about her feet, beetles, spider, rats or worse perhaps, but of course there was nothing.

The air inside the tomb was stale and the limited oxygen that had rushed inside with her was steadily depleting at Minnie's every desperate breath. With a heave and a groan she pulled herself to her feet, standing for a moment to collect her thoughts; if she could only make it known to Essy or her fellow tourists that she was somewhat trapped. 'Helloooooo!' she attempted to call but her voice lacked the strength to penetrate the hard stone walls that encased her. 'Essyyyyyyy, anybodyyyyyy!' Stooping, she rummaged amongst the tomb's numerous antiquities, tugging out a carved wooden totem the size of an average table leg and whilst disregarding its apparent value began to hammer at the exquisitely painted wall. 'Hellooooo it's me, Minnie, I'm in here!' she yelled as best she could, but very soon tired. 'Pleaaaaaaase!' she added, lowering her makeshift club. 'Hellllllllp!'

Esther had washed in haste and left their room in time to meet two Egyptian police officers in the foyer. 'Cooeeeeee!' she called to them. 'Have you found her?'

'Found, madam?' one of them asked, unaware of the facts.

'Yes, yes, my sister,' Esther informed them. 'She's missing, you have to find her, I gather that's why you're here.'

'You say your sister is missing, madam?' an officer again asked, taking out his notebook. 'And you are both staying here at the Fairmont, yes?'

'Yes that's right,' Esther said, visibly agitated and her make-up hurriedly applied. 'But I lost her at the pyramids, we became separated you see.' She screwed a cotton handkerchief in her hands, occasionally mopping at her nose. 'Please, you must find her,' she begged. 'You must, she's elderly like me you see and I haven't seen her since yesterday afternoon.'

'Yesterday?' the officer said, raising his eyebrows. 'I see, and you last saw her at the pyramids?'

'Can you give us a full description, madam?' his colleague asked, also making notes. 'Her height, build and clothes, and I take it she is British?'

'Yes of course she's British!' Esther replied sharply. 'We both are, she's about so tall, a tad overweight, wearing a blue spotted dress with a straw hat, like mine in fact, her name's Minnie, now please hurry will you, I know she'll be petrified, the poor dear thing, wherever she is.'

'OK, madam,' an officer said, pocketing his notes. 'We will issue a missing persons immediately but if your sister returns in the meantime do not hesitate to inform us.'

'Yes, yes, of course,' Esther said, ushering the officers out of the hotel. 'Now please hurry, will you, please.'

Cairo's police patrols were issued with Minnie's description as part of their daily duties and yet another official search of the great pyramid carried out, but of course yielding no results.

'What do you mean, you haven't found her?' Esther said on the telephone that afternoon after a further agonising wait pacing their hotel suite. 'How difficult can it be?'

'Madam, madam, please,' the station officer replied in an attempt to calm the ever anxious Esther. 'We are doing all we can, I promise you, every officer at our disposal is looking for your sister, that I can assure you.'

'Just find her and bring her back to me,' Esther said, dabbing at her running nose. 'I'm going out of my mind, I truly am, I mean where on earth can she be, where?'

'Madam,' the officer added. 'I would like to put something to you but, but I don't want to alarm you any further.'

'What?' Esther insisted. 'What is it, tell me, what is it?'

There was a second or two of silence before the officer broached the subject from an entirely different perspective. 'Madam, I have been informed of your, shall we say celebrity status.'

'Yes, yes, what of it?' Esther asked impatiently. 'It's all nonsense if you ask me, but what are you saying, what exactly?'

'Madam,' the officer hesitated again. 'Have you considered at all that perhaps you r sister may have been taken against her will?'

'Against her will!' Esther gasped. 'You mean, kidnapped?'

'Yes, madam,' the office replied. 'For money.'

'My dear fellow,' Esther replied, almost raising a smile. 'You obviously have never met my darling Minnie, have you?'

'No, madam,' the bemused officer confessed, having considered the theory most plausible indeed. 'I have not had the pleasure, no I have not.'

'I thought as much,' Esther replied. 'Well let me tell you, sir,' she added glancing at the clock on the wall. 'It is fast approaching a full twenty-four hours since my sister disappeared so if, as you are suggesting, she has been abducted, I can safely say without a shadow of a doubt she would have driven her captors quite insane within an hour and she would have been swiftly returned, of that I am quite sure, no, no, I tell you she has wandered off somewhere, maybe to the markets as first suggested, she just can't get enough of your ridiculously tacky souvenirs, no offence intended, you understand.'

'None taken, madam,' the officer replied with a smile. 'My mother is a collector too you know, she has travelled to your London capital returning with miniatures of your hilarious double deck bus and your red telephone and posting boxes.'

'I'll have you know, sir,' Esther said defensively. 'These, sir, are replicas of our rich cultural heritage, now I suggest you direct your men to the markets and bazars at once, if I know my Minnie she's lost all track of time whilst haggling the hind leg off some poor blighter, oh to hell with it!' she suddenly cursed. 'I'll go myself, I'll find her just you wait and see.' With this Esther slammed down the receiver, threw her bag across her shoulder and hurried from their suite once again.

But once outside, the sheer scale of the task at hand all but took her breath away. Mile after mile of market tents and back street bazars stretched out before her, and with tourist season at its peak Cairo was a melting pot of foreign nationals, tens of thousands of them aimlessly trawling the capital in search of that one amusing novelty gift for their favourite aunt, mother, brother, sister or whomever they felt may appreciate the ironic sentiment the most. 'Dear Lord,' Esther sighed, descending the hotel steps and deciding to leave Vivien at rest and pound the pavement herself.

No sooner had Esther entered a covered market place than she found herself having to run the gauntlet, or should we say shuffle the gauntlet of over enthusiastic hawkers thrusting their wares under her nose and jabbering feverishly offering an ever decreasing price. 'No, no!' Esther said, swatting them aside. 'I said no, I don't want it, thank you!' she added when a string of gaudily painted camels was placed around her neck. 'I'm looking for my sister, have you seen her?' she asked, producing a crumpled photograph of the two of them taken some years earlier at her grandson Richard's third birthday, Richard himself in floods of tear in the snap after Minnie had blown out the candles on his marshmallow Mickey Mouse birthday cake. 'That's her there,' she pointed out to another trader. 'With the custard on her cardigan and the jelly on her chin.' Elizabeth could also be seen fuming behind the pair having witnessed Minnie fishing her false teeth out of the strawberry trifle. 'Have you seen her?' Esther again asked, to which the unanimous reply was 'No, madam, but come look, I give you good price,' a line echoed throughout the known universe by traders in an attempt to charm the pennies from the public pockets. 'Good price, very good price!'

'No, no, for Pete's sake!' Esther remarked, brushing him aside and wincing at the cacophonous clanging of his camel bells. 'And will you please stop that infernal racket!' she moaned. 'I can hardly hear myself think, I said no!'

The bell peddler soon got the message and raced to greet another potential purchaser. 'Good priiiice, good priiice!' he called amid his calamitous symphony.

Esther eventually tired, having been jostled, prodded and poked with random replicas ranging from the sublime to the ridiculous. 'My good man!' she snapped, bearing down on a particularly persistent peddler. 'I won't tell you again, I have absolutely no use for your pathetic….' She stopped mid-sentence and looked over his shoulder to the rear of his shambolic stall. 'Oooh,' she said, craning her neck. 'Is that, is that a snow globe, oh how charming, I'll take two please.' She hastily rummaged in her bag whilst the stallholder raced to retrieve the pointless paperweights featuring the three Giza pyramids amid a snow storm when shaken. Whilst the vast majority of mankind would fail to see any significance whatsoever, Esther found them 'Simply delightful' were her exact words. 'One for me' she said, dropping them into her bag. 'And one for my….. oh good grief, Minnie!' she said, thrusting a quantity of coins into the trader's hand and nudging several tourists aside to search for her sister once again.

At the Giza excavation site Mike stood scratching his head. 'God damn it!' he yelled, tossing his hat across his open tent. 'We should have found something by now!'

Within the pyramid's bowels Minnie had beaten at the walls with her club and called until she was horse; she paused, panting and hanging her head with one hand resting on the gilded throne. 'Christ, what have I done?' she asked herself. 'Minnie you bloody, bloody fool, you.'

No more than thirty feet now from the hidden tomb, a team of twenty Egyptian workers toiled with pneumatic drills, picks and shovels barely penetrating more than a couple of feet per hour.

Minnie looked up, put a hand to her ear and listened, at one point catching the sound of a distant drill. 'Helloooooooo!' she called croakily. 'Blast!' she added, taking more water to clear her throat. 'Helloooooooo!' she called again, slapping the palm of her hand on the wall. 'I'M IN HERE, HELLOOOOOO, HELLLLLLLP!' but of course her woeful cries were deadened by the dense rock between them, and even if it were to penetrate to the advancing tunnel the jabbering Egyptians with their thumping generators powering the lights and heavy boring equipment would barely bat an eye. 'IT'S ME, MINNIIIIIIIIIE!' she screamed as best she could. 'OVER HERE!' Her legs again began to tire and buckle at her arthritic knees, despite her surgical wraps applied every morning by her loving and attentive sister.

Minnie's pounding on the wall and shuffling feet had produced a plume of centuries-old dust that dried her eyes and tickled her throat, forcing her to dip into her perilously low water supplies leaving all but a mouthful remaining. Minnie had absolutely no idea at this point how long she'd been confined to the eerie tomb but one thing was glaringly clear, if help was not forthcoming and quickly there would be two deceased occupants from entirely opposite ends of the social ladder, one of them a mystery at this point but clearly a person of enormous wealth and standing within their former community, city and continent perhaps, and the other, Minnie, who preceding her recent global adventures was nobody in particular, the two of them centuries and worlds apart, separated by birth right and a one-and-a-half-ton sarcophagus lid.

Three and a quarter hours passed and the drilling and rumbling grew noticeably louder, rather like the tube trains of the Metropolitan Line that ran under Minnie and Esther's Whitechapel home. *Perhaps it is a train*, she thought to herself, growing increasingly stir crazy; was this a dream, was she really tucked up in bed beside her beloved Essy destined to wake at any moment to the all too familiar Westminster chimes of their father's old mantel clock? But the sand at her feet was so real, the stale air and the flaking hieroglyphics and also the searing pain when she shuffled her feet and stubbed her big toe on a large heavy urn or canopic jar as they are better known, used by those entrusted with the grizzly task of embalming the dead and separately storing their vital organs, the heart, intestines, liver, stomach and lungs etc. Each canopic jar featured a different head on its lid, a jackal, a baboon or human form. 'OW, OW, OW!' she cursed, hopping on one foot and thumping the sarcophagus in sheer frustration. Things as it were could not possibly get any worse for Minnie, or so she thought.

Esther had plagued a hundred or more market traders with her tattered photograph. 'Are you quite sure?' she asked another. 'Please, take another look, her name's Minnie and she's missing, you see, are you sure you haven't seen her?' She batted another hand away. 'No, no, no, no, damn you!' she protested. 'I don't want a flipping fez, my own hat is more than adequate thank you, good day to you, I said good day to you, now go away before I call the police!'

As was customary with most dubious traders the mere mention of the authorities was enough to drain several shades of colour from their faces. Eventually Esther purchased a pineapple juice and sat on a doorway step supping through a yellow bendy straw and willing her sister to round an adjacent corner along with the perpetual teaming tide of tourists. 'Ohhhh, Minnie,' she sighed feeling an emptiness growing like a seed within her. The departing of her dear sweet Jack was a bitter pill to swallow but she had Minnie to raise her spirits during her darkest hours. On occasion she would merely have to look at Minnie tossing grapes into the air and catching one in ten in her mouth, and being scolded by the supermarket manager in the process, or shelling peanuts in her wingback chair and depositing much of the debris into her cleavage whilst glued to her favourite period drama, drooling over the handsome woodsman, wriggling and rummaging on occasion for the said debris.

As Esther's heart sank deeper a young girl maybe eight of nine approached her with an armful of cheap plastic bangles, smiling and flashing her wares. 'No, no, thank you,' Esther told her, in no mood. 'I'm quite alright, thank you.'

But the girl who spoke no English was quite insistent, rattling her gaudy bangles and producing a crude cardboard sign cut from a melon box denoting their price, one Egyptian pound.

'No really, dear,' Esther again refused. 'I'm quite alright, thank you.'

The girl, who wore a grubby denim dress and no shoes, brushed her lank hazel hair from her eyes and looked down at the picture in Esther's hands. Suddenly wide-eyed, she began to prod at Minnie with her custard stained dress and pointed back at the covered market fidgeting on the spot.

'What, what is it?' Esther asked, sitting upright. 'Have you seen her, have you seen my Minnie?'

Without understanding the girl nodded and took Esther's hand.

'Oh thank heavens!' Esther cried, clambering to her feet, discarding the pineapple juice and hastily following the young girl in and out of the cluttered stalls, colliding with several browsers en-route. 'Sorryyyyyy!' she called over her shoulder.

The girl, still clinging to Esther's hand, weaved between the mass of bodies tugging Esther and pointing ahead. 'Where?' Esther asked, puffing somewhat. 'Where is she?' Her heart was pounding, desperate for a glimpse of that hapless face, the face she knew so well, those dimpled cheeks and mischievous smile. 'Minniiiiiiiie!' she called ahead, peering over the crowd. 'Minnie it's me!'

The bare footed girl with the grubby face wrenched at Esther's hand. 'Yes, yes,' Esther said with a broad smile. 'Oh thank you, my darling, thank you.' Passing a replica jewellery stall, the girl suddenly stopped and gestured at a clothing stand run by her mother with a rail of floral dresses not entirely dissimilar to the one Minnie wore in the photograph. Proudly the girl lifted the hem of one dress and beckoned to Esther as her mother approached. 'You like, madam?' the woman asked. 'I have all size, what size you?'

'Oh!' Esther said as the devastation gradually sank in. 'Ohhhh no, no, no, I thought,' she said, going weak at the knees. The girl's mother hastily retrieved a chair and slipped it behind Esther as she slumped heartbroken once again. 'I thought it was my Minnie,' she told the mother.

'Minnie,' the woman replied, taking the photograph from Esther's hand.

'Yes, yes,' Esther replied, tapping her sister's face. 'My sister, have you seen her?'

The child's mother examined the snap closely while Esther sat with bated breath beside her. 'No,' the Egyptian eventually said. 'I not see her, sorry, madam.'

'Oh dear,' Esther moaned. 'Dear, dear, dear.'

Weary with heartache and fatigue, Esther made her way back to the hotel, telephoned the police from the foyer and was given the same answer as before. 'I am sorry, madam, we are doing all we can to locate your sister.'

Peshwari Nans Part II

Without reply Esther left the receiver dangling and trudged to the elevator, deflated beyond compare. 'Damn you, Minnie,' she said ascending. 'Damn you, damn you, damn you.'

Minnie sat once more motionless on the priceless throne breathing heavily now and parched, having drained the last of her water. The reverberation and hammering of the workers drills grew in intensity but the seven-foot-wide tunnel had veered several more degrees to the left and if it were to remain on this course it would miss the hidden tomb by a mere yard and a half.

Minnie wriggled on the throne unable to settle, her lower back taut and knotted. Looking about her feet again for creepy crawlies and undesirables, she raised them several inches from the floor, but again her aging bones creaked. 'Blast,' she said, seeking an alternative resting place. With a huff, a grunt and more than a few puffs Minnie climbed up onto the granite sarcophagus lid, but not before selecting two curved Pharaoh's crooks from the surrounding possessions. The crooks like a shortened version of a shepherd's were the ultimate symbol of power among ancient Egyptians and featured heavily in many unearthed hieroglyphics. Minnie, however, clung to them for her own protection, although from what she wasn't quite clear.

Somehow it eased her pain to lie flat gripping the crooks in readiness to defend herself. 'Essyyyyyyy!' she called in a weak rasping voice. 'Essyyyyyy,' Soon her eyes grew heavy, and yawning she once again succumbed to the desire to sleep, but with her fatigue came a more sinister fate. Oxygen levels had plummeted within the ancient tomb and surrounding passageways, slowly draining the life and soul from the once vibrant pensioner. Her limbs now lead-like hung rooted to the sarcophagus and her slender wrinkled neck lacked the strength and will for that matter to raise her weary head.

Whilst Minnie languished in the final resting place of the unknown occupant she couldn't help but wonder if it was to be hers too. Minnie's had been a rich and rewarding life, full of love and laughter and she knew only too well that countless less fortunate souls hadn't had the luxury of longevity that she'd enjoyed, her beloved daughter Sophia for one, her face still as fresh in Minnie's mind as the day she tenderly kissed it goodbye over and over in her pearl white coffin showering her with tears, heart-wrenching apologies and endless 'I love you's dropping to her knees at the graveside and screaming Sophia's name after three white doves were released into a bracing north-easterly wind.

Perhaps it was time, time for them to be together once more, mother and child reunited for all eternity. With what resembled a faint smile Minnie closed her eyes and relished the tender moments they'd spent together like a flickering super-8 movie playing over and over in her mind, Sophia's first tooth, those red patent shoes she simply adored and on occasion slept in, removing the stabilizers on her bicycle and watching her shakily circle the recreation ground yelling, 'Look, Mummy look, I can riiiiiiide!'

'Yes, yes, yes you can, my darling,' Minnie mouthed on her granite bed. 'And I'm so, so, proud of you, my angel.'

Whilst the light from Minnie's serpent head torch gradually dimmed within the tomb, so did the light within this beautiful soul as her sister on occasion described her. Her legacy would be the memories etched within the hearts of all those fortunate enough to have known her, lived, loved and laughed with her. 'Essy,' she whispered, now breathless. 'My love.'

Esther paced their hotel suite with a cerise silk headscarf of her sister's gripped tightly between her hands; the pair had never been knowingly parted in all their years without prior warning. Minnie would call constantly when away from home for culinary tips or advice on matters of the heart, or crossword conundrums even, plaguing Esther at all hours of the day and night with questions ranging from the trivial to the darn right ridiculous. Like the time she rang at three-thirty on a Sunday morning from the cabin of a cruise ship on the Norwegian Fjords whilst fending off her ex-lover Cyril's repeated advances merely to enquire whether at the ripe old age of seventy nine it was necessary to practise safe sex, to which Esther gave a scathing reply having been woken twice the previous night for a recipe for rice pudding and her opinion on tattoos, piercings and breast enhancements for the elderly. But at that moment in time Esther would give anything for the phone to ring and hear her sister's voice, whether the purpose be pointless or otherwise. 'I'll swing for that girl, I will,' she cursed screwing the scarf ever tighter and blotting the unthinkable from her mind, a life alone without Jack or Minnie.

A knock at the door startled Esther. 'Minnie!' she called, hurrying to grapple with the handle. 'Minnie, where on earth have you....' On opening she saw the police chief standing in the hallway with his peaked cap tucked respectfully beneath his right arm. 'Oh,' Esther said, taken aback. 'I, I thought …..'

'Mrs Reynolds,' the chief said in a sombre tone. 'I'm afraid…'

'Oh dear God no!' Esther blurted, covering her mouth and jumping to conclusions. 'No please, not my Minnie, no, no, no, no, no, no.' Assuming the chief had called personally to inform her of her sister's tragic demise, Esther backed away from the door reaching behind her for the chair. 'No, no, please God, no.'

'Mrs Reynolds, please wait,' the police chief said, following her into the suite with a raised hand. 'I merely came to say we have failed to locate your sister.'

'What?' Esther sobbed, removing the scarf from her face. 'You mean, you mean she's not...' Esther clutched at her pounding chest.

'Are you alright, madam?' the chief asked, hurrying to her side. 'Let me pour you some water,' and moments late he slipped a glass into Esther's shaking hand. 'Please, do not think that way,' he told her.

'Well where is she?' Esther asked angrily. 'Why haven't you found her, tell me why?'

'Madam, I have no answer for this,' the chief of police replied. 'But it is too soon to assume that she may be…' He hesitated.

'Don't say it!' Esther urged. 'Please don't say it.'

'Very well,' the chief agreed. 'As I say, there is still time to find her, Cairo is a big city and there are a thousand places she could be, it will take more time for my officers to make a thorough search.'

'A thousand places,' Esther said despairingly. 'Her place is here, with me, right here, damn it,' and she slapped the seat beside her with the palm of her hand. 'That's it!' she then said, wrenching herself to her feet. 'I'm going back.'

'Back?' the chief asked. 'Back where, madam?'

'To the pyramids,' Esther informed him. 'To retrace our steps, I can't just sit her, for Pete's sake.' She grabbed her bag and Vivien's keys

'But, madam!' the chief exclaimed. 'We have searched the pyramids from top to bottom, I assure you, and besides it is too late,' he added, following Esther out of her suite.

'Precisely!' Esther snapped. 'It is getting late and she's still out there, I have to do something, I have to, I tell you.'

'But, madam, you should wait here.' the chief implored her. 'It is for the best, please.'

'Don't!' Esther barked, raising a hand and glaring at the chief. 'Don't tell me what I should and shouldn't do, my Minnie is missing and I mean to find her if it's the last thing I do, now, get out of my way.'

The chief raised his hands in surrender, watching the defiant Esther shuffle toward the elevators. 'English,' he said raising his eyebrows.

As Esther climbed back into Vivien and buckled her belt, the team of Egyptian tunnellers were just feet from the concealed tomb but a full ten degrees off course at this point, unaware that a vast wealth was slipping through their fingers. Mike himself was coming under increasing pressure from the investors back home in the United States, who on several occasions threatened to pull their funding and terminate the dig which would mean that it could be years if not decades before the Egyptian government would allow another excavation of the great pyramid and thus sealing Minnie's fate within the chamber of secrets as it were.

Esther arrived as night began to fall and a steady stream of tourists snaked away from the ancient site, boarding taxi cabs and coaches, having captured hundreds upon hundreds of images between them of the captivating structures. Esther was buffeted as she made her way against the flow. 'Excuse me!' she said, turning side on. 'Coming through!' Approaching the entrance, she was barred immediately by the pyramid guards.

'Closed,' was their only remark.

'What?' Esther asked, puffing. 'What do you mean closed, I need to look inside.'

A second more approachable guard appeared. 'I am sorry, madam, the pyramid is closed now,' he informed her. 'You will need to return tomorrow.'

'No, no, no, no, no, no, you don't understand,' Esther insisted. 'I'm looking for my sister you see.'

'You sister, madam?' the guard replied. 'Madam, if you mean the English woman the police have explored every inch of this place, every inch, there is nobody here, I promise you.'

'But I need to see for myself,' Esther asked, peering over his shoulder. 'Please, for my own peace of mind.'

'I'm afraid that will not be possible, madam,' the guard said with his hands firmly lodged on his hips. 'We have rules, I am sorry.'

'Sorry!' Esther said, growing hotter under the collar. 'Sorry, what about my sister, are you sorry for her, are you?' Please I just need to take a quick peek, I'll be out in no time I promise you.'

The guard stood his ground whilst Esther attempted to side-step him.

'You don't understand!' Esther said, wrestling against his muscular arm. 'I have to know for sure!' But try as she may there was no reasoning with the stone-faced officers. 'Damn you!' Esther cursed, turning away and descending the steps. 'Damn you, damn you.'

Mike then called out whilst on his way back to the dig. 'ESTHER, OVER HERE!' he signalled, waving his arms and approaching. 'Esther, what are you doing here, and where's Minnie?' he asked, assuming she'd been found the previous day, but then seeing the look of heartfelt anguish on Esther's face he put an arm around her. 'You haven't found her, have you?' he said, taking off his hat. 'Oh Jesus, Esther, I'm sorry, I can't imagine what you must be going through.'

'Hell,' Esther said with a trembling lip. 'I'm going through hell, Mister Mike, sheer hell.'

'Come with me,' Mike told her. 'I'll fix you some tea.'

'Have you anything stronger?' Esther asked, her nerves rattled and frayed.

'Whiskey?' Mike suggested.

Esther nodded and accompanied the American to his floodlit encampment on the far side of the great pyramid.

'Here,' Mike said handing Esther a tin mug and offering her a chair. 'My Granddaddy's recipe,' he informed her, then smiled when Esther coughed and spluttered. 'Take it easy,' he chuckled, 'My daddy used to run a combine and a Chevy pick-up on this liquor.'

'Strewth!' Esther remarked with her eyes clenched shut and her throat on fire. 'That's hardly a single malt is it, Mister Mike?'

'Moonshine,' Mike proudly informed her whilst draining his own mug and pouring another measure.

'Oh no, no, no, no,' Esther said, placing a hand over her mug. 'I'd rather not if it's all the same to you,' and she sat staring into the flickering flame of Mike's oil lamp whilst he conversed with his foreman pleading for increased progress.

'But, sir, the men,' Tariq replied, wiping his forehead with a sweat-stained rag. 'They are tired and need to rest.'

'Outta the question!' Mike insisted. 'Work them till morning, Tariq, work them hard and I'll double your pay, hell, I'll double everybody's damn pay, just find that tomb will ya!'

'Double, you say?' Tariq said with renewed vigour.

'Yes, yes, God damn it!' Mike said, ushering Tariq back toward the tunnel. 'Have your men dig like their lives depended on it, you hear.'

'Yes, yes, sir,' Tariq replied, hurrying inside to rally his men.

'I'm sorry, Esther,' Mike said, returning to his seat. 'Tell me about your sister?' he asked, pouring yet another drink. 'Tell me about Minnie?'

'Minnie?' Esther said, sipping her illicit liquor tentatively. 'Where to begin, Mister Mike?'

Mike's eyes widened as Esther began to divulge the kaleidoscope that was her sister's colourful life. 'You're kiddin me!' he said more than once. 'She did what?'

Within the pyramid Tariq's men were sat taking on water allowing their heavy drilling equipment to cool and breaking bread between them, grateful for the fleeting moments of blissful silence before their next gruelling shift.

Barely a few feet away Minnie had become delirious, drifting in and out of consciousness. *'Daisy, Daisy'* she moaned at one point, the colour now draining from her lips. *'Give me your answer dooooooo.'*

A labourer on the other side of the stone wall pricked up his ears mid bite and looked all around, continuing with his meal when Minnie fell silent.

'Daisy, Daisy!' Minnie sang again, writhing on the slab.

Three more tunnellers sat upright, removing the cotton wads from their ears.

''Give me your answer dooooo,' Minnie groaned.

One by one the men stood and scoured the tunnel, pressing an ear to either side.

With what little strength remained and while conscious Minnie puffed her chest. *'There'll always be an England!'* she crowed, high pitched, *'And England shall be freeeeeee!'*

'HERE, HERE!' an Egyptian cried on the other side of the wall beckoning to his friends. 'HERE!' A dozen or more ears were pressed to the wall listening over the constant ringing, completely flabbergasted at the faint melodic rant. One of them grabbed his pick and swung at the wall while his colleagues backed away, dubious to say the least. 'COME, COME!' he yelled at them. 'Here!'

Inside Minnie slumped semi-comatose once again, motionless, her breathing now heavily laboured and an ashen tone to her cheeks. The oxygen within the ancient tomb was all but spent as were the batteries in her headlight.

Several of the men outside backed to the opposite wall fearing a pharaoh's curse, one that had claimed the lives of many of their forbears, but the frantic Egyptian swung his pick, assuming the eerie sound could possibly be the wind whistling down a ventilation shaft into the very tomb they so desperately sought. 'COME, COME!' he yelled, goading his colleagues with the promise of vast riches, and one by one his wary brethren took up their tools motivated by greed and joined him at the wall swinging with their backs dripping wet but making good headway, clambering over the fallen rock chippings at their feet.

Minnie's heart beat slowed to a perilous rate as she lay oblivious to the hammering on the sandstone wall, her eyes were closed and her head gradually fell to one side and the light from her torch flickered and faded.

Suddenly a pick point broke through, and then another and another. Sensing a void beyond and a possible tomb, the men fell over one another to hack at the wall. The tomb soon filled with dust as larger fragments of stone collapsed until a tunneller's face appeared passing an oil lamp through the hole. His friend pressed their faces against his and all screamed in unison at the mountain of gold before them, taking very little notice of the lifeless old lady laid out on the sarcophagus. With bulging eyes and pounding hearts the men grappled with the loose rock, passing it hand over fist behind them, jubilant beyond words at their discovery.

The vacuum caused by the sudden breach immediately drew a gust of fresh Egyptian air into the great pyramid and consequently the tomb itself. Within minutes the buoyant burrowers had made short work of the dividing wall until they were able to clamber through, picking their way amongst the debris and the king's ransom in antiquities, hugging one another and punching the air.

'Look, look!' one of them exclaimed cautiously, approaching the sarcophagus and the dust-covered figure ghostly figure. Minnie looked every inch a deceased Egyptian Queen, her aged skin almost mummified in appearance, she clasped the two crooks crossed on her chest with her serpent headdress on her forehead.

The labourers' lamps flickered within the tomb playing tricks on the eyes of those gathered around. Could this really be her, could this haggard relic really be Cleopatra herself and had the mystery that had dogged so many historians and archaeologists finally been solved; if so then this was truly a momentous day, a magnificent day. With a trembling hand one man reached with his heart in his mouth to touch the face of the woman immortalised in legend by his people and the entire world. The tomb fell silent as his friends looked on clinging to one another, but were then startled when the young man gasped at the apparent flexibility of the skin although cracked and weathered.

What was to follow would also become immortalised in legend, as opening her eyes suddenly Minnie drew a long wheezing gasp of air and slowly turned her head, evoking near cardiac arrest in those gathered at her side. 'Oh hellooooo,' she said clearing her throat when seeing the group dressed in their white robes with the bright tunnel light behind them and assuming the Lord had sent a party of angels to escort her to the pearly gates. 'I'm coming, my dears,' she added groaning as she pushed herself up to the sitting position.

There was a deafening scream within the tomb as each and every man fell over his countryman to exit the tomb, wailing with their hands in the air and sprinting back along the lengthy tunnel and attracting the attention of those outside.

'Excuse me, Esther,' Mike, said rising from his seat to leave his tent and Minnie's distraught sister to confront his fleeing workforce.

Esther, still clutching her tin mug of moonshine, left also but turned in the opposite direction seeking solitude with her thoughts and walked several meters into the desert to stare up into the starlit sky to pray for a miracle.

Minnie, now alive once more and positive she had crossed to the other side as it were, reached into her bag to retrieve her lipstick, so that if she was to meet the Almighty then she would at least look presentable. Weak and bleary eyed, she crudely applied the cosmetic looking almost clown-like by the time she'd finished. She swung her legs to one side and slid stiffly from the sarcophagus with yet another grunt. Minnie stood for a moment drawing breath after breath and tossing her bag over her shoulder, braced herself for the final walk to salvation and the promise of eternal life. 'I'm coming!' she called, shuffling toward the light which burnt at her eyes.

Outside Mike attempted to stop his stampeding labourers. 'WHOAAAAA, WHOAAAAAA'!' he yelled, waving his hands. 'What is it, what is it, God damn it!'

The words 'CLEOPATRA!' and 'CUUUURSE!' were all that Mike could decipher.

'Cleopatra!' Mike gasped, stopping dead in his tracks. 'You're kiddin!'

Despite the commotion behind her Esther stood in a world of her own, unable to stem the flood of tears running down her flushed red cheeks. 'Pleaaaaaaase, pleaaaaaaase' she quietly begged toward the moonlit heavens.

Mike followed behind his departing tunnellers once again. 'You found her!' he cried. 'Hey wait up, come on, you guys, tell me, did you find Cleopatra?'

Minnie stumbled blindly over the fallen rocks drawn toward the light, turning zombie-like into the freshly dug and now deserted tunnel. Straightening her back and raising her chin proudly, Minnie trudged toward the promised land like a moth drawn hypnotically to a flame. The light grew brighter on approach and although weak as a kitten Minnie refused to falter, driving herself step by agonising step, for soon she would be reborn, made whole again and reunited with those dear cherished souls that had departed her life taking with them a piece of her heart, her mother, her father, her Sophia.

Peshwari Nans Part II

Having skipped the majority of religious education classes, Minnie was a late convert and her choral knowledge was inadequate at best, so she dreamily hummed a favourite melody of her mother's, one she would chirp whilst stood at the china butler's sink running her daughter's Sunday dresses up and down the washboard. *Silver Threads amongst the Gold* an old time music hall song sung by Foster and Allen but dating back to 1873 and a favourite of the American barber shop quartets.

Minnie cleared her throat still blinded but the vision of her mother swaying from side to side in her pink pinnie still fresh in her mind.

'Darling I am growing old
silver threads amongst the gold'

She coughed and cleared her throat once more before continuing,

'Shine upon my brow today
Life is fading fast away
But my darling you will be, will be
Always young and fair to me'

Minnie emerged from the pyramid staggering dust-covered and drowsy, but proud and ready to meet her maker.

'My darling you will be, will be
Always young and fair to me'

Esther, while pacing and kissing her sister's scarf with sodden cheek, soon found herself singing along to the familiar distant melody.

> 'But my darling you will be, will be
> Always young and fair to me'

Both sisters, unaware of the other's presence, raised their voice an octave or two for the chorus.

> 'Darling I am growing old
> Silver threads amongst the gold,
> Shine upon my brow today
> Liiiiife is faaaading faaaaast awaaaaaay'

Esther suddenly stopped, rigid, and listened. Turning slowly, almost daring not to look whilst Minnie struggled to focus, squinting and shielding her eyes in the hopes of catching her first glimpse of the Lord or the bountiful heavens beyond.

> 'Shine upon my brow today'

Minnie mumbled,

> 'Life is fading fast awaaaaaay'

'Minnie?' Esther said, rooted to the spot at first with a high voltage bolt of pure emotion surging through her from top to toe. 'Minnie, oh my God, MINNIIIIIIIIIIIIIIIIIIIIIIIIE!' Stumbling herself and bawling uncontrollably, Esther started back toward the pyramid and the sister she had all but given up hope of ever seeing again. 'MINNIE, OH MY DARLING MINNIE!' she sobbed.

'Essy?' Minnie suddenly said, bemused to say the least. 'What, what, what are you doing here?'

'MINNIE, MINNIE!' Esther called, racing as best she could. 'Oh, Minnie, my darling, my darling.'

'But I don't understand,' Minnie said stopping in her tracks. 'Essy, did you die?'

'Die!' Esther said, approaching with arms outstretched. 'What are you talking about, Minnie, of course I didn't die, and neither did you.'

'I didn't?' Minnie asked. 'Are you quite sure?'

'Yes, yes!' Esther replied, crying tears of unadulterated joy now. 'I'm sure, my dear, I'm sure.'

Minnie could now make out the familiar face of her beloved sister. 'Essy, is that you? Is it really, oh Essy, Essy, Essy, my love, my love!' She too flung open her arms and the pair embraced tighter than they'd ever embraced in their entire lives, a long lingering swaying embrace that only reunited siblings would know.

'Oh Minnie, Minnie, I found you, I found you,' Esther blubbed. 'I found you.'

'Essy, I thought....' Minnie said, her head spinning. 'I thought I'd see my Sophia once again, dear, I truly thought I'd see her again, Essy, I truly did.'

'Oh, Minnie my darling, you will, you will,' Esther said, kissing both of Minnie's cheeks and then her ruby red lipstick-smudged lips. 'You will one day, darling, one day, but for now you're going to stay here with me, do you hear, with me, with your sister.' She kissed her sister again and again. 'My Minnie,' she said in floods of tears. 'My dear sweet Minnie, where have you been, I've been worried sick?'

Mike then returned with one or two of his less apprehensive men. 'Minnie?' he too said. 'Is that, is that you, ma'am?'

'Yes, yes it is,' Minnie replied over her sister's shoulder. 'How lovely to see you, Mister Mike, I thought I was dead you know.'

Mike took the ancient crooks from Minnie's hands. 'Minnie, where did you get these?' he asked whilst his workers gave her a wide berth.

'I didn't steal them,' Minnie replied, tugging at her sister's handbag. 'I say, dear, do you have any water?' she asked.

'Oh yes, yes of course!' Esther said, hastily cracking open a plastic bottle and watching her sister drain every last drop.

'Minnie?' Mike insisted, examining the crooks closely. 'Please, where did you get these?'

'I found them,' Minnie replied, wiping her chin. 'Just before I stubbed my toe on those blasted jars.'

'Jars!' Mike said, wide-eyed. 'Canopic jars!'

Esther cupped her sister's dishevelled face in her hands. 'You remembered,' she told her, 'Mother's song, you remembered, Minnie, *Silver Threads*.'

'Yes of course,' Minnie replied, clinging to Esther's hands. 'Look at us, Essy,' she added, caressing her sister's hair. 'We have silver threads of our own now.'

'We certainly do, dear,' Esther smiled, hugging her sister once again as though she'd never release her. 'We certainly do.'

Mike fizzed with excitement. 'If you'll excuse me, ladies,' he said, starting for the tunnel.

'Of course,' Esther called after him with a wave. 'Of course, Mister Mike.'

Minnie's aching bones in addition to her lack of nutrition could no longer support her. 'Essy I, I...' she stammered, losing consciousness and slumping into her sister's arms dragging the both of them to the ground.

'Minnie, MINNIE!' Esther cried, grappling to support her. 'Oh no, MISTER MIKE, MISTER MIKE, HELP ME, HELP ME PLEASE!'

Although on the verge of a spectacular discovery, Mike slowed in the tunnel,

stopped and turned. 'Esther, Esther what is it?' he called, running back to the sisters in time to scoop the limp Minnie up into his arms. 'Somebody call an ambulance!' he barked. 'NOW!'

'Oh, dear, please no,' Esther said, fraught once again, following Mike to his tent and gripping Minnie's dangling hand. 'Stay with me, dear,' she told her. 'Stay with me, damn you, I won't let you go again I won't, I won't, you hear!'

Minnie's prolonged confinement had well and truly taken its toll on her, the hours spent laid flat out on that granite slab brutalized her frail body leaving hideous pressure sores and a much reduced flow of blood through her tender veins, and the additional delirium experienced muddled her mind leaving her in limbo, somewhere between reality and fantasy.

Mike laid Minnie in his canvas camp bed, prising the bottle from her hand and offering it to her lips. 'Minnie, Minnie can you hear me, Minnie?' he asked, getting no response. 'C'mon, darling don't let go, Esther's here so you hang on to that.'

'Yes, yes, darling, I'm here,' Esther added, squeezing her sister's hand. 'I'm here, please, Minnie, please stay with me, I need you more than you'll ever know, I need you, Minnie.'

Mike rose and put a hand on Esther's shoulder. 'Stay with her,' he said before dashing from the tent. 'WHAT ABOUT THAT AMBULANCE?' he yelled toward his workers.

'But, sir, the tomb,' one of the tunnellers said, eager to delve into the riches once again. 'Shouldn't we…'

'To hell with that!' Mike insisted. 'Get me a God damn ambulance double quick, ya hear me!'

Minnie's eyes fluttered and she reached into space. 'There you are, Sophia,' she said, unwilling to fight a moment longer. 'Oh darling, I've missed you, Mummy's here now, Mummy's here, my angel.'

'No, Minnie now!' Esther snapped, rubbing the back of her sister's hand vigorously in an attempt to rouse her. 'Minnie it's me, your sister Essy, remember, Minniiiiie!'

'Sophia,' Minnie said with a smile. 'My Sophia, yes, yes, darling, Mummy's coming, Mummy's coming.'

'No, Minnie!' Esther said, nudging her younger sister.

'No, you're staying with me,' she said, her heart was breaking and bursting within her chest. 'You can't, Minnie, you can't go, I forbid it, do you hear, I forbid it, I'm your big sister, so you do as I say.'

Minnie's reaching hand fell slowly to her side and her smile subsided.

'NO, MINNIE, NO!' Esther cried. 'YOU DO AS I SAY, MINNIE, YOU STAY WITH ME, YOU STAY

WITH ME, DAMN YOU, STAY WITH ME, MINNIE, PLEAAAAAAAAASE!'

Moments later an Egyptian ambulance crew hurried into the tent escorting Esther to one side. 'Wait, wait, I'm her sister!' she called over their heads. 'I'm her sister!'

Mike ushered Esther from the tent and held her close to his chest, real close, and the pair of then flinched three times on hearing the defibrillator charge administered to Minnie's motionless chest. 'Oh God!' Esther said, burying her face into Mike's shirt.

Suddenly the tent flaps were swept back and the crew hurried out with Minnie strapped to a stretcher. 'She is with us,' one of the men said, holding a drip and line above Minnie. 'For now.'

Esther broke from Mike and scurried after them. 'Her name's Minnie!' she told them in a flap. 'She's my sister, take me with you, please.'

'Sorry,' was the only response from an ambulance man.

'Hey, man!' Mike said, confronting the crew. 'You heard the lady, she's her sister, God damn it, you gotta take her!'

With Minnie's vital signs critical it was agreed that Esther should accompany her to the hospital in case, heaven forbid, those were to be her last moments. 'Thank you, Mister Mike,' she said as he helped her aboard.

'Good luck,' Mike said, closing the rear door and watching the ambulance depart amid sirens and flashing lights.

En-route Esther leaned from her seat to comfort her writhing sister. 'It's alright, dear, it's alright,' she said, stroking her hand. 'I'm here.'

Minnie opened her eyes, hallucinating unbeknown to her sister. 'Essy I know you're here' she said, putting her sister's mind at rest momentarily. 'We are all together now,' she added crushing Esther once again. 'You, me, Sophia and Jack, together again, Essy, together.'

'Ohhhh, Minnie,' Esther sighed, brushing her smiling sibling's brow. 'Minnie, Minnie, Minnie.'

Minnie lay beaming and rocking her head from side to side humming, *'Daisy, Daisy'* and occasionally breaking into tuneless song. *'Give me your answer doooooo.'*

A medic tapped Esther's arm. 'Jack, Sophia?' he asked.

Esther shook her head in reply slumping back into her seat as the ambulance swung into the hospital grounds closely followed by fleet of news vehicles whose crew had gotten wind of the whole affair, several stopping at the pyramid to cover Cleopatra's discovery but the majority chasing the bigger story, a critically ill Peshwari Nan, it really didn't come any bigger at that moment in time. In fact life could have been discovered on our neighbouring planets, the true culprit in the JFK assassination could have been finally brought to justice and Elvis discovered working in a five and dime in downtown LA and the world would not have batted an eye, Minnie, their Minnie was close to death and nothing else mattered.

'Esther, Esther!' a news hound called as she followed the stretcher inside. 'Esther, can you tell us how Minnie is?'

'Esther, what was she doing in the pyramid?' another journalist eagerly called.

'God only knows,' Esther replied, clinging to Minnie's hand. 'God only knows.'

Meanwhile Mike and those brave enough rushed inside the excavated Giza pyramid armed with pry bars, blocks and tackle and hounded by the remainder of the world's media. Mike stood poised at the sarcophagus side, bar in hand addressing the crammed gathering. 'This is truly a momentous occasion,' he told them, trembling in doing so and the culmination of a life's work. 'But,' he added, struggling for an explanation for the bizarre turn of events, 'I'd like to be able to take full credit for this historic find but I'm afraid I can't, you see it appears I was pipped at the post by the British.' The cameras rolled, capturing Mike's every word. 'I'm sure by now,' he continued, 'Many of you would be familiar with the Peshwari Nans, well Minnie, Minnie should receive the credit, and applause for that matter for this, this galactic discovery and I for one salute her.' There was a rapturous round of applause from within the tomb as Mike and his men prepared to open the giant sarcophagus while all around held their breath; whose remains were they about to lay eyes on for the very first time, could it really be the former Queen herself, Cleopatra?

Over at the hospital Minnie's deteriorating mental state was giving her sister and doctors alike grave cause for concern, as was her fluctuating pulse and irregular breathing. 'Mother, Mother!' she called, delirious. 'Mother, will you plait my hair like Jenny Robbins, oh pleaaaase, Mother!'

Esther clung to a young Egyptian doctor. 'Oh whatever's gotten into her?' she asked despairingly. 'Is it, is it dementia, doctor, is it?'

'Only time will tell,' she was told. 'Please, allow me to examine your sister, if she recovers it may be necessary to request a physiological evaluation.'

'Oh I can tell you, doctor,' Esther said at his side. 'She's quite mad, quite mad indeed, but I mean in the sweetest most adorable way, if you get my drift.'

The doctor didn't get Esther's drift as it were and ticked his clipboard whilst Minnie was carefully transferred to a hospital bed and further saline drips attached to both arms. 'She is showing signs of severe dehydration,' the doctor informed Esther. 'I must warn you the next twenty-four hours are critical for your sister's chances of making a full recovery, I only say this so you can prepare yourself for the worst.'

'The worst,' Esther exclaimed. 'What do you mean, the worst, look at her, she's alive isn't she, even if she goes completely gaga I'll care for her till my last breath, my last breath I say.'

'Yes she is alive, madam,' the doctor agreed whilst looking closely into Minnie's eyes. 'But there may be internal complications, organ failure perhaps.'

'God no,' Esther said, clutching her chest.

'Look, dear,' Minnie said, tugging at Esther's arm. 'Mother's going to plait my hair.'

'I know, dear,' Esther said, appeasing her deranged sister, 'Just like Jenny Robbins, I heard you.'

'Who, dear? Minnie asked.

'Jenny,' Esther reiterated, 'Jenny Robbins, you remember, the two of you were inseparable in school.'

'You're mistaken, dear,' Minnie said, releasing a nurse's reddened hand. 'Suzie Farthing was my best friend, I thought you knew that.'

'But, but you hated Suzie Farthing with a vengeance, dear,' Esther attempted to refresh her sister's hazy memory. 'Surely you remember, she put a live toad in your lunch box and you've despised her ever since.'

'Don't be ridiculous, Essy,' Minnie said, swatting an attentive nurse's hand. 'Suzie would never do a thing like that, we were as close as two friends could be, closer than you and I at times.' Minnie's mind was obviously askew at this point because the rift between her and her fellow pupil Suzie Farthing lasted throughout their formative years and even into adulthood, when the pair were once seen scrapping in the supermarket having collided trollies in the frozen food aisle and opened old wounds. 'It was that cow Jenny Robbins,' she added menacingly. 'She planted that blasted toad in my tuck box, she did and I'll never forgive her for it.'

'Doctor, do something,' Esther begged the young physician. 'Please.'

'I will give her a sedative,' the Egyptian replied, summoning his nurse. 'It will calm your sister while we examine her fully.'

Esther sat at her sister's bedside fraught with worry, a position she had found herself in on countless occasions, more so ever since they left their safe and snug East London home. She had finally found her sister in body but now risked losing her in mind, or possibly worse.

The mood, however, at the great pyramid tomb was joyous as the massive sarcophagus lid was prised aside by no less than six strong men with heavy lifting and levering equipment revealing several layers of gold leaf-encrusted papyrus. Necks were craned and all eyes and cameras were trained on this remarkable scene.

Wearing forensic latex gloves, Mike and his team painstakingly removed the papyrus with their hearts in their mouths, delving deeper and deeper into the unknown. There had been much contrary speculation that if such a tomb were to exist then in all probability it would belong to a family member, perhaps a little known child of the great Khufu himself for whom the pyramid was built over a period of twenty years. But whilst meticulously unravelling the mystery and a second inner wooden lid there was a unanimous gasp, the broadest of smiles and the throwing of hands in the air.

TV cameras were rolling, beaming the phenomenal images live around the world. 'She did it!' Mike said breathlessly, raising a clenched fist in salute to the aging Londoner. 'Ladies and gentleman!' he proudly announced with a lump in his throat and a tear-strewn face. 'I give you, CLEOPATRA!'

The resounding gasp within the tomb echoed a million-fold around the globe. She did it alright, Minnie had stumbled inadvertently, blindly, foolishly onto the tomb of the last great Queen of Egypt thus solving the centuries-old conundrum, although Minnie herself may have fallen foul of the very curse the Egyptian labourers so frantically fled from.

Cleopatra had literally been under the very noses of prominent archaeologists the whole time until the oddest series of events sparked by the squabbling Peshwari Nans unearthed her.

This discovery would dwarf that of the boy king Tutankhamen himself, beginning a media frenzy that would span vast continents and stirring the imaginations of billions from princes to paupers. Following the inevitable floodlit press conference outside the pyramid and calls from his ecstatic investors, Mike raced by taxi to the hospital to thank Minnie in person. 'Esther, Esther she did it!' he shrieked, bursting onto the ward. 'Minnie did it!'

'Shhhhhh,' Esther replied with a finger to her lips. 'She's sleeping, Mister Mike.'

'Oh really,' Mike said, peering down at her gaunt and frail sister. 'Gee I'm sorry.' Mike sat at Esther's side and putting an arm around her lowered his voice. 'She did it, Esther,' he whispered. 'Minnie found her.'

'Found?' Esther asked, her mind elsewhere.

'Cleopatra!' Mike said excitedly. 'Your sister found Cleopatra, Esther, do you know what this means?'

'Mister Mike,' Esther said, turning to look him in the eye. 'My sister Minnie is as I've always said a force of nature, and while I agree Cleopatra is a magnificent find, if my sister were anywhere within the vicinity I'd bet my last farthing that she'd be the one to stumble across her, inadvertently or otherwise. Given half the chance, Mister Mike and knowing her as I do, I wouldn't put it past her to root out Bigfoot, the Lost City of Atlantis or the perishing Loch Ness Monster for that matter.'

Mike looked the unassuming slumbering patient up and down. 'She's quite a gal, that's for sure,' he agreed.

'That she is,' Esther replied, clinging to Minnie's limp hand. 'That she is.'

Whilst the American archaeologist enlightened Esther as to the spectacular contents of Cleopatra's tomb and the remarkably preserved mummy within the sarcophagus, Minnie moaned and stirred. 'Mmmmm, Essy,' she said, opening an eye. 'Essy, oh Essy, my love.'

Mike sat bobbing with enthusiasm, 'Minnie, Minnie ma'am, you did it, you found her!' he said wide eyed.

'No, dear,' Minnie said a little more coherently whilst jostling her sister's hand. 'We found each other, didn't we dear?'

'Yes, darling, yes we certainly did,' Esther smiled. 'And I missed you, my dear, terribly.'

'Essy, I'm hungry,' Minnie said, bringing a broader smile to her sister's cheeks.

'Oh that's wonderful, Min,' she said, encouraged by her sister's returning now legendary appetite. 'Nurse, Nurse!' Esther called. 'Do you think you could fix my sister a bite to eat?'

'Ahem,' Minnie said, attracting the nurse's attention. 'Whatever it is,' she said, sipping at her water, 'I'll go large.'

'No, no, no, you found her!' Mike exclaimed. 'Minnie ma'am, you found Cleopatra, you, Minnie, you.'

'Who?' Minnie asked, still thinking about her impending meal. 'Essy, who is this man?' she then asked suffering an amnesic episode.

Esther's heart sank once more assuming her wandering mind could signal the beginning of the end of the sister she knew and adored. The bright bubbly vivacious soul who had been at her side during the happiest and saddest days of her life, but, and a monumental but at that, with Minnie you just never knew.

Suddenly a wry smile broke out across Minnie's face. 'Hello, Mister Mike,' she said cheekily. 'I had you going for a moment there, didn't I.'

'Ohh, Minnie!' Esther sighed. 'You had us both going you, you loveable fool you, but I swear, Minnie, one of these days I'll…'

'Essy, Essy,' Minnie said, interrupting her sister. 'I love you.'

These three words that Esther had been longing to hear during her sister's self-inflicted confinement melted her heart to the very core. 'And I love you, dear,' she confessed. 'With all my heart.'

Mike took Minnie's hand. 'Look, Minnie if and when you're well enough to leave this place,' he told her sincerely, 'You come by Giza, there's a whole heap of people dying to meet you.'

Esther hastily pre-empted her sister. 'Oh I don't think that's such a good idea, Mister Mike,' she told him with her sister's best interests at heart. 'Minnie has been through quite enough, rest is what she need and rest is what she is going to get, right, dear?' she asked her sister.

'Nonsense,' Minnie scoffed, 'I'd be delighted, Mister Mike, absolutely delighted.'

'But, but, Minnie,' Esther protested. 'I really must object.'

'Ah, ah, Essy,' Minnie said, silencing her het-up sibling. 'It was a petty quarrel that got us into this scrape in the first place so let's just agree to see eye to eye on this occasion, what do you say?'

'Petty quarrel!' Esther remarked, immediately forgetting the recent harrowing events. 'You stole my shoes, I'd hardly call that grounds for a petty quarrel.'

'Ladies, ladies!' Mike said, coming between them to prevent another rapidly escalating altercation. 'You're together again, surely that's all that matters.'

'I know that, Mister Mike,' Esther relented. 'But…'

'Ah, ah,' Mike himself now said, raising a finger, 'You're sisters, remember, and from what I hear you love each other very much, am I right?'

'Yes of course,' Minnie chirped without hesitation. 'That goes without saying, Mister Mike.'

'Esther?' Mike asked Minnie's hesitant sister. 'Estherrrrr?'

'Ohhhh alright,' Esther finally agreed. 'Of course I love her, she's the bane of my life but I suppose I wouldn't want it any other way.'

Mike rose from the bed safe in the knowledge he had unified the sisters once more. 'Like I said, come by the pyramid,' he told the two of them. 'Hell, you ladies are more famous now than you've ever been, do you know that?'

'You mean my sister is, don't you, Mister Mike?' Esther replied, refusing to share in the limelight.

'Now, now, Essy dear,' Minnie said adamantly. 'I couldn't have done it without you, well more to the point your shoes, what I'm trying to say is that you have as much right to the find as I have, we are a team, dear.'

'Poppycock!' Esther scoffed. 'It's yours, Minnie, now do as I say and get better, then go out there and relish it, do you hear?'

'Yes but…' Minnie stammered.

'Do you hear?' Esther said a little louder and with conviction and a wagging finger, the finger that Minnie had seen on countless occasions, more than she cared to remember in fact.

Mike returned to the melee at the great pyramid and the media carnival arriving in ever increasing numbers. Officials from the Egyptian government and the Cairo museum were also there to oversee the remainder of the works and claim the Queen's remains as their own, having previously ridiculed the Americans for their foolhardy and altogether costly venture.

Very soon tens of thousands of Egyptian nationals interspersed with a myriad of foreign tourists flocked to the Giza sight, albeit in the middle of the night, to be part of this meteoric occasion, and again the historic event was captured live and wirelessly in glorious technicolour and viewed on a record-breaking billion devices the world over.

Cleopatra was the word on everybody's lips, along with Minnie of course from Norway to Nairobi, Ontario to Okinawa.

Esther sat at her sister's bedside patiently peeling black grapes for her and shelling walnuts, when the pair heard a commotion out in the corridor.

'One at a time, please!' the doctor could be heard addressing the growing tide of reporters. 'The patient is still very weak and under observation at this time,' but the young medic was almost bowled over in the stampede and the doors to Minnie's ward flung open.

'What the devil?' Esther shrieked, spinning to see the bustling news crews.

'Minnie, Minnie!' they called to her, jostling one another for position. 'Minnie, how are you feeling?'

Minnie gave them the thumbs up which was captured by dozens of flashing cameras.

Esther rose hastily to confront the invasion. 'Get out!' she yelled, waving her arms. 'Get out, all of you!'

Minnie reached for her sister's hand. 'It's alright, Essy,' she said, fixing her hair with her free hand. 'I don't mind at all, honestly.'

'Yes but, darling, you need to remain calm,' Esther informed her sensibly. 'Isn't that what the doctor told you?'

'Ohhhh, Essy,' Minnie smirked amid the almost pyrotechnic display of flashing bulbs. 'When have I ever done as I were told, eh, hardly ever that's when, and I'm far too long in the tooth to begin now so settle yourself down and take a chill pill as Richard and his young friends say.'

Although peeved, Esther was inclined to agree and stepped aside. 'Alright, dear,' she sighed 'Have it your way.'

'Minnie, Minnie, how did you find Cleopatra!' a newshound asked thrusting his microphone toward her bed.

'Was it an accident like some suggest?' another asked, crammed between his colleagues.

'An accident!' Minnie said, deeply offended suddenly. 'Of course it was no accident, what do you take me for, a fool?'

Esther looked down at her sister and rolled her eyes. 'Heaven forbid,' she mouthed.

Minnie wriggled in her bed and prepared to impart her, shall we say twisted version of the truth. 'I've always had a nose for this sort of thing, haven't I, Essy?' she said, looking to Esther for support. 'I said I've always had a nose dear?' she insisted, putting Esther on the spot.

'Oh, oh er,' Esther replied, red faced. 'Yes I suppose you have, dear.'

'You suppose!' Minnie exclaimed. 'Essy, was it not I who found our grandmother's engagement ring in the garden amongst the rhubarb, and Uncle Freddy's war medals in the bottom of the wardrobe amongst his mucky magazines.'

'Yes, yes but…' Esther attempted to intervene, having locked Minnie in the wardrobe in the first place after her tiresome sibling irreparably tangled the string on her prized yoyo and refused to apologise for cheating yet again at the board game Snakes and Ladders, winning ten consecutive games in a row by deception and distraction.

'As I said,' Minnie replied to the media mob, disregarding her sister in the process. 'I have a nose for these sorts of things you see, I merely deciphered the, the erm, the whatsits.'

'The hieroglyphics,' a reporter piped up.

'Yes, yes,' Minnie smiled. 'The hiero-thingiess, it was simple really.'

'Simple!' several onlookers smirked. 'Minnie,' one said above the rest. 'Cleopatra's whereabouts has been one of the greatest mysteries of all time, perplexing the finest archaeological minds and scholars, but you found her, Esther, you must be immensely proud of your sister,' he said, turning to confront Minnie's startled sister.

'I'm sorry, what?' Esther asked, wincing at the flashing lights. 'Proud, oh, oh yes of course, very, very proud,' and she did her upmost to sound convincing for her sister's sake. 'But she's modest too, aren't you dear?' she added, tongue-in-cheek.

'Oh to hell with modesty, Essy,' Minnie laughed. 'Yes I found her, it was me, now come closer all of you and I'll fill you in on my perilous feat.'

There was a spontaneous surge and Esther was swept aside leaving Minnie engulfed and loving every minute of it. Her tale got taller and taller and more absurd with every passing minute.

'A thousand scarab beetles, you say?' one wide-eyed reporter asked.

'Yes that's right,' Minnie boasted, 'Creepy crawly little blighters, and the vipers, did I tell you about the pit of venomous vipers?'

The notes hastily scribbled by the news-hungry hacks soon resembled a script from the likes of Indiana Jones, Lara Croft or James Bond with all ears trained her way. 'Yes, yes a lava stream, I tell you,' Minnie continued, possibly still delirious from her ordeal.

Before Minnie descended further into complete and utter fantasy, Esther stepped in. 'That's quite enough, ladies and gentlemen,' she said with her hands raised. 'My sister must rest, doctor's orders, you see.'

'Minnie, Minnie!' a voice called from the back of the room. 'Cleopatra is being removed from the pyramid tomorrow, will you be there?'

Esther again intervened. 'Well we'll have to wait and see,' she replied, concerned for her sister's health and of course her mental state.

'But of course,' Minnie chirped. 'Just you try and stop me, young man.'

'I wouldn't dare,' the reporter joked as cameras flashed furiously once again, capturing Minnie's hearty wave from her hospital bed, an image sure to delight her legions of fans.

Preparations were underway at the Giza pyramid for the Queen's removal, and what an occasion it was set to be. A grandstand had been hastily erected for visiting dignitaries and honoured guests and the day was to be declared a national holiday throughout the country by Egypt's rulers.

Flights into Cairo airport had seen unprecedented demand as enthralled travellers flocked to the Middle Eastern country, a swarm from the four corners of the globe and enough almost to shift it from its axis. For the first time in two thousand and forty years Cleopatra Philopator would see the light of an Egyptian day and take pride of place in a gilded case beside the boy king in the Cairo museum.

Back home in Whitechapel, London, Esther's grandson Richard was sitting at the breakfast table spooning Coco Pops into his mouth and watching the morning news before school when suddenly Minnie's smiling face and that of Esther appeared. 'WOAW!' he cried, spitting chocolate milk across the table.

'What is it, dear?' his mother Elizabeth asked at the kitchen sink with her back to the TV.

'Oh, oh nothing!' Richard swiftly replied, leaping from his chair to switch the channel.

Elizabeth had recently been allowed home for a trial period from the secure unit she'd been housed in since her earlier breakdown and her son feared for her fragile sanity.

'Nothing, nothing, Mum,' Richard explained again.

But before Richard could locate the remote control Elizabeth turned with a baking tray in her hands and froze momentarily before letting out a piercing cry, letting the blackened tin slip from her fingers and clatter to the floor. 'Arrrrrrgh, Mother, Aunt Min!' she cried, rushing to the television in time to hear the news crews' version of events. 'EGYPT!' she screeched. 'RICHARD, WHY DIDN'T YOU TELL ME THEY WERE IN EGYPT FOR GOD'S SAKE?'

'I er, I didn't want to worry you with it, Mum' Richard pleaded. 'Sit down please, Gran's fine by the looks of things, Mum, please!'

'Fine!' Elizabeth scoffed. 'Fine, they are in hospital, damn it, how on earth can they be fine, EGYPT, EGYPT I thought they were coming home, Richard.'

'Mum, please!' Richard begged, seeing his mother's eyes begin to glaze over, a sure sign an episode was imminent. 'Here,' he added, reaching for her tranquilisers. 'Take your meds, please, Mum and try to relax, remember what the doctors said.'

'Relax!' Elizabeth cried, swatting the brown bottle from her son's hand. 'How can I relax, God damn it, look!'

Richard attempted to explain the colossal significance of Aunt Min's discovery but as expected his mother was oblivious.

'I don't give a rat's arse about Cleo-bloody-patra!' she snarled. 'I want my mother and Aunt Min home right now, right now, Richard, right now!' With a simple swipe Elizabeth sent every kitchen utensil from the worktop crashing to the tiled floor. 'I know what they're doing, Richard, I know!' she cursed.

'Mum, please don't.' Richard pleaded, following his mother about the place whilst she embarked on a wholly destructive spree, tearing their framed family photographs from the walls and toppling her beloved Swarovski display case, shattering much of her crystal collection.

'NO, NO, MUM STOP!' Richard implored her before reluctantly reaching for the telephone to hastily call the hospital. 'Hello, hello!' he said frantically while ducking a flying vase. 'Yes it's my mother, Mrs Reynolds, yes that's right, Mrs Reynolds, please, please come quick!'

Suffice to say Elizabeth, after putting up a prolonged fight with four hospital porters, was eventually sedated for her own protection, restrained and placed back in her bolted room. The porters were themselves treated for minor cuts and bruises sustained when attempting to relieve Elizabeth of her brass toasting fork.

At the Cairo hospital several thousand miles away Minnie, having regained a little colour after eating, had been delighting the doctors and nurses alike with tales of their extraordinary travels.

'Yes, yes, a Bollywood movie,' Esther added. 'Minnie here of course stole the show, didn't you, dear?'

'Oh come now, Essy,' Minnie objected.

I thought you gave an Oscar-winning performance as the Duchess, Elizabeth Taylor herself could not have done the part greater justice.'

'Oh,' Esther said, taken aback momentarily by her sister's generous compliment. 'Thank you, thank you, dear.'

'Tell us again about the tiger?' an enthusiastic nurse asked as she and her colleagues shuffled closer.

'Yes, yes, the tiger!' another called.

'Oh that moth-eaten old thing,' Minnie said dismissively. 'It'll take more than an oversized ginger Tom to get the better of us won't it, Essy dear?'

Esther was sat rigidly reliving the nightmare scene when she literally thought they were done for.

That evening Esther refused to leave her sister's side, or let her out of her sight for that matter in light of recent events. 'I tell you, I'm not leaving,' she told the night nurse, 'And that, my dear, is that.'

Reluctantly the nurse made up the empty bed beside Minnie's and presented Esther with a matching surgical gown as a makeshift nightie. 'Thank you, my dear,' she said tucked in snuggly beside Minnie.

'Blueberry muffin, dear?' Minnie asked, offering her sister a treat from her mountain of tasty gifts sent by concerned well-wishers and devotees of the Peshwari Nans.

'Ooooh I don't mind if I do,' Esther replied, the pair then wriggling with delight whilst sharing Minnie's sumptuous pile.

Esther reached for her sister's hand. 'You silly old fool' she said with a heap of cookies balanced precariously on her bed sheets.

'I know and I'm sorry, dear,' Minnie replied, her own bed littered with crumbs. 'I do put you through the ringer at times, don't I.'

'At times!' Esther said, shaking her head. 'Every day, Minnie, every day of my entire life.'

'Really?' Minnie asked, blissfully unaware of the majority of time of the stress and grievance she'd inflicted upon her doting sister, the one true love of her life, and with whom she'd planned to spend the remainder of her days, however many, or few for that matter. 'I, I hadn't realised, Essy,' Minnie said solemnly, 'I am a fool aren't I,' she cursed.' 'A damned fool but, but sometimes, Essy, I just can't help myself, remember when we were children and I'd jump in every muddy puddle no matter how deep, and without wellington boots too.'

'Yes, Mother would be furious with you,' Esther reminisced. 'But you did it again and again, didn't you, and I had to be there time after time to pick up the pieces.'

'Well I'm going to make you a solemn promise, Essy,' Minnie said sincerely.

'Oh really!' Esther replied, having heard it all before. 'What is it this time, don't tell me, you're going to mend your ways and finally curb your enthusiasm, surely, Minnie, that would be too much to ask.'

'Oh no, dear,' Minnie remarked, cramming the last of her muffin into her mouth. 'When we get home,' she mumbled, 'I'm going to buy me those wellington boots.' All her life Minnie had been drawn to puddles and perilous situations causing her sister no end of sleepless nights, stress and anxiety. Like the time at age nine she climbed the neighbour's towering conference pear tree to retrieve an escaped budgerigar, a sky blue answering to the name of Percy and a close companion of their Aunt Edith. Skinning her shins and tearing her taffeta dress, Minnie clambered hand over fist out onto a precarious limb whilst her sister angrily voiced her objections from the opposite side of the fence. 'I know what I'm doing, Essy!' were the last words Minnie called down before Percy fled her reaching hand and the aged bow broke with a resounding crack, sending the startled girl crashing to the ground completely obliterating their neighbour's award-winning dahlias due to be shown at the church fete that very afternoon. Suffice to say Percy was never seen again, the neighbour refused to speak to Minnie's parents from that day on and Minnie herself sustained a fractured wrist and collarbone and spent three agonising nights in the Royal London Hospital. Aunt Edith cut her stay short and left for the Cotswolds in floods of tears, after all it was Minnie who'd released Percy from his cage to act out a pirate parrot fantasy, but of course Percy had other ideas. And at age ten and three quarters Minnie foolishly climbed the guard rail around Brighton Pier to retrieve a red balloon entangled in the rusting supports. Her mother's fraught shrieks were enough to startle Minnie and cause her to release her grip and plummet seaward, balloon string in hand. The retreating rip tide surrounding the pier toyed with the young screaming girl before whisking her out to deeper water, and immediately their father leapt over the rail himself yelling her name while Esther pressed her face to the railings reaching a hopeless hand for her younger sibling. The coast guard was rapidly alerted and helicopter scrambled when Minnie's father was beaten back by the pounding waves. Almost a mile out to see it was the red balloon that was first sighted by the vigilant airmen and then Minnie's body floating face down. In the nick of time the young girl was winched from the swell and treated within the returning helicopter whilst the balloon floated free from her hand toward the heavens and the family wept in a dishevelled heap at the end of the pier.

Esther's heart had been wrenched this way and that throughout their years together and her sister had ridden her luck without so much as a care, disregarding all sane advice and warning. In truth her advancing years only increased her mindless abandon and of course Esther's heart rate. 'Wellington boots,' Esther sighed. 'Oh really, Minnie, what am I to do with you?'

An hour or so later Esther had nodded off, emotionally and physically drained, when she felt Minnie's nudging hand. 'Essyyyyyyy,' Minnie whispered in a whining tone. 'Essyyyyyy'

'Mmm, mm what, what is it, Min?' Esther said dreamily. 'What's wrong?'

'Thank you, dear,' Minnie smiled. 'Thank you for never giving up hope.'

'Hope?' Esther asked, half asleep.

'Of ever seeing me again,' Minnie added, leaning from her bed.

Esther rubbed her eyes and rolled to face her sister. 'Minnie there was never any question of me giving up hope, me darling,' she told her sister. 'I'd have drawn my last breath here in Cairo before throwing in the towel, I'll admit I was worried sick for you for the majority of the time, Min, but somehow deep down, deep down dear I knew you'd appear, and you did, a little worse for wear but that's nothing new, and look at you now, a packet of biscuits, a treacle tart and a box of After Eight mints and you're as right as rain.'

Minnie arched her aching back. 'Oh I don't know about that, dear,' she confessed, scooping a handful of crumbs into her mouth. 'Although having said that,' she added, brushing the remainder onto the floor. 'I am itching to get back to the pyramid to see Cleopatra for myself.'

'Me too if I'm honest,' Esther replied. 'Now get some sleep, will you, you've been through rather a lot of late, haven't you?'

'Right you are, dear,' Minnie agreed, inching further beneath her sheets. 'Night, night, Essy dear,' she said with a smile.

'Night, night, Min,' Esther replied, tugging the hem of her blanket up beneath her chin and shaking her head one last time before closing her eyes.

Very much fatigued, the sisters were left to sleep the following morning surrounded by a heavy hanging curtain. 'Minnie love, how are you feeling?' Esther asked when first to wake and watching her sister with her head resting on her hand until she stirred.

'Ooooooh,' Minnie groaned, stretching as best she could. 'D'you know what, Essy,' she said, wiping the sleep from her eyes. 'I don't feel half bad, Nuuuuurse, nuuuuuuuurse!' she then called, shuffling up onto her bottom and waiting expectantly until a friendly face appeared.

'Good morning to you,' a nurse said, swishing back the curtain. 'And how are our honoured guests today?'

'Hungry,' Minnie said, a sure sign she was well on the road to recovery. 'Very hungry so please tell me we haven't missed breakfast.'

'Well I'm afraid you have,' the nurse replied, plumping Minnie's pillows and pouring the sisters a glass of juice. 'But there is always an exception to the rule.'

'Thaaat's the spirit,' Minnie smiled, rubbing her wrinkled hands together 'Now as long as it's non meat and dairy I'll have it, all of it.'

'All of it?' the nurse asked, wide-eyed.

'Yes, dear,' Esther agreed. 'My sister would like all of it.'

'All of it,' the nurse said again. 'And for you, madam?' she asked Esther.

'Oh,' Esther said, caught unawares and sitting up herself. 'Just tea and toast, my dear, thank you, and em….' She hesitated. 'I don't suppose you have any marmalade, do you, thick cut of course.'

'Do you know, madam,' the nurse returned her smile, 'I believe we do.' She left the sisters and returned to the hospital kitchen to prevent the cook from leaving, explaining that the ordinarily stringent dining regulations had been bent to accommodate their esteemed guests.

Minnie slid from her bed with the help of her sister and the pair headed off to find the ladies lavatory hand in hand to change out of their hospital gowns .'Steady, dear,' Esther told her sister when she insisted on quickening her step.

'I'm sorry, dear,' Minnie replied. 'But I need to spend a penny,' she said as she bobbed with a pained expression. 'Come to think of it, Essy,' she added, 'I doubt I'd get much change from a shilling, it was my dream, you see.'

'Your dream?' Esther asked, attempting to keep up in the corridor. 'What about your dream?'

'I was curled up in a cider barrel, you see,' Minnie replied, scrutinizing every door in passing. 'Ahhhh, thank heavens,' she then said, disappearing into the ladies.

'Minnie, Minnie!' Esther said, scurrying behind her having had her curiosity pricked.

'A cider barrel, what on earth?'

Minnie had rushed into a cubicle slamming the door behind her.

'Minnie?' Esther asked, slipping into the adjacent stall and thumping on the flimsy wall. 'A cider barrel, what were you doing in a cider barrel for Pete's sake?'

'I'm sorry, dear, what?' Minnie asked in return whilst hurriedly sanitising the lavatory seat with a wad of toilet tissue and hitching up the hem of her gown.

'The cider barrel!' Esther remarked, raising a leg up and hoisting herself up onto the pan to peer over the wall and down at her sister. 'What on earth were you doing?'

'Oh!' Minnie said, startled at the intrusion. 'I say, dear,' she added, 'I appear to have used all of the toilet tissue, would you mind awfully?'

'Oh for Pete's sake!' Esther cursed, reaching to slip her roll from its holder and hand it to Minnie. 'Now come on, out with it?' she insisted.

'Out with what, dear?' Minnie asked, lowering herself onto the gleaming seat, she then proceeded to drown out the trickles and sprinkles with a chirpy chorus of,

'Daisy, Daisy give me your answer dooooooo'

'Minnie, Minnie damn you!' Esther barked, unable to maintain her grip on the wall and dropping into her cubicle. 'Ooooh one of these days, young lady,' she grimaced, hitching up her own gown. 'One of these days.'

'I'm half craaaaazy
all for the love of youuuuuuu'

Minnie warbled. 'Oh that reminds me, Essy,' she eventually said, flushing the lavatory and watching the cascading water. 'Did I tell you about my dream?'

The pair exited their cubicles together and washed at adjacent sinks. 'There I was in this cider barrel,' she told her peeved sister.

'AND?' Esther asked aggressively.

'Patience, dear,' Minnie calmly replied whilst applying far too much liquid soap to the hands and struggling to remove the lather.

Esther glared at her sister, which as always was a complete waste of time and effort,

'Well there I was,' Minnie said, standing shoulder to shoulder with her sister.

'Yes, yes, in a blasted barrel!' Esther intervened. 'I know that, you fool, what I don't know is why in God's name were you there in the first place, come to think of it,' she added, splashing water onto her face, 'I don't want to know now, in fact I'm past caring,' and she dried herself and disrobed in readiness to dress.

'Oh but, Essy,' Minnie moaned, following suit. 'I was just getting to the best bit.'

'NO, no you weren't!' Esther replied, wriggling into her petticoat. 'You weren't getting to anything, you were dithering like a fool as always, now help me with my zip, will you.'

Leaving the lavatory having freshened up, the sisters returned to the ward to find the doctor waiting beside Minnie's bed. 'Good morning, ladies,' he said with a smile. 'I see you are on your feet, Miss Minnie, how are you feeling today?'

'Tickety boo actually,' Minnie replied merrily. 'I slept like a lamb which did me the world of good.'

Esther rubbed her bottom, having endured a wayward spring in her mattress and her sister's symphonic snoring the entire night.

'Wonderful,' the doctor said, taking his stethoscope from around his neck. 'If I could just ask you to take a seat on the bed for me I must examine you before you can be released.' He shook his head in disbelief when Minnie's vitals seemed normal in stark contrast to the previous evening when it seemed death's door was but a stone's throw away. 'Remarkable,' he said. 'Quite remarkable indeed.'

Minnie eyed the handsome young doctor. 'As long as you warm your hands, dearie,' she smirked, unbuttoning her blouse a little lower than Esther would have liked.

'Minnie!' her sister blurted, tugging her sister's attire together. 'Have you no shame, woman?'

'I believe you know the answer to that, Essy,' Minnie giggled.

Esther gathered their belongings whilst her sister was given a thorough examination, and laughing when Minnie was quizzed as to her mental state. 'Doctor,' she said, folding her bed sheets back, 'To say my sister is unhinged to the point of insanity would be a gross understatement, if I were to elaborate you would indeed have her committed in a heartbeat, in a heartbeat I say.'

Minnie patted the doctor's knee playfully. 'Don't listen to her, dearie,' she told him, looking into his hazel eyes. 'She's a terrible grouch in the mornings, I said you're a terrible grouch in the mornings, dear!' she said, peering over the doctor's shoulder with her wrist in his hand.

'A grouch!' Esther exclaimed. 'For my sins I have you for a sister, Minnie, God, sometimes I wish I were an only child.'

'Essy!' Minnie snapped, wrenching her hand free. 'You take that back, that's a frightful thing to say!'

'Well it's truc,' Esther confessed. 'How simple life would have been if you'd never been born.'

'Oooooooh, how utterly mean!' Minnie retaliated. 'After all I've done for you.'

'Ha!' Esther scoffed again. 'Minnie, I went grey at the age of forty because of you, I've lost every friend I've ever had because of you, I had food poisoning and nearly died, because of you!'

'Oh come now, dear,' Minnie said, interrupting her sister's endless rant. 'I told you I followed Mrs Beeton's recipe to the letter, to the letter, dear.'

The young doctor stood bewildered between the warring sisters.

'Yes, yes you did, didn't you!' Esther said, seething. 'But the wing of skate was a week old and damn near decomposed.'

'Oh, Essyyyyy,' Minnie said, dismissing her near fatal culinary calamity. 'I do wish you wouldn't rake up the past, I said I was sorry, didn't I?'

'Sorry!' Esther raged with her own pulse rising steadily. 'Sorry, I could have died, Minnie, died, do you understand, I spent three horrendous days in the London Hospital having my stomach pumped and bedpan after bedpan rammed under my blasted bottom and you're sorry, well it's not good enough, Minnie, not by a long chalk.'

'Ladies, ladies!' the doctor said, raising his hands. 'Please, you are sisters after all, you should love one another.'

'I do,' Minnie agreed. 'I love my Essy dearly but for some unknown reason she doesn't feel the same way.'

'Unknown reason!' Esther replied, looking to the ceiling for divine guidance. 'Unknown reason, Minnie, I could give you a dozen reasons right here right now off the top of my head, no two dozen at least.'

Minnie was then distracted when a nurse rattled the breakfast trolley towards her. 'Oooooh,' she said with a glint in her eye. 'Not before time, my dear,' she added, rubbing her hands together. 'Not before time.'

The trolley with its abundant contents of cereals, toast, prunes, waffles, flapjacks, crepes and fresh fruit was placed between the sisters as a peace offering almost. 'Tea, dear?' Minnie asked, turning the pot three times as her mother always did.

'Ohhhh, I suppose so,' Esther replied, simmering somewhat.

The doctor continued his examination of Minnie whilst she meticulously devoured much of the feast before her in next to no time at all as Esther nibbled on a single slice of wholemeal toast. 'Marvellous,' Minnie said, patting her stomach contentedly. 'Well thank you, doctor, for a very delightful stay,' she told him with another lingering pat to his knee. 'Very delightful indeed.'

'It has been our pleasure, madam,' the doctor replied taking a ballpoint from his breast pocket and requesting the sisters sign his hospital whites.

By now upwards of seven thousand people had flocked to the giant Giza pyramid, many of them journalists and news crews, of which a handful stood with cameras poised outside the Cairo hospital.

'MINNIE, MINNIE, OVER HERE!' they called when the sisters emerged into the mid-morning sun. 'MINNIE!'

'Hellooooo!' Minnie called back with a regal wave and shielding her eyes. 'Lovely day!'

Whilst Minnie appeased the gathering with her ever overblown version of events, Esther herself was also quizzed. 'Esther, Esther, you must be so proud of your sister!' one reporter called, thrusting a microphone under her nose.

'Oh, errrr' Esther reluctantly replied, a little camera shy but watching her sister skilfully play to her audience. 'Yes, yes I suppose I am really,' she eventually agreed.

By the time Minnie had finished she had the reporters believing she was a seasoned and tenacious treasure hunter dwarfing the likes of Howard Carter and his trivial boy King Tut. 'It's in the genes you see,' she added. 'My grandfather was a mudlark on the river Thames and Uncle Ray used to metal detect on Margate beach, I'll have you know he had the finest collection of bottle tops in the south of England, I say had because the fool dug up the ice cream parlour's mains cable and blew himself to smithereens, DO YOU REMEMBER, DEAR!' she called to her sister several yards away. 'UNCLE RAY, BLEW HIMSELF TO SMITHEREENS!'

'Yes, the damned fool,' Esther agreed while many of the surrounding reporters looked at one another bemused, having never heard of the south coast, nor their uncle Ray for that matter whose cloth cap and brown ale bottle tops were found strewn across the beach.

Returning to Giza in Vivien, the sisters were given a hero's welcome with the swelling crowds parting and clapping enthusiastically. 'Hellooooooo!' Minnie called from her open window. 'Lovely day!'

The stage was set for Cleopatra's removal from the pyramid with the world and countless camera lenses trained on the open tunnel while perspiring news anchors narrated the tale of Minnie's discovery and the young queen's life and loves. Esther and Minnie were invited to the VIP tent where they were greeted by various foreign dignitaries. 'Hellooooo, hellooooo,' they said, in awe of their esteemed company, shaking several hands and sipping at their free champagne.

'I must say this is awfully exciting,' Minnie said, letting out a little burp.

Esther soon had to curtail her sister's enthusiasm and alcohol consumption after the fourth glass. 'That's quite enough,' she said, placing a hand over her flute. 'Remember you are still on medication, my dear.'

'Ohhhh poppycock,' Minnie scoffed. 'Father used to wash his gout tablets down with a tot of rum if you remember rightly.'

'Yes well, that was, Father,' Esther quite rightly pointed out. 'You haven't his constitution have you?'

A fanfare then struck up from a visiting band as the time came for Cleopatra to emerge from her resting place and the loudest of gasps rang out with a surge of bodies held back by Egyptian military police; there followed a resounding cheer and a chill to each and every spine present at the very first glimpse.

Once again the queen was adored as she had been thousands of years previously. 'Ahhhhhh,' Minnie sighed. 'That's nice isn't it, dear?' Whilst Esther watched the proceedings, Minnie swiftly poured herself another champagne, swearing the smiling waiter to secrecy with a finger to her lips.

Cleopatra was taken to a waiting flower-laden coach amid all the pomp and ceremony her beloved country could afford her, watched by billions around the world and the carnival that was rapidly getting underway at the Giza site.

Esther and Minnie wandered from the hospitality tent smiling at the dancing revellers. 'I do love a party, don't you, dear?' Esther asked, turning to see an empty space where her sister had just been. 'Minnie?' she asked. 'Minnie!'

Suddenly there was a rumble from within the pyramid and the timber props supporting the excavation began to buckle and splinter, as amid loud gasps the tunnel entrance collapsed sending a cloud of thick dust into the air and several tons of stone crashing to block the opening. 'Minnie, Minnie!' Esther said, jostled by the startled gathering. 'Minnie where are you?' After a frantic and fruitless search Esther slowly turned to the pyramid. 'Of dear God no,' she said, clutching her heaving chest. 'Not again,' and she pushed her way through the crowd to within several meters of the pyramid which had been hurriedly cordoned off. 'Let me through, let me through, I say!' she told the police who stood firm.

'Please, madam, stay back!' she was warned. 'It is not safe, stay back!'

'MINNIIIIIIIIE!' Esther cried with her hands cupped to her mouth. 'MINNIIIIIIE, DEAR!'

'YES, DEAR,' was Minnie's reply moments later.

'Oh thank heavens,' Esther said, grabbing a police officer by his lapels. 'Hurry, my sister's in there!' she told him. 'You have to get her out, do you hear, you have to!'

'Madam, please stay back,' the officer ordered, restraining Esther. 'Please.'

'MINNIE, ARE YOU ALRIGHT, DEAR?' Esther called with a concerned crowd gathering around her.

'NO, DEAR, I CAN'T GET OUT!' Minnie replied, her voice echoing somewhat.

'DON'T WORRY, DARLING!' Esther yelled over the officer's head. 'WE'LL GET YOU OUT, MY LOVE!'

Onlookers broke through the police cordon and began removing rocks, but the majority were many tons in weight and impossible to move without mechanical assistance.

'ARE YOU HURT IN ANY WAY, DEAR?' Esther asked, fraught once more.

'I'M FINE, DEAR,' Minnie replied in an anguished tone herself. 'I JUST CAN'T GET OUT, HELP ME, ESSY, PLEAAAAAAASE!'

'I AM, DEAR!' Esther replied, stooping to lift a hand-sized rock. 'WHAT ON EARTH WERE YOU DOING IN THERE, YOU FOOL!' she asked handing the stone behind her.

'SPENDING A PENNY, DEAR!' Minnie called back, stopping Esther dead in her tracks.

'Spending a penny?' she remarked whilst more eager hands helped clear the smaller debris. 'BUT, MINNIE DEAREST!' she called to her trapped sister 'THERE ARE PORTABLE LAVATORIES HERE FOR THAT SORT OF THING, YOU MUCKY MINX!'

'I KNOW!' Minnie said, growing increasingly frustrated. 'I'M INSIDE ONE OF THE BLASTED THINGS, NOW PLEASE GET ME OUT WILL YOU!'

Esther stood with another rock in her hands, frozen for a moment before dropping it to the ground and turning slowly to observe the row of plastic temporary lavatories, one of which was rocking from side to side.

'Minnie?' she said, perplexed. 'MINNIE, IS THAT YOU IN THERE?'

'NO!' Minnie yelled back. 'IT'S THE QUEEN OF BLOOMIN' SHEBA NOW HURRY UP AND OPEN THIS BLASTED DOOR, ESSY!'

Whilst would-be rescuers tried in vain to open the pyramid tunnel once again, Esther approached the rocking Portaloo and wrenched at the handle,

'Oh thank you, dear,' Minnie said, emerging red faced and flustered. 'I tell you, that cheap champagne goes straight through me, it does.'

Esther stood mortified in utter disbelief.

'What?' Minnie asked. 'Did I miss something, dear?' She glanced over her sister's shoulder at the collapsed tunnel. 'Oh dear, oh dear, dear, dear,' she added. 'I do hope there was nobody inside.' She then bypassed her gobsmacked sister and tottered back to the hospitality tent to scavenge a spot of lunch, leaving Esther secretly wishing her sister would take Cleopatra's place in the tomb for another thousand or so years.

CHAPTER NINE.

'Oh there you are' Esther said a short while later, tracking her gluttonous sister down and finding her with a fully laden plate.

'Look, Essy, they have guacamole,' Minnie said, dipping a stick of celery and crunching greedily. 'I do believe it's avocado but it looks more like mushy peas to me.'

'Come away, will you,' Esther said, tugging Minnie from the head of the queue to allow those behind to select what little her sister had left.

A familiar voice then called out to the sisters. 'Esther, Minnie, hi!' It was the young American entrepreneur Karl Bodine accompanied as usual by his entourage of minders and minions.

'Oh hellooooo!' Minnie called, waving the remainder of her celery. 'Look, Essy, it's young Mister Karl!'

'Hello, my dear,' Esther added. 'How lovely to see you again, I suppose you heard,' and she gestured to her sister.

'Gee, who hasn't!' Karl said excitedly. 'Cleopatra, Minnie, Cleopatra, that's incredible!'

'Hmmmm,' Minnie said nonchalantly whilst reaching back for a fistful of dates.

Karl ushered the sisters to a nearby table. 'I suppose you're wondering why I'm here,' he told them. 'Besides the obvious, that is.'

'Well, well yes,' Esther replied. 'I know you live an awfully long way away, but then again so do we, don't we dear?' She got no response from her gorging sister.

'And half of the hangers on here, I'd imagine,' she added gesturing to the dining dignitaries.

'Freeloaders,' Minnie scoffed having taken full advantage of the Egyptians' bountiful buffet herself.

'Yes, quite,' Esther remarked, pinching a sweet pepper slice from her sister's plate. 'So,' she then said licking her fingers, 'You haven't just come for Cleopatra then, Mister Karl?'

'Actually no,' Karl confessed. 'I got a proposition for you ladies, how would you like to go live, twenty-four-seven?'

'Live?' Esther asked. 'But we are alive, for the time being anyway.'

'No liiive,' Karl insisted. 'On the internet, look you two are the hottest thing since, since…' He struggled to find a noteworthy comparison to the sisters' global notoriety.

'Frankie Sinatra,' Minnie piped up, spitting a date stone into her hand. 'Ooooh now there was a man that floated my boat, I did it myyyyyy wayyyyyyyy,' she warbled whilst snatching a flute of champagne from a passing waiter.

'Ohhh no you don't,' Esther said, relieving Minnie of it. 'Any more and I'll lock you in that lavatory myself, do you hear.'

Karl raised a hand. 'Hotter than Sinatra, wayyyy hotter, anyway I've had an idea,'

'Another one?' Minnie said, interrupting, 'My, you're a clever lad aren't you,' and she turned to her sister. 'He's had another idea, Essy,' to which Esther merely replied with a glare. 'Would you like a date, Mister Karl?' Minnie said, offering a sticky hand.

'No thanks,' Karl declined, 'Anyway, like I said I got this idea.'

'What is it, what is it?' Minnie said, bobbing.

'Minnie!' Esther barked. 'Let the young man, finish will you!'

'Oh, oh yes, sorry,' Minnie replied, taking another glass of champagne whilst her sister's back was turned.

'Carry on, dear,' Esther told the young American. 'We're all ears, aren't we, dear?' She turned to catch Minnie hastily quaffing the bubbly. 'Damn you,' she said, snatching the empty flute. 'I swear you have a problem with drink, Minnie, I really do.'

'No problem at all, dear,' Minnie replied, mopping her chin with a smile.

'Ladies, please!' Karl interjected. 'If I could just explain my idea.'

'Yes, yes, get on with it,' Minnie told him, impatient to hear it. 'Don't keep us in suspense a moment longer.'

'Right,' Karl sighed. 'Like I said, you ladies are hot property, damned hot and your fans are crying out to see more of you.'

'WHAT?' Minnie exclaimed. 'Do you mean they want us to go topless, the mucky devils!'

'No, no, no, no, no, no, no!' Karl quickly replied. 'Good God no,' he shuddered at the mere prospect. 'No, no, Minnie, no, not topless, they want to be with you on your travels.'

'With us?' Esther asked, bemused entirely. 'My dear boy, Vivien creaks, squeaks and groans with just the two of us on board, I very much doubt she'll carry anyone else.'

'No, no, not with you,' Karl replied, growing increasingly exasperated. 'They want to be able to see you, online.'

'Ohhhhhh, online,' Minnie said, pretending to understand. 'Essy, they want to see us online, dear.' She thought for a moment. 'Mister Karl?' she then asked. 'Errrm how exactly?'

'Yes,' Esther added, curious to say the least. 'How exactly would they see us, online?'

Karl reached into his pocket. 'With these,' he said, producing two tiny cameras, no bigger than a pea. 'Nano cams.'

'Nano what?' Esther asked raising her spectacles.

'Cameras,' Karl explained 'Minute high definition cameras, powered by a life-long lithium battery and the very latest software, they have GPS so we can track you wherever you go.'

'Track us?' Esther asked. 'You mean if one of us gets lost,' she looked at her sister, 'Or accidentally entombed?'

'Yes exactly, anywhere in the world, I designed them so they'll fit right on the side of your glasses and they're super light so you won't even know they are there, may I?' He reached to remove Esther's glasses from her face and clipped one of his Nano cams to the side arm and replaced them. 'Now watch,' he told them, taking a laptop computer from his assistant and tapping at the keyboard; suddenly his face appeared. 'Look around, Esther,' he told her, and sure enough everything within Esther's line of sight appeared on the screen. 'I call it Nan Cam,' Karl chuckled. 'And hopefully with your blessing I'm gonna launch this worldwide and charge viewers a monthly subscription to follow you, what do you think?'

'Oh I don't know,' Esther said, having grave reservations about privacy and such like whilst Minnie eyed Karl's shiny new laptop.

'You like it?' Karl asked her. 'It's yours, Minnie.'

'Mine!' Minnie gasped. 'For me?'

'Yeah, I know how you like to surf the internet and chat to your Mister Google right?' His entourage smirked.

'Yes, yes I do,' Minnie said, wide-eyed.

Karl ran his hand across the keyboard. 'Well this is the latest bit of tech,' he told her, 'It'll do everything your tablet does and heaps more, heaps, Minnie.'

'Heaps more,' Minnie gushed.

'Yeah,' Karl informed her. 'For starters it has eight gigs of memory.'

'Eight gigs of memory!' Minnie echoed, completely unaware of the significance. 'Essy, did you know that?' she said, tugging her sister's sleeve. 'It has eight gigs of memory.'

Esther sneered at her sister. 'My dear Minnie,' she said in a condescending tone. 'If anybody needs more memory it's you, that reminds me, where are my pearls, you borrowed them in Medina and you haven't returned them?'

'Are you sure, dear?' Minnie asked, having no recollection of the said pearls.

'Quite sure,' Esther said abruptly. 'You promised I'd have them back by morning, now where are they?'

'Pearls, pearls?' Minnie pondered. 'Do you know, dear, I haven't the foggiest idea,' she confessed.

'I knew it, I knew it!' Esther said, launching into another of her raging rants.

Karl beckoned and whispered to his PA. 'This is pure gold,' he said, knowing full well that tens of thousands of his viewers would pay handsomely to witness the Peshwari Nans' now legendary love-hate relationship. 'So what do you say, ladies?' he asked them again. 'Of course you'll have an equal share of the profits.'

Minnie clutched the laptop to her chest, just itching to expand her internet horizons. 'Pleaaaaase, Essy, please let's do it,' she moaned. 'I promise I'll find your pearls and return them to you, can we do it, can we, can we, can we, can we, Essy?'

'Yes what do you say, Esther?' Karl said, applying a little more pressure.

'Ohhhhhh alright,' Esther eventually relented. 'But I want those damned pearls, Minnie, do you hear?'

'Yes, yes, yes, of course, dear,' Minnie agreed. 'If I could only remember where I put them.'

'What was that?' Esther asked.

'Nothing, dear,' Minnie swiftly replied. 'I remember now,' she added, lying through her dentures. 'I know exactly where they are.'

'Splendid,' Esther sighed. 'They were an anniversary present from Jack so I'd hate to lose them.'

Karl fitted a Nano cam to Minnie's spectacles. 'And I'll need to fit Vivien with a rear and front facing camera as well,' he told the sisters.

'My Vivien!' Esther remarked. 'Oh I don't know about that, Mister Karl.'

But Minnie quickly interjected. 'Yes, yes that's fine, Mister Karl,' she said, clinging lovingly to her new laptop. 'Don't worry, dear,' she reassured her sister, 'I'm sure they'll be gentle with her.'

'Of course,' Karl added. 'I assure you, ma'am, she won't feel a thing.'

'Oh well, if you're quite sure,' Esther reluctantly agreed. 'I dread to think what the MMOC would make of it, mind.'

'MMOC?' Karl said, bemused, 'I don't follow you.'

Esther looked at Karl with complete surprise. 'The Morris Minor Owners Club of course,' she informed him in no uncertain terms. 'Jack and I are lifelong members.'

'Wow,' Karl said with little or no knowledge of the prestigious automobile collective, 'Well like I say, Esther, we'll take real good care of your Vivien,' he assured her. 'Real good care.'

'You see, Essy,' Minnie added enthusiastically. 'You have nothing to worry about.'

'Faantastic!' Karl said, clasping his hands together. 'Well I must tell you, you are live as of now.'

'Now!' Esther gasped. 'But I haven't done my hair.'

Minnie bobbed happily in front of her sister's camera. 'Helloooooooo, cooeeeee!' she said, waving.

'Get away from me, you fool!' Esher said, swatting her sister aside.

Karl's team left the hospitality tent to commence Vivien's camera set up.

'Seems like a waste of time if you ask me,' Esther said, venturing outside. 'What with us heading home and all.'

Minnie hadn't heard her sister, tottering behind with her new computer. 'Eight gigs of memory,' she said delighted with her present. 'Eight gigs!'

Karl also hadn't been privy to Esther's plans conversing with the remainder of his team, thrilled at the onset of a new and exciting business venture that would undoubtedly quadruple his enormous net worth. 'All done, ladies,' he later said when give the thumbs up by his technicians. 'Happy travels and er, just keep on doin' what you're doin'.'

'Yes quite,' Esther remarked, shoving her sister into Vivien's passenger seat having been heavily quizzed by the surrounding media circus. Slamming her own door closed, Esther turned the key as the crowd parted for them once again, cheering and waving ecstatically to the two departing pensioners.

'Goodbyyyyyyyye!' Minnie called to Karl who waved also along with his team. 'Goodbyyyye, Mister Karl!'

Heading away from the Giza pyramids whilst Minnie tinkered with her new toy, Esther stopped at the site entrance to rummage for her driving gloves.

'Right,' Minnie said, slapping both knees. 'Where to now, dear?

'Ohhhhhh no!' Esther replied defiantly. 'Ohhhhh no, we are going home, Minnie, and that's final.'

'Home?' Minnie asked, shell-shocked. 'Home, Essy, but why?'

'Why!' Esther said, wide-eyed. 'Why, I'll tell you why shall I, Minnie Moo, since we foolishly set off from Raipur instead of returning home as I suggested we've been attacked by a Bengal tiger, almost drowned at sea, and you, you, Minnie, were imprisoned and publicly flogged, and then, then, Minnie, on top of all that you were trapped inside a blasted pyramid, THAT'S WHY!'

'Well, well yes but...' Minnie stammered. 'We had ourselves a hoot too, dear along the way, you can't deny that, Essy, can you?'

'Oh it's been a hoot alright,' Esther said, tongue-in-cheek. 'But the dangers have far, far outweighed the thrills, no I'm sorry, Minnie, but home it is, and I won't hear another word on the matter, alright, alright?'

'Ohhhh alright,' Minnie sulked. 'But...'

'Ah ahhh!' Esther warned her. 'Not another word I said, you and I are heading home, and not a moment too soon if you ask me.'

'If you insist, dear,' Minnie said sheepishly.

'I do!' Esther snapped, having gone beyond her tether on more times than she'd care to remember on the second leg of their journey.

Minnie managed to remain silent for a full two and a half minutes as Esther drove from the pyramids. 'How about Rome, dear?' she eventually blurted out of the blue. 'I hear the Coliseum is not to be missed.'

'THAT'S IT!' Esther stormed, slamming on the brakes. 'THAT'S IT, MINNIE, I'VE HAD IT UP TO HERE WITH YOU!' She threw her hands in the air and in doing so dislodging Vivien's aging roof lining and a startling revelation. Both sisters gasped when a brown manila envelope dropped down onto Esther's knees. 'What?' she said, taken aback.

'Essy, Essy, what's that?' Minnie asked, looking up at the tattered lining and then the envelope.

'How the hell should I know?' Esther replied, apprehensive at first.

'Open it, open it, Essy!' Minnie shrieked in anticipation. 'Go on, open it!'

'Errrr yes, yes of course,' Esther said with far less exuberance. 'Yes I will.'

'What is it, what is it?' Minnie plagued her sister, who cautiously examined the envelope, turning it over to slip her thumb beneath the flap. 'Hurry, Essy!' Minnie added, bobbing yet again.

'Quiet!' Esther said, tearing open the flap and peering inside.

'Well?' Minnie asked, craning her neck and positively fizzing. 'Essyyyyyy?'

Esther tipped the envelope's contents into her lap; one dog-eared photograph and a key.

'Is that it?' Minnie asked, dejected and somehow expecting a greater, more significant find.

Esther handed Minnie the key and raised the photograph closer to her eyes. 'Jack?' she said, adjusting her spectacles. 'Minnie, it's my Jack!'

Minnie glanced across whilst scrutinising the lone key. 'Who's that with him?' she asked.

There were two men standing beside Esther's late husband in the vintage photograph, one unknown gent in an expensive Italian suit and another Minnie recognised instantly. 'Sammy!' she said, completely flabbergasted.

'What?' Esther asked.

'Dear Lord, don't you recognise him?' Minnie asked her sister whilst prodding the photograph. 'It's Sammy, my first true love, wait a minute!' she exclaimed. 'Essy, Essy is that the Statue of Liberty behind them, yes, yes it is, Essy, they were in New York, for Pete's sake!'

'Don't be ridiculous,' Esther scoffed 'My Jack has never been to New York in his entire life.'

Peshwari Nans Part II

'I'm telling you, Essy!' Minnie insisted. 'Look, look dear.'

Esther examined the snap closer still, and sure enough her late husband and an old flame of Minnie's were stood smiling in a room with the iconic statue clearly visible from an open window. 'But, but…' Esther stammered also, 'What on earth was he doing in New York, and more importantly why did he feel the need to keep it from me?'

Minnie fondled the key. 'Perhaps it has something to do with this, dear,' she said, reading the stamped inscription. 'Chase Manhattan,' she pondered, 'Essy, I've heard that name somewhere before I know I have, Chase Manhattan, Chase Manhattan,' and she opened and tapped at the laptop keyboard, posing another question to her friend Mister Google. 'Essy!' she gasped, 'Essy, it's a bank!'

'A bank?' Esther asked, looking again inside the envelope for further clues to shed light on the mystery, but there were none. 'I don't understand.'

Minnie took the photograph from her sister, stroking Sammy's face fondly. 'We never did find out what happened to Sammy, did we, dear?' she said with a lump growing in her throat. 'I loved him, you know.'

'Yes, yes I do,' Esther said, bemused to say the least. 'He must have gone home to the States.'

'But why, Essy?' Minnie asked. 'Why would he just leave without even saying goodbye, I knew he felt the same way about me, I just knew it, he said it on countless occasions, Essy, we should go.'

'Go!' Esther exclaimed.

'To America,' Minnie suggested. 'Essy, this is a safety deposit box key, look!' she said, turning the computer screen to face her sister. 'Look, dear, we must go, we must, if there is a box that matches this key, Essy, whatever's inside could tell us everything we want to know, why your Jack kept his trip to New York a secret and why on earth my Sammy just up and left me, oh pleaaaaaaaase, Essy, pleaaaaaaase can we go, can we can we?'

'Absolutely not,' Esther said, donning her gloves. 'We're going home just like I said, now let's forget all this foolishness, banks and safety deposit boxes,' she scoffed, 'I say we let sleeping dogs lie, Minnie, and return to our normal lives as soon as humanly possible.'

Several of Karl Bodine's early subscribers to his Nan Cam channel were yelling at their computer screens. 'GO, GO TO AMERICA! GO TO AMERICA!'

'Oh, Essy, please, I'm begging you,' Minnie pleaded. 'You know how I felt about Sammy, he broke my heart in two when he disappeared, pleaaaase pleaaaaase, I promise I'll never ask for another thing, Essy, I promise.'

'Minnie!' Esther replied, finding the whole matter completely preposterous, but a little curious herself as to why indeed her husband would have kept such a secret. 'No, Minnie, I'm sorry, darling, I just don't think it's a good idea at all.'

'Pleaaaaaaaaase,' Minnie begged with her hands clasped in prayer as did their viewers, hungry for further adventures. 'Please, Essy,' Minnie continued doe- eyed. 'If I could find my Sammy again I'd be the happiest woman alive, I know I would.'

Peshwari Nans Part II

Esther looked across at her sister, remembering how devastated she'd been, inconsolable even when Sammy suddenly disappeared out of her life without so much as a note. It had taken her several weeks to coax her sister out of her room and a further fortnight to get her to leave the house. 'But, Minnie dear,' she said, patting her sister's knee. 'How do we know he's still alive, after all he was a year or two older than you, do you remember?'

'Essy, I have to see him,' Minnie insisted. 'Alive or dead,' and she proceeded to beseech her sister for several more minutes until she eventually broke.

'Alright, alright!' Esther said under mounting pressure. 'We'll go for a couple of days and then home, do you hear me?'

Karl's paying viewers cheered collectively, knowing they were in for a feast of entertainment.

'Yes, yes, yes!' Minnie shrieked, kissing the photograph repeatedly. 'I'm going to see my Sammy again, I just know it, I know it, Essy.'

'Hmmmmm,' Esther mumbled, shaking her head in disbelief at being swayed by her sister once again. 'Alright then,' she then sighed. 'Have a word with that computer thingy of yours and find out how on earth we're going to get there.'

'Ooooh yes, yes, of course dear,' Minnie said excitedly. 'I'm on it like a bonnet, dear, on it like a bonnet!'

Esther set off under Minnie's instructions until the two of them were once again on the open road with Minnie grinning like the proverbial Cheshire cat. 'Daaaisy, Daaaaisy,' she began to sing. 'Give me our answer dooooooo.' She swayed in her seat, pressing the photograph to her bosom. 'Do you know, Essy?' she told her sister. 'Sammy used to sing this to me and tell me how he was going to marry me and whisk me off to America to raise a whole bunch of children,' and she hummed the ditty for a while until Esther smiled and joined in with the rousing chorus, en route to America, and uncertainty.

'Daaaaaisy, Daaaaaaisy
Give me your answer doooooo

The two sisters sang and swayed in time, smiling to one another,

'I'm half craaaaazy all for the love of youuuuuuu,
It won't be a stylish marriage
I can't afford a carriage
But you'll look sweet
Upon the seat

The pair held hands and raised their voices,

'OF A BICYCLE MAAAAAAADE
FOR TWOOOOOOOOOOOOOOOOOO!'

The End.

Peshwari Nans Part II

Acknowledgement

A special thank you to Derek Mutch
of Bavaro Art
www.facebook.com/BavaroArt.
for the wonderful Peshwari Nans
cover artwork.